RETURN TO DENTHAN

BOOK 3 OF THE DENTHAN SERIES

To Othea Millie
from

Sam Wilding

SAM WILDING

D1407100

Published by Olida Publishing
www.olidapublishing.com

First printing: April 2010

Printed in the United Kingdom

Cover Design: Jeremy Robinson

ISBN: 978-1-907354-04-5

For maps and other Denthan material, visit Sam Wilding on the World Wide Web at: www.sam-wilding.com

For help and advice in dealing with asthma, please visit
www.asthma.org.uk

ATTENTION: SCHOOLS AND BUSINESSES
Olida Publishing's titles are available at bulk order discount rates for educational, business or sales promotional use. They are also available for fundraising projects. Please e-mail: olidapublishing@gmail.com for details.

Return to Denthan was written for anyone who ever went on holiday with Father (Joe Wilding). A different vicarage every year, a thousand churches explored and a million happy memories. Thanks Mum, Dad, Stewart, Angie and Auntie Jan. Thanks Father...

ACKNOWLEDGEMENTS

To Tiny, Ryan, Emma, Joe and Ruth for your patience.

To my friends, for a glass held high and a kind word.

To Scobie, for your hard work and editing prowess.

To Traci from Arizona, for your support.

To author, Gregor Addison, for getting me started.

To Allan, for your unbridled enthusiasm.

To all the libraries and schools who support my workshops.

To Gordon Brown, of Asthma UK Scotland, for his support.

To my really old friends; Charlie, Craig, Ian and Gary.

CHAPTER ONE

THE TIGER TRAP

"If you stay still, perfectly still, they won't see us," said Helen. She gripped her brother's hand and shushed him, pressing her forefinger tight against her lips. Wee Joe was prone to outbursts that, in this situation, could prove fatal.

"But..." he protested.

Helen made her eyes as big as she could and mouthed the word 'no'.

Ahead of them, barely visible in the undergrowth, a fully-grown Bengal tiger flicked its giveaway ears. The furry, black tips stood proud of the khus grass. The rest of its bulk was submerged in green, sluggish water that stank of sewage and rotting cabbage.

Helen watched excitedly as two more tigers, a big she-cat and a scrawny male, edged through pea soup scum to join the first. She wondered if they were part of the same family group. Mendel had told them about tigers being solitary hunters.

A pair of brilliant white egrets flapped skyward as the first tiger rose from the stagnant water.

"Are you sure we're safe here?" whispered Wee Joe.

Helen tightened her lips and gave a sharp nod. She pointed down at the plastic brandy barrel and winked.

All three tigers were now free of the water and in full view.

The big male snarled at the wounded water buffalo and began to circle.

"We can't just sit here and lets them kill it," hissed Wee Joe. "You said we would save it. You said Mendel would do magic and…"

The scrawny male lifted his head and stared directly at their hiding place. The other two, ignoring the gasping buffalo, roared and broke into a run.

"Mendel!" Helen snatched up the plastic barrel and pulled Wee Joe back. There were less than fifty yards between the tigers and the safety of the ruins. "C'mon Joe, run faster!"

Wee Joe tucked his chin into his chest and ran full pelt. Now almost six, his long, unkempt hair trailed behind him.

"Mendel!" Helen screamed again into the barrel's plastic window. Trying desperately to keep her footing, she prayed for a glimpse of the golden scales. *I was stupid to get so close to the tigers. We'll never make it to the ruins and it's my fault.*

The first big male was only ten feet behind them. Its roar filled her ears.

Wee Joe caught his shin on a twisted vine and tumbled forward into the long grass. Helen could smell the tiger as it leapt over her. She twisted round, covering Wee Joe with her body.

"Wwwstonewwwrightww!" she blurted.

Crack! Crack! Crack!

Three loud cracks shook the jungle. Like exploding shells above their heads, dust and grime rained down on them. Momentarily transformed, the warm breeze took the form of a raging tornado that sliced through the khus grass.

Helen's long mousy hair was thick with dirt as she eased away from Wee Joe. Yellow butterflies danced over the three piles of dust that marked the last living moments of the Bengal tigers.

"Are they gone?" whispered Wee Joe.

Helen listened as the chattering ibis, spoonbills and egrets resumed their relentless din. "Of course they're bloomin' gone." A mixture of anger and relief welled up inside her. "Mendel!"

A big, orange, googly eye pressed against the window of the brandy barrel. "I had no choice, Helen." Mendel's voice sat perfectly in their heads, totally detached from the splashing goldfish before them. "How many times have I told you not to wander far from the ruined city?"

"Never," said Wee Joe.

"I certainly have, and now you've forced me to kill two perfectly healthy Bengal tigers."

"Three," corrected Helen.

"Two," replied Mendel, in that aloof way of his. "The undernourished male had degenerative bone disease."

"Degener...what?" asked Wee Joe.

"It would have died soon anyway," explained Mendel.

"It doesn't matter if it would have died anyway. You still killed it," said Helen.

Wee Joe edged back from Helen, dusted himself down, and picked up the crystal shard that had fallen from his pocket.

In shock, Helen began to shiver. "We just wanted to..."

"Look at the wildlife?" finished Mendel. "Your big brother, Craig, would have done exactly the same thing."

Helen felt a twinge of sadness at the mention of Craig's name. She missed him. Tears blurred her vision as she watched Mendel flick his golden fins before disappearing back into the gloom of the barrel. No more than eight inches long by four inches high, the barrel had been the old wizard's home for the last two years. Helen knew she'd been stupid to disobey Mendel. The frustration and anger she felt was aimed at herself, no one else. Now almost ten, she thought back to the first time she'd met the old wizard. From Denthan, a world that had been destroyed by one of its dying suns, Mendel had been trapped in the shape of a goldfish for the whole time she'd known him. James Peck, her big brother's best friend, had found him while searching for his missing father.

"Helen, yous dreaming. Wake up!" Wee Joe punched her in the arm.

"Awch! Do you *always* have to hurt people?" snapped Helen.

"Yeh. What are you going to do about it?" Wee Joe replied.

With a reluctant sigh, Helen sat up in the swaying grass and gazed across at the rose-coloured temple. Adorned with clinging vines and scrambling ivy, Mendel had told them it was very old. It was there that they'd discovered a ring of ancient statues. Curiously, they were arranged in the same positions as the standing stones back home on Bruce Moor.

Wee Joe straightened. "I said, what are you going to do about it, Sis? Think you can beat me?" Wee Joe adopted the stance of a boxer.

"Shut up and bring the crystal," she barked, not once taking her eyes off of the crumbling temple walls. She felt a hail of dirt hit the back of her legs. "What the...?"

In a fit of temper, Wee Joe had just kicked one of the piles of dust at her. Yellow butterflies danced around his dirty face. "You said wes were safe. They could have killed us," her brother protested.

She looked beyond her stupid brother at the water buffalo. It was dead. Vultures and ugly adjutant storks were squabbling over the entrails. Her eyes refocused on the three pitiful piles of dust. "Mendel, can't you turn them back into tigers?" She heard Mendel grumbling to himself. "Mendel, I said..."

"I know what you said. I'm not deaf, Helen."

"You are when yous want to be," said Wee Joe.

"What time is it now?" asked Mendel.

Helen twisted her brother's wrist until she could read his cracked watch. He wriggled annoyingly. "Six fourteenish..."

"I don't do 'ish'," snapped Mendel. "I need the exact time."

"I know what you need." Wee Joe pulled his hand away from Helen and shoved the face of his watch against the window of the barrel. "Read it yourself!"

"Helen, bring me the Key of Artilis, take Wee Joe and get behind the city wall. Wait there until I've finished."

"Finished what?" asked Helen.

"Now!" screeched Mendel.

It had taken almost a year of tinkering with the key to affect a repair after their crash-landing in the jungle. Bumped and bruised, they had all just been pleased to be alive after the last confrontation with their nemesis, Dendralon. Bound by magic to that one part of the jungle, both of them missed their mum terribly. They had, however, resolved themselves to the situation, safe, in the main, under Mendel's care.

Helen, her eyes still wet with tears, made for the crumbling city wall, reached over a broken lintel, and pulled free the package.

"Quickly, Helen!" shouted Mendel.

She undid the shoelace that fastened the hemp sack and rummaged about until her fingers found the golden key.

"I only have twenty-two seconds before it's too late," said Mendel.

"Found it!"

Pulling Wee Joe down behind the city wall, she saw the key begin to move and blurted the word, "Wwwthgirwwenotsww!" Like the sound you get when you ping your lips and try to speak at the same time. She thought she recognised the spell 'stonewright'. The only difference was that she'd said it backwards.

They both gasped as the roar of a tiger echoed through the jungle. Wee Joe made to get up, but Helen yanked him back down. "Behave! Mendel said to wait until he'd finished."

Wee Joe glared at her.

A second roar echoed through the jungle.

The golden Key of Artilis stopped spinning and dropped back onto her outstretched hand.

The next sound she heard sent a shiver of dread down her spine. She looked at Wee Joe, who simply threw her a stare that said - *Whatever that is, I'm not going to look.*

Helen peered over the broken wall. There, just beyond Mendel's barrel, two tigers skulked back into the long grass. Nearer, however; at the exact spot where Wee Joe had kicked the pile of dust in a rage, a hideous, skinless creature wavered. Every muscle and vein quivered in the bright sunlight. Fresh blood oozed out of its quivering flesh and drizzled down onto the ground. The creature tried to open its fang-ridden jaws. Helen winced. Its lower jaw became detached from its skull, and a terrible howl shook the trees as it crumpled and then fell completely still.

"Mendel...that was horrible!" She sobbed.

Wee Joe stood up just in time to see the raw corpse fade back into dust and blow away. "Yucky."

"It was too late for that wretch," explained Mendel, his voice full of sadness.

"Why?" asked Helen.

"Why?" Mendel left the word hanging for a few seconds before explaining. "Because, the Key of Artilis can only work on a graduated scale."

"I still don't understand," said Helen.

"Its effectiveness is linked to the lifespan of the thing it brings back to life."

"Talk properly," moaned Wee Joe.

Helen picked up the barrel and then, once safely inside the ruins of the city, slouched down against an Ashoka tree.

"Let me try to explain," said Mendel. "A tiger lives for approximately fourteen years, in the wild. There is, therefore, depending on the age of the animal or thing in question, a set window of opportunity in which the key can reverse death or destruction."

Helen closed her eyes and said, "Eh, so, the third tiger was too old or too young?"

"Too young, and it had degenerative bone disease," answered Mendel.

"None-the-wiser," said Helen.

"More importantly, I've been thinking about the Key of Artilis ever since we discovered it last year." Mendel glided up to the plastic window of the barrel. "You see, Denthan was a planet that existed for three billion years before its sun exploded."

Helen passed Wee Joe a drink of water. "So it was really old. What are you saying, Mendel?"

"I'm saying that Denthan might yet be saved."

"But Denthan exploded. Everything on the planet, all life, ended two years ago."

"True. By my estimation, however, we still have one thousand one hundred years left to use the key. It may be possible to turn back time, to stop Denthan being destroyed."

Helen looked at Wee Joe and shook her head. "I don't get it. We were all there, two years ago, when it happened. Are you saying that you can go back in time, change things somehow, and save a whole world?"

Wee Joe looked down at his feet. "So you have lots of time to save *your* world and stuff, but yous can't get us back home to Drumfintley?"

"I'll get to that. Look, there is never enough time, Wee Joe."

"But you just said that you had thousands of years to go back and save Denthan."

"Yes, but the key deducts the distance between here and there," added Mendel. "There is an adjustment for distance on the time left to go back."

"Which means?" pressed Helen, confused.

"Well, we are one thousand and ninety-eight light years from the spot in the universe where Denthan used to exist."

"Too much gobbledygook," snapped Wee Joe.

"Now that we have proved the key is operational again, and applying the maths, we have days, perhaps weeks left to save Denthan. No more. As soon as we can, we will have to return to Denthan at a suitable point before the explosion and have the protection in place that will allow the planet to survive this time."

"So we're cutting it a bit fine?" asked Helen.

"Well..." began Mendel.

"How the heck...?" Helen issued a sigh that soon turned into a yelp of excitement. She shielded the barrel from Wee Joe. "So, can you get us back to Drumfintley? Can you get us home to be with our mum?"

Strangely, for a fish, Mendel grunted. "Ahumm... I told you I would get to that. I need the crystal we found in the ruined city."

"Here it is!" said Wee Joe. He held it up to the bright sunlight.

"Just tell me Mendel, are we going home or are we going to Denthan?" asked Helen, excitedly.

"We have the crystal, the Key of Artilis is working, and we found the ring of stones we needed," said Mendel. "So, yes, I think I should take you both home first of all."

"Yes!" Wee Joe punched a fist into the air.

They'd acquired the Key of Artilis the year before. Unlike any other key Helen had ever seen, this key could change shape; open any door, but more importantly, it could unlock time itself. It could, according to Mendel, open up a gap in the universe that let a person step backwards and forwards between dimensions. Mendel had explained to Wee Joe and herself that a dimension was like a layer of an onion. There could be lots of them in the same place, overlapping each other.

It suddenly occurred to her that Mendel might have planned the whole tiger episode, just to test the key. She knew he was capable of such mischief, especially if a whole world was at stake.

Helen looked down at the golden key. It whirred and spun in her hand, constantly changing shape. Encrusted with three gems; one blue, one red, and one yellow, it took the form of two golden shafts that blurred then merged into a different key every few seconds. Right then, it whirred like the ends of a food mixer and formed a key with four square prongs and a triangular end. There was a hiss, and it changed again. This time, the end of the key had two circles on stalks that bent round and formed a cross.

"It's my shot to play with the key," moaned Wee Joe.

"I'm not playing," snapped Helen.

"Oh no?"

"No," said Helen. "I'm watching, listening, and trying to learn things far too complicated for you to understand. You're only six."

"And yous only stupid," barked Wee Joe.

Helen studied her brother. Under duress, he often reverted back to his baby talk, but he was no baby any more. Not after a year in the jungle and Mendel as his tutor. He knew most of the animals' names; he could blend in with the jungle, if need-be, and he could wield a mighty punch. His long, golden curls were matted by many months of hiding in the jungle, and his freckled face was filthy, caked in the red-tinged mud that lined the rivers and streams of this place.

Her younger brother's clothes had long since deteriorated, and he'd adopted the bright orange loincloth of the local tribes. The only vestige of his life in the Scottish village of Drumfintley was the remains of his cotton shirt, still stained with the blood of the Kraken they'd encountered almost a year ago. Helen thought back to last time she'd seen Drumfintley, to the last time she'd seen her mother and, to the awful events that led to their disappearance. Mendel had told them that their banishment would last until they'd repaired the Artilian Key, found a suitable crystal and, most importantly, discovered another gateway to take them back home. They were locked into their present location with no way of contacting their family until all these things had been achieved. Now that Mendel had used the key to bring the tigers, or at least some of them, back to life, everything seemed to be in place. They'd unearthed the yellow crystal three months previously, deep in the bowels of the deserted Indian city and, to Mendel's amazement, they'd even found a ring of statues, all set in the correct position to act as a gateway home. She felt her heart quicken as she thought of her mum, Jean, and her big brother, Craig, and their dog, Bero. She knew Wee Joe, like her, had nightmares about the Hedra wizard, Dendralon, and about the monsters he controlled on Artilis. She knew, also, that Mendel worried about Mrs. Peck, James's mum. She'd been left behind on that horrible world.

"Helen." Mendel was beginning to move around in his barrel. "It's time to go home."

"At last." Helen stood up.

Wee Joe shook his head. "It won't work."

"Don't say things like that. It *will* work. Everything is ready. Tell him, Mendel."

Mendel flicked a golden fin and sighed. "We can but try."

"Brilliant," moaned Helen.

"Helen, place the yellow crystal at the base of the biggest statue," said Mendel.

Helen lifted the roughly hewn gem and laid it gently beneath the statue. Mendel had told her the statue was of Surya, the Indian sun god. Helen stared up at the ancient figure. Its legs were carved in patterns that showed him wearing a pair of decorated leggings. He held two large flowers, which Mendel told her were water lilies, and there was a circle behind his head, that she always supposed depicted the sun. *He looks kind,* she thought. Mendel had told her that he was supposed to bring luck and that his third and fourth hands were held out to beckon worshippers and bless them. Trapped by the wizard, Dendralon's magic, they had lived in an area of jungle known to the local tribesmen as the 'land of the dead'. Only panthers and moon bears ventured inside the zone and, of course, the occasional tiger.

"Set the crystal in place," said Mendel.

"Hurry up, Helen," nagged Wee Joe.

They'd rehearsed this many times, and now Helen was beginning to tremble with anticipation. She turned the yellow crystal until it pointed toward the Banyan tree and lifted Mendel's barrel until it was level with the glyphs on the statue. Only then did she take her brother's hand.

"Wwwwyouwwarewwthewtemwwple!"

The dirt and stones shook beneath their feet before peeling away from the bedrock like apple skin. Jumping to avoid the rubble, they bumped down onto a smooth sheet of glass. It wavered beneath them.

"To think that this is a membrane between two worlds... It's fantastic, isn't it?" shouted Mendel.

Helen gripped tighter onto Wee Joe's hand, too scared to answer. She'd fallen through one of these before.

"Are wes really going back home?" shouted Wee Joe.

Helen caught his wide-eyed gaze and gave him a tight-lipped nod. She gasped as the hairline cracks spread out from beneath their feet. She hated this bit.

Wee Joe, on the other hand, loved it. He stamped his feet and whooped for joy as the glass surface fractured then failed.

They fell and fell, further and further into the dark abyss...

CHAPTER TWO

DRUMFINTLEY

The service in St. Donan's Episcopal Church had been pitched carefully. Less of a remembrance service, it had more of a 'hope to see them one day soon' kind of feel. Father Michael had, in James's opinion, done a very good job in the end.

James Peck had felt very strange over the last eleven months, what with his mum last seen on Artilis and MacNulty dispatched by the Kraken, the year had been, to say the least, a downer. To top it all, Dendralon had cast a spell in his final throes, which had resulted in the disappearance of Wee Joe, Helen, and Mendel.

With no sign of any of them over the last year or so, Father Michael had suggested that it might be best if everyone *moved on*, hold a special church service. This, of course, went down like a lead balloon. Jean Harrison was distraught and his dad was little better. There was, however, a practical side to the proposed event.

"I suppose if we held a service, it would let the insurance people know that we don't expect them back," his dad had relented. "We... The group who travelled with Mendel, know there is still a chance of their return, but it would send a message out to the rest of the world."

His dad had given up his job and cashed-in his pension very early, just to remain at home. "It's what your mother would have wanted," he'd said. Unfortunately, with no sign of any bodies, Archie, his mum, and the young Harrison children were still classed as 'missing'. With his dad unable to claim his mum's life insurance, their pot of money was running out. There had to be some semi-official line drawn under it all. The church service ticked this box.

As with the service, almost a year previous, Sergeant Carr again paid tribute to Archie MacNulty, the man who'd saved his life. None of the people, in-the-know, could have possibly told the village, never mind the rest of the world, that a forty-foot, immortal Kraken had actually eaten Archie MacNulty, so it was all spun differently.

It had been Ephie's idea. The missing villagers, it was explained, had been: 'blown to smithereens in the gas explosion that had ripped through Drumfintley the previous summer.'

The old sergeant read a passage from Exodus in memory of the man who'd saved his life, a telltale tear dripping from his big red face as he closed the Bible and retook his seat.

The lectern, however, was still too daunting for James or his dad. It was Ephie, Father Michael's wife, who said a few words about Cathy Peck. "A strong woman…" she'd begun, "who never gave up and never compromised."

James couldn't look at his dad during Ephie's speech. He kept his head bowed and his eyes fixed on his feet so his best friend Craig couldn't throw him a sympathetic glance. That would just have set him off.

Now almost thirteen, they'd both grown a little taller. School had kept them preoccupied but there wasn't a day where one of them didn't say something that reminded them of the disaster the previous summer.

Worst of all was Mrs. Harrison. With no sign of Mendel ever returning to Drumfintley, Jean Harrison was trying to come to terms with the loss of her two youngest children, Wee Joe and Helen.

At the end of the service, Father Michael met them all in the vestry. He locked the chalice and collection basket in the safe before speaking softly, "Look. We all know how resourceful Mendel is." He ducked out of his vestments and fixed his thinning hair. "Personally, I don't believe they're dead. I just had to…"

"We agreed," interrupted David. "We agreed we'd go through with the service for the sake of the rest of the villagers. None of us really believe they are…" He glanced over at Jean.

She nodded. "I know."

James felt a funny sensation build in his chest as his dad clasped Craig's mum's hand.

"Look," interrupted James, "we know Archie is gone for good, but I'm sure I saw Mum in the tunnels of Artilis."

"I'm not convinced," said Craig.

James ignored him. "We all hope that when Mendel and the kids disappeared, he took them somewhere safe."

"If he could," added Craig. "They were sent somewhere on purpose. Dendralon might just have... You know?"

James bristled. "Can we try and keep things positive, Craig?"

Craig examined his feet. "Yeh, if you like."

"I like," snapped James.

Jean seemed to melt. She steadied herself on the old wooden vestry table. "They were so young. How could they possibly look after themselves?"

Light streamed into the vestry through the single stained-glass window, throwing coloured patterns over their faces.

James could hear shouts and cheers outside. "What's that all about?"

They all looked at each other as the racket intensified.

The heavy back door of the church creaked open.

"Whoever it is, they're coming this way," said Michael. "Stand back."

All the shouts and mutterings died down before there was a soft knock on the vestry door.

James pressed his ear against wood.

Father Michael adopted a vicar-like tone. "Just a moment."

But the brass handle turned and the heavy door swung open.

There, amongst a huge crowd of Drumfintley villagers, bathed in coloured light from the stained-glass windows, stood Helen and someone who looked like... Wee Joe.

Jean screamed out – "Joe! Helen!"

Everyone, including James, burst into tears and hugged the children.

Appearing between a throng of legs, Bero, the Harrisons' golden retriever, whined and wagged his tail, excitedly.

Through a series of sobs and bear hugs Helen said, "We wondered why...you'd left Bero...in the house all by...himself."

James noticed the plastic brandy barrel. The well-worn object housed Mendel, the wizard-goldfish who'd taken them on all of their crazy adventures. It hung down like a pendulum from Bero's collar.

"A bit of privacy!" exclaimed Father Michael. "Give the children a bit of privacy." He beamed and ushered the children and Bero inside the vestry.

The heavy door clunked shut.

"Any sign of Cathy?" said David.

Helen nuzzled free of her mother's wet cardigan then, peering over bleary-eyed at James's dad, whispered, "Sorry, Mr. Peck."

"Ah, I see." His dad looked genuinely sad.

Mixed up, James was too confused, drained and relieved all at the same time to decide how he really felt. He gulped and, with more than a hint of trepidation, knelt down to look into the barrel's plastic window. "Where have you been, Mendel?"

An orange-coloured goldfish appeared at the window as the familiar voice began to echo round in his head. "James, my boy. Good to see you again. Good to see you all again!"

"Mendel, what happened?" he pressed. James could tell by the look on everyone's faces that they could all hear the wizard now, too.

"We should have been sucked into the void that led back to Artilis, with Dendralon, but I managed to do a little spell through Helen."

James still experienced a series of annoying pangs every time Mendel spoke about Helen in this way. *How selfish am I? To be jealous of Helen's ability to perform Mendel's magic, when that's what saved their lives...*

"I managed to change Dendralon's spell enough to reset our trajectory."

"Your what?" enquired Craig.

"Our destination," emphasised Mendel.

"Ah," grunted Craig. "Why didn't he just say that then?" Craig looked round for someone to back him up, but nobody did. They were all too flabbergasted and thankful to be bothered.

"The children should have been killed by the spell. Split into a million different pieces but the Kraken saved them."

James didn't understand. "How could the Kraken save them? We killed it."

Mendel floated nearer to his window. "Yes but..."

"But the Kraken's blood was on our clothes," explained Helen.

"Still is," added Wee Joe. He pulled his filthy shirt away from his chest to show everyone the black splodges.

"It made us immortal," said Helen.

There was the sound of Mendel clearing his throat. "Not quite, Helen. But it protected you enough to keep you alive, and it gave me some time to focus my thoughts. It allowed me take us back to Earth. To a place where I could re-gather my strength, safe from Dendralon's attention."

"The only problem was," piped up Helen, "that we got stuck there. We were kind of locked in a certain bit of land. Mendel explained that we would have to find a crystal to get home and that we shouldn't try to get home until we'd fixed the Key of Artilis. It got damaged. We had to use both to get back."

"Archie's golden key," said Father Michael. "I remember now."

Wee Joe tugged on Craig's sleeve. "There was tigers and panthers and…"

"Yeh, right!" said Craig, waspishly. He began to laugh, but soon stopped when no one else joined in.

"Was!" blasted Wee Joe.

David listened to the vestry door before asking, in a whisper, "Who else stood in that mess? The Kraken blood must have been on all of us. Come on, who can remember? Hands up!"

James felt a pang of embarrassment. He hated it when his dad assumed the 'rah-rah' tones of the Scout Leader.

Everyone in the vestry put their hand up, though.

"Better include Bero in that roll-call," said Craig.

"Wonderful," said Father Michael, an uneasy expression forming on his face. "When you say immortal, I take it you mean…?"

"The person can never die," finished Mendel. "But I'm *not* convinced immortal is the right word. It could just have given us the protection we needed at the time."

"So, it just made us temporarily immortal?" blurted Ephie.

"Not sure," said Mendel.

"Ah, that's all right then," said Father Michael.

James wondered why Helen was looking down at the barrel suspiciously.

"And you…?" enquired Helen.

"Ah… Well, I was, of course, protected from any such good fortune. Being hermetically sealed in this barrel I had to rely on my own inner magic."

"Mendel means that the barrel is air-tight," added Ephie, seemingly for Craig's benefit, but James was glad of the explanation, too.

"In fact," continued Mendel, "in my current form, I can only expect to live for another few weeks."

"Bummer," said Craig.

James felt guilty for even asking the question, but he had to. "What about Mum? Is there anything you can do for her before you…?"

"Snuff it," finished Craig.

Everyone leered at him.

"What?" protested Craig. "Mendel's just told us that he's only got a little time left."

James took a deep breath. "Never mind him, Mendel. What can we do to help? You and Mum, I mean."

"I have a plan in mind that would bring everyone back to the way they were a few seconds before the destruction of Denthan."

"Even MacNulty?" asked Father Michael.

"Not MacNulty," replied Mendel.

"Ah…" sighed Father Michael. "That's a shame."

"It's one of the rules, you see," said Mendel.

"Rules?" asked Craig.

"It's one of the rules that governs inter-dimensional physics. Loretta Maginata proposed the theory back in…"

"We get the drift," said Craig, mournfully. He began to fidget with Bero's collar.

"It will be difficult and dangerous for us all, and nothing can be guaranteed." The wizard goldfish sailed past his plastic window, eyeing them all. "There is, however, a small chance that we could save a whole planet. Over one trillion life forms, good and bad, all saved. What do you all think?"

"Let me get this straight," said Craig. "Instead of living forever, we can risk everything and perhaps save a few million monsters?"

"Craig!" snapped Jean. "That's enough! You really exasperate me sometimes."

He bowed sheepishly. "Sorry, Mum. I was only trying to summarize things."

"Well don't!" she barked.

James stifled a grin and nodded. "I'm in!"

"Me too," said Father Michael, "only I don't know what the bishop would make of me being immortal. Not exactly politically correct, is it?"

"We've just got Helen and Wee Joe back. Should we really be thinking of setting off again?" said David.

"Dad. We can't give up on Mum."

"No... I never meant it like that. I just think we should regroup, let things settle a bit, think it through." He sighed and ruffled his dark hair nervously. "Okay, hands up all those who want to try out Mendel's plan."

Everyone jerked their hands up and leered at David, who eased his own up above his head until it wavered just below the naked bulb that hung down from the vestry ceiling. "Fine. Just checking."

"So we have some consensus?" said Mendel. "Excellent. I've had a long time to think it over. We have the Key of Artilis. I've tested it and it works. We have, however, only three days and eight hours left before it will be too late."

"That's pretty specific," said Father Michael.

"Trust me, I'll tell you as we go along," said Mendel.

"You mean, you'll think of something as you go along?" said Craig.

James knew that if Mendel could have smiled, he would have.

"As you say, Craig; I'll think of something as I go along."

They bustled out of St. Donan's surrounded by a throng of puzzled villagers. The graveyard abounded with a whole range of questions that could never be easily answered. Gauser, the village drunk, shouted something out about 'the usual big con', while others talked of government cover-ups and, 'the slightly too close for comfort', alien abduction stories.

It will take a while for all this to calm down, thought James.

CHAPTER THREE

ARTILIS

Final adjustments to the stone circle inside the pyramid of Ra had taken longer than Dendralon would have liked. The Racnids, covered in downy hair and set high on six legs, clicked their cup-like hands in excitement. They had turned the tables on their old masters, the humanoid Artilians, and now relished in the irony of making *them* do all the repairs and work needed. Slave had become master and master had become slave.

"The burns I endured on Denthan have almost disappeared," hissed Dendralon, his long, black tongue forking out between his needle-sharp teeth. Tall and muscular, like a man, his face was covered in grey scales that shone dully in the amber light. His cheeks and throat, he could see, were well on the way to recovery. His damaged scales had re-grown over the last two years and had knitted themselves back round his wide nostrils. His yellow-slit eyes blinked as he gazed at his reflection. He traced the surface of the polished copper mirror with his long, cold fingers and viewed his bride.

Dark, inky hair fell over her shoulders, partly hiding her golden breastplates, while an assortment of pewter bands and bangles circled her waist, arms and legs. Her skin was as white as snow, and her eyes burned with a fury that hinted at an incredible inner strength and determination.

He'd emptied her mind of all previous lives and experiences and had replaced them with his own template of memories.

A long, green plume fell away from her golden crown. It flicked in the fading light as she shooed away the fussing Racnid females. They tried, in vain, to offer her perfumes, bitter Artilian wine and the finest of delicacies.

Elhada, the most senior Racnid in Dendralon's court, bowed toward her master's new queen before shuffling towards him on her six spindly legs. She lowered her reptilian head in reverence. "Sire."

"Speak without rasping like a withered old maid, Elhada," said Dendralon.

The black-furred Racnid bristled then began to speak in exactly the same manner. "The Artilian wizards have repaired the gateway in the pyramid of Ra."

"At last," hissed Dendralon. "And how have you managed to install such obedience in the wretched magicians of Artilia?"

"My children have captured Junera. She is in your dungeon." Elhada withdrew a pouched hand from a hair-covered slit in her side. It held a simple silver crown. "The Artilians seem to set great store on her pathetic existence."

Dendralon took the silver trinket and spun it round his long scaled fingers. "You see, Beldam, there is always a key that will unlock the most stubborn of doors."

She offered him a tight-lipped smile before biting into a ripe peacherine. A cluster of fluttering Artilian Wasps with yellow antennae busily mopped up the juice that spilled from her crimson lips. Their gossamer wings fanned the still air and cooled the sacred space around the throne.

"What are you going to do with the gateway, Dendralon, now that the Artilian wizards have succumbed to their fears?" Her brown eyes glistened in the pink glow that filtered in from the open window.

"I intend to reclaim what is rightfully mine," he answered.

Beldam suddenly assumed the look of the woman from Drumfintley. "But I thought this was the world you sought."

"It is, but there are still many other worlds to reclaim, my Queen." He reminded himself to repeat her therapy; make sure that she had forgotten her life in Drumfintley.

Beldam smiled.

She was growing to like him, he decided. He would make sure that her former life was no more than a mist that seeped into the occasional dream.

The Racnid, Elhada, had remained motionless, fixed in her awkward bow.

"Dendralon turned to look down on the Queen of the spiders. "What of your princess, Elandria? How has she eluded your spiderlings for all this time?"

Elhada exposed her teeth, the folds of her reptilian lips riding high. "Elandria is still at large. I have even tried the truth serum on Junera but she still reveals nothing."

"Indeed." Dendralon feared no one, but he felt uneasy about Elandria being free to move against him. She possessed magical powers that puzzled him. He also felt uneasy about Eethan Magichand and his master, Mendel. He would soon move on the city of Gwendral. He'd finally established its new location.It sat on the surface of Ebos, a barren planet in the Ephlos system.

"Prepare twenty thousand of your children and fifteen thousand Inubian dog-men for battle. The Denthan city, which escaped its planet's destruction, will fall first. All inside will perish."

"Yes, my Lord. But it will take time to send all these troops through the pinnacle of Ra without a proper gateway on the other side. I don't see how…"

Elhada suddenly flayed at her open mouth with her pouched hands. "Can't…breathe."

Dendralon closed his eyes and hissed menacingly. "Assemble the army. I have selected a site that will ensure they all get through swiftly."

Elhada backed away, faltering on her skidding legs. "Sire, I do not want to upset you but…"

Reading her mind, Dendralon's eyes widened. "I know it will leave the Artilians partially unguarded. You should select carefully which Racnids you leave behind, for you will die if they do not guard the Artilians well."

"Of course, my lord."

He watched Elhada scuttle out of the coronation hall, with its towering marble pillars, ornate fountains and golden ceilings. Her black and crimson down bristled as she passed the jackal-faced Inubian guards.

He turned to the nearest Inubian. "Tell me that she will be more useful to me alive than dead. Sometimes I think the sand worms should enjoy a royal feast." He used his tongue to snatch a piece of meat from a silver platter. The tiny spines that lined his gullet rippled, forcing it down into his belly. He flicked his eyelids to the side and homed in on her heat trace behind the marble wall. He could still hear Elhada cursing him as she left the palace.

CHAPTER FOUR

ANOTHER JOURNEY

James felt a pang of regret as he walked past the flaking façade of Galdinie's shop. It was boarded up and the letterbox hung, limply, at an angle, from the battered-looking twin doors. According to Gauser, the local tramp, Mrs. Galdinie had moved back to Italy. Drumfintley just wasn't the same without her.

"But we're immortal," explained Wee Joe. "We can come this time because…" He paused, not looking entirely sure what the word 'immortal' meant.

"…we can't be killed," finished Helen.

"Dinny let immortality go ti yer heed, wee laddie," added Craig.

One of the most annoying things about Craig is his pathetic persistence in faking a Scottish accent, thought James. "That was just rubbish, Craig."

"What, the accent or the advice?" asked Craig.

"Both!" James shook his head and stepped into the underpass. Dank and dark, he sidestepped a broken bottle and noticed that some idiot had spray-painted 'The Drummy Young Team Rules' on the walls.

"How many volunteers do we have with us this time?" asked Mendel, in a weary voice.

"There's me and Dad, the four Harrisons, Ephie and Father Michael. Oh, and there's Bero; so that's nine."

The tunnel shook as a lorry rumbled overhead on the by-pass.

"There's no sign of Sergeant Carr," said James, emerging into the sunlight at the other end of the tunnel.

Everyone shrugged.

James was wearing his favourite light blue football shorts, a tatty top and, as usual, he carried his battered, green rucksack. Craig wore a pair of jogging bottoms. James stared at them thoughtfully.

Craig caught his gaze and grabbed hold of the thick material. "Moth-proof."

"Yeh, but we don't have any man-eating Denthan moths waiting on us up in the woods this time, numpty."

Craig continued to look smug. "How do you know?"

James moved back beside Bero. "Mendel, I've just thought of something. We don't have a crystal to take us through the Jesus Rocks."

"I'm going to try something else," said Mendel.

James felt his pulse quicken. "You mean the key?"

"Exactly. There is a small degree of risk but, as I've pointed out, there's a good chance you're all immortal."

"A good chance!" hissed James. "You never put it across like that earlier, back in St. Donan's."

"I'm sure I said that the matter of immortality was far from a certainty," said Mendel.

"Well, I'm sure that you never." James closed his eyes. "I thought you'd tested it out?"

"I've tested the key. I've already brought two and a half fully grown Bengal tigers back to life using that." Mendel sounded impatient.

"What do you mean, two and a half?"

"Trust me, you don't want to know," interjected Helen.

"Look, James, the key will work and, if the legends are true, your spattering of Kraken blood should make you immortal."

James whispered in an anxious tone, "Firstly, when have you ever seen a Kraken killed, apart from last year? Secondly, give an example of someone splashed with its blood who cheated certain death."

"It is written," snapped Mendel.

James felt his face flush. "Lots of things are written."

Ephie's voice echoed out across the hillside. "I need to rest." She plumped herself down on a moss-covered tree stump and rummaged in her pockets.

James's frustration subsided.

"Tablet?" asked Wee Joe.

"I bought Mrs. Galdinie's last batch. I keep it for special occasions: walks, weddings, Christmas…" Her words trailed away as, distractedly, she peeled off the greaseproof paper and broke off a piece of the honey-coloured fudge for the kids. "There you go."

The adults, all panting with the strain of the climb, looked expectant.

"And the big kids, too," she added, dishing out some more.

James had noticed that she'd regained a few of the pounds she'd lost after marrying Father Michael. She'd looked a bit ill after losing all that weight the first time. She suited a little more roundness, he decided. It made her look kinder.

"Best get going," said his dad, checking his compass.

"Dad, we don't really need a compass to find the Jesus Rocks."

His dad smiled. "Sorry, Son. Just a habit."

"Well *I* think it's very sensible, David," said Jean. "You never know where we'll end up."

Craig and James exchanged knowing looks. They'd discussed 'it' before. 'It' being the fact that his dad and Craig's mum seemed to get on a bit too well.

As if reading the boys' minds his dad added, "I wish your mum was here, James."

"You do?" blurted Ephie. "I mean, of course you do." She wiped some crumbs from her shoulder.

The change of emphasis made no difference. Everyone knew his mum was hard work. The village of Drumfintley, however, wasn't the same place without her. It was sterile, lifeless, and mundane. People genuinely missed her. And James knew that they could have done with his mum on this adventure too. She was braver than any of them. He hoped that this plan of Mendel's would bring her back. Craig would try to cheer him up sometimes, saying things like: "I bet your mum's got Dendralon permanently grounded. He's probably just as desperate to get her off Artilis, as we are to get her back."

James fought off a series of nervous coughs as they entered the Tank Woods. The shadows seemed to move of their own accord, assuming the shapes of Tree Trolls, reptilian Hedra and the sloth-like Osgrunfs they'd encountered on Denthan. The monsters' howls and screams drifted around in his mind as they made their way deeper into the gloom.

Helen tapped James on the arm. "I've got the key. You know, the Key of Artilis."

"Good, Helen. Keep it safe." James saw that she'd grown up a lot in the last few years. She was almost the same age he'd been when he first made the journey to Denthan. Her hair was much longer and she'd become much less narky. He noticed that they'd dropped behind the main group so he took the opportunity to ask her something that was niggling at him. "Can you still do Mendel's magic?"

"Yes, when he wants me to," she answered.

"Do you get the knocking sensation?" James felt embarrassed. "You know, the pain in your head and stuff just before it happens."

"Eh, no. The words just come out of my mouth. There's no warning. Sometimes..." she had to step over a fallen branch. "Sometimes, I get a wonderful sense of flying."

"Really," said James, in a quiet voice. Now he was totally depressed. *How come she didn't have the headaches? She actually felt better when she did the magic. Had Mendel found his true magical partner in Helen Harrison?*.

"There they are!" exclaimed Father Michael. He loosened his vicar's dog-collar and steadied himself on a fallen Larch.

The silhouettes of nine standing stones were framed by a deep red sky.

"It's sad, isn't it?" said Craig.

James flicked a cleg from Bero's back before it bit down with its scissor-like mandibles. "What's sad?"

"The graffiti; the 'Jesus Saves' thing. It's going to fade away now that Archie's gone."

"I suppose," mused James. He screwed up his eyes and focused on the biggest stone. "Well, someone's done it. Look!"

There, in the exact spot it had always been, was the message 'Jesus Saves'. The fresh white paint gleamed in the dusky light.

"So, who's done that, then?" asked James.

Craig ran forward. He shuddered to a halt at the stone, Bero close on his heels. He ran his fingers along its orange tinted surface until they brushed the bold letters. "It's still wet. Look." He wiggled his fingers close to James's shirt."

"Get off!" snapped James.

"It must have been one of us," said Ephie.

"Well, it wasn't me, dear," sighed Father Michael.

"Nor me," said David Peck

"Not guilty," piped up Jean.

"We was in di jungle," explained Wee Joe.

James and Craig looked at each other at the same time and said, "Eethan?"

"I don't think so," interjected Mendel. "But you can ask him yourself in a few moments."

"We're going to see Eethan again?" asked Helen, excitedly.

"That's the plan, my girl." The goldfish swivelled past the window of the barrel in a kind of wobbly wiggle as Bero bumped to a halt.

"Right, everyone stand in the middle of the stone circle," instructed Mendel. "Helen, place the Key of Artilis at the base of the biggest stone."

James felt another pang of jealousy pester him.

Helen lifted the key, still whirring, out of its new box and placed it down as instructed.

James felt the knocking sensation in his head. It was building. For once he was glad to experience the thudding pain of Mendel's magic. "Wwwjeswwuswwsaveswwww. Wweboswww!"

Everyone stared at him as the fishy sounds filled the air.

The golden Key of Artilis spun so fast that it became a blur. It changed from gold to bright yellow then, to James's horror, it disappeared. His heart sank as the turf beneath his feet began to roll back from the bedrock.

Only teetering for a few seconds, they all tumbled backwards into the black abyss. There had been no crystal sheet to suspend them, as usual. They were already falling.

"Mendel!" James yelled. "This isn't right. What's gone...wrong...?"

CHAPTER FIVE

THE STONE LARTHS

The great, white dragon, Whindril, sailed over the high citadel of Gwendral. Huge, but still wonderfully elegant and graceful, the dragon banked hard to her left, disappearing round the shining alabaster tower. With a tremendous roar that shook the windows of the small houses and terraces below, she reappeared at the base of the edifice. Her talons clicked on the cobbled courtyard as she lighted.

Leaping up onto her back to join a tall reptilian figure, Eethan, a tiny blue-skinned man with a shock of white hair, flicked the dragon's golden reins and whispered his instructions, "Flich na hath tan Oribianus."

With two huge beats of her snowy wings Whindril was soon above the city once more, and heading due east. Oribianus was the only range of mountains for thousands of miles. Mendel had told Eethan to look there for the creature. Alone and long abandoned by his own race, the creature had been left to survive amongst the Mountain Wraiths and Stone Larths. Whindril would have to be careful when she dropped them off. Beside him, on the ornate dragon saddle, sat his companion on this particular quest. A Hedra captain who'd proved his worth many times in the past, Jal. The giant Hedra, almost eight foot tall, held on fearfully. Eethan knew how his Hedra friend hated riding on the backs of dragons.

"When will we get there, Eethan?" he shouted. The wind cut into their faces as they pushed on through the low cloud.

"Eet weel bee another hour or so," Eethan answered. The vowel 'e' of Eethan's words was always stretched out in a high-pitched whine.

Below them, through gaps in the dust clouds, a vast desert covered the once-lush valleys and hills. Eethan noticed the aberration first. Great lines meandered over the dunes. On the march, thousands of the insect-like Sorabs headed west toward Gwendral and the remaining temperate lands. The desert had become too barren even for the Sorabs and now they were swarming. It wouldn't be long until they reached the outlying Yeltan villages and then Gwendral itself.

"There are more than I imagined," shouted Jal. He gripped on tightly as Whindril dipped forward. Losing height the huge snow-white dragon dived for a thousand feet before holding position above the swarm. Ant-like in appearance, the Sorabs walked on two legs. They had hideous, misshapen heads with an array of different tubes that fell away from their necks. Some of these appendages, Eethan knew, could spray deadly jets of acid, while others were tipped with an array of suckers and hooks that could attach to their foes and pull them into their horned jaws. He could see their wings lying flat across their backs. Unlike the wings of the Artilian wasps he'd encountered the year before, these appendages seemed to be vestigial or perhaps purely for display. He had never seen or heard of any Sorab ever using them. They preferred to scuttle across the sand in their long lines.

"They ees only two or threeee days away from Gwendral." Eethan pulled on the reins and Whindril climbed. Ominous looking mountains loomed on the distant horizon. A cluster of twenty or so sharp peaks towered up from the desert floor. Snowy clouds gathered between their rosy summits, and mist streamed down over their barren slopes.

"Have these peaks been explored?" shouted Jal.

"No. Theeres no mention of what else leeves there apart from thee wraiths and larths. Only that thee creeture we are seeking was last seen theere in a cave. A flyer told of it. Eet ees said to be living in ee cave below thee highest peak."

The tallest mountain was less jagged than the others that formed the outcrop of Oribianus. More volcano-like, with a flattened top, it had two massive shoulders that stood proud of the other peaks.

"Wees will land neeer thee top and go down by foot. Eet weel be less threatening that way. Can you sees a cave down theere?"

"Nothing yet, my small friend, just rocks and shale on this side of the mountain. We will find the cave."

With a command in dragon tongue, Eethan pulled on the reins until Whindril found footing on a slope just above one of the rocky shoulders.

Jal dismounted with a sigh of relief. "What does this creature look like?"

"Well," began Eethan, shielding his face from the biting wind, "eet's like a horse, only eet has six wings and the face of a dragon."

Whindril arched her snake-like neck and moved her head between them to listen. She blinked her big black eyes.

"Is it dangerous?" urged Jal. He unsheathed his curved Hedra sword and tested its sharpness on a clump of heather. It sliced through the woody tussock with ease.

Eethan shook his head. Patches of hardened snow dotted the slope glistening like Whindril's scales every time the sun cut through the fast-moving clouds.

"Thee creature ees special. Eet can act like a crystal, like mees. Golden yellow light, eet sheds."

"And your light is blue, Eethan, just like your skin. Are you not cold up here?"

"Neever cold." Eethan pushed his thumb up his left nostril and surveyed the massive peak. "Wees should go this way." He pointed to a dip in the heather about five hundred yards away. "Whindril, you stay here feer now." Eethan began to chew on a lump of yellow grot he'd extracted from his nose. "Waste not want not," he tittered.

"Ye che snath," growled the dragon.

Eethan smiled and turned to Jal. "She will come if we call her."

They moved off towards the dip as fast as they could, snow whisking into their faces. The clouds had thickened.

Jal came to a halt and raised his sword before jabbing it into the hard ground. The blade shuddered on the rocks. "This ground is frozen solid."

"And thees place looks promising," said Eethan.

They were standing on a plateau just below the summit, and there was a dip ahead about fifty yards deep and a hundred yards wide. In the middle of the hollow a weathered stone circle stood proud of the heather and rocks. Perfect in every way, it had eight stone lintels that held the nine stones an equal distance apart. Eethan had seen such a structure once before. As they moved closer, Jal became agitated. "What is that?" He was pointing to a carving on the thickest stone. It depicted a battle between two great armies all set within the outline of a six-winged horse. The horse seemed to have a dragon's head.

"Thees ees thee creature," whispered Eethan, his voice full of wonder. "Thee Hipposaur."

"What battle is this?" asked Jal. "I can see Manimals and Yeltans." The human-like Manimals seemed to be on the same side as the diminutive Yeltans.

"And ee can see Racnids and Stone Larths," added Eethan, tracing the figures with his long, gangly fingers. The wind blew his pallid hair about his face. The snow was becoming heavier. Eethan nodded as he stared at the figures. "Thees ees not a battle that has been, these ees a battle that ees yet to come. Racnids have neever met Yeltans or Stone Larths eever before."

"And the Hipposaur?" prompted Jal. "What side does it fight on?"

"Ee cannot tell…"

There was a rumble of stone behind them. It sounded as if the whole mountain had opened up.

Wincing in the blizzard, they turned round slowly to face over a hundred Stone Larths.

Ogre-like in appearance, the Stone Larth's skin was encrusted with lumps of granite that acted like a layer of impenetrable armour. Jal braced and pushed his back against the biggest stone. This, however, did not seem to please the Stone Larths. At over twenty feet tall, the most vicious looking of the creatures smashed his fist down into the snow-covered heather. He snarled at Jal, widening his bright green eyes and baring his blackened teeth.

Eethan mumbled a charm. Blue light soon filled his hands and then crept over the rest of his puny body.

The big Stone Larth growled and took a step back.

"Ees not here to hurt you," proclaimed Eethan. "Ees here to talk with thee Hipposaur." He pointed to the outline on the stone. Ee needs to meets weeth *eet*."

The lumbering creature, nearest to them, shook his heavy head and bellowed out a kind of laugh. The sound was like two great stones sliding over each other.

Jal slashed his sword through the snowflakes as a warning.

The Stone Larth stretched itself taller. "Why would the Hipposaur see you?" it bellowed.

Jal lowered his sword.

"Wees have a proposition for eet."

"The Hipposaur is our god. He does not listen to propositions from..." the Larth hesitated, "...from strange creatures that come up our mountain with swords and a dragon." He glanced back down the slope at the outline of Whindril. "Just because you can make light cover your little body does not mean that you scare us enough to disturb our god."

Eethan was beginning to realise that these Stone Larths were not only huge and powerful but that they were intelligent too. The lead Stone Larth gave a signal, and his kin began to surround them. The hulking creature stretched out his bulky arm and made to pick up Eethan but Jal lunged forward and cut down with his curved sword. It shuddered off the Larth's stone-encrusted hide and fell from his hand. "Eethan, fall back!" Jal dived round the back of the largest stone but came face to face with another Larth. It thumped down its fist, just missing Jal by inches. Jal rolled over the hardened snow and stood up, drawing the black bow from his back. The arrow was already nocked and aimed. The Larth shielded his eyes with one hand and lifted a heavy boulder with the other. Jal drew back the bowstring but yelled out as the first Stone Larth picked him up like a toy. The other Larth laughed and dropped his boulder.

Eethan raised his hand and the huge creature, holding Jal, flew backwards into his kin.

Jal jumped free and sprinted back to Eethan's side. His bow lay crumpled at the Larth's feet.

With a chorus of roars that shook the stone circle the Larths righted their leader and attacked.

"Wait!" The leader of the Larths pulled on the shoulder of an advancing Larth, bringing him to a dead stop.

"What now?" whispered Jal.

Eethan took a step forward and bowed. "Wees do not want to fight weeth you and wees are sorry eef wees have upset you. Eee humbly ask for an audience with your god."

The leader of the Stone Larths made his way to the fore once more. He drew a long, ugly-looking sword from his belt and plunged it deep into the snow-covered ground. "If you promise to show our god the proper reverence, I will ask him if he wants to see you."

"Of course wee weel. Of course, great leader of the Larths." Eethan remained prone, never once looking up.

There were many growls and groans of discontent from the other Stone Larths.

"Silence!" bellowed the leader.

Out of the corner of his eye, Eethan could see the giant form of Whindril appearing. Like a huge phantom, the dragon stepped forward through a curtain of snow behind the Larths. She stretched out her wings and arched her slender neck, holding her stance at the edge of the hollow. Her speckled, white wings looked ghostly amongst the flurries of snow that spiralled round the crater.

"The snow dragon is going to attack us," moaned a thick-set Larth.

"Not eef ee tell her not to," sighed Eethan. Slowly, he lifted his head to meet the gaze of the Larth leader.

"Stop!" shouted Jal. One of the Larths, to the rear of the group, was running towards Whindril, his sword raised.

Whindril pulled her head high above the charging Larth causing it to skid to a halt before her heavily scaled chest.

The Larth threw his sword up at her.

Eethan watched it spin in mid air, smiling as her jaws snapped down on the sword. It broke in two. Then, with a rapid movement of her front foot, she caught the Larth in her talons.

"Whindril. No!" Eethan waved his hand to stop her but it was too late. Whindril brought her talons together and the writhing Stone Larth exploded in a shower of dust and gore that spattered down over his kin.

Whindril roared out, *Raaaar!*

"Enough Whindril!" Eethan made a signal with his hands that she understood. The great white dragon drew in her massive wings and roared back in answer, a series of yelps and chirps interspersing the call.

"Lower your weapons," urged Jal. "We cannot control this snow dragon completely. Do not antagonise her."

The Stone Larths laid their weapons down on the snow.

"I am sorry for your loss," said Eethan, an anxious look on his face.

The Stone Larth leader looked confused and frightened. "You lie. You cannot control this animal."

"My dragon meeerely defended heerself," said Eethan.

"We just need to talk to your god," Jal reminded.

The Stone Larth glanced up at the darkening sky. "It will soon be nightfall. I doubt even your pet will be able to fend off an attack from the Mountain Wraiths. The peaks are theirs after the sun goes down. Come, we must go further down the mountain. I will see if our god, Elcar, will see you." With a reluctant sigh, the lumbering Larth waved his arms until his kin had made a path for them.

The light that surrounded Eethan began to fade. He smiled at the leader of the Larths and followed him out of the stone circle. Jal clumped onwards by his side, cursing the bitter-cold wind, while Whindril made her way through the Stone Larths, who scattered fearfully before her.

CHAPTER SIX

THE REUNION

When James Peck opened his eyes he instantly knew where he was. He looked down at his feet and saw the stone scales carved into the floor. This semi-circle of scales had once formed the vision-pool of the main Council chamber. They were back in the city of Gwendral.

"Craig!"

"Yeh, I know. And look, they've fixed the seats that the Mertol smashed in the fight with the Raptor." Craig was already walking down between the empty rows of wooden seats where they'd fought Dendralon for the blue crystal two years before.

Michael and Ephie looked round in trepidation, while James's dad just stood stalk still, his mouth agog. "Where...? What is this place?"

"This place, Dad, is Gwendral. You're in the main Council chamber high up in the most beautiful citadel in Denthan."

"Only we're not on Denthan anymore, are we Mendel?" shouted Craig. His words echoed off the high ceiling as he wandered down an ornate aisle. "They've done a good job on these seats."

James knelt down beside Bero and peered into the barrel. "Where are we again, Mendel?"

The tiny goldfish slid into view. "We are on the planet of Ebos. Eethan transported the city here after he dropped you all off in Drum-fintley two years ago."

Craig ran back towards the group. "So where *is* the wee nose-picker?"

"Eethan? Not here, I sense," said Mendel.

Everyone turned as the main door of the Council chamber swung open.

"Craig? James!"

Cimerato ran in to greet them, his long blond hair swaying as he patted their backs. "It's so good to see you, boys. And..." He knelt down beside Bero, scrunching up the Retriever's golden fur. He squinted into the barrel. "Still a goldfish, old friend?"

"I'm afraid so," answered Mendel.

Cimerato looked well, decided James. The tall Manimal captain, decked in his yellow armour, beamed with excitement. He ushered them into the ante-room where his father, Lord Eldane, fussed over a thick book.

"Michael, Ephie, James, Craig... You're all here." The old man seemed genuinely pleased to see them again.

"Lord Eldane," said James. "This is my father, David."

"How do you do, Mr. Peck?"

"Pleased to meet you, Sir," said David.

James could see that his dad was staring rudely at the Manimals' strange eyes. He cleared his throat loudly and then whispered, "Dad."

David Peck shook his head and backed off a little. "S...sorry."

James continued. "It's my mum that's missing this time, Lord Eldane."

"Oh dear..." The studded wooden door of the ante-chamber creaked open and Lord Eldane waved the creature in. "You've met Elandria."

James eyed the large Racnid, Elandria. She was the outcast princess of the vicious Racnids that lived on Artilis. Craig and James had dis-covered, the year previously, that Artilis and Mars were one-in-the-same place. Her green and purple down rippled as she scuttled over on her six legs. Elandria bowed her turtle-like head in deference to James, offering him a hand of sorts. James took it and shook it gently. "Elan-dria, nice to see you again. Is Eethan here?"

"He is, young James. And look…" She'd spied Craig. "My old cell-mate, Craig. Still not had an honourable death yet, my boy?"

"Don't start that again," sneered Craig.

James could tell his pal was pleased to see the spider princess again.

"Eethan?" Mendel prompted.

"Ah. Gone on a journey with Whindril and Jal."

"To the Oribianus Mountains?" asked Mendel.

"Indeed. They've gone in search of the third creature that you said dwelt there," answered Lord Eldane. "As you indicated, Elandria is an Orphan of Light, the same as Eethan. We now hope to find our own Orphan of Light here on Ebos."

"Excellent," said Mendel. "How long have they been gone?"

"Only a day," interjected Cimerato.

James watched Helen wander into the ante-chamber. She'd been listening-in from the open door, he suspected.

"What is the third creature? I mean, I overhead…" She sat down on a scarlet window-cushion and looked out across the city of Gwendral.

Cimerato coughed and said, conspiratorially, to Mendel, "Ah, well, I don't know how much they all know…"

"I will tell them now, Cimerato," said Mendel.

"Tell us what?" pressed Craig.

James heard Mendel clear his throat. It was an unpleasant bubbly, hacking sound that made James cringe.

"Eethan, as you all know, managed to take the place of the Denthan crystal when the sun Tealfirth exploded. He became as bright as any crystal and allowed us to escape the destruction."

"What?" David Peck looked bemused.

"Bear with us Dad," said James. "Eethan became the light of Denthan. His very body transformed into such a powerful beam of magic light that he literally saved us all. He balanced the crystals that sat on the magic scales and enabled the city to function as a giant ark."

"Ah," said David, obviously none-the-wiser.

"I remember," said Jean dreamily.

Everyone looked at her briefly then, after a noisy splash, resumed staring down at the brandy barrel that hung round Bero's neck.

"Elandria performed a similar function on Artilis. If it wasn't for her crimson shield we wouldn't have been able to get back to Drumfintley and tackle the Kraken," said Mendel.

"She produced dat big curtain of red light," said Wee Joe.

"The shield. Correct!" snapped Mendel. "But she is capable of much, much more; aren't you Elandria?"

The Racnid bowed. "Perhaps."

James's head was beginning to ache.

Mendel swished past the barrel's plastic window. "Let us go back into the main chamber and look into the vision-pool."

They all followed Bero, James, and Helen towards the stone semi-circle of scales that spread out from the throne.

James said the word, "Wwwwviswwwonwwpoolww."

Instantly, a patch of mist swirled over the stone scales. Blown away by a blast of wind that ruffled their hair and clothes, they now looked down on a huge mirror. James could see himself. Now almost thirteen he was beginning to look more like his mum. His hair had darkened from mousy brown to deep chestnut, and his eyes had the same orange clouds round the pupils. He still hoped his face would catch up with his nose and put it in proportion somehow. He looked across at his dad, however, and realised that he was probably stuck with his honker the way it was. Bero plodded over to the edge of the vision-pool just as Helen said, "Wwweethawwnww!"

A cold shiver ran down James's spine as a mixture of anger and embarrassment washed over him. The mirrored surface of the pool rippled until Eethan appeared in the picture. About three feet tall with grey-blue skin and a shock of white hair, he looked the same as he always had.

"Sis did well there, eh?" bayed Craig.

James felt his face flush. "I think she did very well," he lied. "After almost a year with Mendel…"

"She's made you redundant," Craig jibbed.

"Hardly. You know you really are a complete and utter nump…"

"Enough, boys," snapped Mendel.

The picture turned back into a mirror for a second before it moved to another scene. It showed Jal, the eight-foot Hedra warrior who'd helped them back in Denthan. None of the Drumfintley contingent had seen him since then. James saw the expression on his dad's face and remembered that his dad had never seen him before.

"He looks a bit like Dendralon, Dad, but he's on our side."

"Oh. If you say so, Son."

"Jal!" shouted Craig.

"He can't hear you, numpty," snapped James.

Jal walked behind Eethan and some kind of monster that seemed to be made out of grey, lumpy stone.

"It's a Stone Larth," explained Lord Eldane. "Never actually seen one in real life before, only drawings."

"They seem friendly enough," mused Cimerato. He looked concerned, though.

Other Stone Larths came into view, walking through the thick snow.

"There's Whindril," said Craig.

The dragon's gigantic, leathery wings were partially opened, as if she was ready to take to the air at the slightest hint of trouble. Her white mane was covered in fresh, powdery snow. Surprisingly, she tilted her head, as if she could see them all peering down at her. She blinked her big, black eyes before shaking off the snow. It fell down, like a mini blizzard, over the Stone Larths. The thick tufts of hair between her talons stood up like the hackles on Bero's neck when he was angry.

Everyone in the Council chamber stared as Eethan, Jal, and Whindril arrived at the entrance of a dark cave.

Wee Joe pulled his green water pistol from his belt and pretended to fire at the Stone Larths.

"This is as far as we dare go," bellowed one of the Stone Larths. His voice boomed out across the rock face. His tone was rough and hollow, as if his lungs were made of granite and gristle.

"Yuck," exclaimed Wee Joe. "Why doesn't Whindril squish him?" He closed one eye and took aim.

Jean prickled with embarrassment. "Shh... It's trying to help Eethan."

They saw Eethan bow then follow Jal into the cave.

"It could be a trap," said Cimerato, his big fists clenched tight.

"Let's hope not," said Mendel.

James was still annoyed at the wizard for using Helen to do his magic, but his anger was melting into self-pity, which was much worse.

Bero growled as the vision-pool went dark. The pattern of scales reformed on the floor of the chamber. Wee Joe tested it with his foot.

"No, Joe!" Jean gathered him into her.

"What's wrong with the vision-pool?" asked Michael.

"We don't seem to be able to follow them into the cave. There must be some kind of charm protecting it," explained Mendel.

"Can't you tell us what kind of creature lives in the cave, Mendel?" asked Helen. She stood in between Michael and Ephie, a cheeky expression on her face.

"It's called a Hipposaur," said Mendel, a golden fin brushing the plastic window of the barrel. "Part dinosaur and part horse, they were an evil race that fed on the children of men."

Jean gripped Wee Joe a little tighter. "Why would you want to ask such a hideous creature for help?"

"This particular individual was outcast by its race; orphaned, just like Eethan and Elandria, for refusing to be so cruel and heartless. The Hipposaurs are long since extinct. Elcar is the last of his kind."

"I hope Eethan is careful," added Cimerato.

James now found *himself* staring at the Manimals' eyes. As black as jet with vertical white-slit pupils, they mesmerized him.

It was Jean who tapped him on the shoulder.

"I… I'd forgotten how wonderful this place was," said James, pretending to examine the ceiling.

"So James, I heard you had another close shave with Dendralon?" said Cimerato.

"Eh? Oh, yes." His throat constricted and his chest tightened. "My mum wasn't so lucky. She is still…"

The tall Manimal shook his head mournfully. "Eethan explained what happened. I'm sorry to hear that there is still no sign of her."

"Yeh," interrupted Craig. He tilted his head and shook it mournfully. "The whole village misses her. Not the same without her, you know."

"Craig!" snapped Jean, trying to avoid David Peck's gaze, "That's enough."

Craig brightened. "I only meant…"

"I know what you meant, Craig," whispered James. He began to walk over towards the balcony. Set high in the citadel, the view over the city and the surrounding landscape was breathtaking. Eight more towers surrounded the white citadel of Gwendral, arranged exactly like the stones on Bruce Moor. Two years before, Craig had been the first to notice the similarity in layout to the Jesus Rocks. Beyond the walls of Gwendral, however, the view was quite different than before. In Denthan there had been the Gortan Sea to the West and the huge forest of Eldane to the East. There had been a lush plain in front of the city too. Here on Ebos, however, the land was barren. More like a tundra covered in a patchwork of red and brown scrub, the outlook seemed much more bleak. Far to the South, James could just make out a vast expanse of black shadow. "What's that?"

"That is the Halsian Desert," explained Cimerato. "Volcanic ash and rust crawling with Sorabs."

James had no idea what a Sorab was.

The giant Manimal captain placed his elbows on the balustrade. "I am truly sorry to hear about your mother. Eethan has said that you shouldn't give up hope."

"I've not... I don't know what to think." Distractedly, James traced the serpentine carvings on the balustrade with his fingers. "We left her on Artilis. The place was swarming with Racnids and jackal-headed warriors called Inubians. Dendralon has her now." Feeling tearful, he fumbled for his inhaler. He pulled it free of his rucksack and placed it to his lips.

"What is that thing you drink?"

"This? I don't drink from it." James held up the blue inhaler and smiled. "It's my puffer. I have asthma."

A puzzled expression fixed itself on Cimerato's face.

"I can't breathe very well sometimes. I was fine in Denthan because you had loads of extra oxygen compared to Earth, but I'm not so good here. It's probably the dust."

"And this device can fix your illness?"

"It helps," said James. He pressed down on the inhaler and breathed in. The excess white mist fell from his lips as he turned to see his dad.

"You okay, Son?" his dad enquired.

"Yes. Fine." James coughed and asked, "What about the rest of the Manimals and the Yeltans?"

"All fine," answered Cimerato. "We Manimals only venture out of the city to hunt. The Yeltans, however... Well you know what they're like. They like to be underground, out in the wild. They settled out there." Cimerato pointed to a patch of vegetation. A small gnarled wood sat on the edge of what looked like a wall of cloud.

"What is that? Is it mist?" asked James.

"That is The Yelding," said Cimerato.

James looked up into Cimerato's strange eyes. "And that's where the Yeltans live? Is it dangerous?" He often dreamt of the little Yeltans, with their blue eyebrows and yellow-mottled skin.

"The Yeltans live on the edge of the Yelding, an endless cliff that drops into some kind of abyss. It stretches as far as you can imagine North and South. We don't know how deep it is, or if anything lives down there. The clouds you see are mainly composed of steam, so we think there may be some lava streams that perhaps pour into some kind of sea or lake. My father thinks that a meteor may have struck long ago causing some kind of rift. The edge of the Yelding is getting closer, though."

"It's moving?"

"The cliff is breaking off and falling into the void. The Yeltans lost two hundred souls a month ago when the most recent slip occurred. It may not be long before Gwendral slips down there too."

"So why are the Yeltans still there? Why are you still here?" said James.

Cimerato sighed. "We all still believe that there may be a way back to Denthan. A way home."

"How? I mean I know about Mendel's plan but..."

"You have doubts?" pressed Cimerato.

"I don't know." James stared out over the Yelding before turning back into the Council chamber.

His dad gripped his shoulder. "The vision-pool is working again, Son."

"I suppose Helen got it working?" asked James, dolefully.

"Yes," said his dad, a daft smile on his face. "She said some word or other and it started to show a picture again."

James got there just in time to see Eethan and Jal running out of the dark cave. Something big was crawling out behind them...

CHAPTER SEVEN

ELCAR THE SIX-WINGED GOD

Cathy hated the smell of the place. Especially when *he* came near her. No matter what perfumes or scents they gave her to bathe in, the reptilian whiff lingered in her hair and on her clothes. There was no way to describe the smell other than a mixture of stale hamster cage and ammonia. She was stuck on this horrible world with a delusional, seven-foot lizard-man who thought *she* was his Queen.

Dendralon, the monster, and that's what he was, had to be cajoled. She had to play along with his delusions or… Well, she would never see her family again. He'd convinced himself that she was someone called Beldam, so that's who she had to be for now; Beldam, the Queen of Artilis.

"Dendralon?" It was one of the hissing Artilian spider-like creatures. A Racnid.

As soon as he stirred, the smell of ammonia intensified. She stifled the urge to wretch and instead smiled demurely. She listened with interest to the Racnid's words.

"We are ready to move, Sire. The gateway is prepared, and the army is assembled."

Dendralon opened his mouth to yawn, exposing concentric rows of rotting, black Hedra teeth. Unlike any other Hedra Cathy had ever seen, he had long, black hair that hung down over his muscular back and shoulders.

She watched as his cat-like pupils widened.

"Excellent news, Elhada. We will go immediately."

After dismissing the Racnid, he summoned six Inubian guards to fetch his armour and make ready his chariot.

"I have prepared a chariot for you too, my Queen," he said. Dendralon clasped her hand and lifted a pair of beautifully decorated swords from a marble table. "Another gift for you."

She took a sword in each hand and felt their weight. They were well balanced and razor sharp. Thoughts of slicing his head off there and then raced through her mind, but she forced them back. She had to wait until she was safe in her own world or at least with someone like Mendel, who could take her home.

"We will make our way to the apex of the pyramid," said Dendralon.

"Of course," she replied. Having lived in the pyramid of Artilia for almost a year, she knew her way around. She'd seen the surviving Artilians, almost identical to humans, put to work under the whip and sting of the Racnids. Young and old were punished horribly if they did not perform their tasks. This was not the time or place to reap her revenge. She sheathed the swords in her specially made scabbard and marched down to the main atrium. Her chariot was waiting. Two Inubian jackal-headed charioteers stood on the wide footplate in anticipation. She knew they would have been instructed to take care of her on pain of death. The one good thing going for Dendralon was that he was never flat line. Not like David, her husband back in Drumfintley, who only ever became animated about his precious Scouts. The Hedra wizard was psychotic and completely delusional, but never boring. She hated boring.

Winding their way up the newly constructed cobbled paths inside the Artilia, she eventually reached the apex of the pyramid. Composed of some kind of glass, the tip of the pyramid pierced the surface of the red planet. An orange glow emanated from the barren red sands outside, but inside the pyramid another kind of light caught her attention. A ring of stones, exactly like the ones on Bruce Moor, the Jesus Rocks, shone out from the gloom of the chamber. Behind her, the pathway to the apex moved with a seething mass of Artilian Wasps, their gossamer wings glinting in the crimson light. Passing her chariot, the Wasps, along with their oversized Queen, streamed into the red glow enclosed by the ring of stones, and then disappeared.

Where were they going? Her heart leapt with a mixture of excitement and trepidation at the thought of Dendralon taking this army back to Scotland, back to Drumfintley. Not exactly the return she'd envisaged. Thousands of Inubians followed the grisly-looking Artilian Wasps, Dendralon to the fore. Soon his chariot levelled with hers and they watched the procession together. Behind the Inubians, the Racnid army pulled an array of siege weapons and equipment. They scampered up the giant pathway and into the rosy glow of the stones.

"We will attack Gwendral and win this time," growled Dendralon.

"Gwendral?" asked Cathy.

Dendralon did not answer her, he merely hissed at his Racnid steeds to pull him into position.

How could they be going to Gwendral? Where was the city now? Her mind raced as she considered the possibilities. *Was Gwendral somehow on Earth or was it on some other world with Eethan and...* She gasped. *Would James and David be there?*

As her chariot approached the open gateway, a cold breeze caught her hair and made her shiver. Her Inubian charioteers whipped the Racnid steeds, and they charged through the portal.

A second later, a bitter wind caught her breath, and she bumped down onto the ground. Snowflakes streamed down from a dreich, dishcloth coloured sky. They were on some kind of moor.

Holding back, she watched as the remainder of the massive army from Artilis poured out onto the moor through the ring of stones be-hind her. These stones looked different from the ones on Artilis or even on Bruce Moor. They were much more uniform and joined, in a ring, by lintels of matching stone. Cathy scanned her surroundings. They were in a large hollow, and as the clouds parted and the snow eased, she could see that they were on the side of a high mountain. One of her drivers handed her a cloak. Cathy pulled the furs over her shoulders and felt its warmth. Dendralon was about a hundred yards ahead with the Inubian generals. She pointed to his position and her drivers flicked the reins. Snow flew up into the air as her chariot skid-ded to a halt beside him.

Dendralon turned to face her. "We will camp here in this hollow. In the morning we will move down the mountain and onward over the desert." He stood high on his chariot and bellowed, "Tomorrow we will feast on Manimal flesh!"

The whole mountain shook with a mixture of roars, screams and the rasping of wings. Cathy feigned a smile and tapped one of her swords against her shield, Inubian style.

***

Further round the mountain, on a north-facing lee, Eethan and Jal stared at the Hipposaur. It cocked its massive head on hearing the strange cheer from above and blew hot steam from its leathery nostrils.

"You have brought death with you, Eethan Magichand."

"Ee don't know what that sound ees," said Eethan. He'd been just as surprised by the sudden noise as the Hipposaur.

The Stone Larths were grumbling. They kept their eyes lowered when the Hipposaur was in their presence.

"And you've brought a dragon of Hest with you," the Hipposaur continued, stamping the ground with his saucer-sized hoofs. A pair of membranous wings that protruded from its neck fluttered in the cold breeze.

"Ees Whindril," announced Eethan, performing a theatrical bow in the direction of the great, white dragon.

Whindril snorted irreverently.

"Our transport," explained Jal.

Whindril narrowed her eyes.

A Stone Larth edged forward and tapped the Larth leader on the shoulder. "Tertan," he grunted, without looking up, "a whole army of the strangest looking creatures I have ever seen have appeared in the sacred gully. They surround the stones of worship."

Eethan clawed at the air and then licked his fingertips. "Artilian."

Jal peered behind the ranks of Stone Larths.

"Defeneetly Artileean," stated Eethan. He faced the Hipposaur, Elcar, and asked, "Weel you help us?"

Elcar unravelled the large wings folded over his back. He craned his neck and began to circle Eethan and Jal.

"Eethan Magichand, is Mendel with you?"

Whindril's head slid forward over the Stone Larths. She looked down at the Hipposaur, hissed and said, "Nar chan Mendel, arketh."

"Good," said Elcar. "In that case, I will help you."

"Mendel is here?" whispered Jal.

"According to your dragon, he watches us from a vision-pool, here on Ebos." Elcar whinnied like a stallion and then roared. With a sudden bound, he took to the air and hovered above them. "All of you must leave the mountain. If Mendel has asked us to help him, then we must. Besides, to remain here on this mountain will be impossible now."

"What of the Mountain Wraiths?" asked Tertan, his eyes still averted from his god.

"They will be delayed on the slopes above us. They will feast on this army from Artilis. Tertan, you should take your kin from this place. Follow the old route behind the overhang and make your way down the mountain, over the desert and on towards the Yelding." Elcar cocked his head and eyed Jal. "You should accompany Tertan, my Hedra friend." The Hipposaur sprouted a third pair of wings from his horse-like head and flapped off into the blizzard. "Come Whindril. Come Eethan. Follow me."

As Eethan leapt up onto Whindril's neck, Jal cursed and sheathed his curved sword. He looked up at the tall Stone Larth. "It seems that I am with you, Tertan. How many are you?"

Tertan spread his massive stone-encrusted arms. "This is all that is left of our race. Two hundred souls, no more."

Whindril and Elcar soon disappeared into a thick curtain of swirling snow.

"Come, Jal," said Tertan, "before the Wraiths awaken."

CHAPTER EIGHT

THE BATTLE IN THE SKY

Cathy Peck hated tents, especially when they reeked of reptiles and Racnids. Two of the huge spider-like creatures hissed and chattered in their high-pitched voices as they stood guard at the entrance. She was just about to get up from her bed of furs and pour herself a drink of water, when a series of screams began to echo out across the camp. It was still dark outside and with the wind and snow whistling over the canvas she wished, more than ever, that she were back home in Drumfintley. Another hideous screech made her sit bolt upright. She stared across at Dendralon. He edged out of his bed in the far corner and reached for his armour.

"What is it, Dendralon? What are those noises?"

Dendralon stretched and then cocked his head, clicking his vertebrae into place. "I am not sure."

"Sire!" A dark skinned Inubian rushed into the tent. "We are under attack."

"From what?" snapped Dendralon, clipping on his breastplate.

The Inubian sniffed the air nervously and flattened his long, dog-like ears. "We don't know, Sire."

Dendralon threw back the flap of the tent and peered out into the storm. Cathy edged in beside him. *Perhaps it's James,* she thought.

"There!" Dendralon pointed to a group of Racnids scurrying away from a ragged cliff face.

It seemed to Cathy that fleeting shapes or perhaps shadows were peeling away from the rocks above the Racnids and then dropping down amongst them. These shadow-creatures wielded stone swords that hacked off the rickety legs and limbs of the terrified Racnids. The creatures flew through the blizzard with ease, emerging from the storm like fleeting phantoms in the amber light of the dying fires.

"Mountain Wraiths," spat Dendralon.

Cathy watched as he closed his eyes and held his gnarled staff high. He mumbled a jumble of strange words before shouting out, "Brilliato!"

A blast of brilliant white flew out from the end of his staff setting the whole plateau aglow. It was suddenly just as bright as any summer's day in Drumfintley. A hundred stone swords clattered onto the rocks or buried themselves in the peaty ground. The shadows had disappeared.

Obviously shaken, Elhada, the Racnid Queen, scampered up to Dendralon. "We tried to fight back but we could not touch them. They were just like the Dust Goblins on Artilis. Our stings passed straight through them."

The snow had stopped falling and the first signs of morning cut a thin, pale line across the eastern horizon.

Dendralon seemed drained. His voice was low and husky. "Mountain Wraiths cannot be harmed, only warded off by light. What is the damage?"

Elhada bowed a little lower. "One hundred and ninety, Sire. No more."

Cathy scanned the assembled force. The Artilian Wasps were clambering over their Queen in an effort to keep her warm while the Racnids checked the sticky webs and traps they'd set the night before. Something similar to a Mountain Hare, only with horns and a long tail, seemed to be the main catch.

"Elhada," Dendralon hissed. "Tell the Wasp Queen to send one hundred of her flying scouts ahead to Gwendral. They must fly due west."

"Yes, Lord," snivelled Elhada, backing away.

Cathy wrapped a second cloak around her shoulders, as she made ready to board her chariot. Inside her chest, her heart leapt at the prospect of finding James or David.

Her Inubian attendants fussed round her but she shushed them away, kicking one hard that came too close. She wasn't a morning person. She unsheathed her swords and waxed the blades before slipping them back into their jewelled sheaths. "Get away from me, you dogs," she screamed.

As the Inubians ducked and cowered before her, she saw Dendralon smile. She had to keep up the pretence. Just a few days more and perhaps she could reap her revenge on the monster wizard. She'd avoided drinking any wine prepared by Dendralon's slaves, choosing instead to abstain or make her own blend. The wine, she discovered, let Dendralon into her thoughts and memories. The tainted drink gave her razor sharp images of ancient Egypt and of Beldam, the Queen Dendralon had once loved. She'd even seen Dendralon 'the man'. For he had once been human-like in appearance until he'd chosen immortality in the form of a Hedra wizard. This, he'd later discovered, had not been necessary and it galled him even to this day. Mendel had found a way of gaining immortality without having to change. He still remained in his original form, or at least he had done so until Dendralon turned him into a goldfish. Dendralon hated Mendel; that was clear. In Dendralon's eyes, Cathy was this Beldam. It was probably the only reason he kept her alive, so she wasn't going to fight it, not yet.

Still lacking the sleep she'd needed, she stepped up and took the reins herself. Over the last eleven months she'd practised, or as Dendralon put it, rediscovered the skills of warfare. Riding a chariot, sword fighting, throwing the javelin, using a whip, and even hand-to-hand combat had been mandatory. It had all helped to pass the time on Artilis, keep her mind off her most painful memories. She still dreamt of Drumfintley and her son. She even missed David. She longed for his stupid comments and even wished she could find a smelly sock or two, dropped where they shouldn't have been or prized down the back of her sofa in a pathetic attempt to avoid putting them in the washing basket. Her thoughts darkened as she saw the Artilian force take shape in the gully. *Will I have to fight today or tomorrow? Will I have to kill?* She would be expected to do both. Beldam would have fought bravely, so she would have to act the part out as well as she dared. She'd practised fighting with Artilian Wasps and Racnids but, to her, when she'd killed *them*, it had just been pest control. Today, however, it might be different. She might have to face a Yeltan or even a Manimal. What if she had to face someone she knew? They would hardly recognise her in her new armour. *What will I do then?*

One of the Inubians ran up to her chariot and held up a polished piece of copper for her to admire herself in before setting off. They did this every day. She looked quite scary, she decided. She wore a green-plumed copper helmet with cheek-guards that accentuated her light brown eyes. She also wore a moulded chest-plate with matching arm and shin guards, all carved with snake patterns and glyphs that she didn't understand. Her armour matched Dendralon's exactly, and she genuinely felt like a Queen in her over-elaborate garb. She waved the attendant away and looked behind her. The tents had been packed away, and the various races had bunched together as they filed past the ring of stones. The Racnids, to the rear, were the greatest in number. The Inubians, mainly black or dark grey in colour, surrounded her position. They jostled round her chariot trying to avoid the deadly scythes on her wheels. They had their own chariots too, about two hundred or so, that trundled over the snowy ground, skidding from time to time as they bumped over hidden rocks and boulders. Ahead, the Artilian Wasps crawled down the slope of the mountain, their wings vibrating in unison. This vibration formed a low base drone that struck fear in her heart. *Would James be in Gwendral? Would he have to face this army of Dendralon's?* She could just make out a black cloud of flying insects heading due west against the drab sky.

***

James heard the bell ring out from the main gate. Someone had sounded the alarm. As he ran along the battlements with Craig and Bero, Mendel's voice filled James's head. "Why are they ringing out the alarm? What can you see?"

Fighting for breath, James stopped and hung onto the parapet. There was nothing on the ground; no sign of the Sorabs or Jal or… "Look!"

Blinking between the rays of the rising sun were the silhouettes of two huge beasts, flapping and gliding towards the city. The first, James could tell, was Whindril, Mendel's dragon. The second creature was the six-winged Hipposaur he'd seen in Mendel's vision-pool, the night before. The closer it got, the more it resembled the giant figure of a winged horse. About half the size of Whindril it was somehow more bulky and threatening. It blew flames from its nostrils as it flew over the city walls.

"Eethan!" screeched Craig, waving like an imbecile.

Elandria, the Racnid princess, moved in beside them on the parapet and hissed her approval. "We are all gathered in one place at last."

Whindril landed in the courtyard behind them, followed by Elcar the Hipposaur.

Eethan jumped free of the dragon seat and ran in his own spider-like fashion straight up the inner wall of the battlements to greet the boys.

"Eee, eets James and Craig. Good to see yous. Weel be needing your magic soon." Eethan waved his hand over the boys' faces.

James instantly felt his arm sting with pain.

Craig cursed. "Awch! I wish you would give us some warning before you do something like that, Eethan."

James examined his trembling hand. There, he saw the familiar crimson tattoo of a griffin. It had returned, and so too, he realised, would his sword, Firetongue, whenever he called upon it.

"I don't know why we can't swap this time. You always get the sword." Craig rubbed the green worm-like dragon tattoo that wound round his wrist. Greenworm, his magic spear would appear upon command now, too.

Eethan knelt down to address Mendel in the brandy barrel. "Theere are thousands of Sorabs swarming thees way. We weel have to warn Garlon and his people."

"Yes," replied Mendel. "The Yeltans will be safer within the city walls for the time being."

"And Dendralon?" pressed Mendel.

"He ees here too, with his whole army." Eethan shook his head before sticking his thumb up his nose. "Wees have enlisted the help of the Stone Larths, but they ees not many."

"I know of the Sorabs," said Mendel in a distracted voice.

James took a deep inhalation from his puffer. "What are you think-ing, Mendel?" He asked this while watching Wee Joe and Helen walk across the courtyard below towards Whindril.

"I have an idea," said the wizard. "We may be able to stall Den-dralon's advance."

"How?" asked Craig. "If Dendralon has brought his pet wasps, they'll just fly over the city walls like they did in Artilis. And if he has Racnids..." Craig saw Elandria bristle. "No offence, Elandria, but they'll just climb up and over the walls too."

"That's why we have to take the fight to them before they reach the city," said Mendel. "Eethan, are my potions and powders still in my old chambers?"

"Yees, I think."

"Craig, you and your sister Helen will come with me," said Mendel.

James's heart sank. "And me?" he asked, meekly.

Mendel answered in a stern voice, "James, you stay here with the Drumfintley group. Warn the Yeltans as soon as possible about the oncoming threat."

James lifted a finger. "I..."

"Craig, I need you and your sister to get Bero and myself up onto Whindril's dragon seat straight away," said Mendel.

James let his finger fall before grabbing Craig's sleeve with his other hand. "What's he up to?"

Craig shrugged then bolted down the steps towards Helen. "Come on, Sis. Looks like you've been picked to do some more of Mendel's special spells."

James fought back the urge to lob a rock at the freckle-faced numpty that called himself his friend.

Reluctantly, he clambered down into the courtyard. Cimerato was there now, too. James stood with his dad and watched as Helen and Craig hauled Bero up onto the dragon seat. Whindril was snacking on an undistinguishable lump of meat.

"Cimerato," said Mendel, "can you get me the blue bottle from my laboratory marked: phero-X2?"

"Of course, but what...?"

"If we can spray the pheromone over the advancing Sorabs, an ant-based life form, we should be able to confuse them enough to stall them until the Artilian Wasps arrive. When they meet, the Sorabs will be charged full of thermatol."

"Therma-what?" snapped Craig. He put a leather strap round Bero's chest and clipped it onto Whindril's seat.

"It will cause the Sorabs to attack the Artilian Wasps."

"And...?" pressed Craig.

"And, Craig, with a little magic from Helen and myself, we should cause enough chaos to let James and Cimerato gather the Yeltans and get the defences prepared."

Cimerato was well across the courtyard at the base of a dilapidated tower.

"Mendel's old quarters?" asked James.

A Manimal guard nodded.

By the time Jean, Michael, and Ephie arrived on the scene, Cimerato had returned with the blue bottle.

With a series of waves and cheers of good luck, Whindril spread her wings and leapt up into the cool air. James watched as the figures of Helen and Craig became smaller and smaller.

As the hipposaur, Elcar, moved forward, the Drumfintley contingent edged back a little.

"James Peck?" Elcar's voice boomed out over the cobbles. It had the ring of an old, over-theatrical drama teacher, thought James. In fact, he had a teacher who sounded almost identical back at Drumfintley School: Mr. Dundee.

He looked into the Hipposaur's dragon-like face. It seemed skinless, like looking at the blood and muscle underneath. "Y...yes," he stuttered.

"Do not be threatened by the girl, Helen. She is merely a vassal for Mendel's magic. You were once thus." Blood oozed out of the creature's face as it spoke.

James felt like puking but he didn't want to be rude. By the way it had just talked about Helen, it could obviously read his mind. "But you don't even know me," he continued.

Elcar folded the largest of his wings behind his back and swished his horse's tail. "I know that you feel like being sick. I know that my appearance scares and disgusts you."

James flushed.

"Everything that Eethan Magichand knows, I know too," it continued.

"Ah..." blurted James.

"You are to keep the Orphans of Light safe until Mendel returns."

"I am?" said James.

"Eethan, Elandria, and myself, of course."

"Lord Eldane read us the prophecy," said Ephie.

"Not five minutes ago," added Michael.

"Right," said James, cagily. "And it said...?"

Eethan and Elandria had now joined the crowd that had formed round James and Elcar. Elandria shuffled to the fore. "You see, according to Lord Eldane's manuscripts, it seems possible that the three Orphans of Light may join as one. Eethan has the blue light of Denthan, Elcar has the yellow light of Ebos, and I...I possess the crimson light of Artilis. All three of us are orphans, in a manner of speaking. Outcast by our own kind, but somehow endowed with the magical power of light."

"Light?" James was growing agitated.

Lord Eldane touched him on the shoulder. "Mendel thinks that there is a chance for Denthan. He thinks that by acting as one, Eethan, Elcar, and Elandria have enough power to divert the killing blast of Tealfirth that wiped out our planet. Listen to the words of the prophecy." Lord Eldane cleared his throat. "*A boy; the son of a Dark Queen, shall bring the Orphans of Light to the Dragon Chamber. There, together, before and after a world has died, the mother dragon and the ever enduring light will defeat perpetual night.*"

"Eh?" James let his mouth fall open.

Michael pointed to the mass of gathered Manimals that surrounded them. "They think that this boy mentioned in the prophecy is you, James."

Still burning with a mixture of rage and embarrassment at being left out of Mendel's company, James tried to comprehend the meaning of the rhyme. "I think I understand the 'Orphans of Light' bit. I've seen what Eethan did to save Gwendral and what Elandria did on Artilis but, 'the son of a Dark Queen'. That's definitely stretching it a bit. I mean, Mum is hard work and stuff, but she's hardly a Dark Queen. I mean, who made the prophecy?"

Lord Eldane's brow furrowed. "The prophecy was first uncovered on a stone on the hill of Dunnad."

The sound of James's dad rummaging about in the green rucksack broke the embarrassing silence. "I thought we had to warn these Yeltan things about the creatures, the thingies, the...?"

"The Sorabs," interjected Lord Eldane.

"Quite," said David.

"Yes, but, Dad, they think that Mum is some kind of Dark Queen. That means she might still be alive," he continued, "it means that she..." James was struggling to keep calm. His dad handed him his blue inhaler but he shook his head defiantly. "I'm fine, Dad. Are you listening?"

His dad had begun chatting to Jean Harrison.

Annoyed, James traced the griffin tattoo on his wrist with his fingers and then caught Eethan by the shoulder. He eased the little blue man away from the group. "Eethan, why is Mendel using Helen to do his magic?" he whispered.

Eethan tittered and slapped his thigh, pirate fashion. "Ees that what you're worried about?"

"Well..." James tilted his head and nodded down at his feet.

"You can perform magic by yourself now. Hasn't Mendel told you?"

Behind Eethan, steam drifted up from Elcar's nostrils. James's mouth went very dry. "I...I can do what?"

***

Helen was the first to spot the swarm of Artilian Wasps. They were on a collision course with Whindril. "Quickly, Craig. Pour that stuff on those things down there and let's get out of here. I don't like the look of those wasp thingies; they give me the willies."

Craig was busy emptying the contents of Mendel's blue bottle over the disgusting ant-like Sorabs below them. "I don't want to miss them and it's hard enough trying to balance on this dragon without you pressurizing me."

"You don't have to be too accurate," said Mendel. "The pheromone will dissipate over the desert below. They will pick it up on their feet."

"Hurry, Craig. The wasps have seen us," cried Helen.

"We will have to fight," bellowed Mendel. "Whindril, na seth te tche!"

Helen gripped the dragon seat as hard as she could. On hearing Mendel's instruction Whindril arched her supple neck and hissed until a jet of flame leapt from her jaws. Scorching hot, it was blue, like the one on her mum's gas cooker, only this flame was about fifty-foot long. "Whoaw!" She felt the heat on her face.

"Amazing," said Craig.

"Say your word, Craig," reminded Mendel.

Craig hesitated for a moment before blurting, "Greenworm!" Instantly, a beautiful green-tinged spear appeared in his right hand.

Mendel's voice rattled in Helen's head. "Helen, take what's left of the pheromone and throw it at any wasps that get too close."

Helen took the bottle from her brother. "Why?" she asked. Fear was building in her chest and she could feel her bare legs shaking.

An Artilian Wasp buzzed straight in between Whindril's wings, its sting primed.

She jerked out a dollop of pheromone from the bottle, but the wasp veered to the right and came straight at her. The word, "Wwwwswarmwwkillww!" burst from her lips. Only inches away from Craig and her, the wasp froze along with another ten or so that were within range. The air crackled like hot fat before a series of red droplets sprouted over the wasps' compound eyes. Their wings ruptured and split before they spun down, like giant sycamore seeds, onto the Sorabs below.

Suddenly, Whindril beat her wings much more forcefully, causing Craig and Helen to hold on even tighter. Bero's straps took the strain and Craig just managed to keep his balance. He drew back his spear and launched it at another group of wasps to their left. It sailed through the sky in a huge arc, puncturing three of them before returning to his hand.

"Ooh!" He flicked the yellow liquid from his fingers. "Wasp guts."

Whindril blasted another twenty with her blue and purple flame. The wasps' wings crumpled as they fell, trailing black smoke, down onto the confused Sorabs. Flipping over onto her back, the great, white dragon used her massive talons to grip and crush as many more as she could reach.

Helen held on with her eyes closed, praying for Whindril to right herself. Feeling as if she was going to throw up, she opened her eyes and screamed out, "Mendel! I can see Jal and..." She didn't quite know how to describe the other things that were with him. She was still upside down. "Those stone thingamabobs."

Craig's green spear sliced down inches from her face, cutting through a glistening abdomen. Her mouth was suddenly full of black pus.

Whindril righted herself and snapped another wasp in two that was just about to sting Bero.

Helen coughed and gagged before puking up all over the dragon seat.

Bero growled and barked behind Craig, who dived up and hacked off a wasp's head. He landed awkwardly, almost losing his footing.

"Craig!" Tears were streaming down Helen's face. She just caught him before Whindril banked hard to her right.

"Whindril, fly lower," commanded Mendel. We have to bring the wasps within range of the Sorabs.

Whindril instantly went into a death-defying dive. They all clung on for dear life, Helen and Craig both gripping Bero's fur as the dragon suddenly swooped up and then held its position about twenty feet above the ant-like Sorabs.

Below, and further on towards the mountains, they saw the rest of Dendralon's army. Thousands more Artilian Wasps began to take to the air. Jal and the stone creatures looked to be trapped between Dendralon's army and the Sorabs.

"Get ready!" shouted Mendel. "We have to help Jal and the Stone Larths."

Helen's mouth opened involuntarily. "Wwwinviswwibitywww!"

Everything went hazy before they all turned completely invisible. The attacking wasps buzzed round their position, totally flummoxed by the turn of events. Helen remembered Craig telling her how horrible it was to be invisible on Whindril. The sensation made her feel like vomiting again.

Now the Sorabs could only see the Artilian Wasps flailing around in mid air. They rustled and vibrated into a huge cluster of writhing, shiny bodies. Helen saw the horrible tube-things that hung down from their necks rise up and squirt great jets of liquid fifty feet up into the air. As soon as the gunge hit the Artilian Wasps, it burned right through them.

"We need to fly higher!" shouted Craig.

"Hold my hand!" yelled Helen. She groped about until she found her big brother's hand.

The Artilian Wasps were now joined by even more of their kind all dive-bombing the Sorabs, stinging as many as they could. The Sorabs, in turn, swarmed over any fallen wasps, quickly ripping off wings and tearing at their spindly legs with their powerful jaws.

"Ah!"

Helen recognised her brother's voice.

"What's wrong, Craig?

"My leg is burning. The acid stuff is…aah."

"Be quick, Helen. Pour the remainder of the pheromone over his leg," said Mendel.

"There isn't much left. Besides, I can't see his bloomin' leg," Helen howled.

"It's an alkali," explained Mendel.

"Give me it," screamed Craig.

She felt his hand move along her arm until he gripped the bottle. She heard him struggle to get the last few drops free. "Craig, are you okay now?"

"Ah. Got it!" blurted Craig.

"I said are you…?"

"Just tip top, Sis. What do you think? It bloomin' hurts…Whooo!"

Whindril twisted violently before Craig managed to finish the sentence. Still invisible, the dragon snapped and crushed more wasps in mid-air. Their crumpled bodies spiralled to the ground. Swooping lower, the dragon produced another blast of blue fire that ignited Sorabs and wasps alike.

Helen, her knuckles numb, saw Jal and his troupe of giants take advantage of the mêlée. They charged the left flank of the Sorabs and cut their way through. Jal hacked into the ant-like Sorabs with his curved Hedra sword while the giant Stone Larths wielded heavy stone swords as long as clothes poles.

She gasped as Jal twisted away from a jet of acid that grazed his breastplate. The acid caught an unfortunate Stone Larth full in the face. The giant roared in pain and then fell. Helen shrieked and gripped Craig tighter.

As Jal's column forced their way onward, thousands of Artilian Wasps poured down from the sky onto the frenzied Sorabs.

"Climb higher, Whindril!" Charged with exhilaration, Mendel's booming voice echoed over the battlefield as they jerked upwards and through the clouds. The dragon slowed and then hovered high above the carnage.

"Wwwviswwiblitywww!"

Whindril shimmered then became completely visible. The thin clouds parted below them, and Helen could suddenly see everything. Amongst the great army that stretched all the way back to the mountains, she recognised the Inubian dog-men. She saw their chariots rolling across the frozen tundra toward the fight below. To her horror, behind the Inubians, a great host of Racnids scampered along in a long, dark line. "Craig, they're from Artilis. What are they doing here?

"Duck, Sis!"

Helen bent double just in time to avoid Craig's magic spear as it sliced through the head of an angry looking wasp. Its antennae quivered as it fell back, its sting lunging forward at her face.

With a rush of air, Whindril's head whipped round and snapped her deadly jaws shut over the stinging remains of the wasp just in time. Hissing blue smoke, the dragon flicked her massive head twice and swallowed.

"Back to Gwendral!" announced Mendel. He sounded downhearted. "We must use the Artilian Key before they breach the city walls.

Looking grey and washed out, Craig held onto the dragon seat. "Those Racnids will scale the walls of Gwendral, no bother. I saw them do it on Artilis. Oh…"

"What's wrong?" asked Helen.

"Just feeling…sick," Craig gasped.

"What about Jal?" asked Helen.

Mendel swivelled round in his barrel as Bero barked incessantly at the fighting below. "Jal and the Stone Larths will break free from the mêlée soon. He will be safe."

Helen stiffened. "But how can you know…?"

"Trust me, Helen."

"I take it the Stone Larths are on our side," said Craig.

"It would seem so. They will be a great asset," replied Mendel.

Helen pulled her brother closer. "I thought you liked riding on dragons?"

"Yeh, but not when I've had a swarm of giant wasps attack me, been turned invisible, and had half my leg bloomin' burned off!"

Helen screwed up her eyes and looked down at his leg. "That means we are not immortal then. Doesn't it, Mendel?"

"It's not a good sign in that direction, no," he replied.

"It still stings like mad," said Craig.

"Looks all right to me," said Helen.

"Yeh, well, it doesn't feel all right. Okay!"

"Boys," sighed Helen. "They always make out things are worse than they really are."

CHAPTER NINE

THE FIRE OF RA

Garlon opened his arms to greet James. "It's the blinder of the Tree Trolls, James Peck!"

James looked down at the little Yeltan he'd met two years before. A flash of blue above his eyes and an equally garish shock of sapphire-coloured hair jolted his memory. Garlon, the leader of the Yeltans, wore a smart green suit, cut at the knee.

James remembered how Garlon had once repaired the barrel in which Mendel had survived for so long. The little creature loved gadgets and had already begun to fidget with James's dad's compass.

David Peck unclipped the compass from his belt and watched as Garlon's tiny fingers turned it over in his yellow hand.

"This is my dad," James announced.

Distractedly, Garlon looked up from his tinkering. "Mr. Peck, it's an honour to meet you. I'm so pleased James found you after all his trials and tribulations on Denthan."

"So am I. Just in the wrong place at the wrong time," explained his dad.

"So I believe. James, however, was in exactly the right place and just in time to save our people. If it were not for James helping Mendel…" Garlon smiled and handed the compass back to David Peck. He turned his attention to Cimerato and his band of Manimal fighters. "Something is troubling you, Cimerato."

Cimerato had to stoop low to enter the covert of trees that formed Garlon's quarters. "We are going to be overrun by a huge army, Garlon."

"Well, the prophecy said that we would be," said Garlon, matter-of-factly.

James sensed some tension between them.

Cimerato continued, "In about six hours, a massive Artilian force will attack Gwendral. You can remain here at he edge of the Yelding if you desire, however..."

"That would be very ungracious of us," finished Garlon. "After all, Gwendral saved us all once. The least we can do is to try and repay the favour."

James could tell that Cimerato did not really think that the Yeltans would make much difference in the fight by the way he avoided Garlon's stare.

"Your help would be most welcome, Garlon. The plan is to hold the Artilian army off as long as we can. Dendralon is behind this."

Garlon sat down heavily in his chair and closed his eyes. "My father, Landris, is still missed terribly."

"Yes, I'm sorry," mumbled Cimerato.

"Will you come with us?" asked James.

"We will," said Garlon, "but I have to tell you that we have explored some of the Yelding."

"You have?" said Cimerato.

"With the help and protection of the Mertol," explained Garlon.

"A familiar sound echoed across the glade. " Bak!"

With a mixture of excitement and trepidation, James followed Cimerato and Garlon out into the sunlight.

"Bak!" The Mertol nodded its ape-like head in James's direction before stretching out an orange, matted arm.

James backed away. He'd forgotten how wild and dangerous-looking the fifteen-foot high Mertol appeared. He stared, mesmerized, at its pitted face. He watched, unblinking, as the various holes in its cheeks fluttered open and shut in intricate patterns. "Hello, again," he muttered.

The hair-covered creature opened its jaws to reveal its terrible fangs.

Cimerato craned his neck, staring up at the Mertol. "Dendralon is upon us again."

"Bak! Bak!" The Mertol screeched up into the brightening sky.

"Exactly," said Cimerato, smirking. "You haven't forgotten his betrayal on Denthan then, my big friend?"

James remembered how Dendralon had once ordered the Mertol to be killed after it failed to despatch his mum and the group from Drumfintley.

"Bak!" The Mertol's pouched face puffed up as it snapped its menacing jaws.

Cimerato turned and pointed to Gwendral. "Garlon, can you tell me what you found in the Yelding on our way back to the city?"

"Let me summon my people, first. They should know of this renewed threat and what may be expected of them." Garlon walked over to a wooden bar that hung down from an old weathered tree. He beat it twice with a heavy hammer of stone. The dull chime rang out across the stunted forest and the familiar babbling sounds of the Yeltans soon filled the air. Tiny creatures sprang out from every conceivable nook and cranny, old and young alike. James beamed as a Yukplug waddled into the clearing. Resembling a yak on two legs, it bounded forward and crouched down just enough for Garlon to scramble onto its shaggy back. Once aboard, Garlon motioned for silence. "We have been called to arms to help the Manimals and Gwendral!"

The murmurings bubbled up in intensity until Garlon raised his hand again. "Dendralon is still alive."

More murmurs…

"Although Dendralon advances with a terrible army, it is my wish that we defend Gwendral and the honour of all those who died on Denthan. Are you with me?"

There was a huge cheer and a frenzy of activity as the Yeltans gathered up their armour and piled their possessions high on rickety carts.

The singsong sounds of the Yeltans increased as Cimerato motioned them forward towards Gwendral. More Yukplugs appeared as they walked onward and the Yeltans dug out a series of poison-tipped spears from various underground hiding places along the route. James reckoned that by the time they'd cleared the stunted forest, the Yeltans were more than a thousand strong. He ran ahead to catch up with Garlon and Cimerato, who were deep in conversation. "What did you find in the Yelding, Garlon?" he interrupted.

Garlon pointed to another Yukplug and told a nearby Yeltan to help James up onto its back. "There is another world down there, James. Once you pass through the thick mists, about five hundred feet below the ridge, there is a river of super-hot lava and black mountains of ash. Beyond this obstacle, there is a route through to lush valleys and great lakes."

"How did you find your way through the lava?" asked James.

"The Mertol found a single path that cuts down through the fault. We found large bridges formed from the rock and well-worn ashen paths that skirt the danger."

"Well-worn?" said James. Something caught his eye high above them.

"Whindril," said Cimerato. He cupped his strange eyes and focused on the distant speck of white. The dragon wove across the cobalt sky before spiralling downwards.

James bobbed towards the great ivory gates on the back of the Yukplug. He pulled on its ragged mane. "Whoa there, boy."

"Girl," corrected Garlon.

"Whoa there, girl," repeated James, flushing.

The Yukplug snorted.

Whindril beat her huge wings above their heads in an effort to slow her descent.

"There! Back above the Yelding," shouted Garlon.

James screwed up his eyes and realised that what he'd thought had been a wayward cloud was actually a great swarm of flying insects. He recognised their outlines as they moved closer. "Artilian Wasps," he gasped.

"What on Ebos are those things?" said Garlon.

"They're not from Ebos," said James.

It was unlikely, he thought, *that either Cimerato or Garlon would have seen these creatures before.* James called on Firetongue and felt the sword's weight in his hand. Its crimson, leather hilt was warm to the touch.

Whindril banked round above them and then raced back toward the oncoming swarm. James could see Craig and Helen holding on tight as Whindril reared up and blasted the insects with a searing jet of blue flame. A good number of the Artilian Wasps fell from the sky, singed and blackened.

James galloped towards the flailing insects, his sword held high, the Yukplug's rope-like mane whipping his face. He had to duck, however, as the Mertol bounded over his head. Spinning and stamping like a dervish, it crushed the fallen insects and wailed up at the remainder of the swarm.

"Bak!" Two whizzing spheres sped out from the pouches in its face, whirring as they curved upwards into the midst of the wasps. Then, with a crack, the spheres exploded like gunshot, ripping through wings, antennae and shiny brown carapaces.

Completely shredded, what was left of the swarm spiralled down to the ground.

The great gates of Gwendral swung open and James saw his dad and the rest of the Drumfintley group rush out to meet them.

"Impressive," panted his dad. "Scary, but impressive."

His dad was obviously wary of the fifteen foot tall Mertol. "Dad, that's the thing that turned Ephie into a blancmange a couple of years ago. At least that's what Helen told Craig."

David Peck winked and said, "Pretty cool, eh?"

James felt a pang of embarrassment followed by a blast of guilt. His dad just didn't fit in. Especially since his mum had disappeared. His mum would have been in the thick of the fight by now, whereas his dad... Well, his dad wasn't really a fighter. Avoided hassle like the plague.

"James, ye numpty."

James shielded his eyes as Whindril lighted on the ashen earth beneath the city gates. Craig, Helen, and Bero slid down off the ornate dragon chair. Craig was limping badly. "What happened?"

"Chemical burn, but Mendel's going to tell mum how to fix it," explained Helen.

"Where does she get all that terminology from, eh? Chemical burn, indeed," mocked Craig. "You've spent too much time with Mendel, Sis."

"I would just let him suffer," said Wee Joe. He wandered out from a group of Manimals brandishing his green water pistol. "Pow! Pow! Take that!"

"Nice," said James. "You can always depend on Wee Joe for a bit of sympathy."

"Not!" blasted Craig.

The boys laughed as the great gates of Gwendral swung open further to receive them. It took a good half hour for the Yeltans to file in.

They babbled while they walked, pulling their carriages and herding their Yukplugs.

"Why don't the Yukplugs pull the carriages?" said Helen.

"Maybe they can't see too well," suggested Craig. "Or... Or maybe they are too special; you know, like Indian cattle or..."

"What a load of tosh you talk," said James.

"He is correct," said Garlon. "Yukplugs can only be used for riding, not labour."

"See!" blasted Craig. "Two points to me!"

$* * *$

Inside the city, Jean Harrison and Lord Eldane began applying a poultice onto Craig's burn. His tracksuit bottoms had protected him to some degree but it was still bad. Mendel had asked Cimerato to bring up some potions and powders, which Helen was busy mixing together under the wizard's instructions.

Mendel seemed to be distancing himself from James yet again. James had been told he could perform his own magic now, however, he was unsure about the whole thing and too scared to try. What if he blurted out a spell and made a complete hash of it? He knelt down beside Bero, who was busy licking Wee Joe's face, and squinted into the barrel. "Mendel, can I ask you something?"

"Of course," the wizard replied.

"Elandria and Eethan have both said that I can perform magic by myself. If this is true, I have no idea how."

"It will take time for you to understand the process, make the necessary connections, and until then, I will still need you, James."

"It doesn't seem as if you need me much these days." He tried his best not to look at Helen but he was finding it difficult.

"Well I *do* need you. Do not be envious of Helen. I'm just giving her some experience. I will need you again for a much greater task."

"Oh, I see," said James, suddenly feeling stupid and petty. "I'm not envious of her," he added.

There was a blast from a trumpet on the gate-towers. Cimerato looked up from the courtyard. A soldier shouted down at him. "Jal has returned. Shall we open the gates?"

"Open the gates! Let him in," shouted Cimerato.

"And the giant stone things?" pressed the soldier.

Cimerato glanced down at Mendel's barrel.

"And the Stone Larths, Cimerato," Mendel reassured.

Cimerato frowned and shouted up at the soldier. "Let them all in."

* * *

Ahead of her, Cathy could see the black dust cloud. Dendralon had raced on with a contingent of Inubians to see what was going on. She knew, however, that Mendel would have set something in motion to delay them. She felt sure that James and the wizard goldfish were here. She even sensed that David was here. It was hard to explain, but a kind of calmness rested on her heart for the first time in almost a year. She barged past the Inubian footmen and caught hold of the reins. "I've told you before, I will drive this damn thing myself," she yelled.

One of the Inubians growled. "But my Queen..."

"I'm not your ruddy Queen!" she blasted.

They both quailed and handed her the whip. Anger building inside her, like an uncontrollable wave of fire, she pushed the protesting Inubians off the footplate and flicked her reins. The Racnid steeds doubled their efforts. Her chariot cut across the tundra-like plain until it skidded onto the black ash of the desert and slowed. The Racnids, however, soon changed their gait and, well used to the deserts of Artilis, stepped up a gear. Her golden chariot was designed for this type of terrain. She gripped both reins in one hand, dropped the whip, and pulled the brass-tipped javelin from its clip. Ahead of her, the black dust cloud dissipated and she was able to see the full extent of the battle. The Artilian Wasps were totally interlocked with some other race of insects. She saw one of these creatures break free of the fight. It had a row of slithery grey tubes that hung down from its neck. Like a set of writhing snakes, they whipped outward and jetted dark liquid. Its head was misshapen but not unlike a giant ant in appearance. It stood up on two legs and had a further two sets of limbs and a pair of leathery wings folded behind its back. In its hand, it carried a staff or spear of sorts. As she closed in, it tilted its head in her direction. *It's seen you now. Remember your training, Cathy.* Juddering though the black sand she took aim as best she could. She tried to ignore the flecks of dust and grit that ricocheted off her armour and stung her face. Still clutching the reins, she crouched and slid her shield onto her left arm. *Keep your eye on the target.*

"Uh!" She threw her javelin.

What!

The point of a heavy spear thudded off her shield. Her legs buckled. Her helmet had dented where the shield had kicked back. Shaken, she gripped onto the side of the chariot and pulled back the reins. Gasping for breath, she looked at her target. Her javelin had found its mark. The creature wavered, three feet of bronze protruding from its chest. Still full of adrenalin, she flicked the reins and urged the Racnid steeds in closer to the flailing creature. She dug her heels into the corners of the footplate and drew her double swords. Racing past, with inches to spare, she sliced down and back, removing the creature's head. At the same moment the scythes on her wheels did their horrible work.

"Argh!" Her shield was burning her arm. "Argh!" She shook free of the leather strap that held her arm in place and stepped back. The shield began to dissolve in front of her eyes. She kicked it off the footplate and pressed on into the mêlée. Cutting down on the creatures while being careful not to slice through their strange neck-tubes, she made a path towards another group of Artilians. Ahead of her, a swarm of Artilian Soldier Wasps guarded their insect Queen. They teemed around her, stinging and biting down on the ant creatures, undeterred by the jets of acid that burned through them.

The Wasp Queen, almost thirty feet long, trampled through the tangle of bodies inadvertently slicing many of the enemy in two with the sword-like hairs on her long legs.

Cathy's chariot bumped over a rock and locked together with an Inubian chariot to her left. The Inubian charioteer, however, took a spear through the throat and fell off his chariot. Blood sprayed over her armour as the wretch was caught up in the rotating wheel blades. Indiscriminately whirring round, these horrible blades caused a huge amount of damage as she raced forward. Then she saw him. "Dendralon!"

His scales were covered in the jelly-like acid from the enemy creatures yet it did not seem to affect him. "Beldam, come onto my chariot. Your wheel is about to..."

With a shearing sound the left wheel of her chariot buckled under the weight of the unmanned vehicle and came loose. She bumped down roughly onto the black ash and fell free of the footplate. Spinning round with both of her swords drawn, she backed towards Dendralon's chariot.

"Forget the injured Racnids; stay close to me. These other creatures are called Sorabs. Their acid will burn through your tender skin. Be quick. Come aboard."

Cathy slipped on the jelly that covered Dendralon's footplate, her scaled boots wedging tight against the sides of his chariot. The boots did not burn.

"Raptor skin," said Dendralon. "Impervious, like my own." He put his arm around her and whipped his Racnids onwards. "I've been to the frontline and back," he continued. "There are far too many Sorabs. We will sacrifice the wasps and move round this force."

"What about the Wasp Queen?" she found herself asking.

"I will get her out of the fray. She must be protected at all costs. She has the next generation in her belly."

With these words he picked Cathy up and dropped her onto an empty chariot racing by in the opposite direction.

"Wait! Dendra…" She spun round but he was soon well behind her. Dendralon whipped on his steeds and sped off towards the struggling Wasp Queen.

A Sorab spear arced down onto her chariot and found the spokes of the wheel. With a terrible jolt the whole chariot whipped over the Racnids steeds in front and threw her to the side. For the second time in so many minutes, she bumped down hard onto the ash. She rolled into a mixture of scrub and fallen Artilian Wasps. Sorabs were already swarming over the Racnids trapped in the wreckage of the chariot, spraying them with their deadly liquid. She pulled a dead wasp over herself and lay still until the Racnids' screams subsided.

"Beldam!" It was Dendralon once again, his deep voice bellowing over the battlefield. She edged out from her hiding place a little until she saw the giant Wasp Queen. Dendralon was riding on its neck, his staff held high. Beams of red light shot free from his gnarled staff, throwing waves of Sorabs to the side as he approached.

She kicked the dead wasps away and stood in the open. Her breastplate was tarnished with streaks of acid, and her hair was matted to her head, caked in the black blood of her Racnid steeds. The giant Wasp Queen walked round her and faced back towards the main fight. Dendralon slid down from its neck and called another chariot forward.

"Well done, my Queen. You have earned your place beside me on my chariot."

Whoopee doo, she thought, forcing a smile and a bow. *How will I ever escape this mad wizard?*

Once she'd climbed aboard his golden chariot, Dendralon pulled back further from the main fight with the Wasp Queen and several thousand soldier wasps. He closed his eyes, lifted his staff, and bellowed, "The fire of Ra!"

She watched in amazement as a blast of crimson light shot from his staff towards the battlefield. It hit the fray at its most violent, tangled spot and spread out from there. The living red flame, bursting with explosions, wreaked havoc on any caught in its path. The screams and hisses rose to a crescendo as the cracking of carapaces and the wretched howls of the dying tore into Cathy's skull. There was a sudden blast of white light and then... Then there was complete and utter silence.

Everything had turned to dust, indistinguishable from the ashen desert. She had no idea that Dendralon was this powerful.

"See, my Queen. Nothing shall stop us this time."

"You've killed your own troops too," she whispered.

"They're of no importance. Already forgotten. Like whispers lost in the wind." Dendralon laughed at his own words.

"Of course," she sighed, still mesmerized by the complete annihilation of over ten thousand creatures in less than five seconds. "Oh, no. James, David," she whispered anxiously.

"My Queen?"

"Throat," she replied, still dazed, "ash sticking in throat... Not good..."

"Ah," sighed Dendralon.

They waited until the main Inubian flank had caught up with them. Behind that, Cathy saw the main Racnid force, some twenty thousand in all. The giant Artilian Wasp Queen lumbered along beside them as their chariot edged forward. The smell of pear drops was completely overpowering. "What is that stench?" Cathy blurted.

"Ketones and esters," explained Dendralon, in a very Mendel-like way, she decided.

The dark wizard's long, black hair blew into her eyes as he gripped the rim of his chariot.

Dendralon glanced over at the huge Wasp Queen. "She has a weapon that will seal our victory," he hissed. His warped delight in the way he said these words sent a shiver down her spine. *What did he mean? What was the secret weapon?* The dark wizard's excitement was blatantly obvious as he whipped his Racnid steeds harder. The golden chariot began to pick up speed.

CHAPTER TEN

THE PLAN

Annoyingly fastidious, Lord Eldane placed his books and maps back into a large, jewel-encrusted chest. James and Bero waited on the rest of the Drumfintley contingent to gather round, as Mendel had picked out the relevant documents and was about to tell them his plan.

Craig walked in first. He gave James a stupid wave that was like someone flicking flies away from their face and then knelt down to unclip the barrel from Bero's collar.

"Craig, put me somewhere high up, so I can see the whole chamber," said Mendel.

Craig placed the barrel on a stone pedestal in the middle of the Council chamber and withdrew.

The chamber was packed with Manimal dignitaries, Yeltans and a host of other creatures, some of which James had never seen before. James saw the tall figure of Jal make his way to the fore with a creature called Tertan, the leader of the Stone Larths. James wondered if the floor of the Council chamber would take the Stone Larth's weight.

Mendel's voice permeated the whole chamber. His tone was clear and authoritative. "We are in very strange times, where threats upon us have, once again, been exacerbated by Dendralon Pendragon. Although he is in Hedra form and I in my current guise, we are, of course, brothers."

There was a series of gasps and sighs. James knew that many in the chamber would be surprised by this fact. All eyes were on the blob of gold in the barrel.

"It will take me six hours to prepare the magic scales that, with Eethan's help, will transport us back to Denthan.

Cimerato stepped forward to hush the confused and complaining Manimals. "Give Mendel a chance to explain."

"But we will go back to nothing. Denthan is lost!" yelled a Manimal woman councillor. She clutched a young child close to her chest.

Cimerato shook his head. "Let him finish, Herfala."

Mendel cleared his throat. "The difference is, that we will not simply return to an area of space devoid of a planet that exploded, we will return to a living, fully complete Denthan two weeks before its destruction. Before the supernova."

"What's the point of that?" shouted one of the councillors. "We might not make it off the planet this time. We could be going back to our death."

"How can we go back in time?" shouted another.

This time Lord Eldane signalled silence.

"Thank you, Lord Eldane," said Mendel. "Firstly, the reason we can go back in time is because we have recovered a special talisman: The Key of Artilis. According to my calculations, and as I have already said, we will arrive back in Denthan two weeks before its destruction. So the time and place are set."

"What do you mean 'according to your calculations'?" said Herfala. "You were over ten feet out with your positioning of the water fountain in the main square. We had to dig it up…"

"Yes, yes," interjected Lord Eldane.

"So how do we know you've got this, slightly more important calculation right?" pressed Herfala.

James saw Craig grip his tongue with his teeth and screw up his face in thought. He hoped his friend wouldn't say anything stupid.

Cimerato shouted out above the din. "Look what happened when we doubted Mendel the last time. Dendralon fooled us all, and we banished Mendel to another world. If it had not been for James and Craig, the two boys standing here before us, we would have all perished. Dendralon and his Hedra cur would be standing here now."

Jal hissed.

"No offence, my big friend," added Cimerato.

There was a murmur of agreement.

"The second reason my plan will work," continued Mendel, "is that we have the three Orphans of Light: Eethan, you all know; Elandria from Artilis, and Elcar, the Hipposaur from this planet. I believe that the three together can form a shield that will protect Denthan from the inevitable shock wave produced by the death of Tealfirth, our beloved sun. Zalion, Denthan's second sun is more than capable of sustaining us after the blast has subsided."

"What about your brother?" shouted a Yeltan.

"Dendralon is almost upon us," agreed another.

Mendel splashed round in his barrel then stopped. "We will have to stall him."

The voices chattered loudly and the wails of the Yeltans intensified.

"There is a whole lot of conjecture and hope in all this, Mendel," announced Herfala. "I lost my first husband on Denthan one day before we made our escape. He fell in the Battle of the Black Lake."

"He was a brave man," said Mendel.

Cimerato eyed Herfala with a mixture of impatience and, what James thought might be, admiration.

"Where do we stand at this precise moment? What are our choices?" she pressed.

James watched Cimerato, the Manimal captain, pace the floor. "Dendralon is four, perhaps five hours away from our gates with fifteen to twenty-thousand Racnids, thousands of Inubians and a sizeable force of Artilian Wasps, despite Mendel's and Craig's best efforts."

"And my best efforts," said a small voice. It was Helen.

Cimerato smiled at her and nodded. "And Helen's…."

"But, Cimerato, Mendel has just told us it will take him six hours to get the great scales of Gwendral working," pressed Herfala.

"I did," agreed Mendel, "and that is why…"

"What is your plan, Mendel?" Herfala interrupted.

"My plan, Herfala, is to delay Dendralon's advance and then move Gwendral, and all who are inside the walls, to Denthan two weeks before its destruction. Once there, and with the help of the Orphans of Light, I will perform the magic needed to form the shield that will protect Denthan. So…"

There was complete silence in the chamber.

"...I need volunteers to stall Dendralon's advance. It will take him about four hours to reach the city and prepare his troops so I need one or two extra hours, that is all."

"These volunteers will be trapped outside the city walls and will perish," said Garlon, the Yeltan leader.

"Not necessarily," said James, firmly. "I will go outside the city and help stall Dendralon." He turned to Craig. "I need to see if my mum is with him."

"I will go with James," added Craig, his magic spear, Greenworm, already in his hand.

"Craig!" protested Jean.

"Be careful what you promise, boys," added Michael.

James saw his dad stumble forward. "You don't know what you're doing, Son."

"I do, Dad. I know she's out there. Don't you want to see if Mum is with him? Don't you want to see if she's still alive?"

"Of course I do, and I will come with you if you really think that Cathy is here." David Peck took a step forward.

"I'll come too," said Helen.

"No," said Mendel. "I need Helen to stay with me. Wee Joe and Jean should stay here in Gwendral too."

James felt that familiar wave of jealousy wash over him again. Helen was to play some special part in Mendel's plans yet again. He caught the beginnings of a sneer on Craig's face and whispered, "Don't even think about it."

Craig, unable to stop himself, blurted, "Why Helen and not James, Mendel?"

Mendel let the question drift up into the rafters of the chamber, un-answered.

"Numpty," whispered James.

Michael broke the silence when, speaking in his best vicar's voice, he announced, "I think I speak for all of us when I say that the Drumfintley contingent will be happy to help in whatever way we can."

James's dad issued a nervous cough.

Michael straightened, "Mark, chapter four, verse..."

"Yes, thank you, Reverend," interrupted Mendel. "I just need Helen with me now; and I'm not going to explain why, Craig. As far as the rest of the children from Drumfintley are concerned... They must be careful, as Michael says. You see, Craig's injury on Whindril proves that they are probably not immortal."

"Bummer," sighed James.

An excited murmur echoed through the great hall.

"I love the way he says *probably not immortal*," whispered Craig. "He's not the one who had to test it out."

"Lucky you didn't get a big spear in yous head, or get chopped in two by a big monster," said Wee Joe.

"Yeh, lucky old me," said Craig.

Ephie grimaced.

Mendel cut through the din. "Do what you feel you can, but do it quickly."

"We will help on the battlefield!" The voice came from the back of the hall. James peered over the crowd until he picked out Garlon, the Yeltan leader.

"Why would you do such a thing?" pressed a tall, disgruntled-looking Manimal, decked in the same armour as Cimerato.

Craig dug James in the ribs. "I met him earlier," said Craig. "He's a captain, like Cimerato. His name is…"

"Uzarto," finished Lord Eldane.

"That's it." Craig nodded.

Stepping round the diminutive figure of Garlon, Uzarto made his way to the front. "You want to remain here on Ebos, don't you, Garlon? Found a lost paradise beyond the Yelding. At least that is the rumour."

"Yes, we would like to remain here on Ebos as a clan," explained Garlon. "If your plan to save Denthan is successful, however, we will send a group of volunteer Yeltans back to Denthan one day."

Uzarto looked down at the barrel. "What state will Denthan be in if you *are* successful, Mendel?"

"If I am successful, Denthan will go back to the way it was 1.2 seconds before the destruction point. All life will resume. However, all deaths previous to that point and after it will remain unchanged. In fact…" Mendel paused and adopted a more sombre tone. "We should not expect any who perished to return."

Wee Joe tugged on his mother's sleeve. "Mum, I thought Mendel said that Archie MacNulty come back to life? I don't remember."

Mendel swam across to the window in the plastic barrel. "I'm sorry, Wee Joe. I have re-read the scripts and, regretably, there is nothing I can do. The Hedra will appear outside the city of Gwendral, as before, wailing at their inevitable doom. But this time they will be saved."

"So…" began Garlon, "you will save our enemy but not my father."

"What is done is done," reminded Mendel. "Anything alive in that 1.2 second period when we resume our positions in Denthan will be saved. Anything or anyone who died previous to that point, or after it, as I have explained, will remain lost."

James shook his head as he thought of old MacNulty. "Isn't there any way that…?"

"No," snapped Mendel. "The reason I have shifted my calculations is to minimize any fate-time shifts in reality."

"None-the-wiser," whispered Craig.

James saw the worried faces of his friends and asked, "What about us? We will have counterparts in the old Denthan. What will happen to all the things we have done over the last few years, what will happen to our memories?"

"Our counterparts, back on the original Denthan will be no more. They will fade as we appear. Our memories will be intact. At least that's what the texts say. Simple Pathian Physics."

"Simple?" barked Craig. "You lost me about five bloomin' minutes ago."

"Well, that wouldn't be hard," whispered James.

Helen sniggered.

Craig stared into the barrel. "So, my old wizzy friend, we get to stay and fight Dendralon here, outside the city, while everyone inside Gwendral, this lot," he flicked his hand in the direction of the Manimals, "get to go back, safe and sound?"

"Are you saying we are cowards?" snapped Herfala.

"That's right. Got it in one, my lady." Craig sniffed, defiantly, nodding his head for emphasis.

This did not go down well. They were frog-marched, there and then, from the Council chamber.

"Nice one, numpty," whispered James.

"What?" protested Craig. "They're leaving us to do all the hard stuff while…"

"Well, we said we would. You volunteered," snapped James.

Jean Harrison gripped Wee Joe's hand as the soldiers ushered them out with the boys. "That's enough, Craig. You need to learn to think before you speak."

"Ha!" guffawed James. "That'll be the day."

Ephie sat down beneath one of the great stained-glass windows. Michael joined her on the window seat. "Ostracized, thanks to Craig's glib comments," he muttered.

"You sound just like Mendel, Father," said Craig. "Speak plain English."

"Ostrich-ized!" said Wee Joe. "You've been ostrich-ized," he repeated with glee.

"Sounds painful," mused James. He took a piece of tablet from Ephie and popped it into his mouth. "How much time do we have until Dendralon gets here again?"

"About four and a half hours, according to the gormless guppy," Craig grumbled.

Wee Joe kicked his big brother's shin. "Stop being so rude about Mendel."

Craig lifted his hand to cuff Wee Joe but received a withering stare from his mum and lowered it. He sat down on another stone window seat and, for no apparent reason, began examining Greenworm. The green-tinged spear sparkled in the dappled light.

"Why would you call on Greenworm just now? There's no need," said James.

"You never know," moaned Craig, eyeing Wee Joe. "I might feel like a bit of practise." He spun the shaft of the spear faster between the palms of his hands.

James stood up. "Look, nump…"

"Call me a numpty one more time and I'll…"

"You'll what," said James, his heart quickening.

"Now, now, boys," interjected Michael.

James felt the griffin tattoo burn his skin. He was desperate to call on his magic sword, Firetongue.

Craig just stared at him, spinning the spear even faster between his hands.

James lunged forward and gripped Greenworm.

Craig jerked to his feet and tried to tug the spear away.

James held on tightly.

"Enough!" Jean Harrison barged in front of James and grabbed Craig by the collar of his grimy shirt. She dragged him away from the window seat. "If you ever threaten any of this group again, Craig Harrison, I'll ground you for a whole year; a la Cathy Peck! Got it?"

Craig broke away from his mum and moved away from the group.

James opened his mouth to speak but just shook his head instead. What was he thinking? He'd never laid a hand on Craig's magic spear before. For a moment he'd felt its power, felt the rage that accompanied the talisman. Perhaps the spear was changing his best friend. Was Firetongue having the same effect on *him*? Were they both going crazy?

The Council chamber door creaked open. A Manimal guard pointed to Helen and asked, "Would the young lady accompany me back into the main hall?"

Helen looked at her mother for approval.

Jean Harrison solemnly nodded her head. "Be careful, Helen. I love you."

Helen flushed. "Don't worry, Mum. Mendel will look after me."

Craig shifted awkwardly; squinting up at his sister as she walked through the huge door.

CHAPTER ELEVEN

THE GOLDEN CHARIOT

This was going to be the first time that the boys would be alone on an adventure, without Mendel that is, for a very long time. They'd become separated from the wizard years before, on Denthan, and James knew it was going to be tough. Especially since Craig and he weren't exactly on the best of terms.

The Yeltans, in less than one hour, had dug a tunnel that stretched out in a semi-circle round the main gates. Just under the surface of the compacted ash that surrounded the city, it would act as a hidden ditch, should any chariots or bigger creatures attack head-on.

Craig would help with the defences to the left of the main gates, along with one thousand Manimal volunteers and the Mertol, while James, with Jal, would take a similar force of Manimals and the Stone Larths to the right of the main gates. Whindril, along with Ephie, Cimerato, and Michael would watch the skies and direct operations. Jean, David Peck and Wee Joe had been given the task of watching the underground lake, which James hoped would remain undisturbed.

The Yeltans were amassing some five hundred yards from the city walls in a curved, set of horns, formation. They hoped this would bring the enemy in towards the hidden pit. Behind that force they also had a division of two hundred Yukplugs that would act as extra protection for the main gates.

James could see the dust cloud now. Like a great, grey curtain, it drifted steadily towards them, flecks of reflective wings and insect carapace flashing in the sunlight.

"It will be best if the Stone Larths and myself meet the enemy first," hissed Jal. "Mendel says that the great flash of light in the distance was Dendralon's magic. We were lucky to get away when we did." The giant Hedra warrior adjusted his belt, pushing a further two daggers behind the taut leather. Against the grey, ashen ground the Stone Larths became practically invisible with their rock-encrusted hides. Standing over twenty feet tall, James imagined two rhinos standing on top of each other and decided they must weigh at least six tons each. They left large indentations after every step yet still appeared fairly agile. The Manimals kept their distance from these hulking beasts and their huge swords. James was relieved that these formidable creatures were on his side. He'd faced the Artilian hordes before and didn't relish another encounter.

"You should build up your strength before Dendralon arrives," said Garlon. "There's another three hours yet before he reaches our defences. We are going to have some supper. Yeltans never miss an opportunity to eat. Any excuse will do."

Craig pawed a small, velvet pouch on his belt.

James saw that his friend was trying to suppress a smile. "You've still got it, haven't you?"

"What?" said Craig.

"Lugpus," said James, coyly. "The Yeltan stuff that makes you laugh."

"I reckon we could do with some," said Craig.

James thought back to the last time they'd sampled this Yeltan speciality. They'd almost died laughing. It had been given to them in the form of a bubblegum-flavoured drink. They'd drank too much of the stuff and would have collapsed if they hadn't been given the antidote, a yellow powder called Nose-squeeze.

"I can't exactly offer you a banquet," said Garlon, "but you're welcome to join us."

So, sitting round a table of sorts, fashioned from the compact earth and ash of Ebos, James and Craig were soon munching on some of the local delicacies.

James sniffed the contents of a small glass and handed it to Craig. "Are we still friends?"

Craig sighed. "Of course we are. I just get…"

"Loud and stupid sometimes," finished James, rather wishing he hadn't.

There was a pause while Craig downed the familiar bubblegum-flavoured drink. "Yes, I suppose I do sometimes." A grin instantly stole across Craig's freckled face. "I'd forgotten what it feels like when you drink this stuff. It's brilliant."

James looked at his own glass for a moment and took a more cautious sip. He tittered. "You were never tempted to try that powder you've got on your belt back in Drumfintley, then?"

Craig giggled. "Nope. This is Nose-squeeze not Lugpus. I'd have climbed St. Donan's tower and jumped off in a fit of depression." He made a series of small circles with his forefinger an inch from his temple. "I used the Lugpus on your mum, back on Denthan the first time. She was having a panic attack in a tunnel."

James ignored the obvious reference to his mum's craziness and finished the rest of the glass.

"What is that disgusting rubbery thing, Garlon?" Craig pinged a large slug-like object on the table.

"It's a Mudlegrub," said Garlon. "Delicious with Whindleroo and Difersaw, a herb that suppresses the confusing properties of the cooked flesh. Try it." The Yeltan pointed at James's plate.

Both of the boys guffawed and began to shake with laughter.

"I'll try a bit," said James.

"So will I," wheezed Craig. "Don't tell us what Whindleroo is. I'd rather not know."

"No, tell us," said James, swigging another glass of Lugpus while giggling at the same time.

James bit into the slimy flesh of the Mudlegrub. "You know," he tittered, "it's not that bad."

"Mmm," Craig agreed. "It's just the name that puts you off. You should call it something more inviting, like crème de slug or grubby guts or…" Craig's face contorted. "Prams and pyjamas, space ships and doodle bugs…"

James looked at Craig's face, which had wrinkled into one big freckle. "What are you talking about?"

Garlon shook his head. "Craig, you need to eat more Difersaw."

"He's talking gibberish," said James, his eyes streaming.

"I don't do greens," laughed Craig, "or yellows or purples or giant flying pandas…I hate the taste of those things. Where am I?"

James was beginning to choke with laughter while Craig was becoming more and more confused.

Garlon snapped his fingers, and two Yeltans ran towards the earthen table. The first blew Nose-squeeze into James's face while the second little creature opened Craig's mouth and stuffed in a bunch of bright green Difersaw. Craig wriggled for a moment and then swallowed.

James felt the uncontrollable feeling of elation begin to fade. The giggles and titters soon became bearable and he took in a large gasp of air. Through the blur of his tears he saw Craig steady himself on the table and stare at him.

"Why is Yeltan food so bloomin' dangerous?" Craig whispered. His eyes were still looking slightly vacant.

Garlon shook his head. Yeltan food is delicious, but it requires discipline, it requires…"

"A bloomin' government health warning," finished Craig.

It was now Garlon who looked confused.

James wiped his wet face with his shirt. "It was very nice, Garlon, but you need to explain things a bit better next time." James picked up one of the glasses in front of him and then, thinking better of it, placed it back on the table. "I think I'll stick to the water."

"Me too," said Craig.

"All you need to do to keep safe is to eat a balanced diet," said Garlon.

"We get that spiel at home," said Craig. "Mostly from my mum."

"Well, listen to your mum," said Garlon. "Your own food may not send you into fits of laughter or make you confused to the same degree, but I would guess there is a balance to be found there too."

"Mmm…" mused James.

Garlon sighed. "Look, try one glass only."

The boys stared at the tray of glasses suspiciously.

"So, it will be okay if we just have one glass each?" asked James.

"Try," said Garlon.

Hesitantly, James and Craig downed another glass each of Lugpus. They were fine for a few seconds but soon began laughing again. They laughed at the size of each other's noses, they laughed at the shape of the table, they laughed at anything, even when Garlon mentioned Dendralon, they just burst into fits of giggles.

Garlon looked them up and down before sliding the tray of glasses away from the boys. "Your constitution must be very different from ours. You just can't handle our pick-me-ups."

"I'd like to see you try," blurted Craig.

James screwed up his face. "See him try what?"

"Pick... Pick... Pick me up." His eyes were streaming and his fingers were searching for the pouch on his belt.

Garlon and the surrounding Yeltans, who were a good foot smaller than the boys, shook their heads. "We have more strength than you would imagine," said Garlon. With this, he stood to his full three feet and wandered round the table until he was behind Craig.

"He's going to..." hissed James. "S,s,s,s,s..."

Garlon climbed onto the table and lifted Craig off his seat with one hand. Then, stretching until he caught James's shirt, he hauled him up too.

James felt himself being pulled to his feet and then he left the ground. His legs dangled but Craig, being a good bit taller, stood perched on his tiptoes.

Both boys shook with laughter.

"Yeltans are much stronger than humans," said Garlon. He laughed too before nodding to a fellow Yeltan.

Through a stream of tears, James saw the yellow-skinned creature unclip Craig's pouch and remove a pinch of power. The Yeltan climbed up on the table and blew it into their faces, one at a time.

At once, the boy's uncontrollable laughter subsided into a random stream of intermittent giggles.

Garlon dropped them back on their seats. "Don't give them too much Nose-squeeze, Forndal. It's good to see these two boys behaving like friends for once."

James wiped his eyes and patted Craig on the back. "Numpty."

Craig smiled and patted James in return. "Numpty boy."

The odd titter escaped, as they finished their dinner, not much minding that they were eating giant slugs, green Difersaw, or Whindleroo, which turned out to be a creature not unlike a hamster with six legs.

"Glad your dad's not here," said Craig.

"Yeah, he wouldn't approve of the Whindleroo," tittered James. He thought about Scotland and home. He thought about the odd time his mum and dad were actually happy. Sitting in front of a real wood fire or having a picnic beside Loch Echty. He held onto those memories as he stretched out on his seat. He was tired now. His eyes were becoming heavy.

"No time to rest now," said a deep, hissing voice.

James felt the presence of someone very tall standing behind him and spun round to face an anxious-looking Jal.

"You'd best come up to the surface and see what we're up against," said Jal.

Still groggy, the boys called on their magic weapons and followed Jal and the Yeltans out of the tunnel. They winced in the bright sunlight.

Artilian Wasps were already closing in. They buzzed and dived menacingly in a thickening swarm above the jackal-faced Inubians.

A feeling of dread gripped James at the thought of facing these creatures again.

Behind him, the battlements of Gwendral bristled with Manimal archers. Jal explained that they were under instruction to fire on the wasps first. "The archers will allow us some cover." Jal looked around the trench. "Garlon!"

The Yeltan leader ducked out of the tunnel entrance behind them, into the light.

"You should train your poison-tipped spears on the Inubians," said Jal. "I'm told that is what they call the dog-faced creatures."

James looked behind him to see the dragon, Whindril, waddle through the open gates of the city. Cimerato sat on the dragon seat clutching a longbow. He pulled on her reins and guided her out through the ivory gates. Yelping like a seal, Whindril opened her wings, stretched her long neck and shook her mane. Blue steam seeped from her gaping nostrils as she hissed at the sky and leapt up in the direction of the enemy.

"I thought Ephie and Michael were supposed to be with Cimerato?" asked Craig.

Jal pointed to the citadel. "I know that Mrs. Harrison and the children are up there now. Mendel suddenly decided it would be too dangerous to place them anywhere else."

"Good. I didn't like the thought of Mum down at the Black Lake," said Craig.

Jal scanned the city walls. "I'm not sure where Ephie and Michael are."

James held Firetongue. He felt the raw energy of the magic sword course through him and wondered again about its long-term effects on his sanity. A towering Stone Larth eyed it suspiciously before falling in line with the rest of the grey giants. James reeled back as the Larths held their enormous swords aloft and bellowed out an earth-shattering cry. It reminded him of a bunch of Vikings he'd seen in an old film, or maybe it was the Scottish rugby fans at Murrayfield. He couldn't decide.

Whindril circled high above the Artilian Wasps, a distant speck of silvery white, before dropping back down towards the city again. She took her position above the shining alabaster citadel of Gwendral, circling a good thousand feet above its alabaster balcony.

"Whindril will let the Manimal archers loose three waves of arrows before making her attack," explained Jal.

"And what do we do?" asked James.

"We wait and watch for now." Jal's movements were slow but deliberate as he edged over the rim of their trench to get a better look. James saw a second pair of translucent eyelids blink vertically across his yellow-slit eyes. He knew these filters allowed the Hedra warrior to see in the infrared spectrum.

The enemy were obscured by billowing dust clouds that surrounded their position. Soon, however, Inubian chariots came into view amongst the swirling curtain of hoary ash.

Spider-like Racinds pulled the chariots over the rough ground, their spindly legs making easy work of the uneven desert terrain. The Inubians had begun their terrible din, banging their shields in unison. It sounded, as it was supposed to, like the war drum of some terrible god.

"Look," yelled Jal. "I can see Dendralon's chariot. It must be the one covered in gold."

"And he has a new captain," said Craig.

James could just make out a second figure standing beside the Hedra wizard on the footplate. The smaller figure was dressed in golden armour too.

Craig shielded his eyes. "You don't think…"

James refocused, however the billowing dust clouds suddenly obscured the chariot. He felt his mouth become dry. He screwed up his eyes to see if he could catch another glimpse of the figure but the crimson sword, Firetongue, distracted him. It flinched and vibrated in his hand, ready for the fight.

A rush of cool air on his neck signalled five thousand arrows arcing overhead. He ducked instinctively and then watched as they wreaked havoc amongst the milling Artilian Wasps. They tore through gossamer wings and split the tough carapaces of the giant insects before dipping down onto the Inubians below. The Inubian banging stopped as they hoisted their shields above their heads. A hundred tattered corpses battered off their turtle-like formation amongst a hail of arrows. Howls and hisses echoed over the desert as the Manimal arrows dug deep into the Racnid steeds or juddered into the exposed limbs of an undisciplined Inubian.

James raised his sword in preparation for the remaining wasps that flew straight at their positions.

Behind him, a whir of wings caught him by surprise, but his sword arm jerked upwards, slicing the Artilian Wasp in two. The Stone Larths beside him swung their long swords, cleaving many more. Some of the wasps tried, in vain, to pierce the Larths' tough, stone-encrusted hides. However, they were easily caught and crushed by the Larths' football-sized fists or trampled beneath their troll-like feet.

His heart racing, James shouted out, "Come on! Come and see what you get!" His mind, though, kept drifting back to the mystery figure on Dendralon's chariot.

Strangely, the Inubian chariots slowed and then parted to make way for something. There was no sign of the Racnid force yet, except the ones used as steeds by the charioteers. A writhing wasp clattered down on top of him. The bulky creature took his breath away and knocked him to his knees. The sting pulsed menacingly close to his face. He kicked the orange abdomen away from him but the half-dead wasp rallied and arched to deliver its final blow.

"Take care, boy!" Jal hacked off the tip of its abdomen and kicked it away. "Look behind as well as to the fore."

"Thanks," wheezed James. Ducking down he scanned behind him. A flash of yellow light from the citadel indicated that Mendel was at work, but he felt no knocking sensation in his head. He prayed that the city wouldn't disappear. *Not yet*, he thought.

"Those Artilian Wasps have brought their Queen to the fight," shouted Jal.

James let his mouth fall open in dread as he saw the reason why the Inubian chariots had parted and slowed their advance. A massive wasp-like creature clambered forward, surrounded by thousands of workers with bright crimson antennae. Even as she advanced they fed and tended her.

"What are we going to do now, Jal?" asked James.

"Duck!" cried Jal.

The second wave of Manimal arrows whizzed over their heads.

Instantly, the worker wasps completely covered the Wasp Queen and absorbed the deluge of the arrows. They dropped off the Queen, dead, to reveal her massive form once more. Completely unharmed the Wasp Queen continued to lumber towards them.

"Dendralon will have brought her for a reason," said Jal.

"What about the Yeltan pit?"

Jal lunged at an angry wasp. "Just focus on your nearest foe. Cimerato and Whindril will have to think of something." Jal punched James on the shoulder. "Look, your friend has broken ranks."

James looked to his left to see Craig running back from a wasp that lay a good fifteen feet in front of their trench. He cut through another wasp as he came to a stop then pointed at the Wasp Queen. "She's nearly as ugly as you."

"And you're supposed to be sticking to a plan," said James. "Jal told us to hold our positions." He eyed Greenworm.

Craig slipped back into the trench. "It stuck fast in that bloomin' wasp. I had to go and get it."

"How far can you throw that thing?" asked James.

Craig shrugged.

"Could you hit the Wasp Queen from here?"

"Maybe," said Craig.

"Don't lose your spear a second time, boy," said Jal.

"What's she doing?" asked James.

The Wasp Queen had come to a halt. She was unravelling two long, tube-like appendages.

"I don't like the look of this," said Jal. He turned to a Manimal captain. "Mendel told me to watch out for his precious Manimals. Can you hold your men in position?"

"Watch out for yourself, snake-man. And we know how to follow orders, unlike some." The Manimal grimaced at Craig.

James hunched. Above them the third wave of Manimal arrows raced over their heads and hammered into the flying wasps. This time Whindril dived after them, almost reaching the last of the arrows as she blew her deadly fire into the midst of the oncoming swarm. The high-pitched screams of the wasps masked the incessant drone of the Wasp Queen. James and Craig sidestepped to avoid several frazzled wasps dropping on their heads.

One of the Stone Larths roared out in pain as a burning wasp ignited the down on its back.

James and Craig watched in awe as Whindril spun round and dived again. This time she snapped wasps in half with her fanged jaws while Cimerato aimed his bow and dispatched many more.

"She's good at that," said Craig. "Just eats them whole sometimes."

"Now what is that thing doing?" barked James. He pointed at the Wasp Queen

The Wasp Queen had raised herself up on a pair of elongated back legs. The loud base drone from her huge wings intensified as she raised herself higher above the Inubians. Then, to James's utter surprise, there was a noise like a giant cork popping from a bottle.

"Everyone, get down!" shouted Jal.

Greyish, torpedo-like shapes flew over their heads and thumped onto the city walls. Stuck fast, the strange objects wobbled and then began to shake violently.

"Are they maggots?" yelled James.

Craig shook his head mournfully. "If they're anything like the maggots on Artilis, they can probably tunnel through stone."

"They can *what?*" exclaimed Jal.

Half the Manimal force on the battlements had peered over to watch the long maggots. They began to burrow straight through the thick city walls. The smooth stone crumbled and fell away as time after time more living torpedoes flew over the Yeltan trenches and began to eat away at the walls of Gwendral.

Bemused, some of the Manimals in the trenches with James and Craig began to move back towards the city.

Jal jumped up on a nearby rock and yelled, "Hold your ground!" He looked round until he found the leader of the Stone Larths. "Tertan, take half your force and cut those things to bits before they get a chance to burrow any more holes in the walls."

"Come!" Tertan waved his massive arms. "This section, fall back to the walls."

James watched as the rear line of Stone Larths stripped away from the tightly-packed group and bounded back to the city walls. The Manimal archers had disappeared from the battlements, presumably busy killing the wasp larvae as they emerged from the inside of the walls. James shuddered as he saw a huge hole appear in the wall where several larvae had burrowed through together.

Crash!

Rock and rubble tumbled free of the smooth city walls.

A yell rose up from the Inubians and they charged. The jackal-faced infantry ran just as fast as the chariots. James picked out Dendralon and his consort in their midst. Firetongue lurched upward, pulling him towards the fight.

"No," snapped Jal. "The Yeltan pit is in between us and them. Hold. Let them come."

Whindril bore down on the Wasp Queen, frazzling her antennae with a blast of blue fire but a crimson shield rose up from the charging masses and doused the flame.

Dendralon's magic, thought James.

The great dragon spun round and landed heavily near to James's position. The ground shook. Cimerato shouted at his men, "Keep in line. Leave the Stone Larths to their task."

The Stone Larths were doing a good job against the wasp larvae. Their extra-long swords and exceptional height proved a good combination.

The Mertol beat its chest and let out a roar as the first of the Inubians tumbled into the Yeltan pit. Over a thousand of the jackal-faced warriors howled in surprise, disappearing below the ground in a cloud of grey dust. Chariots spun to a halt, their scimitar wheels slicing their own as they veered recklessly. James gripped Firetongue even tighter as Dendralon's chariot pulled up just in time.

"It's a female!" hissed Jal.

"*What's* a female?" shouted James, trying to make himself heard above the cheers of the Gwendralin defenders.

"His driver. I can smell her. Look, her black hair is as long as his." Jal's tongue flicked in and out of his mouth before he snapped shut his serrated jaws.

James squinted to see through the dust cloud and remembered that Jal was most probably watching the fray in infrared. He glimpsed the golden chariot, only briefly, through the mêlée. He had to shield his eyes as Whindril flapped skyward again.

A moment later, James saw her. Decked in gold, the woman threw a javelin across the Yeltans' pit, her long hair trailing behind her as the royal chariot changed direction once more. As it regrouped with a phalanx of Inubians something tugged at his chest. He felt nervous and short of breath. A trumpet blew as the golden chariot skidded to a halt.

James wondered what was going to happen next. He could hear the screams of the Inubians as the Yeltans finished off the trapped and wounded in their deep pit. Then he realised what was going to happen. "No!" His voice was lost in the din.

A flash of red light shot out from Dendralon's gnarled staff illuminating the Yeltan trench. All screams and wails inside the pit intensified and then ceased as the two earthen sides slid shut. Over twenty feet wide, the two edges of the Yeltan pit had snapped together, burying all inside.

"How the…" gasped Craig.

"Dendralon has become more powerful," whispered Jal.

The deafening sound of Inubian swords clattering against their bronze shields resumed. The jackal-faced Inubians moved en masse behind the golden chariot, growling and whining with excitement.

Craig ran back to his position beside the Mertol.

Two hundred yards back from what had once been the Yeltan pit, James looked along his trench. To his left the Yeltans babbled relentlessly; their cries of woe almost unbearable. They held their ranks, though, under Garlon's command and drew back their spears. To James's right the trench was full of Yeltans and Manimals. This flank, supposedly led by Craig and the Mertol, spilled over the rim of the trench and launched a blur of spears into the Inubian host. James braced.

Garlon gave the command. "Now this flank; throw!"

The Stone Larths behind him stepped over his head as soon as the Yeltans loosed their spears and broke into a thunderous run. He caught a glimpse of Whindril swooping down to deliver another blast of blue fire directly at the golden chariot. *Could the figure beside Dendralon really be my mum?*

CHAPTER TWELVE

THE SPELL

Cathy Peck tensed as the vibration from the chariot shook her armour-plated legs. She held the reins tight as she saw Dendralon prepare to perform his dark magic. She thought she'd seen James, but she wasn't sure. It was hard to tell. Something that looked like a herd of giants had raced to the fore of the Manimal and Yeltan lines to face them. Above her she recognised the white dragon, Whindril. It was spinning down from the skies towards her position. It was close enough for her to pick out Cimerato, the Manimal captain from Gwendral. Her heart raced with a mixture of exhilaration and dread. He would never recognise her in her armour.

"Brace, my Queen," hissed Dendralon. "My old dragon attacks…"

Cathy's skin prickled with static as the Hedra wizard cast his spell, "Obliteratha!"

By the time Dendralon's spell had left his lips, Whindril's blue fire had already roared out from the dragon's jaws. Cathy covered her head with her shield and waited. Through her half-shut eyes she watched as Dendralon's red flame collided with the dragon's blue. A giant ball of purple flashed above her. She felt the searing heat on her face. The golden plates that hid her face seemed to be melting. She screamed and tore the heavy helmet off her head. It dropped onto the ground, and she sighed with relief as the scalding pain subsided.

A Yeltan spear narrowly missed her leg and buried itself deep in the side panel of her chariot. She knew the Yeltans dipped their spears in deadly poison, so she drew her leg back from the razor-sharp point. The flurry of the poison spears found many Inubians and Racnid steeds, dropping them on the spot.

Dendralon aimed another blast of red flame at Whindril as the dragon banked down at them for the second time in so many minutes. *I wish I could tell them it's me*, she thought. Then she realised that without her helmet she might be recognised. Dendralon's red flame had missed, and she ducked as the dragon's talons swished passed her head.

Dendralon bellowed up at the retreating dragon, "Traitor!" He turned and signalled the main assault. "NOW!"

Terrified of hurting anyone she knew, Cathy searched for any sign of James or Craig, but she was already in the thick of the battle. Behind her the deafening screams of attacking Racnids filled the air. They had lain low behind a ridge of dust and now raced to join the fight. The remaining wasps dived in and stung the Manimals while the Inubians hacked and slashed at the lumbering giants that looked as if they were made from stone.

"Stone Larths!" shouted Dendralon as he reached out and thrust down with his sword. It pinged off a Larth's stone-clad hide. "Hard to kill."

A Yeltan drew up beside her chariot on the back of a Yukplug and threw his spear at her. She twisted just in time and deflected the poisoned tip with her shield. The wild-eyed Yeltan screamed and leapt off the Yukplug, bearing down on her with a second spear. Instinct took over and she cut down hard with one of her swords.

"MUM?"

Her heart jumped as she recognised the voice.

The Yeltan fell dead amongst the Racnids, who quickly devoured his remains.

Dendralon hissed beside her, "This is your moment of truth, my Queen."

Staring into his cat-like eyes, she quickly handed him the reins and leapt free of the chariot. Racnids raced past her on either side then, looking up, she stopped before a towering Stone Larth. The Racnids juddered off of its thick, immovable legs as it lifted an unbelievably long sword above its head. She knew her shield would be useless. The blade was already slashing down at her when she saw him. "James..."

***

High above the battle, in the citadel of Gwendral, Elandria glowed a deep, iridescent scarlet. Elcar shone as bright as any sun while Eethan, just discernible behind the two bigger animals, radiated a blue light that seemed to cool the chamber and cancel out the raw power of the others.

Helen picked up the spinning Key of Artilis. She held it away from her and, shielding her eyes from the increasing golden light, mouthed, "Wwwtakewwuswwfrwomwwthewwmomentww!"

There was a blinding flash of all-consuming, pure white light.

***

The whole battlefield fell silent as Gwendral shimmered then disappeared.

James, still in a state of complete bewilderment at seeing his estranged mother fighting alongside Dendralon, closed his eyes as the blinding light crept over the battlefield.

"No!" The city was gone. "I need you now more than ever. Mendel!" he shouted.

When the light subsided he saw her. She'd twisted away from a Stone Larth's sword and rolled beneath the trampling feet of advancing Racnids. His mum moved like a panther, lunging as she wound her way through the battling creatures. With a sword in each hand she dispatched a further two Yeltans. Tears were streaming down his face as she moved closer. "Mum! Stop it!"

The Stone Larth's sword whistled down at her again but she dived through its legs and hacked into the creature's tendons. Rolling she caught hold of a passing Racnid. James watched in horror as she jumped off the Racnid's back and then removed the Larth's bulky head with a deliberate crossing of her two swords.

"Mu..." He couldn't finish the word. Ducking an Inubian spear Firetongue struck upwards and felled the jackal-faced creature. She'd seen him. He was sure she had. Was it really her? He turned to Jal, but the Hedra giant was too busy fighting to stay alive. The battle had intensified and there was no longer any Gwendral to retreat into. Mendel had left them to their fate. He caught her eye and she his.

James held his crimson sword before him. "Mum, is that you?" Her features were unmistakable but the look on her face was completely unknown to him. It had been a year since they'd been separated.

"Wait!" She hissed the command as a Yeltan spear glanced off her chest-plate. She regained her balance. "Strike me!"

"What?" James didn't have a clue what to do. He quickly scanned for Jal again but found him in the thick of the Racnids. Craig was nowhere to be seen and above him Whindril beat her wings over the fight.

"Strike me!" she repeated. She turned and skewered another Yeltan. "Pretend to stab me. Now, before I have to kill any more!"

He saw her glance nervously towards Dendralon. The wizard's Racnid steeds had fallen under another deluge of Yeltan spears and he was busy fighting his way round his chariot.

His mum's eyes widened as he lifted his sword, unsure whether Firetongue would pretend to stab anyone. Suddenly, two Inubian warriors sliced down at him with their scimitar-headed pikes. His mum fell back as he sidestepped the first attacker and parried the blow of the second. A third Inubian pulled his mum away from harm's way. "Mum!"

Lost in the confusion of bodies and blades, her glinting armour disappeared. James turned his attention to Dendralon. The wizard had just called out someone's name. It sounded like *Beldam*. He saw the dark wizard was in trouble. Jal and the Mertol were circling him while Whindril pestered him from above.

"James!" His mum was suddenly to his right. Without waiting he clambered over a fallen Inubian and lunged at her.

She blocked the blow.

He'd seen Dendralon glance over at her in the same instant.

His mum's technique was faultless but it wasn't just that; he had to fight against Firetongue. It jerked and lunged forward at his mum's throat. "No, stop..."

"Kill the witch!" said Craig.

"It's not a witch, it's my..." James's voice seemed so small against the screams of the battle.

As his mum turned, Craig froze. "Mrs. Peck?"

"Shut up and stab now. Use that stupid green spear of yours."

James saw the wild look in his friend's eyes. "Craig! Don't you dare!"

Greenworm thrust forward and plunged deep into her Inubian guard.

James aimed his blow carefully. He cut down at his mum's shoulder hoping that his magic blade would not pierce her golden armour. Thankfully, his arm jarred. "Craig, just pretend to…" he panted.

"I get the gist," barked Craig. He immediately stabbed down as she hit the ground. His green spear sinking deep into the dusty ground between her outstretched arm and her chest-plate. James saw his mum feign agony before lying still.

"NO!" Dendralon roared out in frustration. "Blinders!" He broke away from the Mertol and ran towards them, pushing all comers out of his way.

"That's what they called us on Denthan the first time," said James.

"Big deal. Now what?" urged Craig, panic etched on his freckled face.

"Throw your spear at him, idiot," whispered Cathy.

Craig jerked Greenworm free of the dirt and launched it at the approaching wizard. He watched in anguish as the green-tinged spear burst into flames, only inches from Dendralon's scaled face. Craig gripped onto the tattoo on his arm and screamed out in agony.

James felt his chest tighten. His temples began to throb.

Dendralon raised his staff, but a set of huge talons snatched it from his grasp. Whindril beat her wings and soared up into the dazzling sunlight.

James's head pounded. "Wwwstonewwwwrightww!" The word flew from his lips before he'd even thought about it. He blinked, as his breath seemed to turn into a cloud of steam and then cover the approaching wizard. As it did, the texture of Dendralon's armour and skin changed. Dendralon shuddered to a halt, bewilderment forming on his hardening face. His huge bulk cracked then, like a fragile china vase, he began to fall apart. Tumbling onto the dust and blood of the trampled battlefield, the lumpy sections of Dendralon's body exploded into a fine powder before the waft of Whindril's wings blew it into their faces. Craig coughed and spat out the grime.

"James?"

His mum's voice seemed to penetrate his thoughts as he fell onto his knees, suddenly exhausted beyond belief. A wave of static swept over him. Every hair on his body stood on end before he sprawled over the dirt and threw up. "Uh. What...?" He could barely hear his own voice through the foggy curtain that dulled his senses.

His mum's voice cut into his mind again, "JAMES!"

Her voice echoed over the battlefield and everything stopped. All eyes were on him. His mum stood up and threw down her sword. Sternly, she looked at the surrounding Inubians and Racnids and gave the signal to drop their weapons. In seconds, the clank and clatter of steel against steel spread across the dusty plain as the Artilian force laid down their arms. Wasps began to fly away from the fight and the huge bulking shape of the Wasp Queen lowered on her jointed legs. The breeze strengthened and soon all James could hear was the wind whistling over the fallen. It flicked his hair into his face. He forced himself up onto his knees and coughed.

With Gwendral no more and Dendralon committed to dust, the Artilian force fell back.

Tentatively, James walked towards his mum. Her hazel eyes glazed as she pulled him close. He began to cry too. "Mum... Where have you been? Are you okay? Did he hurt you?"

His mum's lips curled into a smile. "You're beginning to sound like me."

Shaking with the sheer force of the tears that spilled down his cheeks, he hugged his mum as tightly as he could.

"Kill her!"

James looked up at the Stone Larth.

Craig waved a Yeltan spear in front of the giant creature. "She's on our side now." He hesitated for a moment then added, "I think."

"Cathy Peck, is that really you?" broached Jal.

She pulled away from James and stood to face the Manimal force. Every inch an Artilian Queen in her polished golden armour, his mum looked so different. The wind played with her long, black hair, and her face seemed to shine in the strange light.

Cimerato dismounted Whindril and approached. Herfala walked out from the gathered Manimals with Michael and Ephie. "I found these two in the Yeltan trenches."

Cimerato touched Herfala's shoulder. "Wait a moment, Herfala." He glanced at James and then focused on Cathy. "The prophecy was true, James. You *are* the son of the great Dark Queen."

Then Michael and Ephie walked to the fore, their faces beaming with delight. "Thank God, oh, thank God!" Michael patted her golden armour then hugged Cathy tightly.

James's mum stiffened.

Awkwardly, Michael peeled away, flushing pink. "Nice to see you again, Cathy."

Ephie eyed Michael strangely.

A loud thud distracted the gathering crowd. The Wasp Queen had fallen on her side. As her carapace dulled the worker wasps switched from avid protectors to voracious feeders. They began to devour their dying queen.

There was another thud much closer to their position. "Kill this dark witch!" Tertan, the leader of the Stone Larths moved in next to Cimerato and pointed down at Cathy. "She killed my kin. She must die."

James snapped out of his trance-like state. His head still throbbed but he was regaining his strength. The physical and mental pounding he'd taken had totally drained him and his chest was as tight as a drum. "Stay back, Tertan." James stepped closer to his mum and drew a line in the dust with Firetongue. "Don't cross it, Tertan."

Cathy Peck instantly rubbed the line away with her boot and waved the Stone Larth forward with her long fingers. "Come ahead, if you dare."

"Mum!" James protested.

"I can take care of myself, thank you." She sidestepped James and faced up to the towering Larth. Her two swords still dripped with black blood.

"Enough!" yelled Cimerato.

The Mertol cried out, "Bak!"

Whindril shook her dusty, white mane and thudded forward.

The Stone Larth and Cathy parted to make way for the dragon as it moved between them. Whindril paused to sniff at the dirt where Dendralon had fallen.

"Where is Mendel?" snapped Cathy.

"He's gone," said Craig. "It was Mendel who made the city disappear."

Their attention shifted to the spot where the city of Gwendral had stood.

"Who's that?" James shielded his eyes. A solitary figure walked towards them across the plain.

"But…" began James, "he was supposed to stay in Gwendral, look after Wee Joe, Helen, and Mrs. Harrison.

"Oh, was he now?" spat Cathy, she turned away from the Stone Larth.

James waved. "Dad! Over here!"

"Son!" David Peck broke into a run. As he came closer, however, he slowed.

Ephie broke into a series of nervous coughs and splutters.

David patted her back and asked if she was okay.

James's heart sank.

"So," yelled his mum, "you'd rather help chubby there than come straight over and say hello?"

"No. I…"

"I've only been gone for a YEAR!"

The word 'year' echoed over the whole battlefield. The Artilian worker wasps momentarily stopped munching.

"Bloody typical," slammed Cathy.

"I…" his dad stammered.

"Pathetic, as usual. I should have known you could never change."

James cringed as he caught the look of bewilderment on Ephie's and Michael's faces. His dad tried to speak but his mum barged past Tertan and caught him by the collar. She pushed her face very close to his and whispered venomously, "So, you hid in the city while your son was out here risking his life?"

"No, I…"

"You what? You decided to come for a look, now that the danger is over? You're not only pathetic, you're a coward too."

"Bak!" The Mertol seemed to protest but Cathy drew it a withering stare.

His dad touched her armour. "Cathy, I…"

She slapped him full force in the face.

Everyone gasped.

"You left me to die in the tunnels of ARTILIS!" she blasted.

Smarting, his dad bowed his head. "We couldn't find you, Cathy. You were there one minute and then…"

"And then you decided to carry on without me!" she blazed. "I had to live as *his* wife," she pointed at the dirt, "as his stupid queen, for a whole year!"

There was an eerie silence as everyone contemplated this statement.

Cathy plunged both her swords into the dust. She turned and began walking away.

"Cathy, wait a minute," said Michael.

Ephie pinched his arm and whispered sharply, "Don't you dare try to placate her after what she just called me."

Craig shook his head. "You know, for one small moment I actually thought your mum might have changed. I mean…"

"Shut up, Craig!" yelled James, his face beetroot red.

James took his dad's hand and wandered after her. He saw the last of the Racnids disappear over a rugged ridge in the distance, scampering off in the direction of the Oribianus Mountains. James wondered where they would go. Still vastly outnumbered, the remaining Manimals, Yeltans, and Stone Larths were in no mood to give chase. Everyone seemed to be staring at him. He let go of his dad's hand, pushed him towards his mum, and called out, "We've been very worried about you, Mum, no matter what you might think."

"*We've* been worried? *We've*…" Cathy spun round to face his dad. "What about you? Have *you*, my husband, really been giving a monkey's uncle about me?"

"James?"

More than a little relieved, James turned to see who it was.

A stern expression on both of their faces, Cimerato and Jal walked towards him. Ignoring his battling parents, Cimerato asked, "James, was it you who performed the spell that killed Dendralon? Jal says it was you."

James reeled, torn between sorting his mum and dad out and answering Cimerato's question. "I think it was me," he mumbled, unconvincingly. "The city had already disappeared, so I…"

"How did you do it?" asked Jal.

I don't know how I did it, he thought.

His mum peered over his dad's shoulder at him.

"I… I thought it was worth a try. Mendel said it was possible and…" James was feeling the pressure to lie. "It just happened." He didn't feel like elaborating at that precise moment.

Craig moved closer to listen. "Go on, James. Tell us how you did it."

James really hated Craig sometimes. "Eh, well, Mendel said that my brain was changing and that connections were being made. Whatever that means. Even Eethan and Elandria said I could do my own magic so…"

A coy smile fixed on his face; Craig said, "So let's see some more magic then. I know, turn Jal into a budgie."

Jal eyed Craig suspiciously. "What is this budgie creature, you talk of?"

"Well, it's one of the most powerful, magical creatures on Earth. It can…"

"Craig, will you give it a rest? And stop grinning like a gormless git," said James.

"You destroyed one of the most powerful wizards that ever lived," whispered Cimerato, his voice full of wonder.

"I suppose…" said James, trying his best to ignore his 'best' friend's facial contortions.

"He saved us all," bellowed Jal. "James Peck saved us all!"

"BAK!" cried the Mertol.

A cheer built as the news spread across the battlefield until the whole Gwendralin army sounded as one. "JAMES, JAMES, JAMES!"

Craig patted him on the back. "Nice one, numpty."

Strangely, James felt a smile form on his dirty face as he realised that his family was reunited and that they no longer had to fear Dendralon. "What now?" he muttered, still beaming. He shouted louder, "I mean, look around you. We've been deserted on a world which is…" He paused as the cheers subsided.

"Which is now over-populated with the scum of Artilia," finished Cimerato. "You're right, James. Our celebration is premature."

The mood had completely switched from elation to bleak realisation.

James scanned around him. "Has anyone seen Garlon, the Yeltan chief?"

"I'm here, James." Garlon stepped into view beside the Mertol. The Yeltan closed his nose holes as he passed the giant, matted beast.

"Tell us about the Yelding, Garlon."

"What!" exclaimed a nearby Manimal. "There is only death down there."

"No," said James. "Garlon found a way down. There is a different world down there. Tell them, Garlon."

"There is only death up here," replied the stumpy Yeltan chief, eyeing the Manimal dissenter. He pointed to the dust cloud beneath the far off mountains. "The Artilians might come back. There are, what...?" He jumped up onto a fallen chariot and looked round. "Five thousand of us and well over thirty thousand of them. The spider things had barely joined the battle when..." He beamed at James. "...When James killed their wizard and caused the rout."

"You're right, Garlon," said Jal.

Garlon continued. "We should leave this place."

James took in the full horror of the battlefield. Piles of dead Racnids mingled with the twisted corpses of Inubians, Manimals, and Stone Larths littered the plain. Dead Yukplugs and Yeltans lay only feet from where they stood. The cold winds of Ebos had already partially covered them in the hoary grey volcanic dust so typical of the place. It was as if the world of Ebos was trying to hide all trace of conflict from its surface. James brushed the dust from his clothes and coughed. "Mendel won't just leave us here. He'll come back for us once we've given him the time he needs. Gwendral should now be back on Denthan before the explosion of its sun. He will need us to help him there, too. He..."

A disgruntled looking Manimal captain shook his head. "He may be dead along with everyone else on Denthan. We have no proof that his plan has worked."

"That's enough, Gursor," snapped Cimerato.

Whindril cocked her head and snorted down at Gursor.

"Such talk is not helpful," Cimerato reminded.

"He's right," snapped Cathy. "And besides, Elhada, Dendralon's Racnid Queen will not remain at bay for long." Cathy Peck looked every inch the Dark Queen of Denthan prophecy. She walked with an air of defiance that seemed to affect the Manimals more than the rest of the creatures. They edged away from her, gave her space. "My son and Garlon are right. It would be better to be free of this place."

James thought she talked differently now too. She would never have said something like 'free of this place' a year ago. She sounded like Dendralon.

Michael loosened his dog-collar. "But Cathy, shouldn't we wait for Mendel here? How will Mendel know where we are?"

"Bak!" The Mertol waved its long arms, seemingly frustrated by the conversation and pointed to the piece of land where Gwendral had recently stood. A black shining ball shot out from one of the many pits that covered its face and exploded over the site.

What happened next was beyond James's wildest expectations. He looked on in amazement as the gates of the city reappeared. At first, only the outline of the battlements and the adjoining towers came into view but in seconds, more and more of the city revealed itself.

"What's going on?" blurted Ephie.

Still more of Gwendral came into view and as a second magical ball zinged past James's face and exploded behind the first. Minarets re-emerged, rooftops reappeared and finally the majestic outline of the citadel stood proud over the plain. With a mirage-like shimmer the city solidified and sat, as it had before the battle, dominating the skyline.

James thought he saw a sly expression trace the Mertol's face before it grunted and waved the remains of the army towards the opening gates. Several gaping holes still marked the spots where the Artilian Wasp larvae had burrowed through the city walls.

Unblinking, Craig tapped James on the shoulder. "It was here the whole time?"

"So Mendel did not succeed after all," hissed the dissenter, Gursor.

"Rubbish," snapped James. "It means that Mendel is far more clever than you think."

The remains of the army staggered back towards Gwendral, picking up their dead on the way and tending to the wounded. A troupe of archers that had manned the battlements raced out to help.

Helen and Lord Eldane appeared high above them on the balcony of the citadel. James heard Helen's voice in his head. It was full of urgency. "James, you only have minutes to get everyone inside the city. The magic scales are almost balanced."

"But…" protested James.

"Just get them inside!" Helen's voice reverberated inside his skull to such a degree that it made him wince.

A pang of self-doubt washed over him as he wondered whether he had truly performed the spell that killed Dendralon by himself. Perhaps it had been Helen and Mendel after all.

James yelled at the creatures around him to hurry. "We only have minutes to get inside. Hurry before it disappears for good!"

Cathy Peck ran beside James and Craig, ducking as Whindril flew over their heads. James looked back and saw that Cimerato was staring into the distance. He followed his gaze. There, far over the Halsian Desert, a huge line of Inubians had regrouped on the horizon.

Cimerato soon caught them up. "Who's leading those dogs this time?"

Cathy Peck answered. "I told you before, it will be Elhada. She spent many days and nights preparing this venture with Dendralon. I can't understand why they've turned back from the mountains so quickly. "

"They've seen the city reappear and they may also have spotted *them*," said Jal, his black Hedra armour clanking as he jogged forward.

Cimerato grimaced at the Hedra captain. "Seen what?"

Jal pointed, due west, towards the Yelding. Thousands upon thousands of Sorabs, the ant-like creatures of Ebos, were emerging from the clouds.

Cimerato waved everyone forward with renewed urgency. "Get everyone inside the city, now!"

An incessant clicking sound issued by the Sorabs began to fill their ears as even more of the weird-looking creatures poured out of the Yelding.

"Thank God we never went into the Yelding," shouted Michael.

Half of the Sorab force veered towards James and the remains of the Manimal army as they ran as fast as they could toward the city gates; the other half swarmed towards the advancing Inubians and Racnids.

"The Artilians couldn't have retreated that far," gasped James.

As they ran the last few hundred yards, Gursor, the Manimal captain, took an arrow in the shoulder and fell. Still more arrows rose up into the sky behind them as they poured through the city gates. James and Craig ushered everyone through, their magic weapons deflecting any arrows that came too close. The Mertol barked out a cry as several black arrows sunk into its back. It ripped them out and staggered into Gwendral as the gates began to close. James watched it race up onto the parapets. Three more balls flew from its face and disappeared into the sky. Three explosions shook the ground under their feet.

The distant screams were dulled slightly as the giant gates of Gwendral shuddered together. Inside, James and Craig pushed their backs against the massive gates and slid down onto the ground. James glanced up at the citadel and spied Helen holding something gold above her head. It was the Key of Artilis.

The chains and cogs jarred to a halt and the whole city flashed the brightest blue James had ever seen. He grabbed Craig's arm and screamed as the ground beneath them fell away.

CHAPTER THIRTEEN

THE RETURN OF THE SNAKE

On seeing the city of Gwendral fade for the second time in so many hours, Elhada screamed out her commands in a high-pitched wail that caused the Inubians to flatten their ears. "Turn from the city and attack the Sorabs!"

The line of Inubians that had been giving chase to the retreating Manimals banked round and smashed into the side ranks of the Sorabs, many of whom were badly burned from the Mertol's magic. Their sabres and pikes cut through the tough Sorab carapaces with ease while the Racnids spun silk that tangled their ant-like legs and jammed up their mouthparts. Racing over the struggling Sorabs the female Racnids jabbed down with their stingers until the last of the Sorabs juddered and fell still. Smashed by the full-on attack of the Artilian force only a few survivors managed to seek refuge of the Yelding, disappearing into the thick bank of cloud that marked its boundary.

Elhada ran over the top of her own kin until she reached the spot where Dendralon had fallen. Sniffing the trampled ash, she kicked the dead aside and began to circle the one spot where she'd caught the most discernible scent of her master.

A green-backed Racnid skidded to a halt at her side. "I have been to the city boundary. It has truly disappeared this time."

"Stay back!" Elhada screamed out.

The whole Artilian force made way for the Racnid Queen. Elhada knew what to do. Dendralon had made her rehearse this dance before. The steps were precise and it was important that there was no distraction. An Inubian charioteer leapt free of the footplate and handed her a golden-bound book. She snatched it from him and pierced his neck with her glistening stinger. The Artilians drew back even more. She lapped the fallen charioteer's blood with her long, grey tongue before spitting out a congealed lump of gel onto the dusty ground. She hissed in rage. "The blood of dogs is not good enough. Find me a wounded Manimal. He must be conscious."

A pack of black-downed Racnids scuttled away from Elhada and scattered out over the battlefield.

Elhada opened the golden book and pushed her cupped hand deep into a slit in her side. She produced a black casket and carefully unscrewed the lid. Her eyes bulging in anticipation, she drew a circle in the dirt and moved round its circumference, bobbing on her six spider-like legs.She then poured a dark liquid from the opened casket into the centre.

A high-pitched scream sounded the return of a battered-looking Racnid missing one leg. "I have found one!"

Elhada turned her head to one side and eyed the Manimal captain. Two black arrows protruded from his back and his breathing was laboured.

"What is your name?" she hissed.

The tattered-looking Racnid gave the Manimal a shake causing him to scream out in pain.

"Gursor... My name...is Gursor."

"I need you to remain alive a little longer, Manimal coward." Elhada's long tongue traced his wounds. "Bind him!"

They wrapped Gursor in their thick, silken strands and dragged him into the middle of the circle.

Elhada addressed the host of gathered Artilians. "The reason I signalled the retreat before was to keep this safe." She tilted the black casket over and unscrewed the other end. With a shake, a shining white seed edged with purple hooks fell onto her cupped hand. She held it high for all to see. "We have not lost. We have won."

An initial murmur soon became a cacophony of confusion.

"Silence!" Elhada tilted her head and narrowed her bulging eyes. "This seed will bring Dendralon back to us. We will then follow the Manimals that run and hide and drink their salty blood." She hissed a kind of laugh and positioned herself over the helpless Gursor. A smallish Racnid held open the golden book while Elhada read out the strange script. More like a series of grunts and hisses than actual words, the sound of her chanting grew louder until, with a final scream, she stopped.

The white seed began to elongate and sharpen above Gursor's terrified face. It had taken the form of a long blade. "Unlock the soul of Dendralon! One life for one life!"

The shining white blade hovered over Gursor's chest.

Elhada hesitated for the briefest of moments, poised above the wide-eyed Manimal beneath her.

"Please," whimpered Gursor.

"I should ask you this," hissed the giant Racnid. She lowered her ugly head to within inches of Gursor's face and bared her black fangs. "Where has the city gone to?"

"It's still there," he gasped. "They will be priming their bows and aiming their spears. If you let me go, I will secure your safety."

"Ha!" Elhada raised her abdomen, her sting already dripping poison. "My sisters have searched the plain, and the city is not there, fool." She tilted her head until one bulging eye winked above him. She lowered the white blade until it rested on his chest. Her body was heaving with anticipation. "Last chance. Where is the city, Manimal?"

"D... Denthan," he gasped.

"LIAR!" She jabbed downward with the white blade and Gursor stiffened. His eyes widened and then closed. Elhada began to tremble, then in an eerie, ethereal voice she whispered:

> *"Take this blood to keep you warm,*
> *Take this dust and brave the storm,*
> *Leave the halls of death and pain,*
> *On your throne, to rule again!"*

Elhada held her position over Gursor. The air shifted and a strong breeze whipped the dust up from the ground. The giant Racnid pressed her leathery face against Gursor's cold cheek.

"Dendralon!" screamed Elhada. "ARISE!"

A spinning cloud of dust rose up from the barren ground and spun into a small tornado.

The white blade disappeared. A wisp of smoke left Gursor's open mouth. Elhada waited patiently until every grain of dust gathered into a single, ghostly cloud. "ARISE!"

The dust-cloud shot up the dead Manimal's nostrils.

The body jerked upwards, its chest lifting sharply before falling back down to the ground with a clump. Gursor's shape became indiscernible from the Racnid silk and then caved-in on itself, merging with the blood-soaked earth.

Above the gathered Racnids and Inubians, the sky clouded over and turned as dark as pitch. A crack of thunder threw the whole army onto their knees.

A shadowy form sprouted up from the ground at the Racnid queen's feet.

Elhada exposed a ragged row of tattered teeth and bowed down low.

Dendralon Pendragon was no longer in his Hedra form. Reborn, the dark wizard had resumed his original appearance.

Squinting upwards, Elhada asked, tentatively, "Is it you, Master?"

Light danced round the human-like form of Dendralon. Nothing like the deceased Gursor, his features were noble and distinguished. He stood over seven feet tall, and his body bulged with tanned muscles that looked as if they'd been hewn from the finest marble. His expression was one of unfathomable anguish, his square jaw set resolutely and his eyes closed tight.

"NO! I cannot hold this form... I..." The figure shook his head violently and fell.

The smooth human skin slowly changed into grey Hedra scales. Only the hair that trailed over his shoulders, dark and silken, remained distinct from the reptilian form.

Once more, a dark figure stood tall in the clearing marked out by the Racnid queen.

Elhada scampered back, the murmurs and hisses from the gathered army building until they formed a hellish crescendo.

Dendralon opened his cat-like eyes. "SILENCE!"

All went quiet.

"Where is it, Elhada?"

Elhada scuttled forward. "Where is what, Sire?"

"The magic of the Eden Seeds has trapped it." Dendralon paced the area left clear by the Racnids. "We have been fortunate."

"I don't understand, Sire," said Elhada.

"A talisman was used near this place. Recently. Very recently, and now it is mine."

She glanced behind Dendralon and spied something sprouting from the ground.

Dendralon caught her gaze and snapped his fingers. A golden key whirred free of the trampled earth and floated up into his open hand. "The Key of Artilis has been returned to me, at last," he growled.

* * *

The first thing James felt was a rush of energy as the sweet Denthan air filled his lungs. He was lying about ten feet inside the closed gates of Gwendral.

"Are you okay, numpty?"

James screwed up his eyes in the bright Denthan light and focused on the freckled face of his best friend. "Yeah… Hey look!" He pointed up at the sky. Two suns sat in a powder-blue sky, one smaller and brighter than the other.

"Zalion, if you remember, is the smaller of the two," stated Mendel.

"Well, if it isn't my wee sis," said Craig.

Helen stood beside Bero. The brandy barrel was still swinging from the dog's furry neck.

"Are you hurt?" asked Helen.

"Nah; why would we be? I mean we've only been in a totally crazy battle with poison arrows raining down on us, giant spiders, a mad lizard-wizard and a few thousand well armed rabid dogs." Craig smirked.

"Okay, Craig, they get the point," said James.

James's mum marched up to them and poked Craig in the chest. "You didn't have to live with the mad lizard-wizard, Freckles!"

"Oh, that's nice, Mrs. Peck. Teach the kids to call people names," barked Craig.

Wee Joe pointed at his big brother and repeated, "Freckles, freckles, freckles…"

Helen sniggered.

"See!" complained Craig.

Cathy Peck ignored him and while examining her swords asked, "Mendel… Why are we here? What's the plan? And how long have we got before we can all go home to Drumfintley?" She sheathed her swords and knelt down to address the barrel that swung below Bero's throat. James's dad wandered forward with Michael, Ephie, and Mrs. Harrison.

"I fear we may have a problem," announced Mendel.

"Surprise, surprise," hissed Cathy.

James saw Mendel's fishy eye draw nearer to the plastic window then dart back. As the goldfish neared the window again, however, James noticed something. Mendel's eye was dull-looking, verging on opaque.

Tentatively, he asked, "Are you okay, Mendel?"

"Not really. I'm getting on, you know."

"Yeh. We know. You're ten thousand years old," said Craig.

"Oh, that's not a problem, Craig. It's the fact that I'm a goldfish that's a problem. In this form, I'm almost at the end of my lifespan."

A terrible weight bore down on James. *What would happen if Mendel didn't live long enough to carry out his master plan – save Denthan and get them all home safely?*

That, however, wasn't the only thought in his mind. He'd grown very fond of the old wizard. "How long do you have, Mendel?" he broached.

"Oh, going by the state of my swim bladder, about two days, give or take…"

James felt his throat tighten. "And there's nothing we can…?"

"I shouldn't think so," finished Mendel, matter-of-factly. "I did, however, bring us a little closer to our goal."

Helen almost burped out the spell that caused the huge gates of Gwendral to swing open. "Wwwunwwlockwww."

James braced expecting to see the Hedra army outside. "Where are we?"

"In Denthan," explained Mendel, "just a few hundred miles further north than Gwendral's usual position here on Denthan, and…"

"And what?" pressed James.

"And less than a day away from the destruction point. No more."

Cathy Peck looked at James and let the barrel swing back into position. "Just cut to the chase, Mendel. I couldn't care less where we are, exactly, or when.. I still haven't had a decent answer to any of my questions yet. When do we go home?"

"Mum. For goodness sake, let Mendel finish! We were supposed to have two weeks to sort things out on Denthan, not just a few hours, so…"

Cathy took a swing at James. "Don't you dare back-talk me."

Cimerato and Jal both stepped forward.

"I'll sort this one out," said David Peck, putting his arm between Cathy and the advancing warriors.

"Oh you will, will you?" Cathy Peck eyed her estranged husband with contempt. "That will be a first." She prodded him in the ribs as she advanced. "How many times have I told you to curb his cheek? And how many times have I told you never to undermine me?"

James saw his dad flush with rage.

"That's enough, Cathy!" yelled Jean.

Cathy drew her hand back to slap his dad, Jean, caught the back of his dad's jumper and pulled him out of harm's way. His dad backed in beside her.

"Oh, I see," hissed Cathy. She homed in on Jean Harrison. "Decided to move in on that excuse of a man of mine while I was away, did you? Well, you're welcome to him. He's about as much use as a fart in a blizzard."

As the horrible, embarrassing scenario unfolded, James heard Mendel clear his throat. "Dendralon is not dead!"

Cathy Peck spun round and squatted down in front of the barrel again. "Of course he is. He is…"

"In possession of the Key of Artilis," finished Mendel.

"How come?" enquired James, relieved at the change of focus. His face was still very pink.

Everyone in the courtyard began chattering and murmuring.

Cimerato held his palms open and urged calm. "What are you saying, Mendel? I saw Helen holding the talisman above her head, up on the balcony. You used the Key of Artilis to bring us back in time to Denthan."

"I did," stated Mendel. "But the key vanished as we arrived. Did it not, Helen?"

Helen nodded.

Mendel coughed. A small trail of bubbles rose up past the window of the barrel. "There is a remote possibility, all being considered, that…"

"Your brother, Dendralon Pendragon, has it?" finished a familiar voice.

Everyone turned to see Elandria, her down, the colour of fresh grass, shining brightly in the Denthan sunlight.

"Him or one of his followers," said Mendel. "If he was also in possession of an Eden Seed, then I am certain that he is alive again."

James screwed up his face in confusion.

"An Eden Seed that sprouted on Artilis," finished Mendel.

"Dendralon is your brother?" snapped Cathy. "Your name is Pendragon?"

"I know that name," said Helen. "In a book at school, or…"

"Merlin," said Craig. "It's got something to do with Merlin."

"Mendel, Merlin, whatever," sighed the old wizard.

James shook his head in disbelief. "So, you're Merlin?"

"What? Don't be daft," interjected Craig. "Camelot and all that junk is just a kiddie's fairytale. Excalibur and…"

"And don't jump to any quick conclusions, young Craig," said Mendel.

"Mendel lived in Camelot. Mendel lived in Camelot…" Wee Joe's voice cut through the murmurs.

Everyone stared at him sympathetically.

"Dun Briton, Scotland, actually," whispered Mendel. "Look! We are getting away from the point here."

James pulled his fingers over his eyes and yawned. "I killed Dendralon. I turned him to dust."

"You thought you did," said Mendel. "But he may have cast a blood-wish spell long before that." Before the questions could begin, Mendel pressed on. "It is possible that he nurtured Eden Trees on Artilis from seeds he'd saved from Denthan."

Cathy toyed with the chain round her neck

"It's perfectly possible that he has given someone an Eden Seed, or even several," said Mendel.

Cathy nodded slowly. "Brilliant."

"Once the blood-wish spell is cast and a sacrifice made, an accomplice can resurrect the one linked to the seed. More than that, such spells often attract other magical objects. A blood-wish spell acts like a magnet. Strong magic attracts strong magic."

Helen stepped forward. "The Key of Artilis was in my hand until about three minutes ago. Then it just disappeared."

Craig fidgeted. "So, you're saying that Dendralon could still be alive, even if he was blasted into dust and swallowed…by mistake," he added, sticking out his tongue and rubbing it.

Mendel's voice faltered. "The manner of his death is irrelevant. I cannot think of anyone else who could have taken the key, so we have to assume Dendralon has been resurrected. He might still follow our trail back here from Ebos."

"We've left a trail?" asked Jean, avoiding eye contact with Cathy.

"In time and space," said Mendel. "Resurrection is a fairly consistent theme with my brother."

Michael looked down at the barrel. "I'm not entirely happy with the way you're banding about the word *resurrection,* Mendel."

"Yes, well… Leaving all that, and my husband's obvious adulterous intentions aside, what now?" said Cathy.

James saw his dad shake his head in protest, "It's not like that Cathy."

Elandria pointed a hairy leg at the blue mountains in the distance. "Eethan, Elcar, and myself can still join forces as planned and, if we reach the high plateau safely, use our combined natural magic to shield Denthan from the exploding sun." She raised another hairy appendage and pointed at Tealfith, the bigger of the two suns.

James craned upwards. The Denthan sky was slipping from a pleasantly pale blue to a deep, dodgy orange.

"In theory, you can, Elandria," said Mendel.

"In theory?" yelled Cathy. "I'm sick of all this rubbish."

"Mum." This time James kept out of range. "It's not rubbish," he whispered.

"Mendel ees always right, Mrs. Peck. But wee should theeenk also about Dendreelon. If hee has thee Key…" The small blue figure of Eethan sat in the dip of Whindril's long curved neck as the dragon waddled over the courtyard. "And ee ees cleveer enough to track us, and if Eee ees lucky enough to have other Eden Seeds…"

Cathy Peck pulled on the golden chain that hung round her neck until a circular golden casket came into view.

Everyone gathered round.

She opened the casket and pinched the end of a dazzling white seed, edged with delicate purple hooks.

Mendel pushed his eye as hard as he could against the plastic window of the barrel and blew a stream of bubbles.

"You mean something like this?" said Cathy. "He's got a whole orchard full of these little beauties. Though, I don't recommend the fruit. It make's you hallucinate."

Mendel mpah mpahed against his window. "He made you his bride, Cathy?"

There was a ghostly silence.

"I had no choice!" she screamed, tucking the chain back into her armour.

James's dad looked dazed. "When you said you were his wife, I…"

"You thought I was kidding?" Cathy growled.

Jean Harrison flushed. "So, you're giving David a hard time because he's helped me stay sane over the last year, in a perfectly innocent way I may add, while you… You've been married to Dendralon." She pointed to the chain round Cathy's neck. "You accepted his gifts?"

Cathy bristled. "There wasn't much of a bloody choice!"

Elandria shuffled between them, knocking Cathy off balance.

"Hey!"

"We have to go now," said Elandria.

"Ee agree," said Eethan. "Leets stay focused, now."

Elcar strolled into the courtyard behind Whindril, his leathery wings folded over his broad back. His voice was unnaturally deep, "If Dendralon is alive, as you suspect, Mendel, and if he has these Eden Seeds, he will try to come here. He will try to rescue his bride."

"That is logical," said Mendel.

"How will he know where we are?" asked James.

"As I have said, all magic leaves traces," said Mendel, distractedly. "He will wonder why I have come here, to this place and time."

Cimerato sighed and tapped his long, Gwendralin sword on the stone cobbles of the courtyard. "We should prepare to face him again, if we must. We need to give Elandria, Eethan, and yourself the time you need to journey to the high plateau in the Mountains of Hest."

"What's so special about this plateau, Mendel?" asked James.

"It is where the dragons of Hest used to hold council. It is the one place that the three Orphans of Light can join as one and, with the old dragon magic that lingers there, save this world."

James looked at his mum. She was staring venomously at Jean Harrison and his dad.

The Manimals and Yeltans looked particularly weary. They were still covered in blood and the dust of Ebos. "How long will we have to hold him off this time, Mendel?" asked Cimerato.

"Eighteen hours and seven minutes," said Mendel. "Though, you will hear the wailing sound of Tealfirth as it waxes and wanes well before that."

"Holding off Dendralon weel beee thee eeeasy bit," piped up Eethan, his piercing voice cutting through the din.

"The hard part," pressed Mendel, "will be getting into the dragon's Council chamber."

"Ah-ha," said Craig, "I knew there'd be a catch."

Mendel continued, "I will need James, Craig, and Helen to go with the Orphans of Light. James, you will need to ensure that Elandria, Eethan and Elcar are protected."

"They look as if they can probably protect themselves," said David.

"We will need all the magic we can muster. If Elandria, Eethan, or Elcar dies, Denthan will be destroyed as before."

"No pressure then," smirked Craig.

"I'll be going with them too," said Cathy Peck.

"Now, wait a minute," protested David.

Cathy rounded on him. "Don't worry, you can stay here with your new family." She flicked her fingers at Wee Joe and Jean. "I'm going with my boy."

"No, Joe!"

But it was too late. Wee Joe had drawn his green plastic water pistol and fired. A thin jet of dirty water caught Cathy's chin.

"Bull's-eye!" he shouted.

"Why, you little…" Cathy lunged forward but became instantly tangled up in a sticky web of silk.

"We are not going to get very far if we continue to fight amongst ourselves; are we?" hissed Elandria.

Cathy tried to free her sword, but Elandria simply wrapped her up even tighter. "You can come too, Dark Queen, but you will have to restrain your temper. Your self control is something you will have to work on."

"Ha!" blurted Craig.

"Mum, calm down. You can come, okay?" said James.

CHAPTER FOURTEEN

THE SHINING ARCH

Jal and Cimerato got to work on the battlements while Craig, James, Cathy, Helen, and Bero all climbed aboard Whindril.

"I love this bit," said Craig.

"Not when we're overloaded like this, I don't," said Helen.

"Overloaded?" said Cathy.

"Look at Whindril's expression," said James. "She's worried."

"How can a dragon have an expre…?" Cathy, however, stopped mid-flow as the dragon pushed its muzzle closer to the ornate seat. Smoke drifted up from the creature's wide nostrils as its dog-like face assumed a disgruntled air.

Cathy eased back.

Standing amongst the remaining contingent from Drumfintley, the Mertol barked a goodbye of sorts.

James thought he saw tears in his dad's eyes and felt his stomach tighten. He made to wave goodbye but had to grip on tightly as Whindril beat her massive wings and lurched upwards.

Once over the battlements of Gwendral, the view was breathtaking. The blue Mountains of Hest had to be over fifteen thousand feet high, and they really did look blue. Way off in the distance, to the south, he could just make out the great dark shadow that marked the forest of

Eldane. To the northeast; black, rugged silhouettes formed the impos-
ing outcrop of Nordengate, and on the western horizon James decided
he could just make out the Gorton Sea, where the Salt Trolls came
from. Mendel had explained that this was Denthan, but not the same
Denthan. It was confusing. Mendel had told him that time and space
was like an onion. Different layers could be peeled away. It was still the
same onion just different somehow. Apparently, he was just seeing another version of the same thing. Mendel had explained that even if
they went to another version of Denthan and saved it, they would still
save the onion as a whole.

"I know what you're thinking about," shouted Craig, his face beaming with delight as Whindril banked north. He held the golden reins as
if he was actually guiding the great beast. "You're thinking about that
stupid onion story of Mendel's."

"Yeh, I am. How did you know that?"

"Your eyes are watering!"

"Hardy-har-har." *A mixture of the cool wind and the horrible feeling of leaving my dad behind are the real reasons*, he thought. He shook his head at
Craig and mouthed the word, "Muppet."

"It's getting colder," said Helen.

Cathy Peck cuddled her in and looked blankly into the distance.

What is Mum thinking? wondered James. *What did she endure on Artilis? What will she do about Dad?*

Whindril cried out like a tortured seal as she caught a warm thermal
and soared even higher.

"If you look west now," said Mendel, "you may even see the other
Gwendral."

"I don't get it," shouted Craig.

"Are we there, fighting all those things in the citadel, like we did before?"

"Not yet," said Mendel. "I think we were still down in the Black
Lake."

"This is just all too weird," said Craig.

"You're not wrong," agreed James. "Are you okay, Mum?" His
mum, however, just continued to stare into the distance. "Fine... Okay
then, Mum..." James's words trailed off.

Whindril banked off to the west and drifted down beside Elcar. The
hipposaur's wings, that is to say, the biggest of the three pairs, were red
and leathery. They flapped awkwardly, like two tattered pieces of

skinned flesh, each vein and artery visible through the taut skin. The smaller wings, on his neck and head, fluttered erratically like a pair of jiggling gyroscopes.

Eethan clung onto Elcar's scrawny neck while Elandria sat tight on his back, a strand of thick silk binding her in place.

The temperature dropped as they moved closer to the mountains. Here, jets of cold air caused them to jolt and drop in a very scary way. Patches of snow sparkled below them.

"Look," said James. "There's a path of some kind. Down there!" He pointed to the outline of a track.

That's the dragon's trail," explained Mendel. "We must land here and proceed on foot."

"Why?" Craig moaned.

He sounded just like a little child who'd been asked to get off his favourite fun ride, thought James.

"It is impossible to fly onto the plateau," explained Mendel. "There are great overhangs of rock that enclose it. Besides, it is customary to follow the dragon trail."

"Overhangs or not," continued Craig, "I'm sure there must be a way of getting in on Whindril."

Whindril bounced gently on her four feet as she landed. Elcar, to their left, seemed to bump down more harshly. He let out a hiss of frustration and then folded his crimson wings over his back. Elandria and Eethan were already scuttling away from the ungainly beast.

"What can we expect, Mendel?" asked Helen.

Bero licked her hand as she bent down to look into the barrel.

"I have only walked this way once before. It was with Eethan back then too. It was such a very long time ago."

"Why did you come that time, Mendel?" pressed Helen.

James edged in a little closer. It wasn't that he couldn't hear, he just wanted Helen to know that he was interested in the conversation. His irrational jealousy was beginning to gnaw at him once again.

Mendel continued, "I had to ask the dragons of Hest for their help. You see, young Helen, there was a great battle raging between the Hedra and the Manimals back then, too."

"We saw the tapestry in the Yeltan tunnels," interrupted Craig.

"I had forgotten about that tapestry." Mendel sighed. "It was woven by a great Yeltan Queen. It is accurate enough, though. It depicts the Hedra being driven into the Southern Marshes."

Cathy Peck slid the swords from her double scabbard and examined them. "Dendralon has never forgiven you for that, Mendel, has he?"

"No, Cathy, I'm sure he hasn't."

"Mendeel?"

"Yes, Eethan."

"Thee trail ahead ees moving…"

James followed the little blue man's gaze and then quickly skipped off the main path. The track had dissolved into a mass of fur and whipping tails. Millions of rats were pouring out of the rock face, and they now completely covered the dragon trail.

"They're coming our way," whined Craig.

"You think," snapped James, sarcastically.

* * *

On Ebos, Dendralon stared down at the spinning key. His eyes narrowed. "Elhada, give me my casket!" he snapped.

Elhada offered him the black box that had contained the Eden Seed she'd used to bring the wizard back to life.

Dendralon tapped the black box with the Key of Artilis and watched as its lid popped open to reveal another compartment. Inside, there was a cushion of velvet, on which sat two more hexagonal seeds.

Dendralon pinched the end of one of the seeds and held it up to the light. "Stand back!" He waved the dark army back. Two Artilian Wasps buzzed skyward. "Where did the city of Gwendral go to this time, Elhada?"

The Racnid Queen shifted nervously. "I… I'm not entirely certain. The…"

"Listen!" Dendralon moved closer. "You had a live sacrifice?"

"Yes. Of course."

"And you asked this…this…"

"Manimal," blurted Elhada.

"…Manimal, where the city went to?" pressed Dendralon.

"Yes but…"

"WHAT DID HE SAY?"

Elhada lowered her body submissively. "He said that the city had returned to Denthan, but he must have been lying."

Dendralon smiled thoughtfully and threw the first and then the second seed onto the bloody earth. As soon as they touched the ground, they disappeared. "Stand back." He stared at the swirling clouds above his head and said the spell, "Gnarltheth Starffthe!" A gnarled staff appeared in his hand. "Further back!" he blasted.

Sticking the staff into the dusty earth, he raised the Key of Artilis and murmured another incantation. The ground suddenly lifted then fell back. It began to pulse like a huge beating chest.

"Prepare your troops to go through," shouted Dendralon.

Elhada looked puzzled. "Go through what, my lord?"

The words had just left her ugly lips when the loam shifted a second time. Two thick limbs burst free of the earth and soared upwards towards the heavens. The sky turned blood red as the limbs thickened and intertwined. Pulsing and creaking, the white bark, that covered them, ruptured and sprouted a mass of rootlets. These raw-looking appendages snaked their way down and into the ground, worming their way towards the army. All the creatures yelled and fled back further. There was a shimmering sound like the tinkling of falling crystal, then a soft crackle as a thousand amber-coloured leaves unfolded. They covered the tangled branches and flickered in the breeze. An orange glow emanated from the arch formed by the two trees, intensifying then fading away altogether. The breeze dropped and the sky resumed its normal hue, a drab, dishcloth grey.

"Our gateway to wherever we wish to go," announced Dendralon. "Now…" he pondered, "should we go straight to Earth or should we follow Mendel?" He turned to Elhada. "Tell me."

The Racnid looked uneasy, obviously unnerved by the enormity of the question. "Well…?" he pressed.

Elhada's leathery jaw fell open, "I know…"

"You know very little," snapped Dendralon, his long, thick hair swaying as he caught hold of Elhada's wrinkled face, "so do not try to hypothesize."

"But… But Denthan is destroyed," she finished.

"Yes, you are correct." He fingered his chin thoughtfully for a moment then smiled. "Which means that Mendel has used the Key of Artilis to go back in time. Mendel has managed to go back to Denthan before its destruction." He paced the barren earth. "Tell me, Key of Artilis, is this true?"

The golden Key whirred upwards and nodded at Dendralon.

Dendralon addressed the assembled army. "Will you follow me through the gateway? Will you follow me to a world that is doomed?"

Not one creature dared to look him in the eye.

"Yes, my lord," hissed Elhada. "We will follow you to the very gates of Hades, into the belly of hell, if you request it."

A murmur echoed over the plain, building steadily into a deafening roar that shook the ground beneath their feet.

Dendralon caught hold of Elhada and pulled her in close. "And what became of my bride?"

Elhada hesitated. "She... She went into the city with her son when it reappeared."

"Ah... When you say 'she went', does that mean that she went of her own volition or does it mean she was taken, forcibly?"

Elhada stared down at the ground, unwilling to commit herself one way or the other.

Dendralon felt genuinely sad. His yellow, cat-like Hedra eyes widened as he stared at the shining arch. He took in a long, considered breath, as if trying to find some trace of Beldam's scent in the damp air. "COME! Follow me, onward to victory, onward into the unknown and certain death. For death is the one thing you can all rely on." Dendralon strolled up to the massive archway and hesitated.

"My lord?" enquired Elhada.

He traced the amber leaves of a stooping branch until he found two perfect seeds. He twisted them free of their newly formed stalks and then placed them inside a black silken pouch on his belt.

Elhada offered him the black wooden box.

"I'll keep these ones safe, Elhada." He walked forward and stood directly under the hundred foot high arch. His staff above his head, he turned his scaled face to the peak of the arch. The dazzling orange glow had returned to the Eden Trees. Sparks of gold and silver raced over its splitting bark. Dendralon whispered a silent instruction to the golden key that floated, erratically, at his shoulder, and then he walked through...

CHAPTER FIFTEEN

HULATANIA

These rats, James decided, were quite different from any rats he'd ever seen in Drumfintley. Typically Denthan, they were roughly the size of Patch, Father Michael's Jack Russell Terrier, and possessed the yellowing fangs of a vampire bat. Not the real vampire bats that you get in South America, the ones that might nibble on a sleeping cow or horse now and again, he was thinking more of the vampire bats of his nightmares, the ones that snapped and flapped round Dracula in the movies. Their tails were forked and the smell... The smell that preceded them, he decided, was of rotting cabbage and baby sick.

Cathy tried to cuff Eethan as he barged past her.

He sprung high over the oncoming pack and clung onto an overhang of rock. The rats stood up on their back legs and snapped up at him, fangs dripping in anticipation. A few began to leap higher and snap their tails like whips. One of the more agile of the creatures managed to get within range, which resulted in Eethan receiving a nasty cut to his thigh.

"Eee! Nastee beasties!"

"Eethan, be careful," warned Mendel, "without you we are all lost."

James winced in the sudden heat as Elcar sent a blast of fire across the writhing pack. They screamed, wriggled and squirmed in an effort to avoid the snaking flame. Very few, however, managed to do this. Their screams were deafening.

James covered his ears but then had to sidestep a blazing rat as one landed at his feet. The word Firetongue hissed from his lips and his red and gold sword appeared in his right hand.

Eethan dropped down behind the pack and hit them with a blast of blue fire that froze the whole squirming mass solid.

"Was that really necessary?" moaned Craig. He picked up one of the frozen creatures and turned it over in his hands. "On second thought, we could take some of these home with us and sell them in the village shop as ornaments."

"They're horrible," retorted Helen. "And you're horrible." She shuddered and then began to pick her way forward through the grotesque statuettes. "I mean, you'd have to be totally sick to buy one of these things."

"I'd buy one," said Craig, proudly.

"Yeah, well..." said Helen, stumbling through the last of the effigies.

"Where did the rats come from?" asked James.

"There is a stone door set into the mountain," replied Mendel. "I fear, however, that they were running away from something. They don't usually attack en masse like that. They usually hunt in the deep caves, well below the mountains. Something has unsettled them."

"What do you think scared them out into the open?" asked Cathy. She picked her way through the pathetic creatures.

"Maybe they know that Denthan is about to explode," surmised Craig. "Animals can sense the weirdest things."

"Perhaps, Craig," said Mendel. "I think, however, it much more likely that some creature, much bigger and wiser, may have sensed the demise of Denthan and shifted from her lair."

Quietly, Craig patted Bero and said, "You're telling us that something much worse than this pack of frozen rats is coming our way."

James eyed his glittering blade and braced. "What's coming through the door, Mendel?"

"He won't answer you, James. He's a lofty, ignorant..." sniped Cathy.

Mendel splashed in the barrel. "Just make sure that Eethan, Elcar, and Elandria keep out of harm's way. Without them..."

"We know. This whole cockamamie plan of yours is knackered," finished Craig.

"Quite," said Mendel.

BANG!

James felt the ground shake beneath him. He glanced up at the sky, convinced that Denthan was about to be ripped apart right there and then. Tealfirth was bigger and redder than before. *Had Mendel got his timing wrong again?*

BANG!

The noise was louder this time. He caught hold of Helen's arm as she staggered backwards. "Try and keep on your feet, Helen."

BANG!

A stone door appeared on the mountainside, light emanating from within. It shook violently and then buckled outwards.

"Fall back!" shouted Cathy.

"What the heck is causing that?" yelled Craig.

Whindril hissed in dragon tongue, "Ta ne ta, Hulatania?"

"I fear so," replied Mendel.

Whindril screeched.

James stumbled backwards. "What... What is Whindril scared of, Mendel?"

CRASH!

The rock exploded outwards as a huge head eased out from the darkness. A sizeable boulder whizzed towards Bero and Helen, but Elandria shot a flare of red light that turned it into dust.

The ugly head pushed out even further.

James tried to decide what it looked like.

"It's a dragon," shouted Helen.

"Hulatania!" said Mendel. "She is the mother."

Whindril bowed low and closed her eyes.

James soon realised that Hulatania was absolutely enormous; at least four times bigger than Whindril, judging by her head. He pulled Helen even further back as another huge crack shook the mountain. Like a massive worm, the giant dragon's neck slithered free of the mountain before a heavy, clawed foot thudded onto the track before them. She was a deep russet red and her mane was, like Whindril's, flecked with gold. When her wings broke free of the debris she stretched them out to their full length.

Out of breath and quivering with fear, James had covered the length of a football pitch along with the others in an effort to avoid the emerging beast.Now completely free of the mountain and what was left of the door, the mother dragon, Hulatania, stood resplendent in the crimson hue that was beginning to creep over the land. Her wings were tipped with golden spikes and her tail was encrusted with glittering gems.

"What now?" urged James.

"She is about to flee her nest," said Mendel.

"Not a good sign then?" said Craig.

"But doesn't she know that we're going to save Denthan?" asked James.

"It doesn't look like it," snapped Cathy.

"Whaow," gasped Craig. "You're right, Mrs. Peck, she's nicking off before the whole place goes boom."

Hulatania let out a roar of despair before leaping up into the reddening sky. The back-draft from her wings knocked them all off their feet. Bero yelped. Whindril took to the air and began to follow her, but the mother dragon hissed back at Whindril and beat her huge wings even harder. As Whindril circled downwards, Hulatania became smaller and smaller.

"Where is she going?" asked James.

"She's scared," said Helen, in a small voice. "She's trying to escape."

Mendel spoke, his voice wavering, "I tried to speak to her but she did not want to listen. Helen and Craig are correct. She has gone from this world. It is her instinct to preserve the remaining young inside her."

James tried to pick the dragon out of the blazing sky but it was impossible now. He felt his chest tighten. Even here on Denthan, where the oxygen is plentiful, he was becoming breathless.

Cathy Peck pulled the green rucksack from James's back. "Here!" His mum handed him his blue inhaler.

Craig gave him a 'who's a mummy's boy' look.

"James pressed the blue plastic tip of the inhaler to his lips and breathed in. *What if we fail? What if Mendel was wrong? He's been wrong in the past. What if we're all going to die here on Denthan after all?*

With a trembling hand, Helen stroked Bero and knelt down in front of the barrel. "Mendel, I'm frightened too."

"Don't worry, Helen. We will do what we came here to do." He pushed a cloudy, orange eye against the plastic window of his barrel and waited until the whole group had assembled round Bero. "We must carry on. We must go into the mountain and up to the Dragon Chamber as planned. However... Just in case anything happens to me, you must follow these instructions."

"Nothing's going to happen to you." Helen hugged Bero.

Mendel continued, "Elcar, Eethan, and Elandria; once you reach the Dragon Chamber, you must climb up onto the three great seats of power. You must join, all three of you, into one."

James was confused by the last part but he watched the three creatures mentioned give a solemn nod.

Flippantly, Craig said, "Well, that's that then. It all sounds like a piece of cake. You three go on into the mountain and we'll just wait here and watch the sun explode."

Everyone stared at him.

"Craig, stop talking rubbish," said Helen.

"Rubbish? You weren't here the last time Mendel did a little disappearing act. Giants...Centides...blood...terror...falling...screaming... And that was just for starters. Do you really think that I want to go in that mountain, to face God knows what, without Mendel? He says... He says that he's dying. What happens if we go in there and we're left alone?"

James could see that his mum was brewing for a fight.

Cathy eyed Craig. "Look Craig, if you listen to the gormless guppy, and have half a brain, we might still get out of this mess."

"Half a brain, eh?" Craig flushed. "Greenworm!" The emerald spear appeared in his hand.

"Craig," warned James.

"What are you going to do with that, sonny?" said Cathy. She sneered at Craig and moved closer until the tip of Greenworm rested under her chin. "Go on then. Push it home."

"Mum!" shouted James.

"Craig!" shouted Helen.

Cathy Peck flicked the spear away and gripped Craig by the shirt. "If you were my son, I'd..." Cathy clenched her fist.

"Nice," whispered Craig, his face covered in sweat. "Threaten a child, why don't you?"

Cathy let Craig wriggle free. He staggered back, obviously shaken.

Elandria scuttled forward. "I will take his punishment, Mrs. Peck."

Craig screwed up his eyes in disbelief. "What is it with you, Elandria? Craving an honourable death and all that stuff... She wouldn't dare hurt me." Craig sighed and shuffled closer to James. He stared at Elandria. "What kind of punishment do you think she was going to give me anyway?"

"Well," said Elandria, "on Artilis, answering an elder back is at least twenty lashes."

"Lashes?" exclaimed Helen.

"Or six stick hits..." added Elandria, with an air of longing.

Cathy Peck beamed "Now you're talking."

Craig poked James in the ribs. "Has your mum ever heard of Childline?"

"Are you threatening me?" launched Cathy.

"There you go. That's what she does. I rest my case," said Craig, edging back a little further. "You see, the fact that you've just said 'are you threatening me', in a threatening manner, means that *you* are actually threatening me."

"Verbal abuse is just as bad as physical abuse," added Helen.

"That's six stick hits for you too, young Helen," said Elandria, with a smile. "I'll take both punishments, no problem."

They all stared at the green-furred Racnid, a stupefied look on their faces.

"There's not going to be any stick hits," said James. "Mum's not that bad."

"She bloomin' is!" blasted Craig. "And if Mendel goes, guess who's going to take over as leader?"

Mendel made an audible splash in the barrel. "Will everyone just try to stay calm? I do not intend on leaving you but..."

"We're better to know what should be done, just in case," finished James.

"Just in case," repeated Mendel. "And now that I have told the Orphans of Light what to do, we can we focus on our current predicament. Everyone ready to move on?"

"Yes," replied James.

Ahead, the black, gaping hole that marked the dragon's door into the mountain beckoned. One by one, they walked forward, picking their way through what was left of the rat-like statuettes.

"The sooner we do this, the better," said Cathy, resolutely. "I want to get back home."

"We all do, Mrs. Peck," said Helen.

Cathy stared at Helen for a long moment and then moved forward after Eethan.

They entered the hollowed-out cavern made by Hulatania and followed the three glows produced by Eethan, Elcar, and Elandria. The blue, yellow, and red seemed to merge into one faint beam of white, which was handy.

James could see where Hulatania had widened the tunnel in her efforts to escape, and he wondered what else she might have disturbed in her haste. Strange squeaks and growls echoed out from the gloom as they moved deeper into the mountain.

CHAPTER SIXTEEN

THE SPIDERLINGS

It was Cimerato who first noticed the anomaly on the Southern horizon. A shimmering distortion of the mountains soon became a more discernible outline. "Jal! Come and see this."

A huge archway of blinding amber light now pulsed in the distance.

Jal was beside him in moments, hissing as he caught his breath. "I see it."

"We will need every archer we have, every Yeltan spearman on the city walls now," said Cimerato.

"Is it Mendel's work?"

"I don't think so." Cimerato shielded his eyes and looked beyond the strange apparition at the high peaks of Hest. "I doubt Mendel would have reached the Dragon Chamber yet."

Jal hissed and signalled toward the giant archway. "It doesn't look good."

Cimerato had seen Dendralon fall on Ebos. Killed by the boy, James. The dark wizard, however, had cheated death before. He signalled a soldier to his left to find him a scope. The soldier passed the word along the battlements and soon produced a small wooden telescope.

Jal looked quizzically at the device.

"Mendel's work," said Cimerato. "He made it for me when I was just a boy." He lifted it to his right eye and began to explain what he could see. "It's an archway all right... It looks like it's covered in bark.." He refocused. It looks like the Eden Tree that used to grow here on Denthan, only there are two of them intertwined to form the archway."

"Cimerato, the Dark Queen…"

"Jal, you mean Cathy Peck."

"I suppose. She said that Dendralon processed a number of Eden Seeds."

Cimerato lowered the scope and handed it to Jal. "It can only be Dendralon. He must have followed us here, as Mendel predicted."

Jal looked through the device, unsure how to focus it. "He can't have. He was turned into dust."

"Someone has walked through the arch. Can you see who it is?" said Cimerato. He shielded his eyes and stared over the parapets. A brisk breeze caught the folds of his tunic and ruffled his blond hair.

"A tall figure," relayed Jal. "He has the height of a Hedra."

"And the soul of one, I suspect," murmured Cimerato.

Jal ignored the jibe.

Cimerato snatched the scope back from Jal, cursing as he tried to focus the device.

The first phalanx of Inubians marched through the shining archway in the distance.

"They're unmistakable, even from this distance," said Jal.

Cimerato turned and shouted down over the courtyard below. "Get ready for battle!" A trumpet sounded from the gate-towers.

Garlon ran out into the sunlight and called on his spearmen. The Yeltans poured into the courtyard and made for the stairways. Their poison-tipped spears rattling as they climbed.

"Jal," said Cimerato, "will you command from the East tower? I will give orders from the here. When they are close enough, the look-outs will sound the trumpet once.

"Fine," said Jal. "I will try to organise a nice surprise for any Racnids that may attack."

"Pitch and flame should slow them down," said Cimerato.

"My thoughts, exactly," said Jal.

"Cimerato!" called a high-pitched voice.

Cimerato scanned the courtyard and found Jean Harrison. She pulled Wee Joe behind her. The Mertol, towering over the Yeltans, lumbered across the cobbles beside them. David, Michael, and Ephie followed.

"This is no place for children," said Jal.

Jean shouted up at them, "The Mertol wants to help!"

Cimerato did not need this kind of distraction.

Jean Harrison mounted the stairs but the Mertol picked her and her child up off their feet and bounded up onto the parapet in one leap. The walkway shook as it landed beside him. The rest of the Drumfintley group climbed the ladders.

Michael's bald head appeared first. "I'm not sure what I can do to help," he panted.

"Come on, it will be safer if you all remain inside the citadel," pleaded Cimerato. He eyed the Mertol, distractedly, still uneasy in its presence.

Jal leaned down and addressed the cleric from Earth. "Michael and Ephie…"

"Yes," said Michael, an expectant look on his face.

"Can you use any weapons?"

"Eh, not really," replied Michael.

"We could help with the gates; free up your soldiers there to fight elsewhere," suggested Ephie.

Cimerato considered this for a moment and then nodded at Jal. "Get the tower guards to show them the levers. Our fighters be better deployed on the battlements."

"That will free up another six fighters, big lady, " said Jal.

Ephie bristled.

The Hedra hissed a kind of laugh before adding, "Thank you, cleric?"

"Michael looked up at the tall Hedra fighter. "You're welcome."

"Pray to your god for us all," said Jal.

"I haven't stopped doing that since we arrived." Michael beamed.

Jean tapped Cimerato on the shoulder. "How did they all get here?" She was staring out over the battlements at Dendralon's gathering army.

"They have come through that!" Still more creatures poured through the dazzling archway.

"The Mertol has spoken to Wee Joe," she gasped. "My boy seems to understand it."

"It's easy," Wee Joe said. His eyes widened at the massing army in the distance. "I can go with the Mertol, take care of the doggy-faced things. See if there's another big wasp thing too."

"You can not!" snapped Jean.

"Mum, the Mertol says he will wook after me."

The towering creature beside them, covered in matted, orange hair, grunted. It pulled Wee Joe against its giant leg and patted his head with a huge clawed hand.

Jean flushed. "Joe, there is no way…"

"Your mum is right, Joe," said David.

Jal produced something that resembled a smile and hissed, "Let him go. The beast will take care of him. The Hedra young learn to fight at the age of six."

"And I'm seven, Mum," piped up Wee Joe. "See!"

A soldier shouted out from several yards away. He was looking through Cimerato's scope. "The Racnids are coming through the arch. I'm sure I spotted Elhada, their Queen. The big one with the crimson patch on her abdomen."

"That's her," said Jean.

Cimerato turned to David, Jean, and Wee Joe. "It's up to you, Mrs. Harrison."

Jean Harrison hesitated then said, "I don't think it will be any safer in the city much longer anyway. Go if you think it will help us all." She grabbed a handful of the Mertol's hair. "You look after him, okay!"

The Mertol threw back its head. "BAK!"

Cimerato ducked as the strange creature bounded over the parapet clutching Wee Joe. He shouted down at them. "Be careful!"

The Mertol landed softly on the ground below and ran towards the shining arch in the distance. Wee Joe, hanging over its shoulder, gave them all the thumbs up as he bounced along.

Ahead, the Racnids continued to pour through the hundred-foot-high archway.

"What have I done?" sighed Jean. "I've got a horrible feeling about this."

"I'm not sure you should have let him go, Jean," said David.

"Thanks," snapped Jean.

Cimerato eyed the remaining humans. "You two will have to fight as best you can."

"We can use a bow and arrow, can't we Jean?" said David.

She sighed and nodded, reluctantly. "Why did I let him go?"

"That must be Elhada. She's bigger than the rest," said Cimerato. Ignoring Jean's comments, he pointed at the dark outline of the Racnid Queen. "She's circling…a tall Hedra with long, black hair."

"It can only be him," sobbed Jean. She leaned over the parapet. "Joe! Come back."

"It's Dendralon, all right," said Cimerato.

Garlon's eyes narrowed as he stood on his tiptoes and peered over the battlements. "And he has his staff back."

"It's him," said Cimerato. "I hope James and Mendel do their magic quickly as I fear we are dealing with a much stronger foe than before."

Out on the plain, between the Mountains of Hest and the walls of Gwendral, the Inubian chariots rolled into position. The Racnid steeds made way for the main chariot. Decked in gold and carrying Dendralon, it pulled to a halt beside Elhada. Cimerato saw Dendralon lower his gnarled staff.

Cimerato cupped his mouth and shouted, "Everyone! Get down behind the parapets." In the same moment, however, a familiar voice drifted into his mind. It was Dendralon.

Cimerato glanced round to see if anyone else could hear the voice. They seemed oblivious. He spoke into his hand, surreptitiously, "What do you want with us this time, Dendralon? You have come back to a dying world."

"Yes. Fascinating, isn't it? Why would Mendel use the Key of Artilis to bring Gwendral back in time to its doom?"

Cimerato didn't know what to say.

"You don't have to say anything, Cimerato. I can read your thoughts, such as they are."

Cimerato tried desperately to think of anything else he could but the face of the human boy James Peck kept returning to him; his mousy hair; his wide, grey eyes, and his sword – Firetongue. The way he questioned everything and his mother, his beautiful queen-like mother who never managed to control her rage.

"Yes. Queen Beldam is quite a challenge," mused Dendralon. *"She has not, however, seen me in my true colours, as king of Denthan. My full powers have been restored by rebirth, my desires rekindled."*

"Keep out of my head, you…" Cimerato felt his heart quicken.

"So, the old fool Mendel thinks he can save Denthan, does he?"

Cimerato jerked back and punched his shield in frustration.

"You okay?" said Jal.

Cimerato ignored his Hedra friend. He tried to think his words, rather than say them out loud, *"That is not what he intends to do."*

"Don't deny it. I read your mind, Cimerato."

Jal was eyeing him suspiciously now. "What's wrong, Cimerato?"

Cimerato pressed his finger to his lips and shook his head. Dendralon's laugh echoed round in his mind.

"In that case," pressed Dendralon, *"he can save Denthan for me and my new army. We will rejoin the Hedra masses that, I presume, are still unharmed on the ridge beside the other Gwendral. Yes… Mendel has told you about coexisting dimensions. I see, however, that you struggle to understand."*

***

Dendralon closed his connection with Cimerato and summoned the leader of the Inubians, a warrior called Zanther. "Take your jackals and split them into two ranks. One half must remain here, out of reach of the Manimal arrows; the other half are to follow Mendel and the boy, James, to that plateau. He pointed behind him towards the Mountains of Hest where a flattened peak glistened with snow, now the colour of burnt amber in the reddening light. "Elhada?"

The Racnid Queen flinched. "Yes, Sire."

"You will take your spiders in first. Scale the walls and open the gates for us as soon as you can." Dendralon looked up, once more, at the angry sky. "We don't have much time, and I am not sure what will happen if Mendel is successful. The Inubian force should delay his return from the mountains if he is." He turned to the one called Zanther. "Take the sky-arrows with you. Make sure the machines are set to kill a dragon."

"Yes, my Lord." Zanther bowed low and backed away.

Elhada shuffled in closer. "My Lord, what if the fish wizard is unsuccessful? What if the planet dies once more?"

"You and I will stay close to the archway, just in case. We will return to Ebos and leave them all to their fate."

Elhada snapped her teeth together in ecstasy then faltered. "What about our army? What about my children?"

"What about them?" said Dendralon, a wistful look in his eye.

Elhada lowered her body on her spindly legs and shuffled away, hissing. Within minutes, the Racnid masses were screeching and hissing round a huge mound of grub-like larvae. They tapped on a myriad of silken strands that emanated from the outcrop of rock that bore the weight of the larvae until they began to hatch into spiderlings. Less than the size of a man's hand, the young Racnids swarmed over the Denthan soil, swirling round their mothers as they marched.

Dendralon watched the Artilian Wasps buzz down over his forces, their newly-formed queen to the fore. She was shunted along by a host of workers that spread over her bulk. A living wave of cartilage and shimmering gossamer, they nibbled at her trigger hairs until she began to arch her back and lay. Her larvipositor contracted and slopped forward over her back, clicking every time she fired a spinning larva toward the walls of Gwendral.

At the sound of an Inubian trumpet, the jackal-faced division that remained began to march, their swords smashing off their shields as they moved in unison. This, in turn, sent the spiderlings racing forward, out between their mothers' many legs.

As the slime-covered wasp-larvae thumped against the smooth city walls, they began to burrow through, as they had before.

Dendralon heard the unmistakable sound of the Mertol roaring in the distance.

***

David Peck watched the big, orange-haired Mertol race forward from the city walls, Wee Joe clinging to its matted fur like some oversized parasite.

The Mertol came to a sudden halt about two hundred yards before the first of the spiderlings. It turned back to face the city walls and lifted its bulky arms above its head. Wee Joe stood astride its shoulders and pulled the flaps of skin that normally drooped down from its cheeks further apart. He braced. Then, with a jolt, the Mertol jerked its head back as an array of small balls shot from its face. The balls stuck to the city walls and spread over the adobe stone surface. A blood-like liquid soon covered the stone and began to drip onto the wasp larvae. On contact, the larvae wriggled, as if caught on a giant fishhook, and then dropped down dead. Now, when any wasp larvae thumped into the walls, they suffered the same fate.

Wee Joe pointed down at the approaching mass of spiderlings before squinting up at David Peck's position. "Yous better watch out for thee baby spiders, Mr. Peck!"

Clumsily, David Peck tried his best to nock an arrow. He shouted down to Wee Joe, "I'm not sure arrows are the best defence against those tiny spiders."

"Joe! Joe!" called Jean. "Get back inside the city. It's too dangerous out there."

Wee Joe screamed back up at them. "Set the arrows on fire! I seed it in a western. The Indians did it to the cowboys' wagons." He crouched lower on the Mertol's back as it turned round to face the spiderlings.

David Peck ran along a section of wall past Cimerato and dipped his arrow tip into some burning pitch. His arms trembling, he pulled back on the taut gut string and, with a *thuck*, released the arrow. He watched it arch up then down onto the mass of advancing spiderlings. It missed the spiderlings but the flame ignited the silken threads that covered the ground beneath them. The flame roared out from the arrow as another twenty or so Manimals followed suit, sending their flaming arrows deeper into the mass of spiderlings.

"They's barbecued!" shouted Wee Joe.

Cimerato shouted down at the Mertol and Wee Joe. "Watch yourselves! Some of the spiders are breaking through!"

A wave of spiderlings broke free of the flames.The fire, however, raced back behind them, snaking a deadly path along the silken strands to the waiting line of Racnid mothers.

David pointed at the Racnid Queen, Elhada, as she retreated back into the huddled Inubians. The noise from their shield bashing had abated; instead their howls were intermingled with the hissing of burning Racnids.

"Bak! Bak!" The Mertol's eerie cry sounded over the plain as the first of the spiderlings to break free raced over its clawed feet and up its matted legs. The Mertol clawed at the swarm but soon crumpled to its knees.

"Joe!" Jean found Cimerato and caught hold of him. "Do something!"

Spying a rope, David Peck tied one end round a stanchion and threw the other end over the wall.

Jal pushed past David and made to climb down.

"No!" snapped Cimerato. "I need you here." He caught Jal's arm.

Jal jerked free and peered down over the battlements. "Too late. The Mertol's disappeared."

"NO!" Jean shrieked.

David pulled her close and scanned for any sign of Wee Joe and the Mertol. "I… I can't see them either. Maybe…"

"He's dead!" She pounded David's chest. "You were all too slow. Too slow!"

David felt his heart sink. He only wanted the nightmare to end. He wanted to be home in his bed waking up in a sweat after the worst dream in his life. A Manimal nudged past him, clutching more arrows.

David closed his eyes. "Wee Joe…"

"The Mertol can look after itself. One of my men said he saw it disappear into thin air," said Cimerato. "It promised to protect the boy, so be calm."

"Calm?" Jean protested. "Calm?"

The Racnids were beginning to douse the flames with pouches of water pulled from their abdomens. They were regrouping.

David screwed up his eyes and watched Dendralon flick his staff back and forth until a grey misty cloud spread out over his army. It lifted higher and began to bubble and twist until, with a crack of thunder, it drenched his troops in a torrent of rain.

"The Artilian Wasps can't sting us now," said David. "I remember… Mendel… Drumfintley…" His head was numb. "Mendel told us that the rain renders them harmless." He still couldn't look Jean Harrison in the eye. No matter how convinced Cimerato was of the Mertol's powers, he'd been too slow to act. Jean was right.

CHAPTER SEVENTEEN

THE DRAGON CHAMBER

James wondered how much further the passageway would take them. They'd been walking for hours down the freshly widened tunnel, re-honed by the incredibly huge dragon, Hulatania. Slabs of rock, many tons in weight, smashed down behind and in front as they picked their way through the debris. Fortunately, with Whindril to the fore, most of the bigger boulders bounced off her scaly hide. They only had to dodge the odd one.

"Not long now, boys," said Mendel.

"And girls," added Helen.

"So sorry, Helen, oh, and Mrs. Peck. Still, now might be a good time to explain a few points I may have brushed over before."

"Oh, here we go," snorted Craig, side-stepping a small landslide to his left. "Spit it out then, Mendel."

James stopped and crouched down to stare into the brandy barrel that swung beneath Bero's chin.

Helen shuddered with annoyance. "Craig, do you have to be such a complete nark?"

"He's right for once," said Cathy. "Let's hear it, Mendel. What's the problem this time?"

James saw his mum refocus on Eethan, who was busy nose-picking. She cracked the little blue man across the back of the head, forcing his thumb further up his nostril.

"EEEE!"

"Chuck it!" she warned.

Mendel cleared his throat and waited until the noise of tumbling rocks subsided a little. "There's no problem. I just want to clarify a few things with James. My magic…"

Craig guffawed. "You mean the stuff you do through Helen nowadays?"

James felt his face flush. "Why do you have to wind me up all the time? I thought you were supposed to be my friend."

Craig brushed some dust out of his hair and stood up. "Look, James. I'm your friend. Your best friend."

"Well, it doesn't bloomin' seem like it. You're always trying to put me down every chance you get." James felt his temples burn with rage. "Every one of your stupid, smart-alec comments is at my expense!"

Mendel tried to speak, "I was just going to say…" but stopped mid-flow as Craig almost tripped over Bero in an effort to push his face even closer to James's.

Craig clenched his fists. "You, you, you… I'm the tag on, last minute, never in the limelight, side kick; and I'm sick of it." He glanced down at the brandy barrel. "Why does he never pick me to do his magic? And what's *she* got that I haven't, eh?"

Helen crouched down beside Bero. She let the retriever lick her hand. "Mendel knows best."

"Oh! Sure he does!" snapped Craig.

"BOYS!" screeched Cathy. "Shut up and listen."

Exasperated, the old wizard began, "Time is running out. Helen is correct. I only do things because there is a very good reason. I don't do things just to upset people. There is always a perfectly…"

"…Good explanation. I know." Craig took in a very deep breath and closed his eyes. "I'm sorry."

James waited for the 'but'… Amazingly, none followed.

Zing!

One of the bat-things, that had been pestering them, dropped at Craig's feet, frazzled by a blast of blue from Eethan. Craig bent down to pick it up.

"Not a good idea," said Mendel.

Craig pulled his fingers away from its twitching grey wings.

"Grantaf Bats, *Lornes vamparnes,* are highly charged."

"Highly charged?" asked James.

"Full of static electricity," explained Mendel. "Give you a nasty shock."

"You see," said James. "You're quite happy to explain that kind of stuff but when it comes to my knocking sensation, or whether or not I did the spell that killed Dendralon, you avoid a proper explanation like the plague."

Mendel swam across to the window of the barrel. "I am trying to tell you right now, if you'd give me a chance."

"Oh, for goodness sake," snapped Cathy, "Never mind who can do what magic and who can't, just let the gormless guppy take us to this Dragon Chamber, or whatever it is, and then we can all go home."

"I'll just explain this first, Cathy. If that's all right," said Mendel.

She clattered down onto a rock, her armour twinkling in the eerie light. "Fine. Suit yourself. Explain."

Mendel sighed. "As I have said before, you are simply... a *natural,* James."

"Eethan appeared from the gloom to James's left. "Ee was too!"

Distractedly, James crouched down nearer to the barrel.

Mendel continued. "Your body has gathered every piece of my magic and stored it for a future date. Your synapses..." Mendel seemed to struggle for another way to put it. "Your nerve endings have collected the information and have evolved."

Dreamily, Craig peered ahead into the shadows. "You mean he's changing?"

"Precisely," said Mendel.

James was confused.

Helen's expression switched from inquisitive to concerned.

"You have kept every trace of magic you have ever done inside you. It's stored there. All you have to do is learn how to unlock it."

James decided he liked this explanation. "So I *did* perform the ston-eright spell that killed Dendralon on Ebos?"

Mendel sailed past his plastic window. "No, on two counts."

"Oh," said James, dejectedly.

"Firstly, it was me who performed the spell and secondly, I doubt that Dendralon is actually dead."

"So, my brain isn't ready yet?"

"No, I feel it *is* actually ready. You will do magic all by yourself very soon."

"So, why are you using Helen all the time?" pressed James.

"Helen is at the right age to be a vector for someone else's magic, but you... You have actually absorbed it. There is always physical pain if you take on the mantle. The aberrations of the mind often render the incumbent racked in..."

"Excuse me," said Craig, "plain English would be nice."

Mendel swam out of view. "Magic hurts."

James felt dizzy. "Now I know that I didn't do the spell on Dendralon, I don't think I could ever risk it."

"Oh yes, you could," said Mendel, "If the situation isn't too precarious, I will let you say one of my spells by yourself."

"Yeh, right!" barked Craig. "You're going to risk our lives and let him practise something he might not even be able to do?"

"Exactly," said Mendel.

James balked. "You are?"

"Now let's get going," said Mendel. "We've got a world to save."

"Hear, hear," said Cathy.

As they trundled on, Helen whispered to her big brother, "Maybe Mendel will only let James do magic if the situation is only slightly threatening."

Craig kicked at the dirt. "Fair point, Sis, but there haven't been many slightly scary moments, have there?"

"What about the bat-things?" Helen asked.

"Yeh," said Craig, "I'm not too comfortable with all that bat-zapping stuff going on just now. They don't seem to be much of a threat at all. What's the point?"

The Grantaf Bats, closer in size to geese than the usual mouse-sized ones back in Drumfintley, fluttered over their heads in the direction of the opening they'd come through earlier.

"They're not daft. They're getting out of here too," said Craig.

"Seems to me that we're going the wrong way," said James.

Bero produced an unexpected yelp as Mendel's barrel shifted. "Ah, there is a creature close by that may be a possible candidate, James."

"What creature?" said James, instinctively hunkering down.

Bero issued a low growl.

"There," said Helen. She pointed up a side tunnel, partially lit by the azure glow emanating from Eethan's skin.

A worm-like creature with elongated antennae slithered along the rugged wall, its tube-shaped mouthparts blowing out red bubbles as it moved. James had seen a few strange creatures in his travels with Mendel but this...

"*Venturga glengatus*," said Mendel.

"How helpful," whispered Craig.

"A Cave Whipworm can deliver enough venom to kill a fully grown dragon," explained the wizard.

"Hardly slightly scary, then," moaned Craig. "I knew it."

James tried to focus on the creature. He saw Ethan and Elcar move away from the wall. Elandria bumped into him.

"Sorry, James," she said with a sigh. "I'll just put myself between it and you."

"No, you won't," said Helen. Mendel told you that you have to stay safe. We need you to do the magic that will save Denthan."

Craig shook his head. "Don't let him do it, Mendel."

"Try to use one of the spells you can remember now, James," prompted Mendel.

The worm creature was much bigger than James had first imagined. Thicker than a lamp-post and dripping with slime, it fired a stream of crimson bubbles at them.

"Everyone, duck!" shouted Mendel.

They all dropped to the floor of the cave, pressing themselves as flat as they could against the rock. All, that is, except Bero, who proceeded to snap at the fairy-like suds with all the excitement of a perky pup.

James tugged Bero down and then re-focused as hard as he could - "Wwwstonewrightwww!"

Instantly embarrassed, James braced in preparation for Craig's inevitable taunt.

"Eeee!"

The creature twisted round to face Eethan and lashed out with its long, forked tail before falling off the wall into the darkness.

"Great," snapped Cathy. "Now we can't see a bloody thing."

"I..." James hadn't seen his mum behind Elandria.

Elcar blasted the floor of the tunnel with yellow mist that poured over the stones. This didn't help. It just made it even more difficult to see where the Cave Whipworm had gone. There was a crash as Whindril thumped back towards them.

"There it is!" yelled Helen.

"I see it," said James. The creature was slithering round in circles about four feet away from them.

"Oh no. It can't move," said Helen.

Craig dug James in the ribs. "Cruel pig! You've only turned half of the poor thing into stone."

Bero growled and lunged, but Craig caught his collar and guided the old dog round the Whipworm. Its stinging, forked tail still thrashed and stabbed at them.

Eethan scampered dangerously close.

This time James tried to imagine the whole animal when he said the spell, "Wwwstonewwwrightww!"

There was a sickening crack as the Whipworm's tail sheared off and smashed on the ground, exploding into a cloud of dust.

"Argh!"

"Who was that?" said Cathy. "Did someone…?"

"Well done," interrupted Mendel.

"Cruel pig," reiterated Craig.

Helen's silence was enough to make him feel a pang of regret. Guilt crept over him like a dead man's shroud.

"No need for that whatsoever. And not even a clean kill," said Craig.

Cathy caught hold of Bero's collar. "Who screamed out? And what have you done to my son, Mendel? It's not right. I don't want him to be a freak like you." Cathy's questions hung, unanswered, in the dank air. The passageway was full of yellow mist and dust. It was still hard to make anything out.

"Mum." James found her wrist. "Can we just get going?" James wanted to bring the creature back to life. He hadn't wanted to kill it. It was just that everyone was expecting him to do it.

"Where's Eethan," asked Helen. Her voice wavered as Elcar's yellow mist cleared.

Craig waved away the pungent mist and stepped back. An indistinguishable lump lay on the floor of the tunnel.

"Eethan," said Helen.

James's cloak of regret grew much heavier.

"Is he dead?" asked Helen.

They all closed round the crumpled figure.

Elcar and Elandria strengthened their glows.

Eethan's eyes were closed, and he wasn't moving.

James noticed two tiny black holes in Eethan's bare chest.

Craig crouched down. "The Whipworm must have caught him before you…"

"I'm sorry. I tried my best. I…" James felt faint.

"It's not your fault, James. This is my doing," said Mendel.

James could feel everyone's eyes, like red-hot needles, burning into him.

Cathy knelt down beside the scrawny figure of Eethan and, screwing up her face in disgust, placed her hand on his chest.

"If only we still had the Key of Artilis," said Helen, in a small, trembling whisper.

"Well, we don't," blasted Craig.

A succession of big, lolling tears rolled down Helen's cheeks. They dripped off of her face, landing silently on the dusty floor.

"I'm sorry," whispered Craig.

No one spoke. They all watched Cathy's fingers as she searched for a pulse.

In an ominous, but steady voice, Mendel said, "There will be no pulse."

As an unbearable emptiness washed over him, James knelt down beside his mum and Eethan. Time seemed to stand still. His mum touched his hand. "Mum, he can't die like this." James shuddered in an effort to hold back the tears. "I mean, in an accident. I…"

"There's not much we can do for him now," she whispered.

His mum, certainly never Eethan's greatest fan, sounded truly sad.

Whindril's massive head snaked down until it was level with Eethan's face.

Cathy moved away from the little corpse.

James had never seen a dragon cry before but he decided that was exactly what he was seeing now. Like droplets of black, sticky oil, Whindril's tears flowed across her scaly cheeks until they disappeared into her snowy fur and dripped down onto Eethan's blue-tinged skin. The dragon tilted her head slightly and whispered, "Na te chan te, Eethan."

James knelt down and picked up the little blue man's delicate hand. It was so light, like a bird's wing. "Eethan, wake up. Please…"

"Come on, Son. He's gone." His mum's words unravelled the last knot in his stomach, and he wept like he'd never wept before. Gasping for air, struggling to see, he collapsed against the hard wall of the cave. He felt Craig's hand on his arm. Through a blur of tears he saw Helen and Bero draw closer.

"We need to keep moving," said Cathy.

Mendel's scales glimmered in the half-light. "Your mother is right, James. We need to keep going. Time is not on our side."

Mendel's voice grated inside his head. *How could the old wizard simply leave a ten-thousand-year-old friend behind to rot without even saying goodbye?*

Mendel seemed to pick up on this. "He would not want us to miss the one chance we may have to save a whole world, James."

James felt rage build in his chest. "What's the point?" he yelled. "You said we needed Eethan to do the magic. You said we had to keep him alive. You're the one who told me to try a spell on the whip-worm!"

"I'm sorry, James," said Mendel.

"Sorry?" James cupped the barrel and stared inside. "Sorry doesn't cut it, Mendel. Not now. What are we going to do?"

Mendel flicked his ventral fins and drifted over to the plastic window. "We are going to remain calm and we are going to make our way to the Dragon Chamber. We are going to find another way. There is always another way. So let's get going."

It just didn't seem right to leave Eethan's small, crumpled body in the middle of the tunnel, so James wiped his eyes and scooped Eethan up in his arms. He found a cluster of rocks, to the side, and placed him on the ground behind the biggest stalagmite he could find. At least a cave rat or some other nasty wouldn't stumble across him quite so quickly.

"C'mon, James," urged Craig.

"What's done is done," said Cathy.

He started walking, his legs like lead. "What's done is done? You didn't even like him," he mumbled.

"Don't cheek me, James." His mum caught hold of his wrist but then loosened her grip. "Let's try and save ourselves first. We'll be no good to anyone if we don't do that. According to Mendel, there is only a little time left." She let go of his arm when they caught up with Craig and Helen.

James turned round to face Craig. His best friend's freckled face was wet with tears, just like his own.

"He saved our lives," said Helen.

"More than once," Craig mumbled. "Doesn't seem right to leave him."

James gulped. "We'll come back for him."

"Yeah, right," mumbled Craig.

James saw Bero walk past him. The water, sloshing round in the barrel, reminded James of Mendel's dull eyes, and of how the wizard only had a few hours left to live himself. He felt another pang of regret. He decided to ask Mendel a technical question. He liked explaining things to the boys and Helen. It might cheer him up. "Tell me, Mendel, how does this whole 'save the world thing' work? I mean, you're changing history in a way, aren't you?"

"Yes and no," replied Mendel.

Craig sighed. "Nice one, numpty. Now we're going to get one of his 'clear as mud' lectures."

"Nestler," pressed Mendel, "predicted that when you alter the past by interfering with a set path of fate, you are ninety-five percent likely to be part of the fate."

"There he goes," moaned Craig.

"Shut up, Craig," barked Helen.

Craig gave her a quizzical stare.

James increased his pace. "So what does that mean in plain English, Mendel?"

Craig guffawed, "Ha!"

"What does it mean for us?" pressed James. "Will Eethan come alive again if we manage to stop Tealfirth exploding and destroying Denthan?"

"We will not stop Tealfirth exploding, James."

Bero cocked a crooked ear.

Cathy reached down and caught hold of Bero's collar. She peered into the barrel. "Say that again."

"The sun will still explode," affirmed Mendel.

"So what are you going to do?" she asked.

"Magic, Cathy. Magic," answered Mendel.

"Please, Mum. Let Mendel continue," said James.

"Fine," blasted Cathy, marching off ahead.

Mendel continued his explanation. "A scientist called Nestler had a Space-Time-Fate Theory. I think it was theory number seven. Anyway, applying the basic elements to our situation…"

"See," said Craig.

"I want to hear. So, shut up," said Helen.

James and Craig stared at each other in disbelief.

"Mendel explained loads of stuff to me and Wee Joe in the jungle. Perhaps if you two listened more at school you wouldn't be in the bottom of the class."

"Oh! Below the belt, Sis," said Craig, a sneer joining his freckles together.

Mendel continued, "If we can stop the explosion destroying the planet it should mean that the time-fate index will be altered."

"The what?" asked Helen.

"Anyone inside Gwendral when the fate of Denthan is altered will instantly reappear where they were the moment Denthan broke apart the first time. The exception being anyone whose soul had been separated from their body in the meantime."

"Why the soul bit?" asked Helen. "I'm not sure I understand what a soul is."

Cathy, who'd been listening in, broke into the conversation. "Your soul is your essence. It's the thing that makes you you. Some people think that you are reborn, forever. They think that you just keep coming back, time after time, with the same personality."

Craig visibly shuddered, and then surreptitiously mouthed the words, 'good grief' to James.

"So, what will happen to us and the creatures outside Gwendral?" asked James.

"Mmm…" pondered Mendel. "I believe we will simply remain where we are at the moment of salvation."

"Salvation?" said Cathy. "It's hardly an appropriate word."

"I would say that it is an entirely appropriate word, if you consider that we stand to save over three trillion creatures from total annihilation."

"Including about fifty-thousand Hedra," reminded Craig.

"Yes, well," mused Mendel, "I have some hope in that direction." Mendel floated away from the plastic window of the barrel.

"Rraaaarr!" Whindril's tortured cry caused the whole tunnel to shake until there was an almighty crash. James wafted away the dust from his face and looked up. Daylight streamed in towards them.

"The Dragon Council," announced Elcar. A trail of yellow mist drifted from his jaws. "We are here at last."

CHAPTER EIGHTEEN

THE THREE ORPHANS OF LIGHT

Dendralon turned away from the battle to check the progress of Zanther and the Inubian division he'd instructed to climb up to the high plateau. A few dragons had appeared in the sky, carrying Manimals. This meant, of course, that there were two Gwendrals coexisting on Denthan. "Nestler's theory would have predicted this," he mused. He remembered seeing a few of the Manimal gentry escape the Hedra arrows in such a way two years before. In fact, he'd instructed the Hedra to ignore them.

Pulling his long, silken hair away from his flattened Hedra face, he managed to pick out the thin line of Inubians weaving their way up the mountainside. He wondered about joining them, facing Mendel. He was torn between this notion and the thought of capturing the city of Gwendral in person.

The huge Eden archway glowed behind him. He felt its incredible energy tug on his golden armour, beckoning him back to Ebos and beyond. He was, however, convincing himself that the capture of the beautiful city he'd once helped to build was going to be the better path. He would win back that prize first. Stolen from the Hedra so long ago, it was time to walk through Gwendral's tall, ivory gates, victorious.

The battle was going better for them, now that the Mertol had disappeared beneath the swarm of ravenous spiderlings. The Racnid young could now resume the terrible work they had performed on Artilis the year before. They had obliterated the proud Artilian army so easily. The Racnid mothers would clear up any leftovers in the city. He waved the remaining Inubian rank forward. "When Elhada opens the gates, rush inside and use the full force of your brigade to ensure no male of any kind survives." He lifted his staff and took in the warm, Denthan air. Of all the worlds he'd visited over the last ten thousand years, Denthan felt the most like home. As the Inubians marched forward he shouted, "Do not harm my queen."

The Inubians issued a resounding howl that echoed off the looming mountains behind them and filtered over the plain. Snarling and brandishing their long pikes and cutlasses, they soon broke into a run and charged.

Dendralon reined in his Racnid steeds and measured out the distance between the arch formed by the Eden Trees and his position. He decided that he could reach the gateway back to Ebos in less than fifteen minutes. He also estimated that Tealfirth, the dying Denthan sun, would explode in less than two hours. He remembered well, the deep, ominous drone that preceded the explosion the last time he'd stood on Denthan. The sound caused his stomach to turn and the ground to shake. He had to decide on his next course of action. In some ways it would be much simpler to let Denthan die, return now to Ebos, but he couldn't take the chance that Mendel would succeed and win over the planet that was rightfully his. Mendel had just over ninety minutes to stop the obliteration of Denthan.

He would, of course, have to face the old wizard at some point. Deal with his magic. It was a battle he did not relish. His new wife, however, was a prize worth fighting for. Beldam would come back to him when there were no other options, when she saw him, as he was now, his power fully restored. He would cultivate her love over an eternity. Show her worlds and riches she could never imagine. He tightened his grip on the gnarled staff that had served him so well and aimed at the gates of Gwendral. The huge gates had been hewn from the massive tusks of Saurs that roamed over the Southern deserts of Denthan and then fused by magic. The main gates had served the city well for ten thousand years. *It would be wrong to destroy them now.* He would wait a little longer. The Racnids were already pouring over the battlements. They would soon penetrate the gate-towers. Again, he scanned the Mountains of Hest for any sign of Zanther's Inubians. They had disappeared. Torn, yet again, by an urge to confront Mendel and sensing that his queen, Beldam, was up in the mountains, he wavered. Angry at himself, he turned to Elhada. "Enter the city. I want you to finish off the Earthlings yourself. I sense four adults and a boy."

"But I thought we were to remain and witness the city's demise. I thought we were staying close to the Eden arch, Sire...?" Elhada peered up at the angry sky. "Sire?"

Ignoring the Racnid Queen, Dendralon closed his eyes and let the Hedra magic flow through him. Pictures of his bride flooded his thoughts. She was inside a huge, dark tunnel, scrambling over debris. She was following a dog, two boys, and a girl-child. There were other creatures there too but now a blinding light cut through the darkness and he couldn't see anything apart from his bride. The light spilled over her beautiful form, causing her armour to shine brightly. He opened his yellow eyes and stared down at the cowering Racnid. "You will carry out my orders, Elhada."

"And what if Mendel fails?" hissed Elhada.

"He will not fail," said Dendralon, his dark eyes again fixed on the Mountains of Hest. "Go now and finish this. I am going up into the mountain to rid myself of Mendel and reclaim my bride."

***

Trapped in a corner of a parapet full of dead Manimals, David Peck shouted out for help. His arrows were spent and his options running out. The blaze that had taken hold of the Racnids had been doused by Dendralon's magic and now David was going to die here on a faraway world, eaten alive by tiny spiderlings.

"Mr. Peck!"

He twisted and looked above him, frantically trampling as many of the clicking spiders as he could. "Wee Joe?"

A massive hair-covered hand snatched his collar and hauled him up and out of reach of the swarming spiderlings. Cracking his shoulder on the stone rim of the tower, David yelled out before being unceremoniously dumped at Wee Joe's feet. Jean Harrison, Jal, and Cimerato were all there too. The Mertol let out an eerie cry that made him feel his rescue had only been temporary.

"Thanks." He strained to say the word, his shoulder still burning.

"No bother," said Wee Joe.

David Peck couldn't believe they were all there. "I saw you disappear out on the plain with the Mertol, Joe. I thought..."

"Yous thought wees was munched but wees wasn't. The Mertol's magic brought us up here."

"And now it's time to escape or die," said Jal.

"What about Michael and Ephie?" asked David.

"They are safely locked inside the gate-towers. They should be fine as long as they don't open the thick doors."

"But the spiderlings might climb up the chains or get in the windows."

Cimerato urged them onward. "They have Yeltans in there with them too. Look, David, we all have to look after ourselves here. Are you coming or not?"

David hesitated, gulping when he saw the state of Jal's armour.

Jal was covered in green slime and black, chunky lumps. "All of you, down this rope. Now! Get across to the citadel, get inside, and bar the door."

Hanging from a massive chain, a thick rope dangled down into the courtyard. Half sliding, half climbing, they slid down into a wagon below. David stood up and helped Jean and Wee Joe aboard. He turned and looked up at Cimerato and Jal. "What about you two?"

"The Mertol will get you all inside the citadel. Get up to the Council chamber," shouted Cimerato. Jal remained beside Cimerato. The Mertol was already pulling the wagon forward.

David craned his neck as he peered up at the high citadel. It had assumed a crimson glow, and its smooth alabaster facade flickered as the fleeting shadows of winged reptiles and strange birds traced its surface. "Cimerato, how will *you* get inside the citadel if we lock it from the inside?"

"Look after yourselves. We will find a way."

"Mr. Peck, wees have to get to dat door!" Wee Joe pointed across to a complex, stone archway composed of interwoven snakes. It framed a dark, iron-studded door.

"I know, Son, it's just that they'll be stuck out here with..." He ducked as a Yukplug slammed against the side of the wagon, a fully-grown Racnid biting down through its thick coat. "...those things."

Jean covered Wee Joe's ears as the Mertol began pulling the wagon faster towards the door. The screams of battle and the eerie, continuous drone that emanated from the sky were truly horrendous. Jal and Cimerato had disappeared in the chaos. *Had they gone to help Michael and Ephie?*

"We're nearly there. Keep down," said David. He clung to the frame of the wagon as it trundled over cobbles, and he tried not to think about the unfortunate Manimals falling around them as they rolled faster and faster.

"We're near enough. Jump out!" instructed Jean.

They leapt down from the wagon, as the Mertol held a group of Racnids at bay, and ran at the huge door. They tried to pull on the heavy iron handles but the doors didn't budge. Wee Joe's tattered shoes skittered over the top step as he jerked the black iron knocker.

"It's no use," wailed David.

"Bak!" The Mertol, eased past them and jerked the heavy doors open with ease.

They all slipped inside into the darkness.

The door slammed behind them, and the noise from outside abated.

"What about Cimerato and Jal?" said David.

"They will have to fend for themselves," said Jean, sternly. "David, I need you to focus on Wee Joe." Resolutely, she walked back to the huge doors they'd just come through and slipped two thick iron bolts into place. "That should hold for a while."

The door shook as something big battered against it.

David stared at her in disbelief. "What about Ephie and…"

"Keep focused on him," said Jean, her finger pointing down at Wee Joe.

The Mertol gave a short "Bak" of satisfaction.

Wee Joe looked sad. "I think de Manimals are great warriors but theys never had to face those wee spider things before." He trudged up the first set of stairs.

Jean took his hand. "Let's just do what Jal and Cimerato said. Let's get as far up this tower as possible."

Rrrrooooaahh!

The Mertol covered its ear-holes.

David felt his stomach clench as the deep bass roar shook the stone under his feet. A low, insidious rumble ensued that never really faded away.

"It's the same as before," said Wee Joe.

Jean looked as if she were fighting to keep calm. "Yes, it's the same as before, and Mendel will find a way to save us, just like he did the last time. Isn't that right, David?"

"That's right, Jean. Come on now, Wee Joe. Chin up."

"You get yous own chin up!" retorted Wee Joe, stomping past them to catch up with the Mertol.

David called after him, "Don't forget that Cathy, James, and Mendel and Craig…"

"And my big sis," added Wee Joe.

"And your big sister, Helen, are probably on their way back to us right now." He paused to look down through a high, stained-glass window. "The ivory gates are opening," he gasped.

"Why would they open the gates?" Jean asked.

"Bak!" The Mertol seemed to answer the question by pretending to ring his own neck. He stuck his black tongue out and then feigned death by lolling against the wall.

"Not very helpful," snapped David.

Wee Joe laughed. "He's funny."

The rumble intensified and the stained-glass shook in its leaded frames.

"Going by the last time this happened, we've got less than an hour," said Jean

"About an hour?" asked Wee Joe.

"About an hour until we get back home, of course, and all nonsense is over."

"Or until de sun explodes and wees all get splatterated!" shouted Wee Joe. He ran ahead, blasting invisible foes with his green plastic water gun.

David edged closer to Jean. "He's pretty resilient, isn't he?"

"Yes. Always has been, really." Jean steadied herself against the warm stone, took a deep breath, and then continued up the stairs.

***

The light poured in through a high vaulted ceiling that was joined in the middle by a series of long wavering spikes.

"Spears?" asked James.

"Dragon defences," explained Mendel. "There is a reasonable chance that we will have to trust in fate from now on."

"Unacceptable," snapped Cathy.

"Mum..." James complained. He studied her powdered face. Her skin was still covered in the weird Artilian make-up that accentuated her eyes in a kind of Egyptian way. She'd changed a lot in the last year, he decided.

"It's okay, James. Your mother is quite right," said Mendel. "Where chance is quite random, fate is certainly not. I've made it my life's work to interpret the random events that form round different individuals. You can make an educated decision about fate after a while. You see," Mendel continued, his voice crackly and thin, "I know our fate is inextricably linked to this place. Denthan, I mean. The planet was not meant to die in the fires of Tealfirth."

"You're beginning to bug me," said Cathy.

"Me too," added Craig.

"If we only had the Key of Artilis." James sighed. "Eethan would be here, and there would be no problem." His tongue was suddenly too big for his mouth. "I can't believe he's gone."

"We don't have the Key or Eethan," said Mendel, "but we do have you, James."

"Me?" wheezed James.

"Yes," added Elcar. "You can take Eethan's place."

"He would have liked that," said Helen, matter-of-factly.

"But, how?" protested James.

Elcar opened his scarlet wings and hopped over the debris. He glided for a few seconds and then landed, with a snort, in the Dragon Chamber.

Cathy drew her swords and followed.

James felt Craig nudge him.

"Your sword's disappeared. Call it back again, numpty."

James had forgotten how their magic weapons sometimes fizzled away. If unused for a while, they conveniently went somewhere else until they were needed again. He didn't know where.

"Firetongue!" The crimson sword filled James's palm. Right then, he wished beyond any wish he'd ever made that he'd called on *it* to deal with the Whipworm, rather than test out his supposed magical powers. *Eethan might still be alive.*

Mendel's voice filtered into his thoughts. "Elcar is right, James. You *could* take Eethan's place."

"What, and glow bright blue just at the right time?"

"Yes," said Elandria. "You are from Earth, just like Eethan was, and you are a *natural*, according to Mendel."

A bubble flew past the window of the barrel. "Elandria is right. You are the Earthling who possesses the ability now."

"I haven't exactly proved that I can do anything even close to magic. You did the spell that killed Dendralon and I managed to..."

"You managed more than you take credit for," said Mendel. "Luck was not on your side."

Where Whindril could flap up into the ceiling, like Elcar, to avoid a ten-foot high ridge before the Dragon chamber, the rest of the group were forced to climb up a narrow set of stairs set into the obstacle. They were bunched tightly together.

"Come on, Mrs. Peck, I can't see anything," complained Craig.

"Watch what you're saying," whispered Helen. She widened her eyes in warning.

"I can't see what's in the chamber for her big bahooky," Craig whispered back.

Cathy spun round and caught the tip of Craig's green spear.

Craig skidded to a halt. "Hey! There's no need to get all aggressive."

"Oh yes there is." Cathy reached beyond the spear and caught Craig's nose between two of her fingers. "You've been getting on my nerves for years." Cathy slipped and almost toppled back down the stairs, pulling Craig with her.

Helen covered her smile with her long, blonde hair and stepped past them up into a brightly lit gallery.

James winked at Craig and followed Helen.

Cathy gave Craig's nose a sharp twist and let him go.

"Awch!" yelled Craig. "I've got witnesses." He called up at James and Helen. "Haven't I?"

"Didn't see a thing," said James, the little episode momentarily taking his mind off the sadness and fear that clawed at him.

"Look," yelped Helen. Excitedly, she pointed across a black marble floor at three identical pedestals. "What are they?"

"Those are the three Dragon Thrones of Hest," said Mendel. "Hulatania was the last of her kind. A true mother dragon." Mendel pressed his eye against the window of the barrel. Like a big orange marble, it wavered behind the see-through plastic. "Take me closer, Bero."

Bero wagged his tail and padded into the chamber.

Mendel waited for the barrel to stop swinging. "This place should still possess the dragon magic required to join all of your powers and focus your energy. Elcar, Elandria, and you, James, need to stand on the raised platforms. One each. Elandria, you take position on the far throne. Elcar, the middle, and James, the one nearest to me."

Whindril shook her white mane and hissed.

"What's wrong?" said Cathy.

"Whindril's hearing is twenty times greater than yours," explained Mendel. "What can you hear, my old friend?"

James could hear something now too. Noises. Animal noises. A mish-mash of yelps and howls barely audible above the incessant drone of the dying Denthan sun.

"Jackal heads," said Craig. "I'd know that sound anywhere."

"Inubians, and more of Dendralon's work, I fear," said Mendel.

"I hoped... I mean, I assumed we'd seen the last of him," said James, his heart racing.

"Never assume anything in life," warned Mendel.

Whindril stood her ground at the edge of the marble floor.

"Don't they know that if they stop us from doing this, they will all be killed?" asked Helen.

"I wouldn't bet on it," said Craig. "We'll need to keep them off until those three do whatever it is they have to do."

Tentatively, James climbed up onto the nearest dragon throne and watched on as Whindril spread her wings and arched her neck in anticipation of the Inubian attack.

As the first of the jackal-faced Inubians came into view, Whindril roared and spewed out a stream of flame. Blue fire scorched the first of the Inubians into charred, flailing lumps that burst into dust. The ranks that were not instantly vaporised screamed as the flames caught hold. They fell back, screaming and howling in panic. Five or six burning figures ran out of the fray towards Craig and Cathy. These, however, were despatched by Greenworm or by Cathy's swirling swords.

"Are you ready, James?" asked Mendel.

"No," said James, indignantly. "Ready to do what?" He looked up at the crimson sky through a series of massive black membranous barbs that formed a kind of cage above them.

Ignoring the battle with the Inubians, Bero had sat in a spot equidistant from all three of the dragon thrones.

On the furthest throne from his, Elandria hissed and clamped her curved black teeth together as her greenish down began to vibrate. Bouncing on her six legs, her two cupped hands stretched out before her, she closed her bulbous eyes and shook even more.

James felt nothing.

Elcar too had begun to tremble. His long crimson wings outstretched, he craned his neck backwards and emitted a high-pitched wail.

They both know what to do. I haven't got a clue, he thought.

He saw that Helen had stayed close to Bero. She was kneeling down. She was talking to Mendel. *What is the stupid guppy doing now?* "What do I do now?" he screamed. "Helen!"

Helen's gaze, however, remained fixed on the brandy barrel that swung gently beneath Bero's muzzle.

"Helen!" he called again.

Helen began to shudder, just like Elandria and Elcar had. She gripped on tightly to the brandy barrel and pulled it closer to her face. Her long, golden hair whisked and danced around her as an unexpected breeze wafted down through the cage-like barbs above their heads.

Crash!

A slab of stone fell from the ceiling and exploded yards away from his mum and Craig. Whindril whipped her tail to the side just in time, taking the legs away from a group of Inubians that crawled over the debris. On his pedestal, James stood in place, as instructed. He longed to join the fight.

A blast of shimmering light shot out from the brandy barrel and hit Elandria on her down-covered abdomen. Another, similar blast caught Elcar. A third beam of light struck him on the chest. The force of the beam almost knocked him off his pedestal and he had to fight to hold his position. His chest tightened. His legs buckled, but unexpectedly, an incredible feeling of exhilaration began to build inside him. It hardened his stance and pulled him up straight.

Bang!

The far wall began to fracture. Hairline fissures spider-webbed out from the edge of the tunnel until, with an enormous explosion, the far wall of the Dragon Chamber collapsed. The boulders tumbled into a huge pile. He was sure he'd seen his mum and Craig run back in time, but a thick curtain of dust rose up from the floor of the chamber and he wasn't sure. Whindril was nowhere to be seen.

"Whindril!" he yelled. It looked as if the dragon had been buried beneath the rock fall. "Mum!"

Still caught in Mendel's beam, he looked down at Bero and Helen. Neither had moved.

The growls and barks of the Inubians resumed as far off crashes and rumbles subsided.

Elcar, to his left, had shuddered again and seemed to glow even brighter. Elandria was undergoing a similar transition. Her light was an intense crimson that cut through the dust and gloom of the cavern to merge with Elcar's yellow light. James felt his skin begin to tingle. His eyes nipped and his teeth throbbed. All thoughts and fears subsided as his skin began to glow a deep ocean blue. His blue light fused with the red and the yellow to become one single blast of dazzling white that shattered the long, black barbs above them and travelled upwards into the fiery Denthan sky. Everything in his muddled mind became distant, and he had the sensation of floating. Lifted off his feet by some unknown force, James drifted high over the mountains and forests of Denthan. Over the Gortan Sea he climbed higher still, above the clouds and further still, up into the amber tinged atmosphere of Denthan and out into the darkness of space. Racing through an endless night, his head spun with visions of stars and distant galaxies. Great clouds of coloured stardust towered over him as he travelled toward Tealfirth, Denthan's dying sun. A huge dragon, bigger than a world, spread its wings around Tealfirth. *Was it Hulatania?* He could feel the heat intensifying as he approached the dying star. Then his strength, the feeling of endless power that had surged through him, began to ebb away. He was slipping back down to Denthan again. He couldn't keep up with the light that spun out from Elandria and Elcar. *His* light was fading. He could feel his feet again, standing on the cold plinth of the Dragon Chamber. He could hear the screams of battle. A small, cold hand gripped his ankle.

CHAPTER NINETEEN

THE SECOND SUN

High above the city of Gwendral, in the Council chamber of the citadel, Jean and Wee Joe followed David Peck through the empty rows of wooden seats towards an ivory throne. It was covered with images of twisting snakes.

As Jean followed David Peck's echoing footsteps, she recalled the nightmare that had unfolded in the same chamber two years before. The mutilated face of Dendralon; half serpent, half man, had sneered down at Wee Joe. The look of complete hatred on that monster's face had plagued her dreams ever since. She thought of the vision-pool, still there, a fan of scales set into the floor... Dendralon had fallen into the vision-pool, into the fires of Denthan, yet had survived. She felt giddy.

One of those *monsters* from Denthan was a mere five feet away from her right now. The Mertol leered at her with its deep-set eyes, its pitted face flicking in strange, mesmerising patterns. The growing wail of the dying sun, unchanged from two years ago, gripped her heart like a vice. She took Wee Joe's hand and led him over to the fan of scales on the floor.

"Don't step on thems, Mum. You might fall through," warned Wee Joe.

There was a scream from behind the door they'd just come through.

Jean pulled David and Wee Joe towards a heavy velvet curtain. She remembered that there was a balcony beyond.

As they made for the curtain, Jean glimpsed the Mertol. Its outline shimmered and then disappeared. She could hear steel clashing against steel and still more screams, hisses and howls coming from behind the door of the Council chamber. Jean pulled Wee Joe along. "The Mertol's just vanished. How could it leave us now? Quickly, David, get out onto the balcony." Panic was beginning to grip her.

The heavy drape closed behind them, but through the ever-decreasing gap she saw the main door burst open and the unmistakable shape of Elhada, the Racnid Queen, emerge from the shadows. The spider-like creature scuttled through the massive door of the Council chamber. Her black down was speckled with fresh blood and she was missing a leg. A host of smaller Racnids followed on behind her, scratching and hissing as the deep roar of Tealfirth began to shake the whole city. She whisked the curtain shut and ushered Wee Joe and David back towards the balustrade.

"It's just like before, Mum," said Wee Joe.

They moved across the stone balcony and gripped onto the balustrade.

"Wook, Mum!" Wee Joe pulled himself over the edge to get a better view.

David caught Wee Joe's shorts and held him tight.

Down below, a writhing sea of Inubians and Racnids poured through the open gates of Gwendral. Yeltans and Manimals lay motionless, in piles strewn across the courtyard, unable to halt Dendralon's Artilian army. To their surprise they spied the Mertol. He was back down in the courtyard, his orange, matted fur covered in black Racnid blood. Jean saw Cimerato and Jal dash into the citadel behind the Mertol. The giant creature was single-handedly holding off the Artilians.

"He's still fighting, Mum. He's trying to help the Manimals."

"What about us?" Jean whispered. Her heart felt like a ball of lead, far too heavy for her to carry. She knew the Racnids were already behind the curtain.

Artilian Wasps, fully dried after their dousing, buzzed the flailing Mertol, trying to find a gap between his clawing arms to plant their stings. Ducking low, the Mertol snatched the leg of a dead Inubian and swung the gruesome corpse round his head, knocking the wasps back against the inside of the city walls.

"Bak!"

Wee Joe gasped as a long, black, Inubian spear pierced the Mertol's ape-like arm.

"Why doesn't he use his magic, Mum?" yelled Wee Joe. "Come back up here!"

"Shhh! Keep your voice down, Joe." Nervously, Jean glanced back at the swaying curtain.

"But why is he just letting them hurt him?" persisted Wee Joe.

A second spear caught the Mertol's leg. It roared out in agony.

"Maybe he's run out of magic, Joe," said David. "Magic won't always be there to save us."

Jean saw David Peck peer up at Tealfirth. It had the look of a giant, red eyeball strewn with black veins and ready to burst. The balcony shook violently.

Wee Joe's face was set in a frown. "The Mertol could do his magic if he wanted to," he assured. "He just prefers to fight with his hands sometimes, dat's all."

The Mertol pulled the Inubian spear from his arm and dispatched a further four jackal-face assailants. Black arrows, however, were finding their way through the Mertol's hide and his strength looked to be fading.

A big tear rolled down Wee Joe's face. "Do your magic!" he shouted. "Don't let them…"

The Mertol looked up and caught Wee Joe's gaze. Three more arrows caught its neck and it roared. "BAK!"

Wee Joe sniffed in sharply and nodded.

"What are you doing, Son?" said Jean.

"It talks to me, Mum," whispered Wee Joe. "I hear it in my head. I always heared it."

Jean Harrison stared at her youngest in disbelief.

"What did it say?" asked David.

"It said, not to worry. It said it had to do something. It said it would come up and help us soon." Wee Joe sounded very sad, as if he didn't quite believe the Mertol's words.

When they all glanced back down, the Mertol had gone.

A crashing sound, much closer, made them jump.

Behind the black velvet curtain, in the main Council chamber, the hissing sounds made by the Racnids had intensified.

Wee Joe approached the curtain.

"Leave it," whispered Jean.

"But I can hears Cimerato and Jal," said Wee Joe, excitedly.

David gave Wee Joe a cautionary wave of his forefinger. "Just stay here with us, Wee Joe."

As the sound of Tealfirth's waxing and waning raced to its zenith, however, they all edged away from the stone balcony until they pressed against the curtain again. Jean felt its smooth texture against her bare arms and she stopped dead. "I don't know what to do," she sobbed.

David Peck cupped her with his arm and drew her close.

Wee Joe cuddled in too.

A sudden blast of air caused the velvet curtain to flick open. Inside the chamber, Jal and Cimerato were fighting a group of Racnids and Inubians. The cries of Yeltans could also be heard above the jumble of screams and clanging blades.

David pulled the curtain shut and looked up at the tortured sky.

Wee Joe made to open the curtain again. "Wees should try and help," he said.

"We haven't any weapons," said David. "We can only hope that James and Mendel have reached the Dragon Chamber."

A piercing scream sounded from behind the curtain. It swished open and they ducked. Two Yeltans flew through the air and over the balcony.

"No!" shrieked Jean.

"Sss…" The huge, twisted face of Elhada, the Racnid Queen, pushed through the black, velvet drape.

David crouched down with Jean and Wee Joe.

"Sss… What have we here?" she hissed. She tore down the curtains with her jointed arms and threw them over the balustrade.

David cupped his mouth and shouted as loud as he could, "Cimerato!"

Elhada's ugly mouth formed a hideous smile.

Jean knew there were too many Racnids between Cimerato and the balcony.

Elhada turned her head and eyed Wee Joe. He was staring, fixedly, at the stump of the Racnid's severed leg. It dripped black blood.

"I have another five, youngling. And, besides, it will grow back again if I take a little nourishment."

A long strand of yellow drool eased down from the side of her tilted head and splashed on the marble floor beside Wee Joe. Elhada drew back to strike.

"Leave him alo…"

Jean fell back against the balustrade as the bulky Racnid toppled forward.

Jal was on Elhada's back. He hung on with the two daggers he'd plunged into her hairy abdomen.

Screaming even louder than the deafening drone of Tealfirth, Elhada snapped her jaws shut over her shoulders but the Jal was too quick for her. Part monster himself, Jal bit down on her bulbous eye.

The Racnid Queen crashed down in agony, pushing Jean over the balcony.

"Jean!" David just managed to catch hold of her arm.

Wee Joe was trapped beneath Elhada's legs. He ducked and weaved as her shining black sting darted in and out around his head. A Yeltan spear clattered down beside him. Without thinking, Wee Joe lunged for the spear and jabbed it upward into Elhada's soft underbelly.

"Eeeeeee!"

Her legs flopped uselessly, pushing the Yeltan spear in deeper.

Straining to keep hold of Jean, David reached in under the Racnid's bulky frame and pulled Wee Joe free just in time.

Her fellow Racnids added to her ear-splitting wails and then fell silent.

Elhada was dead.

The other Racnids had stopped fighting. They began to gyrate on their jointed legs, hissing mournfully.

All eyes were on Wee Joe.

The battle had come to a standstill until, with a howl, a large Inubian jumped forward at Jal. In turn, the Hedra hissed with excitement, withdrawing his daggers from the twitching body of Elhada. Leaping to meet the Inubian, Jal performed an amazing pounce and spin that completely disorientated the jackal-faced Inubian. As he swung down with his daggers, however, a hundred silken strands, as thick as rope, whipped out across the Council chamber and held him tight.

Squinting through the balustrade, Jean felt her hands slipping down David's arms. She couldn't hold on.

Straining, David gasped and caught her wrists. He gripped tighter and heaved her up and back over the balustrade. He turned and gasped as Jal's bound body thumped onto the floor at the Inubian's feet. The Inubian sidestepped Jal and waved Jean, David, and Wee Joe away from the balcony. "Come here, rats."

A second later, Cimerato bumped down on the floor of the chamber beside Jal. Both were now wrapped firmly but still alive. They lay on a floor strewn with fallen Yeltans, Racnids, Inubians, and Manimals.

The big Inubian, who'd just escaped Jal, dragged Jean and David to the edge of the vision-pool. A small Racnid caught Wee Joe with a strand of silk and pulled him in.

"Kill them!" shouted an enraged Racnid.

"Not yet," snapped the Inubian. "Dendralon may want to interrogate them."

"That youngling killed Elhada!" screeched another Racnid.

Jean saw Jal's eyes dart in Wee Joe's direction. He hissed approvingly and Wee Joe, still skidding along the smooth floor, punched the air. This victory display, however, only served to fuel the hatred of the Racnids.

"Kill him!"

Jean's arm was aching but she reached out and pulled Wee Joe. The strand flopped to the floor and she hugged him in closer.

"The youngling will die first if that is Dendralon's wish," reassured the Inubian. "If we kill him now, which one of you would like to explain the boy's death to Dendralon?"

The Racnids edged back a little.

"He said to kill every male in the city," hissed one of the Racnids.

"Cowards!" hissed Cimerato.

Jean could see that he could barely breathe. He was bound so tightly.

The Inubian ignored Cimerato, his eyes fixed on the blistering sun. It was framed by the opening that led to the balcony.

The small Racnid that had pulled Wee Joe into the chamber scuttled over and flicked Wee Joe from Jean's grasp. It hovered above him, menacingly. "Dendralon could be dead for all we know," it hissed, "and he gave us the instruction. I say we kill him now."

Wee Joe bit his lip in anticipation.

"Leave him!" yelled Jean. Her legs shook as an overpowering feeling of dread gripped her like a vice.

Outside, the bloated form of Tealfirth expanded to twice its size.

As the light failed and a thunderous roar grew in ferocity, the stone began to crack beneath their feet. It felt as if the whole citadel was breaking up. There was a violent shudder as the balcony detached itself from the face of the citadel.

Shaken to the ground, Jean rolled under the vibrating legs of the confused Racnid and caught hold of Wee Joe's hand. As the floor fractured, however, the Racnid lowered, trapping them both beneath it. The smell of the Racnid above them was overpowering. Only inches from their faces, the soft down on its abdomen crawled with maggot-like parasites. Wee Joe tried to wriggle free but the Racnid spun round and held its dripping sting inches from his stomach.

"Mum!" Wee Joe braced.

Jean tried to push herself up.

The Racnid jabbed down.

* * *

James looked down at his ankle. He'd felt someone touch him but now there was no one there. *Had he been dreaming?* He was still standing on the plinth. He scanned the Dragon Chamber and then caught his breath. The Inubians had halted their advance. They were cowering and whining. Someone was walking from their midst. James blinked and refocused. "Dendralon." He felt dizzy. "But I saw you…"

"You saw me killed and turned to dust. Blown away by the winds of Ebos across a bloody battlefield," finished Dendralon. He laughed.

James knew that time was running out. He glanced up at the sky through the roof of the Dragon Chamber. The light had faded.

Dendralon glanced up at the sky too. His reptilian features hardened and then he nodded. "Less than three minutes."

Elcar and Elandria stopped shuddering and aimed their rays of light at the dark wizard, but he simply raised his staff and sent them flying. Thrown backwards against the wall of the dragon chamber, they slumped uselessly onto the floor.

James didn't know what to do. There was no sign of Mendel, and if Elcar and Elandria's magic couldn't harm Dendralon, what good would his be?

"Stop there!" shouted Cathy.

James watched nervously as his mum closed in on Dendralon.

"Leave my son alone," she whispered. Her voice was soft and threatening.

Dendralon eyed James as one might consider a dog that was just about to be put down for its own good. His voice was full of false concern, "Much as I admire the boy's spirit, he is not our own."

"He is my flesh and blood," said Cathy.

"Quite." Dendralon sneered.

James wondered if this was their first ever domestic. As the tension increased between his mum and Dendralon, James managed to hear a soft command from Mendel. He tried to pick Bero and Helen out from the swirling dust. "Throw your crimson sword over Dendralon's head, towards the Inubians," the old wizard whispered.

James was puzzled by the request. It was never wise to throw your only form of defence away.

"Do it!" urged Mendel.

Dendralon flinched and then watched as James launched Fire-tongue over his head. As the dark wizard's eyes followed the spinning blade, Mendel's words burst from James's lips, "Wwwwcanwwiswwpetriwwdwww!"

James had never heard this spell before, but its effects soon became apparent. Every jackal-faced Inubian shrieked in unison as Firetongue exploded above their heads, showering them with a million crimson sparks. In seconds, the Inubians quietened and then thumped to their knees, turned to stone. The endless rumble from Tealfirth dominated the chamber once more. *It must be ready to explode*, thought James.

"Bero!"

James looked across and saw Craig. He was staring down in horror at his pet dog.

"Bero's frozen solid. What have you done?" Craig, full of rage, marched towards the goldfish wizard's barrel, which had rolled away from its petrified harness.

Dendralon barged past his mum and caught Craig by the throat.

"Arggh!" Craig's eyes nearly popped out of his head.

"There's no time for this!" shouted James.

Dendralon held Cathy at bay with his free hand, a swarm of bees spilling out from the tips of his fingers to form a temporary barrier. He tilted his head and then loosened his grip on Craig. "Just stay there, my little blinder friend."

Craig's feet seemed to be stuck to the floor of the chamber but, worse than that, his throat remained constricted. His face was puce.

Dendralon turned to face James. "So, you are Mendel's medium; James Peck, son of Beldam?"

"Her name is Cathy," James barked. "Cathy Peck!"

Dendralon threw Cathy a venomous stare. The bees formed a window of sorts while he examined her. "Without the boy, Mendel is powerless."

James noticed Elcar and Elandria stir and then, very cautiously, move towards their empty plinths.

"Well done, Dendralon. Your assumptions are, however, flawed." Mendel's voice was rich, like velvet, in James's mind.

James had to distract Dendralon. He had to give Elcar and Elandria the time they needed to resume their positions on the plinths. He would have to try and use his own magic to distract the dark wizard. "Let my friend go, Dendralon!"

Craig was losing consciousness.

"I don't think so, Medium." Dendralon closed his fingers and Craig's eyes bulged even more.

"No!" shouted James. "What do you want?"

"Want? From you?" Dendralon answered his own question, "Nothing. You are but a medium. You are of no consequence, a pawn in a far bigger game."

"It's never been a game!" said James.

Dendralon dropped his hold on Craig. James saw him reach down to the stone floor for the barrel. "You have chosen your side, but has your mother? Well, have you, my bride? Will you submit to my will in the last few dying seconds of this world?"

Cathy Peck shifted nervously. "Only if you spare my son. Let Mendel save Denthan!"

Dendralon laughed scornfully, kicking a petrified Inubian into dust.

The fragments drifted onto James's shoulders, and he felt a surge of adrenaline charge him as he directed his thoughts to Dendralon.

Dendralon examined the brandy barrel before placing it back on the floor. He lifted his foot to crush it, then hesitated. "Ah, you have begun to assimilate…." He turned to face James. "You see, sometimes a medium can acquire the powers of the master." He raised his staff and shouted, "Ath nar te chan tar!"

Instantly, James and Helen fell down. James could feel a great weight pressing down on him. He was fighting for every breath.

Dendralon slammed his foot down on the barrel. It shattered, spilling out the water that kept Mendel alive.

A few inches from the broken barrel a goldfish flicked and arched as the water fell away from its golden scales. Dendralon aimed his staff at the helpless fish.

Cathy moved forward but Dendralon waved his fingers, and the swarm of bees became more animated. She came to an immediate halt.

The drone of Tealfirth intensified.

James tried to mouth the spell, Stonewright, while looking directly at Dendralon. Due to the constriction of his chest, however, he only managed a feeble gurgle that sound more like sniff bite.

Amazingly, this caused the tip of Dendalon's staff to assume the shape of a living snake, which snapped down at Mendel.

The rumble was beginning to dislodge some sizeable rocks from the roof of the Dragon Chamber.

To James's horror, the snake-head he had formed bit down on Mendel's scales.

"No... I..." James's chest was filling up with fluid as he turned towards Helen. She was staring at the tunnel where the Inubians had fallen.

Something moved between the Inubians. There was a flash of light.

As Elcar and Elandria edged onto their respective plinths, Dendralon clutched his throat. A beam of blue light spread down from his grappling hands and threw him backwards. His eyes rolled in agony and then froze in the direction of Cathy before he roared out, "Cha ner tag!"

He disappeared and Tealfirth exploded.

A powerful azure beam instantly joined the blinding lights that now emanated from Elcar and Elandria. Someone had taken James's place on the third plinth.

He stared up at the roof of the dragon chamber as the three colours merged into one radiant burst of white. This time James knew the combined powers had to work. The sound of the exploding sun soon faded into a single, heavenly note that transcended everything. It rose, like the trumpet sound of an angel, until all other sound and energy ceased. The ground shuddered and his head filled with a mass of pictures and lights until the vision settled on the figure of a great grey dragon. Bigger than the sun, it closed its massive wings round an exploding star. The light became so bright that James's head almost burst with the sensation. He couldn't look away. He couldn't bear it.

"James?"

Everything went as black as night until, slowly, one by one, the stars flickered back on to fill the firmament. He took in a sharp breath and opened his eyes.

"James?"

"What...? Who is it?"

Again, he felt a small, cold hand touch his ankle. "What?"

There, right beside him, was the unmistakable figure of Eethan Magichand. Still shimmering with blue lights that traced his damp skin, Eethan smiled broadly, his black, needle-like teeth glimmering in the half-light.

"But you were..."

"Dead? Yees ee was. But dragon tears are very mageecal. Can bring ee back to life, eef they are tears for you."

"Whindril's tears..." James gasped, suddenly remembering what happened before the explosion of Tealfirth.

The small, golden fish lay completely still. Mendel's magic scales seemed dull and lifeless. A gel-like substance leaked out from his gills.

"Salt!" snapped Cathy.

Helen knelt up. "Mrs. Peck, Eethan's alive!"

"Never mind that. We need to get Mendel into salt water," said Cathy.

Craig sprung to his feet. "And where are we going to get salt water in the next few seconds?"

"Ees under your armies," said Eethan, pointing at Cathy. "You ees sweating, aren't you?"

Cathy Peck drew him a withering glance. "How dare you? You little..."

James felt the crushing sensation in his chest subside. "Mum, Eethan's right. It's salt."

"Amongst other things," added Craig, his face concentrated in a frown of disgust.

James lifted the flaccid little goldfish and placed him in a cold, clear puddle of water. Eethan traced his armpits and then dipped his fingers into the puddle. He winked at Cathy. "Yous too, fine ladyeee!"

Cathy traced her bare arms and joined the blue man, crouching down at the edge of the water.

James looked across at the tunnel. He felt sure he'd seen something move. "Mum?"

"Shhh."

"But... Where's Dendralon?"

"We need more salt," screeched Cathy. "More armpits, here, now!"

Helen, Craig and James all began tracing their sweaty brows and arms, dipping their fingers into the puddle. As they performed this fairly ludicrous act, the worry about Mendel, Bero, his dad, his mum, and Dendralon all seemed to lump into one big heavy chunk of rock and press down on James. He recognised this sensation. The energy that always seemed to soar through him here on Denthan had suddenly disappeared. His arms became heavy, and a large tear spilled down his cheek. It plopped into the puddle. The surface rippled, distorting the image of Mendel into a dancing array of gold and yellow dots.

"Where has Dendralon gone?" asked Craig.

"I don't know," said James.

"He's gone. That's good enough for me," said Cathy. Her hazel eyes narrowed as she scanned the Dragon Chamber, suspiciously.

"I was sure ee killed heem," said Eethan. "Maybee ee wild aneemal has taken eem."

"Don't be so bloody stupid!" said Cathy.

Eethan flinched, instinctively.

James's breathing was now plainly audible to the whole gathering. A rattling wheeze that gurgled deep in his chest reminded him that he had much more to fear besides wizards and magic.

Cathy rounded on him. "Just calm down, James. That's enough!"

"And that's supposed to help him?" said Helen. "He's having an asthma attack, Mrs. Peck. Sit him up, undo his collar a bit. Where's his inhaler?"

"Now, look you..." She checked herself and then stood up, scanning for the green rucksack. "It's in his rucksack, on his back." She turned James round and rummaged in the rucksack. "Here, James. Stop making an exhibition of yourself!" Her words echoed round the huge chamber as James took in a deep blast from his inhaler.

Everyone edged back from the puddle where Mendel lay quite still.

"Are you okay, James?" said Craig.

"That helped," said James trying to regulate his breathing. "We're stuck in some kind of huge collapsing cave with the 'Lord of all Darkness' or whatever name he goes by these days, lurking in the shadows. I'm trying my best to remain calm, Mum."

"Yes, well…" Cathy eyed the inhaler. "Give me that." She pointed it down at Mendel and pressed down on the pump. A blast of white mist filtered over the goldfish.

"Mum!" coughed James. "It might…"

"It might," said Cathy, "but, then again, it might not."

Distractedly, Helen stared into the shadows. "Is Dendralon still here?" she asked.

"You mean heer new husband," interjected Eethan, staring up at Cathy.

Craig gulped. "He's probably some kind of undead zombie thing now, ready to pounce at any minute. No wonder James is wheezing like an old man."

James punched Craig in the side and widened his eyes. "Not helping!"

"Not sure what your mum's just done is going to help either," said Craig, helping James stick his inhaler back inside the green rucksack.

The goldfish-wizard remained motionless.

Craig followed Helen's stare. "Maybe Dendralon got covered in some Kraken blood one time. He must be immortal. What am I saying? He is immortal. He's never going to leave us alone." Craig stood up. "What if Dendralon can't die?"

"He can die."

Craig froze.

James peered round Craig to see who'd spoken.

Cathy raised the tips of her swords.

A tall, slim man stood over the puddle.

They all scurried back.

James had never seen this man before, but he was sure he recognised the voice. The man had a square jaw that was framed by a thick curtain of dazzling, white hair. He wore a long, indigo gown embroidered with a gold double helix that spiralled down the shiny material and then wove up round the cuffs and down round the hem.

As the air returned to his lungs, James asked, "Who are you?"

"Ees Mendel." Eethan beamed. "Ees my Mendel."

James and Craig stared at each other, mouths agape, before craning their necks to see if the goldfish they'd known for three years was still in the puddle.

"It's gone, boys." Mendel's face wrinkled into a warm smile. "The goldfish is gone."

"Can't say I'll miss him," mumbled Craig.

"Wait a minute," said Cathy. "How do we know that this isn't a trick? You could be Dendralon, for all we know."

"This could indeed be a trick, Cathy." Mendel's long fingers brushed the blue fabric of his gown. "Let's see… How can I prove to you that I am Mendel, once of forty-five Willow Terrace?"

"Dendralon could have known that," said Craig, taking a step back.

Helen nudged her brother in the ribs. "Shh."

Mendel beamed at Helen. "That's not going to help persuade him, Helen. Here, let me show you." He took several steps towards Craig and then cuffed him round the ear.

"Awch!" Craig yelped. "I wish people would stop hurting me."

"Gormless guppy, indeed. You need some lessons in etiquette, my friend. And…" Craig winced, expecting another clout, "…when I take the time to tell you the full scientific name of a very rare creature, pay attention!"

Craig formed a doleful expression and nodded, "It's him, all right."

Mendel rounded on Cathy Peck. James sensed that his mum had enjoyed Craig's slap, but he could see her bracing herself for a fight.

"Beldam, Queen of Artilis, mother of James and wife of David. A more courageous and honest woman I have never met." Mendel stretched out his hand.

"You forgot beautiful, patient, and resourceful," whispered Cathy, sternly. "And you can keep your *friendly* handshake. I think I preferred you as a fish."

"Ah," mused Mendel, "I should have expected no less."

"All you've ever done is lead everyone who has ever helped you into danger and death," she whispered.

"For which I am truly sorry, Cathy. Now, let's look on the bright side." Mendel opened his arms and stared up at the ceiling of the Dragon Chamber. The golden-stitched double helix on his gown began to move as an unexpected breeze rustled along the floor of the Dragon Chamber. The huge spikes that formed the roof slid apart, like a giant zipper, all the way down to ground level. Soon, the whole area they stood upon was open to the elements. The landscape of Denthan stretched out before them in all directions. It was plain now, in the yellow light thrown down by Zalion, the one remaining sun, that Elandria and Elcar were petrified just like Bero and the Inubians.

Mendel clasped his hands and solemnly bowed his head, firstly towards Elcar and then Elandria. "They will remain as such until some other race in some other time requires their help."

"That's a bit harsh," said Craig.

James cleared his throat and, in as manly a voice as he could muster, said, "And could you not set them free?"

"I could," answered Mendel, "but I'm not going to. They knew the consequences of their sacrifice."

"I suppose that Elandria will be happy enough," said Craig, sarcastically. "Not quite an honourable death, but close."

"Worse, if you ask me," barked Helen. "It's just horrible."

"And Bero?" pressed Craig. "I mean, that was technically your fault."

"Ah," mused Mendel. He circled the stone effigy that was Bero. "A true stalwart. Never complained once in three years."

"Well?" urged Helen.

"Musclama!" said Mendel.

A flash of bubbles erupted from a purple cloud above the golden retriever's head and then floated down. As each bubble burst on the dog's petrified coat, it transmogrified the area back into flesh and fur.

"Impressive," said James.

"Less restricted now," said Mendel. "I can be a little more flamboyant."

"You really did it, Mendel. You saved a whole world," said James.

"We *all* saved Denthan," said Mendel. "All of us."

Cathy had turned her attention to the world outside. Now that the huge dragon-spines had receded and the rock had slipped away around them, they were, in effect, standing on a large marble-clad plateau. She was already looking south towards the forest of Eldane and the hazy spires of Gwendral. A black mass of shadow seemed to surround the city.

"We all performed brilliantly, in every way." Mendel beamed.

"Self-praise is no praise," said Cathy, her eyes still fixed on the scene in the distance. "So the Gwendral we came here in has gone and we are now all back in the old Gwendral? The one that's surrounded by about fifty thousand Hedra?"

"We are here," said Mendel. "Our old selves are also back in that city you can see, but as we near, so they will fade and we will become more defined."

"And what about Wee Joe and Jean and...?"

"They are as we are now, only they are there, not here."

"I'm completely lost," said Craig, "so don't even bother to explain another thing."

Mendel walked forward and took in the scene below. "There are still some matters to put right."

"I'll say," whispered Cathy. "How do we get back home to Drumfintley? Where is David, and the rest of the crew? And..." she turned to the spot where Dendralon had stood minutes before, "Where has *he* gone?"

"Always so many questions at once, Cathy." Mendel teased his bristled chin with a wrinkled thumb and forefinger. "Dendralon? Not sure. Not entirely sure where *he* is."

"Not good enough!" snapped Cathy.

"No, probably not. Still..." He grinned. "A trillion souls, eh? Not a bad day's work." He patted Bero on the head and marched out to the perimeter of the Dragon Chamber.

James followed the tall wizard.

"David and the others should still have three years worth of memories." Mendel screwed up his eyes and pointed down towards a distant ridge next to the Gortan Sea.

James screwed up his eyes in disbelief. "If that's the old Gwendral, where did the other one go again?"

Mendel muttered to himself. "More questions. My, my... Right, well... It seems that part of the Nestler Theory was inaccurate."

"What part?" growled Cathy.

Mendel paced the marble floor. "Obviously, there can't be two Gwendrals... Can't be two of us... there's been a terra... A terrashift!"

Cathy's face was puce. "Will you stop talking mince!"

"Mince?" enquired Mendel.

"Garbage, rubbish, gobbledegook!" she blasted.

"I'm just trying to figure a few things out. You see, a terrashift is when the world adjusts to compensate for the impossibility of two people or places existing at one time in the one place," explained Mendel.

James began to nod knowingly, but Craig shot him a look that said 'yeh, right, liar', and he stopped.

"It's a kind of blend. A blend of realities that makes final sense of the one situation," Mendel finished.

"Are you saying that there is only one Gwendral now?" asked Helen.

"Yes, Helen. Spot on, my dear."

Craig sighed. "So, presuming that my mum, Wee Joe, and Mr. Peck survived long enough, until the sun exploded, they should be in the old citadel with the Hedra outside." He caught his breath. "What about the Racnids and stuff?"

"The Racnids will be back in Artilis. But I must say, well done, Craig. That was a good summation. Not as daft as you look."

"Gee thanks," muttered Craig.

"What will you do about the Hedra? How will we get off this mountain? How are we going to get back to Gwendral?"

"Right, Cathy. Let me have a moment. You see, I'm hoping for a bit of help in all those directions."

James thought that Mendel seemed more confident all of a sudden. Less blasé and lost in thought. He watched the wizard close his weird, white-slit eyes and say, "Ta che led anith, Whindril." He repeated this chant over and over. "Ta che led nith, Whindril."

As Eethan joined in the chant, James scanned the edge of what remained of the Dragon Chamber for any sign of the white dragon.

"If you're looking for Whindril, you're wasting your time. She's dead," said Craig, "crushed under the weight of the mountain. We all saw it."

Mendel put a finger to his lips to signal quiet.

Craig shrugged his shoulders.

James tried not to think about his asthma and waited.

A rumble deep below their feet followed by a crack and an ominous grinding sound caused them all to brace. To his left and then to his right, James noticed a shimmering wall of air rise up from the edge of the huge Dragon Chamber. Higher and higher it grew until the topmost rim of the wall arced over and joined together. Zalion, the remaining sun of Denthan, wavered behind the curtain of vibrating air. Like heat-haze on a hot tar road, everything became distorted.

Bang!

They all gasped.

In the silence that followed, James edged closer to Mendel. "What's going on?" he whispered.

"Didn't expect this," said Mendel. "I fear there may still be some after effects of the Nestler Theory at play here. Then again, I'm trying to remember. It was so long ago." Mendel paced the floor, deep in thought. "Chant never worked… Or…or has it? Eethan is still repeating the correct words. It should work but…"

James edged closer to the wavering shield and peered down at the spot where Gwendral had been. "Mendel, the Nestler Theory is wrong; the Gwendral we arrived here in has gone and we are not back in the original Gwendral surrounded by Hedra either."

"Will everyone stop talking about this Gwendral or that Gwendral? It all gets very confusing. Just admit it, Mendel. You got it wrong," said Cathy.

Mendel opened one eye. "Not completely wrong, Dark Queen."

"I am not a…" Cathy searched for the right words, "Dark, bloomin' Queen."

Ignoring her, Mendel paced about, tapping his chin and anxiously surveying the scene. "The Dragon Chamber has kept us in place, but everyone else will have been moved back to where they were the moment Tealfirth exploded and…"

Bang!

The whole mountain beneath them began to crack open.

"Eee, just like before Mendeeeeel!" screeched Eethan.

"At last," said Mendel. He moved them all back from where they were standing as an ever-widening crack split the chamber floor. "Eethan is right. You are all about to witness a phenomenon that only happens every ten-thousand years!"

"Thee dragons weel bee reeebrorn!" Eethan slapped his thigh, like a pantomime pirate and danced about excitedly amidst the chaos.

With another lurch of stone, they were all thrown on their backs. The rock split even wider apart.

The first thing to slither free from the massive crack in the floor was a huge white creature. Snake-like in appearance, it glistened in the wobbly light, its wet wings folded close against its sides. Another followed, greyish in colour and a good forty-feet long; it was slightly smaller than the first. Still more belched forth from the deep hole in the Dragon Chamber, writhing and wriggling over each other like a mass of squirming worms in a jar. James sat up and found Craig's shirt. He tugged it and pointed into the tangled mass of scales. "Look! There's black smoke coming from their jaws." The creatures hissed and snapped at each other as they unfolded their slimy wings and craned their serpentine necks.

Bero began an incessant barking that seemed to annoy the creatures intensely.

"Can't you shut that mutt up?" shouted Cathy.

Craig found Bero's tail and traced the dog's spine with his fingers until he knelt next to his dog's muzzle. "Shhh, boy. It's okay. Don't listen to the nasty lady."

James caught hold of Mendel's gown. "Is this supposed to happen?"

Mendel was about to put a silencing finger to his lips but faltered before it reached his chin. "This bit? Yes, James. I didn't quite expect all this at once, though. A group emergence on this scale is very unusual."

"So this is the help you expected?" pressed James.

"Yes... Watch out," yelled Mendel.

They all staggered back from a particularly big serpent that shook its neck and splattered them with heavy blobs of clear jelly.

"Yuk!" screeched Craig, slipping on the gloopy mess.

The huge creature, that had just covered them in slime, shook its head again until a dazzling, white mane sprung open behind its slit-like ears. Its wings stretched out to their full one-hundred-foot expanse. Then, with a deafening screech, it meticulously folded them behind its ridged back. It then began to purr and yelp, excitedly, licking its scaly talons like an overgrown kitten until tufts of thick fur sprung free of its massive claws. This was the first of the creatures to really look like a fully formed dragon. James cowered as it threw its head back and roared. "Sshhhaaaaar!"

Nervously clutching their spears, swords, and staffs, James's group moved back a little further.

Bero continued to bark manically.

A blast of blue fire gushed from the dragon's mouth while, behind this, another twenty or so dragons followed suit. The air was roasting hot and sweat was lashing down James's face. "I can't breathe." He gasped.

"Don't worry, James, it will soon stop," said Mendel. He raised his staff and walked toward the white dragon.

The air stank of doused matches.

Mendel stopped beneath the towering beast, completely unprotected. "Tan teth, Mendel. Ech la ti, Whindril?"

Helen tugged on James's sleeve. "It that Whindril?"

Thud!

The dragon stamped down with its massively taloned foot.

"Not good!" Craig called out.

"Get further back," James urged.

"Tath ma, Mendel!" Mendel's hands were outspread and his head remained bowed.

The white dragon, however, only seemed to become more irritated.

"Tath ma, Eethan!" yelled Eethan, his scrawny, high-pitched voice cutting through the increasing din of dragon roars and blasts of flame.

The dragons that saw Eethan all roared and began lurching and snapping down at the little blue man with his ridiculous shock of snow-white hair.

Whindril, though, seemed to recognise Eethan. She turned on her kin and roared louder than any of them, sending a jet of bright blue flame over their heads. "Ssraaaaarr!"

The other newly-born dragons huddled submissively and moved back en masse.

Whindril's head, about the same size as James's mum's Volkswagen Polo, spiralled down until it was level with Eethan.

He's within easy biting distance, thought James.

Helen called out, "Be careful, Eethan!" She crouched low beside Bero and Craig. She twirled Bero's soft fur between her fingers.

Eethan glanced back at Helen and winked before moving even closer to the dragon's menacing jaws. Whindril's see-through fangs dripped a blue-tinged liquid that splashed onto the cracked marble floor.

They all screamed out, as Whindril's jaws snapped tight. "NO!"

She flicked Eethan up into the air, slid her head beneath him and then waited, as the little blue man somersaulted above her.

Eethan screamed and then landed with a jolt, his legs flopping at either side of Whindril's long, scaly neck. He gripped onto a tuft of fur and held on like a rodeo star.

"Whoof!" Bero barked up at Eethan as he waved down at them all, his weird little face set in a manic smile.

The rest of the dragons looked on for a few moments before, one by one, they moved forward and lowered their heads in submission to Whindril and Eethan.

Mendel began matching different dragons to the people in the group. "Cathy and Bero. I believe this dragon is called, Rusufia."

James watched in anticipation as a stocky, red dragon waddled forward and lowered its neck alongside his mum and Bero.

"There are no seats fixed to these dragons yet, so you will have to tie yourselves on using the long hairs on their backs. Straddle the base of the neck and hold on tightly," said Mendel.

"Cool!" said Craig, his face beaming with delight.

"What?" exclaimed Cathy. "How the heck is Bero supposed to stay on this thing?"

Mendel twisted his hand and said the word, "Mergaria!" Unbelievably, the red dragon's long hairs snaked down and lifted firstly Cathy and then a very bemused Bero up onto its nape. The hairs, as thick as hosepipes, then wrapped round their legs and held them tight.

Mendel smiled across at Eethan. "We are going to liberate Gwendral for a second time, my friend."

"Mendel, ees good to be back beside ee en your normal form," said Eethan.

Helen sat with Craig on a dragon as black as a starless night, while James fumbled with the rough hairs on the creature next to his mother's red beast. *His* dragon had elaborate, blue-tinged hooks at the tips of its wings and a thick mane of living snake-heads. These, James found very disconcerting, especially when they snapped at his fingers every time he tried to hold on. "Mendel... I think I got on the wrong one," he broached, panic washing over him. He saw, however, that everyone else was staring at the shimmering curtain of air that surrounded the huge chamber. It was melting away bit by bit. Soon the cool breeze from outside ruffled their clothes and made them shiver. The dragons jostled for position and began baying at the sky.

"Onward to Gwendral!" shouted Mendel.

All the dragons flapped up into the air except James's blue dragon, which circled and whined. "Come on boy. Hup!" pleaded James. He saw the other dragons gaining height. "Please!" He kicked his heels in but quickly thought better of it when the mane of snakes began spitting at him. "Sorry," he wailed. The grumpy-looking dragon curved its head round and snapped its jaws shut a few feet above his head. "Mendel? Help!"

Whindril veered back and hovered above the blue dragon. Mendel and Eethan peered down at him.

"It's not doing what it's being told," shouted James.

"Ah," said Mendel. "Some dragons need to be asked properly."

"And it's got these," added James, pointing gingerly at the writhing snake mane.

"Very rare," acknowledged Mendel. "The word you should use is, 'tethna'. It's like saying 'please' in dragon tongue. Not quite the same but…"

"Okay," snapped James, "I get the drift." He looked up at the menacing face of the blue dragon and said, "Tethna." He motioned with his arms for the dragon to flap up into the air.

The blue dragon sneezed a noxious spray of blue slime over his face and stretched its wings. With a jolt, James was airborne and was soon soaring up towards Craig and Helen.

Craig nudged Helen, giggling as James came alongside.

"Hardie har har!" said James, wiping the grot from his face.

Whindril edged in closer as they gained height. "It's not that unusual," said Mendel. "Most creatures appreciate it hugely if you at least try to speak their tongue."

"No one else tried," said James.

"Some dragons are more moody than others," shouted Mendel.

"Just my luck," moaned James, still unsure of the snake-heads.

Mendel's voice found its way into his thoughts, "Your dragon is called Zurala."

James repeated the dragon's name and continued to pat her neck while struggling to remain onboard. The mane of snakes now nuzzled round his arms. They weaved in behind his elbows and round his back, holding him in place. *Just as well*, thought James, as the dragon made a series of elaborate acrobatics that would have thrown him off, otherwise. After a while, Zurala, seemed to calm down. She sailed to the fore and beat her wings in a more rhythmic fashion, long slow strokes replacing the erratic jolts and jerks that had almost thrown him off. As James began to relax a sense of exhilaration replaced his fear. His spine tingled with something that felt like electricity. "Yes, yes, yes!" he yelled.

* * *

Blinking awake in the highest citadel of Gwendral, Wee Joe looked down at his stomach. He was frightened he would see a mess, but he was fine. Then he became confused. The Racnid above him was gone. He knelt up and looked around.

Outside, up in the sky, red streaks like firework trails arced across a deep blue sky. The angry blood-coloured sun had disappeared. Wee Joe wondered where it had gone. Weirder still, the black curtain that had been ripped down by the Racnid queen, Elhada, had returned to the balcony. It swished as a blast of hot air rushed through the Council chamber.

As he crawled over to his mum, he heard a series of echoed grunts and yelps from outside. Soon, however, a steady jumble of hisses and roars began to build until the air was full of the sound of a great army. Wee Joe shook his mum. "Wake up, Mum." He was suddenly in one of his worst nightmares. The war-drums and hissing cries were unmistakable. These were the sounds of the snake-men, the Hedra.

CHAPTER TWENTY

THE RETURN

With a crack like thunder the wizard, Dendralon, stood amongst the raucous screams of his kin. Moments before, he'd found himself falling into an abyss, but he had homed in on the Plain of Gwendral. Relieved that his magic had worked, he threw back his head and roared louder than any other beast on the battlefield. All other sounds soon died away. The drums stopped beating and the Hedra charioteers reined in their Raptor steeds. All eyes were on him, Dendralon, their dark wizard. The Hedra army, an array of tall, reptilian beasts decked in armour, soon quietened. Their light grey scales reflected the new purple hue of the Denthan sky.

Dendralon raised his staff and began to whisper a charm. Around him, the Hedra, direct descendants of the ancient Saurs that walked the planet so long ago, picked up their weapons and began to clatter their swords and spears against the black steel of their shields. Like the Inubians he had trained on Artilis, these creatures also pounded out a thunderous rhythm, a terrible warning of their deadly intent. Saved from obliteration, fifty thousand Hedra, gathered round the city walls of Gwendral, awaited Dendralon's command. To the Hedra, it had been two minutes, not two years that had passed since the disappearance of their second sun. Dendralon shot a stream of fire from his gnarled staff and all sound died away. He had their attention.

A huge cheer shook the walls of Gwendral and echoed out across the Plain of Gwendral. Dendralon closed his eyes and took a deep breath of fresh Denthan air.

Excellent, he thought, *Mendel has saved Denthan after all.* He had endured no burns or wounds this time, and he could still conquer Gwendral and reclaim his bride. He had the whole Hedra army at his disposal. Mendel had, unwittingly, put him in the perfect position to realise all his aspirations.

He opened his eyes and pointed up at the sky with his staff. "The Manimal sun shines no more in the Denthan sky. Zalion, the true light of Denthan, signals the beginning of a new Hedra age."

Another cheer went up.

"Gwendral shall be reclaimed today. The true founders, the master craftsmen, the *only* Denthan race fit to rule will sit on the ivory throne once more. I chose to assume Hedra form many thousands of years ago. I chose strength, I chose intelligence, and I chose the right to live forever within this skin of scales. We are the true masters of this world, and of many more, as yet unknown to you. We will begin with Gwendral and then move on to other conquests and kingdoms!"

Amongst the roars he surveyed the chaotic state of the Hedra army and gave the orders to fall back one thousand yards. He found eighteen captains and gathered them together. "Who is in charge of the Raptor charioteers?"

A stout Hedra with a pug nose and dullish grey scales stepped forward. He wore the green and black armour of the charioteers.

Dendralon found a patch of dry earth and began to draw out his plans. "Split the chariots into two ranks. Form two crescents, here and here, at the outer edges of the infantry." Dendralon marked out his meaning using a shard of bone. He eyed the captain of the archers. "You will lead your men to the fore of the army. In two lines, five-thousand feet long, you will lay fire on the walls either side of the gates." Dendralon sighed, wishing he had the luxury of a Racnid attack. Scaling walls was no problem for the Artilian spiders. He would adapt. "Charioteer, what is your name?"

"Relfarth, Sire." He bowed.

"Un-hitch the right-hand Raptor from every chariot. They will attack when our archers fire their last volley."

"But…"

"Silence! The remaining steeds can still pull the chariots while the unleashed beasts scale the smooth walls. Can this be done?"

Relfarth lowered his eyes. "With ease, Sire. With ease."

Dendralon raised his hand and scanned the infantry. "I need a Hedra soldier to ride bareback on every free Raptor that scales the walls."

"They have not been trained…" began Relfarth.

"A good soldier will learn quickly. Once over the walls, they will fight their way through the Manimals and open the gates for the rest of the army." Dendralon sighed heavily. "I can't believe I have to take this city all over again!"

Relfarth looked confused.

"How many Hedra do we have left in total?" asked Dendralon.

The captains looked at each other for confirmation but came to the conclusion that there were near to fifty-five thousand souls in all, including five hundred charioteers and three thousand archers.

"Very well…" He counted eighteen captains. "Take three thousand Hedra each. You ten will pour in through the gates and rush the main citadel." He looked at the other eight captains. "The rest of you will hold your divisions outside the city until I command. There may be an attack from the hills beyond Eldane, so you will form a circle that is vigilant in all directions."

"What other force is this, Dendralon?" asked Relfarth.

"Prepare the dragon-killers."

The eight captains fell silent and looked up into the cobalt sky.

"You have twenty minutes," said Dendralon. He followed their gaze. The sky looked like a deep blue sea cut by a thousand crimson scars, the remains of Tealfirth, he suspected. He needed the Hedra to fight well until he regained his strength. He'd summoned enough magic from his staff to escape the Dragon Chamber, pull free of the vision-pool, where he had fallen two years before, and rejoin his Hedra force on the Plain of Gwendral. The extreme energy required for full transference, however, had weakened him. *Had the magic of the Dragon Chamber brought Mendel back to his original form?* He could feel his brother's presence stronger than ever. And there was something else… He looked to the northeast and the mountains of Hest. If there had been an emergence, the dragons would come soon.

* * *

Everyone was now fully awake inside the Council chamber of the citadel. Cimerato began to see Yeltans streaming in through the shattered chamber doors.

"Almost eight-hundred kin," murmured Garlon, the Yeltan leader. No more than three feet tall, his complexion was bright yellow, his eyes a powder blue and his clothes a blend of grubby greens and browns. "The city is back in its original position," he said.

"It would seem so," said Cimerato. He knelt up, his face twisted in concern. "That sound is unmistakable."

"Hedra," confirmed Garlon.

Michael edged in beside them and adjusted his dog-collar. "We've all aged over the last few years," he traced the few remaining wisps of hair that protruded from his temples, "but we appear to be back at the point where we all disappeared the first time."

"The city is back in place," said Cimerato. "I'm not sure that the people are. For example, there's no sign of James or Mendel."

"No..." Michael considered.

"Or my father, Landris," said Garlon. He peered out of an arrow-slit and waved down to a Yeltan who was signalling back using a polished mirror. "He is not in the gatehouse, where he fell two years ago."

"Mendel said that those who had departed before or after the explosion would remain... Well, departed," said Ephie.

"My father was killed just prior to the death of Denthan." Garlon looked frustrated and bitterly disappointed.

"I... I don't know all the answers," whispered Ephie.

"None of us do," said Cimerato. "It is only natural that Garlon would hope that his father could be saved." *There would be a small, irrational voice in the Yeltan's head that hoped for a miracle,* thought Cimerato. He spied a Manimal he knew well. "Elgry!"

Elgry scraped and bowed as he approached the tall form of Cimerato. He looked confused. "We were all on Ebos and then, all of a sudden, we were back in the tunnels that lead to Nordengate. We were..."

"Back where you were the moment Denthan exploded the first time?"

"Just about," replied Elgry.

"No sign of the Manimals we lost in the tunnels three years ago?" Cimerato paused, suddenly embarrassed by the ridiculousness of the question.

Elgry gave a simple shake of his head. "No sign." He looked across at the balcony and followed Cimerato. "Others have tried to find loved ones who have perished since our last escape but..."

"It would seem that Mendel's theory is correct," said Cimerato. "Those who died before or after the exact moment of destruction will remain dead."

On the balcony, they stared out over the Plain of Gwendral at the gathered Hedra force.

"Mendel may have played into their hands," said Cimerato. "What if he has saved Denthan at the expense of Gwendral? This Hedra force is larger than we can cope with."

Michael loosened his collar. He shook his head mournfully. "May the Lord bless us and preserve us."

Cimerato turned from the conversation as the curtain flicked open again. He ruffled Wee Joe's hair but got a kick in the shins for his trouble.

Cimerato laughed.

Wee Joe tugged his sleeve. "The balcony is all fixed again?"

"Yes, little fighter."

"And the holes is all fixed in the walls too," added Wee Joe.

Cimerato surveyed the scene inside and outside the city of Gwendral.

Wee Joe stretched a tentative toe out to test the sturdiness of the balcony. "It was good that the spider things and the dog-men disappeared, wasn't it?"

"It was indeed, little fighter, but we still have that lot to deal with." He pointed out across the Plain of Gwendral at the massed army of Hedra. "And I don't like the way they're beginning to organise themselves."

Jean Harrison couldn't contain her relief. "Thank God, Mendel managed it." She looked down on the Hedra. "I don't care how bad you think it is now, it's still a million times better than it was a few moments ago. What with you all tied up and Wee Joe..."

"We will have to fight again, won't we?" said Ephie, in a solemn voice. She took Wee Joe's hand and leaned against the balustrade.

"It looks like it." Cimerato whisked open the velvet curtain and stepped back into the Council chamber. He spied Jal.

"Have you seen what's happening?" said Jal.

"What do you mean?" asked Cimerato.

"My kin, the Hedra, are splitting the raptors away from the chariots! There are fools out there trying to ride the damn things." Jal clutched his stomach and then examined his fingers.

"And…?" said Cimerato.

"They will try and use the Raptors to scale the walls."

"Garlon," said Cimerato, "take your Yeltan kin down there and use your spears on anything that tries to scale the city walls."

"The Hedra infantry are splitting into legions," said Jal. His Hedra tongue flicked in and out of his serrated teeth.

"And the Yukplugs?" added Garlon.

Cimerato considered the ancient, single-horned Yeltan steeds. "Keep them in the courtyard. If any Raptors do make it over the walls, the Yukplug cavalry will have to pick them off."

"Come!" Garlon signalled his soldiers back down the spiral staircase of the citadel.

"Elgry!" shouted Cimerato.

The Manimal secretary had just found his wife and seven-year-old son, Davado. "Yes, I am counting…" He fumbled with a pile of papers and pens.

"Cimerato, we have close to five thousand able fighters."

Cimerato drew his long, curved sword. "Take three thousand and line the city walls."

"And the other two thousand?" pressed Elgry.

Cimerato pondered for a moment. "Form two cohorts in the courtyard behind the main gates."

Elgry looked puzzled.

"They are coming with me," said Cimerato.

"With you? But your shoulder?" said Elgry. He glanced at Jal and then at Wee Joe. The boy had found a large, crumpled heap of matted orange fur.

"The Mertol is in here," whispered Wee Joe.

"I know," Cimerato whispered back. "If the beast is anything like Jal and myself, the wounds it received before the first explosion, two years ago, will have healed."

"This is all very confusing," said Michael. "We're back at the positions we were two years ago but we've aged and remember everything that has happened in between. Not only that, but you've returned without the wounds you received back then."

"My stomach wound healed in a matter of seconds," said Jal.

"Time is putting things right," said Wee Joe. He now stood with the lumbering figure of the Mertol, clutching its taloned hand. The pits in its cheeks opened and closed in undulating waves.

"Well, why are James and the rest of them not back here then?" said Michael.

"And why am I here and not back in Drumfintley?" said David Peck.

Cimerato eyed the Peck boy's father thoughtfully before saying, "Strange, indeed." He frowned as he turned to stare at the Hedra on the plain. "Where is Dendralon?"

The Mertol became agitated at the mention of the dark wizard's name and let out a mournful cry. "Bak!"

Everyone in the chamber gripped the hilts of their swords. The fifteen-foot magical creature still made everyone very nervous.

Cimerato stared hard at David Peck. "Why *are* you here?"

David Peck shrugged his shoulders.

"Mmm..." For a moment, Cimerato wondered if the Peck man might be Dendralon in yet another disguise. "Not big enough..." he muttered.

"Pardon," said David.

"Nothing," said Cimerato, "Just a thought. We'll need to ask Mendel some of these questions when he returns."

"If he returns," hissed Jal.

Jean Harrison had found some grapes and was trying to persuade Wee Joe to try a few.

"Yuk!" he spat.

"Bak!" said the Mertol, its own face mirroring Wee Joe's expression of disgust.

"We can only presume that Mendel's plan worked. Denthan has been saved," said Jean.

"He may have saved Denthan, but who has he saved it for?" said Cimerato. "The Hedra are regrouping and they seem better organised than before."

Manimals and Yeltans teamed up the stairs that led to the battlements and palisades.

Wee Joe looked from the citadel in the direction of the distant Mountains of Hest. "Hurry up, James. Hurry up, Craig."

"We need Mendel back here now," said Cimerato. "We can only hold that army at bay for so long."

CHAPTER TWENTY-ONE

THE LAST STAND

Although it wasn't the first time James had ridden on a Denthan dragon, it was the first time he'd done so bareback. His short-lived feeling of excitement and energy was beginning to ebb away. To his dismay, anxiety and panic were slowly taking its place again.

With no ornate saddle to snuggle into, he clung to Zurala with every ounce of his strength. The tentacle-like mane of snake-heads weaved round him every time she dived or banked hard. They seemed to hold him fast but he just couldn't relax. He felt the blue dragon scales move over each other as Zurala stretched her neck or changed direction. The ground below looked dangerously far away.

"Stay calm, James," urged Mendel.

"I can still hear you in my head," said James.

"Of course you can," said Mendel.

James found the familiar voice of the wizard comforting. He took a deep breath and tried to relax.

"Everyone!" yelled Mendel. "We need the element of surprise." He pulled Whindril to the fore of the dragons and edged up from his position. His blue robes fluttered in the warm Denthan wind, and his long, white hair whisked out behind him. "Follow me. We will keep low behind the cover of the low mountains ahead until we reach the Forest of Eldane. There we will use the thermals and climb high to gain the speed we need for the maximum impact."

"Impact?" James knew his voice had sounded sheepish.

"Weh hey!" yelped Craig.

James was close enough to see Helen dig her brother in the ribs.

The dragons dipped down behind the cover of Nordengate, skimming silver rivers and banking round grassy slopes. Flying as one, they caused the bushes and trees to bend before them. James glanced across at his mum and was, for a few moments, incredibly proud of her. Still dressed like an Artilian Queen, she looked every inch the warrior on her red dragon. Bero's head rested on her lap, his furry legs and body bound by the crimson strands of the dragon's mane. James noticed, for the first time, that her black, silky hair was longer than he remembered. He thought that her face had altered somewhat too; it was more steely and noble; more resolute and less out of control. She'd always been like a bomb ready to go off, back in Drumfintley. In fact, she'd been a bit like that everywhere. He wondered if she'd ever calm down and become, well, normal.

"Uh!" His stomach jerked upwards as Zurala dropped down a thousand foot cliff face, then, with two giant flaps of her indigo wings, rose above the rocks and rubble at its base. James had to concentrate very hard on not being sick.

* * *

From the gate tower, Cimerato could see that the Hedra archers had drawn back their bows. "Take cover!" He saw the Manimals in the courtyard join shields above their heads. The Yeltans pulled their Yukplug steeds in tight below the battlement walkways. On the battlements themselves, his own Manimal archers pressed their backs against the palisades and braced.

Whoosh!

Even from a thousand yards away, Cimerato heard the catgut of the Hedra bows snap as one.

A great cloud of black arrows reached their zenith and then, spinning slowly at first, fell.

The crackle of black arrowheads against the walls of Gwendral was deafening.

A few screams issued from the courtyard as a number of arrows found gaps in the Manimal shields.

"Close in tighter!" bellowed Cimerato.

A Yukplug bolted out in terror and was quickly felled.

Thankfully, less than a dozen Manimals teetered and fell forward from the battlements.

Cimerato listened for a second volley of arrows, but none came. Instead, he heard the ominous shrieks and screams of the Hedra Raptors. "Damn!" He turned to Garlon. "They will fire their second volley when we engage the Raptors. I've seen them do it before. Their arrows will harvest our fighters while the Raptors' tough hides protect them from harm."

"They may not use such tactics this time," said Garlon. "Look, they have riders."

Cimerato peered through an arrow-slit to see hundreds of the hideous creatures running, full pelt, towards them. Twice the height of any Manimal, the Raptors were partially feathered with long coloured plumes that trailed down from their scaly scalps. A single Hedra soldier gripped on precariously to each of their backs.

"The archers will not fire on their own Hedra riders," said Garlon.

"They will still fire," said Jal. He gasped as a wave of realisation washed over him. "I've seen them do this before."

"When have you seen them do this before?" asked Cimerato.

Jal hissed and exposed his needle-like teeth. "Dendralon is here."

Cimerato shook his head. "No, not again. He may have found us on Ebos, appeared through the shining arch, here on Denthan, but he died in the flames of Tealfirth the first time. Two years ago."

"I feel the dark wizard's presence too," said Garlon.

Jal pointed to the massed Hedra army. "The way they've rearranged themselves, the Raptor riders... He's back. I just know it"

"The riders have scythe-bows and Hedra short-swords," said Garlon. He addressed a hunched Yeltan with greying hair. "Take aim on the Raptors with our poison spears."

"Yes, Sir."The Yeltan relayed the instructions.

Cimerato ran a hundred yards along the city wall until he found the female Manimal called Herfala. "Sound the bell, Herfala. No firing until they are within fifty yards. I don't want to waste any arrows."

"Yes, but your father, Lord Eldane, has told us this already." Cimerato picked out his father down in the courtyard and waved down at him. Cimerato hesitated. "Good. Remember, our arrows will not harm the Raptors, take aim on the riders." He glanced again at his father. He didn't like to see the old man exposed to danger like this.

Herfala sounded a brass bell set into the palisade. Two beats for hold your fire and five more to indicate the yardage.

The Manimals drew their bows while the Yeltan spearmen filtered in beside them.

"Ready!" Cimerato raised his mailed fist. "Hold..."

The lead Raptor was almost at the wall.

"Fire!"

Three thousand arrows whistled out from the battlements followed by four hundred poison-tipped spears.

The screams of the Raptors echoed over the Manimals waiting in the courtyard.

Herfala reported back to Cimerato. "A third of the Raptors have fallen and many more have lost their Hedra riders."

"Fire at will!" bellowed Cimerato.

The Raptors screeched in delight as they dug their razor-sharp talons into the smooth city walls and began to climb.

"Pick as many off as you can, but be careful, the Hedra will fire another volley soon," yelled Cimerato. He snatched up a dead Yeltan's spear and threw it at the neck of an orange-plumed Raptor below him.

The spear sliced over the creature's crimson scales but nicked the animal enough to inject a little of the deadly Yeltan poison. With a mournful wail, the Raptor let go of the smooth wall and thumped onto the ground below.

Many of the Raptors with Hedra riders toppled as they advanced. Slower, they were easier to bring into aim. Only fifty or so Raptors, half with Hedra intact, made it to the battlements, their formidable jaws snapping as they neared the Manimal defenders.

"Here it comes!" said Cimerato.

The crack of several thousand catgut strings signalled another volley of arrows. This wave caught many more Manimals than the first. Some of the Hedra riders toppled, killed by their own side, but the Raptors, a few with Hedra intact, made it all the way to the battlements. The first to breach the top of the palisades was a scarred individual with a long, purple plume and green-tinged scales. It thudded heavily onto the walkway and kicked out with its prehensile claws. The Raptor's talons were much more deadly than its jaws, and three Manimals fell back into the courtyard, disembowelled. Four Yeltan spears found their mark, but as the Raptor toppled, another twenty took its place. Cimerato glanced up at the Drumfintley contingent on the balcony and saw, to his horror, that a further two Raptors were already scaling the alabaster walls of the citadel.

He twisted as a Hedra rider cut down at him. He used his heel to dig into the back of his assailant's knee as he turned.

Off balance, the Hedra gripped onto the palisade.

Cimerato jabbed upward with his yellow, Gwendralin blade but an indigo plumed Raptor bit his blade in two. Cimerato rolled to avoid the creature's deadly killing claws and toppled off the walkway.

"Uh!" Cimerato landed on a woolly Yukplug that yelped out and then bolted. He quickly found his feet and spied another Yeltan spear. He aimed as the Raptor leapt down towards him. Sweating profusely, he waited and then launched the spear. It juddered straight into the Raptor's mouth. The animal convulsed and tumbled, its long tail whipping round and taking his legs away. Winded, he lay on his back as the screams of battle intensified all around him. Another wave of Raptors jumped over the battlements and down into the courtyard. There, the Yeltan riders swung their Yukplugs round to attack. The Hedra riders, however, were nowhere to be seen. He edged up onto his elbows and then onto his knees.

The massive chains that held the city gates shut tight began to creak and groan.

* * *

"Cimerato's all right," said David. "He killed the Raptor with a Yeltan spear."

"What about all dose udder ones?" said Wee Joe.

Michael, Jean, Ephie and David all craned over the balustrade to see the smooth walls of the citadel below them. Four Raptors of various different colours were slowly, but methodically, making their way up the sheer alabaster walls.

David pulled back. "They'll never make it all the way up here. We must be more than three hundred feet up."

"Four hundred, actually," corrected Michael, "And they *will* make it all the way up. They did last time."

"Last time?" said David.

Wee Joe leered at David Peck. "Two years ago when yous were a…"

"That's enough, Joe," said Jean, sharply. She pulled him back from the balcony and turned to the adults. "We need to do something."

"You're right," said Ephie. "But What?"

"Knock 'em off," said Wee Joe. "Throw stuff at dem." He ran through his mum's legs and began firing his green water pistol in between the pillars of the balustrade.

Jean caught him by his belt and yanked him back again. "We'll do that. Keep back before I get mad at you."

"Wee's could use the smashed up chairs," Wee Joe added, wriggling free.

"We could," agreed Michael.

Thirty seconds later, David was the first to get a direct hit. "Yes!"

Wee Joe was next, landing a Raptor right between the eyes with a marble doorstop, knocking it back onto the courtyard.

As the battle raged below them, Michael knocked a third Raptor off the wall of the citadel. A brass lectern caught it square in the mouth and toppled it. "Forgive me, Lord. Oops, it's just hit a Yukplug."

"Oh, Michael, Garlon will be upset," said Ephie.

"Thanks Ephie, that's just made me feel ten times worse."

"Sorry, dear," said Ephie.

They couldn't find the fourth Raptor for a while, being particularly distracted by a horrific battle between an evil-looking, mounted Raptor and two Yukplugs in the courtyard.

"It's not TV we're watching here, you know," reminded Ephie.

"Over there," shouted David. He lifted a broken piece of masonry and launched it at a green-plumed Raptor barely fifteen feet below them. The stone whistled past its head and smacked into its tail. Off balance and taken by surprise, the Raptor screamed and fell backwards, turning head over heels several times before crashing into the fray.

"That beastie must av kiwled one of ours dat time," said Wee Joe, a hint of his big brother's smugness in his voice.

"I don't think so," protested Michael.

"No, it did. I seed the Yeltan get squished."

David lowered his head and sighed. "I…"

"You couldn't help it, David," said Jean. "And I know it's not TV, Ephie."

"I was just saying…"

"Well don't. So let that be the end of it," said Jean.

"I really don't like this," said Michael.

"None of us do," snapped Jean.

"There's another two monsters on the wall," said Wee Joe. "But they're coming up the other side, out of range," he added.

"Brilliant," said David, more than a hint of panic in his voice.

Wee Joe pointed down again. "Wook! The gates are opening."

"Some of the Hedra have got into the gate-towers," said Jean.

"No," said David. "It's Cimerato; *he's* opened the gates."

As soon as the gates were about twenty feet apart, the whole Hedra army began to advance. More than fifty thousand scaled warriors moved as one.

"Cimerato is leading our soldiers out the gates to meet them. Oh my God!" Michael clasped his hands and prayed. "Where is Mendel?"

David shook his head. "They're totally outnumbered. They've got no chance of…"

"There's always a chance," interrupted Jean. She hugged Wee Joe into her and scanned the walls of the citadel below them.

"Where are those Raptors?" said Ephie.

"Where is Cathy?" whispered David.

Everyone looked at David. Tight-lipped, they tried to hide their expressions of surprise.

"Oh, for Pete's sake," he barked. "She's not all that bad."

"Is," mumbled Wee Joe. He tugged his mum's skirt. "I thought she was married to de snake man now. You know Denra…"

"Not any more, Son. She's back on our side now. Isn't she, David?"

David walked round the balcony to its furthest northern edge and gazed across at the blue-tinged Mountains of Hest. "She always *was* on our side, Jean."

* * *

Dendralon raised his left hand and then his right. One after the other, the semi-circles of Hedra chariots raced in to fill the breach between the emerging Manimals and his frontline archers. "What is Cimerato doing?" he mused. "A few thousand Manimals and a bunch of raggedy Yeltans stand no chance against this force."

Something else puzzled him, though. *A distant cloud perhaps.* It wavered far beyond the Forest of Eldane. His reptilian nostrils opened wider and he closed his yellow cat-like eyes, deciding on his next course of action.

He looked westward from the Plain of Gwendral, towards the Gortan Sea. The waters were still and blue. He held his position and raised his gnarled staff. "Ah sth rath! Ah sth Rath! Hemiptera Vendi! Vendi!" His voice boomed out across the plain.

The Hedra around him edged back a little.

"HEMIPERTA VENDI!" he shouted.

More of the surrounding lines cowered away.

He spun round to face them. "Keep in rank and move forward." He flicked his reins and braced as his two Raptor steeds heaved his chariot forward. The scythes on the chariot's wheels spun faster and faster until they were a nigh invisible blur.

As soon as the Manimal force was out on the plain, the huge ivory gates began to swing shut behind them.

"What madness is this now?" cursed Dendralon. He urged his beasts on all the faster. Several Hedra fell screaming, cut down by his wheels as he veered out from the front ranks to join the charioteers on the right flank. "The Raptor riders have failed to keep the gates open," he shouted. "Keep a third of the archers back. Form a circle round the Manimals in front of the gates and pick them off!"

The remaining Hedra archers now performed their secondary duty. They ran closer to the city walls and knelt down. Every fourth Hedra archer in this group had a rope and a hook slung over his shoulder. They broke free of the ranks and raced at the city walls. Those that made it far enough threw up their grappling hooks and began to climb while those that remained kneeling fired at the battlements to provide cover.

The Manimals on the plain had formed a tight shield formation that made it almost impossible for any Hedra arrows to penetrate. "Enough!" roared Dendralon. "Charge!"

Dendralon smashed into the Manimals with such force that he almost reached Cimerato's position in the first few seconds. A Yukplug, however, lurched forward and skewered one of Dendralon's Raptors with its single horn. His chariot catapulted over the dead animal but Dendralon leapt free and joined the fight. The screams of battle drove him on, gave him an unquenchable lust for killing his foes, but every time he felled a Manimal or sliced a Yeltan in two, he glanced up at the skies or over toward the Gortan Sea. *Where are they?* He wondered. Still, he pushed on. His staff had transformed into an eight-foot long, two-handed sword and every creature on the plain soon made space round him in an effort to avoid its deadly arc. Once more, he caught sight of Cimerato through the fray. He pulled a nearby Hedra charioteer from his footplate and took its place, whipping the Raptor steed over the dead and wounded towards Cimerato. *Cut the head off this army and it will fold.*

Hedra archers were still firing up at the city walls while a division of infantry now took the dead archers' places and climbed up the hundreds of ropes they'd secured. A second division of the Hedra infantry, who had held back to let the chariots do their work, now encircled the dwindling Gwendralin force. Keeping a good hundred yards back from the battle, they launched spears into the fray at a safe distance.

Dendralon cut through another two Manimals before spinning his chariot round to face Cimerato. Smiling, he swung his huge sword round his head and cut down at the Gwendralin Lord.

Cimerato leaned back as the heavy blade whistled past his face with only inches to spare.

"Can't you stay dead, Dendralon?" shouted Cimerato.

Dendralon tapped his belt as he dismounted the chariot, his Raptor steed already battling two Yukplugs. "I have the seeds of life, my fated friend."

"Fated?" enquired Cimerato. He ducked to avoid a whirring scythe that had come free of a chariot wheel.

Dendralon cut the spinning scythe in two and pointed to the western gate tower. "Fated to die at my hand: the last of the Eldane line, the last Manimal heir."

Cimerato tensed beneath his yellow armour. "What do you mean?"

"Look for yourself. You are about to become the next Lord Eldane, albeit for only a few seconds."

"My father..." Cimerato glanced at the western battlements. Two Hedra warriors had scaled the trailing ropes and now held his father, Lord Eldane, over the edge of the wall. The old man kicked out and then fell.

"NO!" yelled Cimerato.

With amazing speed, Dendralon sliced Cimerato's sword from his hand and caught him by the throat. He pushed him down onto his knees. "Suddenly weak, my Lord?" mocked Dendralon. "Can't you move your arms or legs?" He jerked Cimerato's head down and pulled the Manimal helmet from Cimerato's head. Cimerato's neck was exposed. Dendralon raised his massive sword as his Hedra kept all the surrounding Manimals and Yeltans at bay. "Enough!" he yelled. "Drop your weapons!"

"Fight on!" wailed Cimerato. He squinted up at Dendralon.

"Look at your city," said Dendralon. "It is overrun and completely surrounded. I want you to see the Hedra take back that which is rightly theirs."

Cimerato looked totally beaten. The sounds of battle began to subside. "No!" he protested. "Fight on! Don't let them take the city!"

"Thousands scale your walls while thousands more wait their turn. A whole division of twenty thousand stand ready for the gates to open. Why were you so stupid? Why did you march these poor fools out here to die on the Plain of Gwendral?"

"Sssrrraaaaaaar!"

The deafening roar cut through the din of the battle.

"To give us more time," spat Cimerato.

Dendralon stepped back and looked up at the citadel. There, perched on the pinnacle, a mighty white dragon flapped its wings and roared out once more. The ground shook at his feet as a whole sky full of dragons roared in answer. A myriad of colours, the dragons soared down over the city walls, spewing fire onto his great army.

Cimerato toppled forward as the sword in Dendralon's hand merged back into wood. Dendralon glanced towards the shining Gortan Sea and smiled. There, amongst a great cloud of spray, an army of giant, water-walking insects raced towards the plain. His staff raised high, Dendralon continued to chant as the insects raced over the brown, sandy beaches and then took to the air in a deadly swarm.

The white dragon toppled off the citadel and opened its wings.

"Mendel!" cried Dendralon.

CHAPTER TWENTY-TWO

DRAGON ATTACK

Whindril swooped down along the city walls, her gargantuan talons scooping up every Hedra rope that hung down from the battlements. Blue fire belched from her open mouth, down over the closely-packed Hedra who screamed and bunched even tighter in their efforts to escape.

James hung on for dear life as Zurala followed Whindril's example, skimming dangerously, along the western wall.

To the rear of the Hedra army, the grey-scaled lizard-men struggled to wheel their giant crossbows in place. James knew these were a real danger to the dragons if they found their mark. He pulled Zurala up using a handful of writhing snake-heads as reins and made for the Hedra directly under the ridge at the far edge of the Plain. He would stop these war-machines if he could.

Zurala was almost ready to blast the siege weapons with a burst of flame when something big hit them from behind. The force of the impact tore him free of the snake-heads, and he frantically grappled for a secure hold. He shot a look behind him. *What was that?*

A flying insect, bigger than anything James had ever seen, even on Artilis, had locked onto Zurela's tail. The weight was pulling them down onto the gathered Hedra below. Their deadly, black arrows we-re aleady whizzing past his face.

"Zurala, fly higher!" he yelled.

James glanced back at their attacker. A long, spear-like tube was growing down from the insect's triangular head. It fluttered a pair of silver wings. A second pair, stiff, with black and orange stripes, bounced at an awkward angle. They were only feet from the ground now. Zurala could not cope with the extra weight and more and more Hedra were taking aim at them.

"Ugh!" James jumped clear as they hit the grassy plain. The giant insect had crawled up the dragon's back and jabbed down, between her wings, with its giant rostrum. He rolled away as Zurala roared and twisted her neck. She sent a burst of flame over her attacker's gossa-mer wings. James shuffled further back but jarred against something. A Hedra was looking down at him. The lizard-creature was about the same size and, he presumed, age as he was.

James tried to call on Firetongue but instead burst into a series of coughs and splutters. He rolled away and patted his pockets in an ef-fort to locate his inhaler.

Confused, the Hedra boy ran back to a rickety cart and lifted a black axe from a pile of rags.

Zurala gave one more scream and then fell limply to the ground. Dust bellowed up around her as a hideous sucking sound ensued. The giant insect, long-legged and glistening in the sunlight, proceeded to suck out the dragon's innards through its giant straw-like rostrum.

James's chest tightened. *The air is thinner in Denthan now… More like Drumfintley… My lungs feel too small… My asthma might kill me if I don't calm down.*

The Hedra boy circled him nervously. The rest of the Hedra had become busy with more dragons that had joined the fight and the boy looked unsure what to do. The sky behind him was full of dragons, huge insects, arrows, and fire. Suddenly a blast of heat caught James by surprise. The ground around him burst into flames. He shielded his eyes. The Hedra boy had taken refuge beneath one of the wagons. He'd dropped the axe and now James picked it up. The boy's eyes wid-ened as James approached. James lifted the axe but… He couldn't do it. The young Hedra looked as scared and confused as he felt. James threw the axe away and was just about to speak to the boy when there was another blast of dragon-flame. James ducked down but when he looked under the wagon again the Hedra boy was gone. The giant sucking insect that fed on Zurala was ablaze. It writhed, screaming, between the dead dragon's outstretched wings. The heat was becoming more intense…

"Numpty boy!"

James had never been so pleased to hear those words in his whole life.

"There's room on our dragon for one more if you hurry." Craig and Helen beamed down at him from their back of a shining, black dragon. The creature's mane shone an iridescent blue and emerald. Craig reached down and hauled James up. "He's a boy dragon," shouted Craig. "This is Nargis; aren't you, big guy?"

The dragon beat its wings and roared deeply.

James felt Helen's arms hug him in. "I can't seem to call my sword, Helen. And my asthma…"

"Have you forgot that you can do your own magic now?" said Helen.

James *had* forgot. "I don't really know what to say or do," he yelled. The sounds of battle were becoming louder again. "I… I only know the stone spell, and I didn't exactly get it right the last time, did I? "

"I'm sure you can do it, if you try again," said Helen.

"I can't do any magic without Mendel," moaned James.

A black arrow whisked past and Helen snuggled in tighter.

"I'll just muck it up," said James.

"Just try it," said Craig.

Ahead, between Nargis and the city walls, half a dozen of the flying dragon-suckers buzzed towards them.

"Mendel says that they're giant pond-skaters," said Helen.

"They're what?" said James. He screwed up his eyes and tried to imagine these pond-skaters whizzing across Loch Echty. "No way."

"Just try the stone spell," urged Helen.

"Yeh, try it now!" said Craig.

"Eh… Stonewright!" James blurted.

Still, the horrible flying pond-skaters whirred closer.

"Concentrate," snapped Helen. "Pretend Mendel is saying it through you. Imagine his voice saying it."

Craig pulled Nargis higher.

James almost slipped off. He had no helpful snake-mane to hold him fast on this dragon.

"Try again!" Craig yelled.

James closed his eyes and tried to remember Mendel's deep reassuring voice. "Wwstonewwwrightwww!"

The lead Skater's wings froze. Its legs wriggled and then stopped. James scrunched up his eyes and focused as hard as he could. Then, from the tip of its piercing and sucking proboscis to the end of its flattened abdomen, the Skater morphed into stone and dropped like a huge cannon-ball. The insect exploded amongst a group of Raptor chariots, decimating their ranks. Only a few spinning wheels and the odd chunk of armour marked the spot.

As James homed-in on the other Skaters they dropped too. One after another, more and more explosions wiped out a third of the Hedra force below them.

"James, you're even better than the guppy," said Craig. "Yes!" He punched the air.

James, however, felt strange. He felt listless and dizzy. He slumped against Craig's back then began to slip.

Craig turned and caught him just in time. "Get him, Sis!"

Helen helped to pull James back into position as Nargis climbed higher. "Well done, James. Just hold on."

James, with great effort, lifted his head. He saw Whindril, with Mendel and Eethan on her back, bearing down on the remaining Manimal force on the plain. He knew Dendralon was in there somewhere. Pins and needles crippled him as the blood rushed back into his arms and legs. He tried to make sense of what was going on. The city walls were free of the grappling-hooks and ropes and the Hedra were in retreat. Several dragons lay dead on the battlefield, surrounded by squabbling Skaters. Many more Skaters lay frazzled on the ground. Upturned, their legs looked like the twisted spokes of a crumpled umbrella. A smell of burnt sugar and spent matches permeated the air. It made him cough. He felt his breathing becoming more laboured again. Helen handed him his inhaler. "Where did you get this?"

"I picked it off the ground in the Dragon Chamber," said Helen. "It was in this." She tapped the green rucksack on her back.

"Thanks, Helen."

Helen tapped his shoulder and pointed. "Look!"

James followed her gaze. "It's my mum!" She was on the red dragon known as Rusufia. His mum was circling the citadel and the dragon was scorching the smooth stone. He tugged Craig's sleeve. "Why is she attacking the citadel?"

Craig sneered. "I bet your dad's in there."

James gripped onto the dragon mane a little tighter. "Very funny."

"Let's go see," said Craig. He pulled Nargis to the left just as a massive arrow whistled up between the dragon's wings. "The Hedra have got their crossbows working."

"Climb higher, then," screamed Helen.

Craig flicked the hairs that flew back from Nargis's neck and the black dragon obeyed.

The sounds of battle soon faded as they climbed high enough to escape the threat from the ground.

"Dad!" yelled James. "Look, he's on the balcony."

"See, I told you he'd be there," said Craig. He shook his head. "A hundred percent nutter."

Helen reached past James and punched Craig on the arm. "That's James's mum you're talking about, so cool it!"

"Cool it? She's trying to fry his dad with an eighty-foot, red dragon."

"No she's not, she's..."

Just then the red dragon carrying Cathy Peck and Bero disappeared behind the citadel. Another blast of flame scorched the white alabaster and licked the balcony where they could now see David, Wee Joe, Michael, Ephie, and Jean Harrison.

"See! A hundred percent nutter," repeated Craig.

At that moment a blazing Raptor edged round the citadel and gripped onto the balustrade. The Drumfintley group pushed themselves against the black curtain as the rail crumbled. Wee Joe lurched forward and stamped on the creature's blackened claw. It screamed and toppled backwards, falling like a writhing torch until it thumped into the courtyard below. The balcony detached from the citadel and hung precariously, with the Drumfintley group screaming and scrambling to stay on.

"Mum!" James yelled. The Drumfintley group was too far away from the citadel to jump back inside.

Cathy pointed at the crumbling balcony and shouted across at Craig. "They'll never make it into the citadel now. Use your dragon. Get them off of there."

"Look out! There's another Raptor coming round the back," shouted Helen.

Cathy's dragon, Rusufia, performed a half-twist and sailed out of sight.

Craig urged the black dragon, Nargis, as close as he could and shouted out, "Mum! You, Mr. Peck, and Wee Joe will have to jump."

The force of Nargis's wings almost dislodged them from what remained of the balcony. "Take Wee Joe," Jean shouted. She stretched out her arm, edging Wee Joe closer.

Nargis flapped as hard as he could in an effort to stay in the one spot.

The citadel shuddered.

Jal appeared at the curtain and tore the material, tugging the curtain from its rail.

Nearest to the material, Father Michael and Ephie caught hold and swung against the citadel. Jal heaved them up.

Whindril rushed past them in a blur of white, Mendel and Eethan riding on her snowy neck.

The citadel shuddered again. Slates and masonry began to whiz past their heads from the turreted roof.

"Quick!" screamed James. "Take Wee Joe and jump now, Mrs. Harrison. There's just enough room." He looked down and saw that Dendralon was a hundred feet below them, riding one of the huge Skaters.

Whindril immediately corkscrewed down and issued a blast of liquid fire.

Dendralon, however, simply raised his staff, and the flames snuffed out in a deafening hiss of sparks and steam. Dendralon's Skater fluttered back and then raced at the tower once more. It slammed into the alabaster, cracking the whole structure.

The balcony crumbled.

What's he doing? thought James.

Jean Harrison stretched out as far as she could and swung Wee Joe out towards Nargis.

James reached out and caught hold of Wee Joe's wrist. With a quick heave, he placed him beside Helen but Nargis had to twist away from the face of the citadel as a heavy piece of stone gave way above them. The dragon caught the huge lump of stone with his claws and dropped it down onto Dendralon, who was battling with Mendel and Eethan. Beams of light burst from the wizards as they vied for position. The lump of stone thumped into Dendralon's Skater and knocked it from the side of the citadel. More and more Skaters, however, began to circle the citadel, relentlessly crashing into the tower.

Craig pushed Nargis back up to the remains of the balcony where Jean and David held on to a small outcrop of broken stone. "Now! Both of you. You've got to jump!"

Jean Harrison turned and caught the black curtain just as the balcony fell.

David Peck jumped out into thin air.

The balcony fell away from the tower and David disappeared. Jean swung on the black curtain.

"Dad!" yelled James. The dust and flames made it impossible to see. "Dad!" James peered down into the swirling ball of fire and filth.

A rush of air knocked Nargis back from the Citadel.

A huge groaning sound filled James's ears. The citadel was going to fall. "Dad," he whispered.

A creature knocked into Nargis from below. It was Rusufia. His mum and Bero had an extra passenger.

"Dad!"

David waved and then clung on for dear life as Rusufia climbed back towards the hole that had marked the spot where the balcony had been.

"It's Jal," said Craig. "He's too busy fighting to help..."

"There are Hedra inside the citadel," said Helen. "Nargis can't get any higher. We're too heavy."

Craig urged Nargis higher.

"Jal, Father Michael, and Ephie have all disappeared inside the citadel," said James. "Your mum's still hanging onto the curtain. We have to get her!"

More heavy-set and powerful than Nargis or Whindril, it was Rusufia who flapped up towards the black curtain as it tore even more.

Another Raptor appeared beside Jean and then pounced out from the wall of the citadel at Rusufia. It ripped downward with its claws at the dragon's underbelly.

Cathy leaned over into mid air, cutting down with her swords. She gripped onto the dragon's neck with her thighs. Her blades caught the Raptor's neck, but it hung on, causing Rusufia to lose height. The weight of the wounded Raptor was taking its toll on the red dragon's strength.

"Hold on," said Craig. He urged Nargis back up into the air and flicked the hair-like reins as he reached Rusufia. Nargis spun upside down and scraped the Raptor from the underside of Cathy's red dragon. A single squeeze of Nargis's talons crushed the creature and it dropped like a stone.

Still screaming, James, Craig, Helen, and Wee Joe all clung on for dear life as Nargis righted and soared downward. James craned his neck in an effort to pick out Mrs. Harrison.

There was a blast of red light from the battle below which hit the citadel with a thunderous snap of stone. Dust and debris bellowed out of the citadel.

"NO!" shouted James. "Mrs. Harrison!"

The whole building collapsed with a roar that seemed to go on forever.

As their dragon spun blindly he heard Craig, Helen, and Wee Joe all scream out in horror, "MUM!"

Surrounded by a cloud of impenetrable grime, soon all James could hear was the constant rumble of falling stone. He only glimpsed the odd flash of red or white that signalled Whindril and Rusufia until, eventually, they cleared the dust cloud. On and on the crashing sounds of falling rock filled James's ears. He looked back at where the citadel had stood but there was only dust and the occasional glimpse of blue sky.

The great citadel of Gwendral had fallen.

"Mum," whimpered Helen. She began to cry.

"What's that?" said Craig, scanning the ground below.

"Is it Michael and Ephie? But, how…?" said James.

"I seed the Mertol grab them just before…" Wee Joe began to sob and cuddle into Helen.

A loud drone signalled an approaching Skater, but it was still invisible in the dust cloud. Then a voice bellowed out, "No one will inherit Gwendral if I cannot!" The eerie words sounded very close. James knew that Dendralon was only feet away. The drone of the beating insect wings grew louder.

"Drop down," said James. "Nargis can't take our weight." The black dragon was faltering, dipping, and then flapping hard to say aloft.

"Where is Dendralon?" said James.

"I'll kill him!" roared Craig. He peered into the dust and aimed his green spear.

"Wait," said James. "You might hit someone else."

"We have to off-load some people first," Helen reminded. She screeched as Nargis lurched downward.

"Your mother is dead, children." Manic laughter sounded from the dust cloud.

"Don't listen to him," said James. "He's trying to get our position."

For a few seconds, the unmistakable figure of Dendralon appeared from the murk and powdered rock. Shimmering like an apparition, ghoul-like on the back of the monstrous insect that had toppled the citadel. James watched the giant Skater's spear-like rostrum elongate.

"Your mother is crushed beneath the rock, Blinder! Ha, ha, ha..."

Dendralon's laugh was a mocking rasp that cut deep into James's soul.

Craig launched Greenworm but the dust closed over the wizard and he disappeared.

James peered into the dust hoping that Dendralon was either no longer there or pierced by Greenworm. *He might have to try his magic on the dark wizard after all, and this time Mendel might not be able to help him.*

"Do it," urged Helen.

"Kill him," added Wee Joe, tugging on James's sleeve.

"I... I don't think he's there," said James, stalling for time. *It was too ambitious to try his magic on Dendralon, but on the insect... He'd managed that before.*

Wee Joe shouted out into the swirling cloud of debris, "She's not dead. My mum is not dead!"

A cackling laugh echoed out from the cloud. "A million tons of rock says you're wrong, boy."

"Ah!" James's stomach lurched as they dropped. "Craig, what are you doing?"

"I need to find Mum. He's lying."

"Of course he's lying," said Helen. "He wants us to be mixed up. The Mertol or Jal will have found a way to save her. She may have jumped onto Whindril for all we know."

"Helen's right. He's lying," said Wee Joe. "The Mertol's magic will have saved her."

James, however, was sure he had seen Jean Harrison fall. He was sure they had all seen her fall. He wanted to tell them what he'd seen but he couldn't. He couldn't say the words out loud.

Dendralon is really close by.

The drone above them wavered as the roar of a dragon filled the air.

Wee Joe punched James in the back. "He says dat Father Michael is okay. And Jal and Ephie…"

"Who says?" said James.

"De Mertol says," said Wee Joe.

"He hears its voice or something," explained Craig.

"Are you sure? I mean we saw the whole citad…" James hesitated.

"Where is it?" said Craig, guiding Nargis over the shattered remains of the gate tower. "Where is the Mertol?"

"Oh, my God," said Helen, "the dust is clearing…"

The citadel had been reduced to a pile of rubble. It had fallen in on itself and over parts of the gate-towers, where the Yeltans had been stationed. "Nothing could have survived that. Not even the Mertol," James sighed.

"Well, it did," blasted Wee Joe.

Huge insect legs sticking out of the debris, like tangled and twisted metal rods, made it plain that the Skaters had been crushed by citadel they'd helped topple.

Nargis soared over the most complete of the two gate-towers and landed on the battlefield. Most of the Hedra near to the walls had been killed, and there was no sign of Dendralon. James could still hear the cries of dragons and, as the sky cleared, they revealed themselves circling high above the plain.

Around him, the bodies of the Hedra lay in charred, ungainly piles but James could see that the main bulk of the Hedra force was already back on the ridge that overlooked the Plain of Gwendral. He counted over twenty dead dragons between him and the remaining force of Manimals and Yeltans. Amazingly, Cimerato's ranks had stood firm despite the carnage around them, some thousand souls in all. He picked out Cimerato, covered in blood and propped up against an overturned chariot. Nargis snorted as James helped Wee Joe down from the dragon's back. James squinted up at the hazy sky for any sign of Mendel, his mum and dad or Dendralon.

"James!"

James spun round and saw the bulky outline of Rusufia. The cumbersome red dragon that carried his mum swooped down and flapped to a halt behind Cimerato and his force

"There it is!" said Wee Joe.

Some fifty yards away, the one remaining ivory gate of Gwendral creaked and then toppled free of its rusting steel hinge.

Crash!

Limping and bent over like an old man, a lumbering, orange mass of hair threw back its head and roared. "Bak!"

Amazingly, people were filing out behind the Mertol.

James saw that it was carrying someone.

CHAPTER TWENTY-THREE

EASY PREY

Dendralon slipped off the back of his Skater on a dark beach next to the Gortan Sea. He had seen the remains of his flying Hemiptera force destroyed by the falling citadel, and having battled his way through the dust to avoid a confrontation with Mendel and his dragon Whindril, he would now have to decide what to do next. He checked his pouch. He still had two Eden Seeds from Artilis, so he had a way back or, if need be, another chance to reincarnate. To reincarnate, however, he would need a well-trained accomplice to perform the incantations and spells. Elhada was dead, and no other would learn the skills needed quickly enough to achieve this for many years. Mendel was, as usual, his main concern and the Key of Artilis was probably buried beneath the rubble and dust of the citadel. There was no way now to bend time. He did have his bride, Beldam, to fight for and the Hedra survivors still formed a sizeable force. The losses caused by the dragons of Hest, however, had caused them to rout. The legends of the Hedra defeat at the hands of these monsters thousands of years before still played on their serpentine psyches.

He knelt down and took a handful of damp sand in his hands. Many things puzzled him. One thing that he couldn't understand was how Mendel had managed to protect the planet of Denthan from the apocalyptic explosion of Tealfirth. He'd seen the light emanate from the three plinths in the Dragon Chamber but it still annoyed him that Mendel had been able to perform such magic, such advanced magic. And as for the aftermath… Although his Hedra had still been gathered outside the gates of Gwendral, as they had been when Denthan exploded two years before, the thousands of dead Osgrunfs and Salt Trolls that had littered the Plain of Gwendral after the battles they'd fought back then had disappeared. Only those who lived were placed back on the planet as it had been prior to its destruction.

A scream sounded behind him.

He turned to see the outline of Whindril flying low over the sea. Mendel was trying to find him. The dragon looked to be wounded. *Perhaps my magic found its mark in the clouds of dust after all?* The dragon faltered and then splashed into the sea.

"Be quick, my water Queen, a feast awaits you." He pointed to the spot where the white dragon had fallen and watched as the Skater closed its gossamer wings behind its back. It snapped a second pair of chitinous overwings shut over these and then bounced in anticipation. Dendralon leapt back up onto the creature's carapace. At first, the Skater began to walk over the water, but soon it gathered speed and moved so fast that Dendralon had to shield his yellow, lizard eyes against the wind. If Whindril were truly wounded she would be easy prey for the giant water Skater. The Hemipterid would tear her apart and suck out her innards while he… He would finally get his chance to deal with Mendel.

* * *

Mendel signalled Eethan to get beneath the waves. "Get out of sight. Dendralon is on his way."

"Eee does not like to leeeve yous," said Eethan.

"Go!" He examined the damage to Whindril's left wing. "I will fix this, my old friend." He waved his hands over the tear and watched as it knitted back together. The thick, membranous tissue then reattached to the dragon's bone and sinew."Now, Whindril, play your part. You must pretend to be wounded," he urged.

Eethan's head appeared above the waves. "Theere ees and island over there. Eet ees small but eet will bee beeter to fight the Skateer on land than on the water, where she hunts."

"Well done, Eethan."Mendel's eyes met with Whindril's. "Swim slowly across to that island. Let us wait there, as Eethan suggests."

The island, no more than a rocky outcrop with a small beach, gave Whindril some footing. She tucked her wing beneath her neck and assumed an awkward gait.

"That's it, girl. We want the element of surprise on our side."

Smoke trailed out from the dragon's wide nostrils.

"Eethan?"

Eethan popped his head out of the water again. "Yees?"

"Do not reveal yourself to Dendralon, no matter what happens. Do nothing until I give you the signal."

"Signal?"

"You will hear my voice in your head," said Mendel.

"Eee…" Eethan bubbled under the water as the monstrous Skater closed in.

* * *

James ran forward and slowed as the Mertol laid the body down on the grass.

"Jal and Ephie are walking behind the Mertol!" shouted Craig. He was desperately scanning the people behind the Mertol. He ran forward and caught hold of Ephie's tattered coat. "Have you seen Mum, Ephie?"

Unable to speak, Ephie's sobs and wails caused the Mertol to growl and whine like a pup in sympathy.

James had never heard the Mertol make these sounds before.

Manimals poured round the tall Mertol as it staggered out of the city.

James saw Craig look up at Jal.

"Jal? My mum?" he asked.

Jal shook his head mournfully.

Sternly, Craig peered behind the tall figure of Jal. "I can't see," said Craig. "Who did the Mertol place on the grass?"

"It's Father Michael," said Helen, already running over to the prone figure.

As James moved closer, he saw no sign of life in Michael's face. It was ashen grey. His eyes were shut tight and his dog-collar hung loosely from his neck, the buttons torn.

"Michael!" wailed Ephie. "Why didn't you stay in the bubble? Oh, no…"

"Bubble?" said James.

Ephie let her head fall limply onto her chest. "It was the Mertol. He pulled those of us he could together and made a green, glowing bubble. It kept us safe. Everything fell; everything went black, and the noise… Why didn't you stay closer to us, Michael?" She beat the Reverend's shoulder and sobbed even louder.

James knelt down beside Ephie as she cupped Michael into her and shook with grief. "Ephie, have you seen Mrs. Harrison?"

Bleary eyed, Ephie raised her head briefly and whimpered, "There was no sign of Jean."

"Wook!" said Wee Joe.

They all stared at Michael's left hand. His fingers twitched.

Cathy caught them up and hugged James.

Bero licked Michael's fingers, and they twitched again.

"There's nothing that much wrong with him, Ephie," said Cathy. "Get out the way." She pulled Michael from Ephie's grasp and laid him back on the grass, opened his mouth, and began mouth-to-mouth resuscitation. Ephie was in too much of a state to help or protest. David and Jal gathered round with Helen, Bero, Craig, and Wee Joe.

Jal, however, became distracted. "Out there!" He pointed out over the Gortan Sea. "Is that Whindril?"

James stood up. "Mendel…"

"Whindril must have been wounded," said David.

Michael coughed and took a sharp breath.

"Oh, thank God," said Ephie.

"Ephie, you can take over from here," said Cathy.

"What is that fing, out on de water?" said Wee Joe.

"It's another Skater," said Jal. "It's closing in on Whindril. Those things live on the Gortan Sea; walk on the water. They kill whales, Salt Trolls and other monsters. A wounded dragon floating on the surface will have no chance."

"Someone is riding on its back," said Helen. She hugged in Wee Joe who seemed to be talking to the Mertol.

"Mum, could you stay with Michael and Ephie?" James asked.

"No chance. If Dendralon is out there I want a piece of him. I spent a year of misery at his beck and call and he's going to pay."

"Don't worry Cathy, I'll stay with Michael," said Ephie, meekly. "On you go. Sort him out."

"Rusufia, Nargis!" called James. "Mum, who should we take?"

"Anyone who can fight," said Cathy.

Seeing Wee Joe pull away from the bulky Mertol, James knelt down beside the small boy and asked, "What did the Mertol say, Joe?"

"He says that my mum is dead."

Everyone stopped in their tracks. The sound of crackling fires from the ruined city echoed over the battlefield.

"I'm sorry, Son," said Cathy.

James didn't know what to say.

"I'm coming too," said Wee Joe.

"Too right you are," said Craig. "You can fight better than anyone here." He punched his brother on the shoulder and, to James's amazement, forced a smile before pulling Wee Joe and Helen in close.

The Harrisons began to sob.

"Look," said Cathy, sympathetically, "you should stay here, Craig. Look after your brother and sister…"

"NO WAY!" blasted Craig. He wiped his face and sniffed. "We are all coming."

James waited for the reaction from his mum.

"Fine, Craig. If that's what you want," she said.

"It's what we *all* want," he replied.

Sniffing, Helen and Wee Joe nodded. They climbed aboard Nargis as Craig wrapped the shining mane round his wrist. "You coming, James?"

James glanced at his mum, who nodded her approval.

"What about Bero?" asked Helen.

"He can come with us," said Cathy. "Rusufia is strong enough."

Cathy, Jal, and David climbed onto the red dragon before hauling Bero aboard.

Cimerato remained with Ephie, Michael, and the remaining Manimals and Yeltans. More dust-covered Manimals were beginning to filter out of the city gates. "I should stay here and rally whatever survivors I can," he said. Cimerato scanned the ridge. "The Hedra will be back. This is far from over."

Cathy wound Rusufia's long crimson neck hairs round her wrist and spun the dragon round to face the Gortan Sea. "We have to make sure

Mendel is okay. He is our only way out of this mess. If he dies we will never get home to Drumfintley, any of us."

Drumfintley seemed like another lifetime to James, but he knew that his mum was right.

"Up, Nargis!" shouted Craig.

The jet-black dragon flapped its gigantic, bat-like wings and lifted. Rusufia followed. Gaining height, James saw that the giant Skater was almost on top of Mendel. Sitting behind Helen, he had no idea what they would do when they got to Whindril.

James glanced at Rusufia and saw his dad put his arm round his mum's waist. Her swords were criss-crossed over her slender back and her hair, a midnight black, flew into his dad's eyes. His dad shouted across at them, "Whindril is trapped on some rocks. Is it an island?"

"Faster Rusufia!" roared Cathy.

The red dragon returned the roar.

"There's not a lot of room down there," said Craig.

"It's Dendwalon," spat Wee Joe.

"Good!" snapped Cathy.

* * *

As the giant Skater smashed into Whindril, Mendel was knocked off the dragon. He landed heavily on the small beach and lay still.

Whindril's tail flicked out and wrapped round the Skater's front legs. At the same time the white dragon flapped both her wings and snapped down with her long fangs, biting deep into the creature's head.

Eethan swam away from the writhing Skater as it splashed down beside him. He ducked under the foam and then broke the surface a good distance away. He saw Dendralon leap high over the grappling giants and land next to the prostrate form of Mendel. Deftly twisting his gnarled staff from his cloak, Dendralon approached the old wizard very cautiously. He held his staff high, ready to strike at the slightest sign of movement.

"Mendel, get up and kneel before me. It's time to swear allegiance to the true King of Gwendral," said Dendralon.

Eethan ducked down as the squirming giants behind him rolled closer. He swam hard before easing up behind a jagged rock. He saw Mendel's eyes flicker open.

"Ah, you're still alive. Good. Will you kneel before your own brother?" hissed Dendralon. His long, grey tongue vibrated excitedly between his needle-spiked teeth.

Mendel slowly shook his head and whispered, "Never."

"No?" mused Dendralon, "I didn't think so."

By now the Skater was fixed on top of the dragon's back, its rostrum easing down from its mouthparts.

Eethan shook with frustration, but remembered Mendel's instructions and remained out of sight.

"So, how then can I guarantee that you will serve me, while at the same time remaining totally impotent? I could turn you back into a goldfish but... I suppose you managed to cause me quite a bit of trouble even then," said Dendralon. "A stone statue...?" Dendralon brought his staff round and placed the tip on Mendel's chest. "If I remove your magic powers... Better still, absorb them for myself, my victory will be two-fold." Dendralon ducked as Whindril's tail slashed past his flattened face. "By turning you back into a goldfish, only this time a completely impotent one, I could place you where you could see Beldam every day. Never able to hold her in your arms, your torment might just satisfy my need for revenge."

Eethan ached to use his magic. He saw Whindril fall back into the waves. The Skater had gained the advantage again and was circling.

Dendralon caught Mendel by the collar of his blue cloak and dragged him across the damp sand away from the battling monsters. "You see, Mendel, if you'd taken on the form of a Hedra you could have remained young, never aged." He pulled Mendel up so that he could see himself reflected in a small pool. "Open your eyes, old man, and look at yourself." Dendralon dropped him into the pool and then jabbed his staff into Mendel's side.

Mendel moaned. "Ah..."

Eethan struggled to keep still.

"Looks like you have a broken rib, brother. There, you see... That's just what I was talking about. A Hedra rib is four times stronger than a Manimal one. The bone is double-woven. You have chosen an inferior race. Which Manimal bone will I pick next? The humerus? The tibia? Perhaps the skull..." He lifted his staff higher.

"Stop right there!"

Dendralon looked up. Two dragons hovered above him; one red and thickset, the other, like a black shadow, oozing a trail of thick smoke.

"Beldam, my Queen. Excellent. I was thinking of keeping him as a pet, but now it may be better if you watch me kill the man who was your first love."

"What?" screeched Cathy. "You are totally deranged."

Eethan heard Mendel's voice in his head. *"Kill the Skater."* Eethan immediately sent a blast of blue light into the Hemipterid. It hissed and slid off Whindril, its crumpled corpse bubbling down beneath the waves.

Dendralon scanned the waves suspiciously then craned upwards again. Now surrounded by three dragons, Dendralon unclipped a silken pouch from his belt. He hunched down beside Mendel and squinted up at Cathy. "Your dragon will not use its fire when I am so close to your lover, Beldam. Ten thousand years ago Mendel and you were betrothed."

Cathy's eyes blazed. "Dendralon, you are going to die for what you did."

"Ha! You should know by now that I never die. I am impossible to kill."

Whindril shook the seawater from her snowy mane and moved between Dendralon and the Gortan Sea.

* * *

With the terrible news about Jean Harrison still racing through his mind James had to struggle to keep control of his anger. Craig, however, was well past the point of restraint. He tugged on the black dragon's mane and pulled him into action. "Kill him!"

James caught his wrist. "No, Craig!"

On Rusufia, David yelled out as Nargis lurched forward, racing towards Dendralon, his long, black dragon-fangs already exposed.

"Rrraaar!" Nargis roared, jerking to a halt as Dendralon raised his hand. The great beast flapped and roared against an invisible wall. Unflustered, Dendralon placed the tip of his staff onto the small of Mendel's back.

The old wizard moaned once more and began to shake.

"MUM!" cried James.

"I can't get any closer. There's some kind of shield round him," she snapped. Now Rusufia flapped against the shimmering wall of air, her russet jaws trying to find an opening.

James held onto Helen and shouted down at Dendralon. "Leave Mendel alone!" He could see that the old wizard was in pain.

Dendralon quickly raised his staff and called out, "Firetongue! Greenworm!"

The boy's arms blazed in pain as the magical weapons appeared and then fizzled away. Their tattoos were gone.

"No more magic to help your wizard friend now, boys," spat Dendralon. He resumed his stance over Mendel, pressing the staff even harder into the old wizard's back.

James rubbed his arm and stared around in panic. A faraway voice floated through his thoughts. *"Now, Eethan."*

Eethan was kneeling, as if in prayer, on a pile of olive-coloured seaweed. A dazzling blue light began to build around him as he stood up. With a flick of his puny arms, a blast of purple sparks flew out from Eethan's hands, crackling over the forcefield that surrounded Dendralon and Mendel.

James heard Eethan's voice in his head. "Dendreeelon ees stealing Mendeeel's magic... All three dragons must use theeer magic fire now!" James tugged at Craig's sleeve. "Craig, we all have to attack at once. The dragons must use their fire at the same time."

Craig pulled Nargis back from the forcefield and nodded, his eyes streaming with tears.

"On my count," said James. "One... Two... Three... NOW!"

A torrent of black, white, and crimson fire jetted into the forcefield that surrounded Dendralon. Eethan's purple sparks raced over its surface and then burst into a lilac flame that merged with the dragon-fire. A multicoloured sea of flame contorted the Hedra wizard's shimmering wall until, with a crack of thunder, it fell.

The dark, demon-like figure of Dendralon looked puzzled. He wavered like a mirage.

James took his chance. As Nargis clipped the rocks, James leapt off the dragon's back and concentrated hard. He focused on Dendralon and pushed the spell from his lips...

"WWWSTONEWWRIGHTWW!"

All energy drained from his body and he fell to his knees. He slipped and caught his hand on the rocks. His lungs felt as if they'd collapsed. He gasped for air. Tears streamed down his face.

Two heavy clumps signalled the dragons landing on the rocks beside him.

Eethan ran right up to Dendralon but had skidded to a sudden stop. His dad had jumped off the red dragon and was already shielding Helen and Wee Joe. His mum now slipped off Rusufia's back with Jal, who'd drawn his large curved Hedra sword.

James managed to stand up. He walked out from behind his position onto the sandy beach. The air was warping and bending round Dendralon. He felt his mum's fingers close over his shoulder. "Move back, it's not safe," she whispered.

Had his spell worked?

CRACK!

There was a sound like a church spire splitting in two.

Everyone ducked.

Dendralon's outline wavered, and Mendel's cloak fell flat to the ground. The old wizard's body had disappeared.

James clenched his fists in frustration. "What have I done?" he moaned.

His mum hauled him further back towards Rusufia. "Keep back, I said."

Like a madman, Craig suddenly broke away from Nargis and ran straight for Jal. He snatched the sword from the unsuspecting Hedra warrior and ran straight at Dendralon.

"Craig!" everyone yelled.

Screaming with rage, Craig pulled the curved blade back at the last minute and then plunged it straight through Dendralon's chest.

There was an almighty scream that seemed to come from everything around them: the sea, the rocks, the air... A shock-wave knocked everyone off their feet.

When James struggled back up onto his knees, Dendralon was staring down at his chest, a look of complete disbelief etched on his face.

Craig was crying. "You... You killed her!" Sobbing uncontrollably, he staggered back from the dark wizard.

In two huge strides Jal covered the distance between himself and Dendralon. He flicked Craig to the side and pulled his sword free, arcing the weapon round his head in the same movement. His legs jumped apart and he brought the blade back round. Yelling out with the effort of the strike, the razor-sharp blade swished through Dendralon's neck. The wizard's eyes flared, and his mouth parted slightly as his scaled head rolled back off his shoulders. A burst of white light shot up from his severed neck before his body slumped to the ground.

"Quick," called Cathy, "cut the black pouch from his belt."

Momentarily confused, James ran forward and knelt beside Dendralon's body, anxiously searching for the black pouch. His heart almost stopped when he saw Dendralon's long fingers move. They traced the ground moving over the blood-soaked earth like some gruesome spider.

Not sure what to do, James stood up and stamped down hard on the fingers. Then he saw it. The pouch was there, tucked under the wizard's cloak. As he cut it loose, however, Dendralon's left hand caught hold of James's shirt.

James gasped and tried to tug himself free.

"Move away from the body," yelled his dad. "The head..."

The yellow eyes in Dendralon's severed head opened.

James broke free but tripped over Craig and fell hard onto the seaweed and rocks. He dropped the pouch. Jal and his mum tried to pull him away but something was dragging him back to Dendralon. The severed head began to roll towards him. *I... I need to do something...*

"Stone... Stone... S... Stone." he just couldn't push the words out. His tongue was stuck to the roof of his mouth. The pouch rolled along the sand and then stopped beside Dendralon's severed hand.

Eethan was running up the beach as fast as he could.

Dendralon's fingers traced the pouch. They wormed it open.

James was sliding across the damp sand towards the wizard. Dendalon's sharp, scaly fingers found his leg and dug into his skin.

"Rrrar!"

The ground shuddered as, in a blur of white, Whindril's muzzle slammed down beside James. She crunched her massive jaws shut. Flicking her head back twice as Dendralon's severed head disappeared down her throat.

Everyone around James stood spellbound. Dendralon's fingers froze.

Panting, James rolled over onto his back and stared up at Whindril. "That..." he began, "should do it."

"Good riddance to him," said Craig.

Whindril waddled back to meet Eethan, who patted the dragon on her wet, dog-like nose. "Good girlee! Good girlee!"

Whindril shook her mane and gave a snort of satisfaction.

James looked down quickly at Dendralon's body. Beginning at the wizard's feet, James watched as the waves lapped over the wizard's body.

"What's that?" said Helen. She broke free from the other dragons and ran straight up to James.

At his feet, James noticed something moving. He yelled and pulled Helen back.

"Is it Mendel?" said Helen.

There, just visible beneath the blue cloak, flicking pathetically on a damp patch of sand, a small goldfish mpuh, mpuhed in desperation.

Helen stooped down. "Mendel?"

"We need fresh water," shouted James.

"Here, Bero. Here, boy," said Craig.

Bero barked and bounded forward, but there was no plastic barrel hanging down from his fluffy neck. It had been smashed in the Dragon Chamber.

Quickly, Cathy knelt down and rummaged around in the seaweed until she found a large shell. She shook the seawater out of it and looked round at the others. "Salt water this strong will kill him."

"One minute we need salt water, the next we need fresh water. Hurry up and make up your mind," said Craig.

Mendel's tail was only twitching now.

Cathy rounded on Jal. "We need fresh water! Jal?"

"I have nothing," said Jal.

David Peck scooped up a handful of seawater. "Are you sure it will kill him?"

Wee Joe caught hold of Mendel's tail and plopped him into the empty shell.

At the same time Helen and Craig yelled, "No!"

From his belt, Wee Joe produced his trusty, plastic water pistol and pumped the trigger. In moments there was enough fresh water to cover the goldfish.

James felt his lips curl into a smile. "You little dancer."

"Brilliant," yelled David. Excitedly, he patted Cathy on the back but she caught him with a death-stare and he backed off. "Fine... okay then... Well done, Wee Joe!"

Once the shell was half-full Wee Joe handed it to James. A smug look on his face, Wee Joe blew the tip of his water pistol, like a cowboy who'd just won a gunfight, and beamed. "Der you go."

James found another piece of shell and formed a lid of sorts. He edged it open and looked inside. A stiff golden tail wavered in the water. James held his breath.

"He's alive!" screamed Helen.

"He ees," agreed Eethan.

"Let me wook!" said Wee Joe.

James gulped back a tear as he thought of Jean Harrison. She would normally have corrected Wee Joe's pronunciation but Helen stepped in.

"Look," said Helen. "The word is *look*. You know how to speak properly, don't you Joe?"

Wee Joe nodded and looked into the shell, distractedly.

The crashing of huge feet caused them all to duck down. The dragons were on the move.

"They have carried out their task," said a voice.

"Mendel?" said James. The wizard's voice was very thin and wispy in his head.

"Is he talking about the dragons?" said Jal.

"It looks like they've had enough," said Helen.

Craig called out, "Come back! Wait!" Nargis, Rusufia and Whindril, however, ignored their calls and clambered up onto the rocks. One by one, the dragons flexed their enormous wings and, with a mixture of roars and barks, they flapped up into the blue Denthan sky.

Solemnly, Craig reached for Mendel's shell and peered inside. "The old man seems to be back on form."

"Not exactly, Craig," said Mendel. "I…"

James felt a kind of emptiness deep in his stomach.

"I can no longer perform my magic," finished Mendel.

"How do you know?" said James. "We can all hear you."

The others nodded.

"I tell you, my magic has gone for good," said Mendel. "Dendralon drew it from me."

"But you can still talk in our heads," said Helen.

"I can only assume that Dendralon wanted to converse with me on occasion. Torture me, taunt me, hear my reaction."

"Don't be so stupid," snapped Cathy. "Where did the magic go? I assume *he*'s dead now." Cathy stared across at Dendralon's limp corpse lolling in the waves.

"Whindril made certain of that, Cathy," said Mendel.

"So where did the magic go?" asked Helen.

Mendel blew a stream of bubbles and sighed. "Back to the Earth, back to the sea and back to the sky... Back to where all magic comes from in the first place."

"None-the-wiser," barked Cathy.

Bero woofed.

Bravely, Wee Joe raised the aim of his water gun in Cathy's direction.

"So, how do we get home?" asked David.

"How indeed?" said Mendel. "There is still much to do here."

"And now we're stuck on this bloody rock with no way off?" said Cathy. "And will *you* stop pointing that thing at me?"

Reluctantly, Wee Joe lowered his gun.

The three dragons were off to the east. They climbed high to join the rest of their kin, soaring over the remains of Gwendral and then on towards the Mountains of Hest.

James took in his surroundings. His mum and dad had wandered over towards Jal, while Wee Joe and Helen huddled in beside Craig. Eethan stood close to Bero. The little blue man was muttering to himself, at least James thought he was. On listening a bit closer and interpreting Eethan's drawn out pronunciation, he decided that he was actually chatting to Mendel. James knew that Mendel could do this kind of isolated conversation. James couldn't hear Mendel's response but he could hear Eethan saying things like, "Why deed you not fight back...?" and "But eee wanted to help...?"

Mendel's voice suddenly sounded in his own head. "You, James, have magic, natural magic. It's in your bones now. You, like Eethan once did, will have to learn your craft. You will eventually know when to use your gift and when to hold back."

"But I only know the one spell, and I'm not even very good at that. It didn't work on Dendralon. It was Craig..."

"It was Craig who used Jal's sword, but he could never have struck if you had not disorientated Dendralon. Your spell had enough of an effect to let Craig's bravery prevail."

"My spell worked?"

"It worked enough and sometimes that is all that is needed. You know more than you think," said Mendel. "Eethan will help you."

"And what will you do?" said James, still unsure how they would get off the small island never mind get back home to Drumfintley.

"I..." Mendel paused, seemingly lost in thought. "I doubt Dendralon intended it, but I am now a very young goldfish, and without the drain of magic on my small body I should live to a good age. I can pass on a huge amount of knowledge and ideas. I have much to share with you, if you want me to."

"Of course I want you to," said James, not really sure what Mendel meant. He saw the Harrisons consoling each other, motherless. He still couldn't believe that Jean Harrison was gone. "And what about Helen?" he asked. "She could do your magic too."

"Helen was a very good host, a most excellent conduit for my magic. Her mind, however, was not destined to absorb the natural powers in the way that yours has. She will no longer perform magic."

James looked over the half-mile of sea, back towards the Plain of Gwendral. The Hedra were regrouping on the ridge. "There is still danger here, isn't there, Mendel?"

Jal followed his gaze and hunkered down beside Bero and Eethan. "They will have seen the dragons fly off towards the mountains. They will try one last attack."

"But the gates of Gwendral are destroyed and the city is in ruins," said James. "What's the point?"

"They will attack," assured Mendel.

"They ees leaderless," whispered Eethan.

"Not necessarily," said Mendel.

James watched Jal stand up and move towards the lapping waves. He sheathed his Hedra sword and stretched. "We are not all bad, you know."

"I'm sure," said James. "There must be more of them like you."

Jal laughed. "Yes..."

"Ee ees thinking," said Eethan. "Ee will go and get us a lift back to thee citee."

"Ah, yes," mused Mendel. "Go and see if you still hold some sway below the Gortan Sea."

"Some sway?" said James. He smiled. "Good one."

There was a splash as Eethan disappeared under the small waves. Denthan did not possess a moon, James remembered, and therefore the breezes and winds that swept down from the distant mountains caused the only waves to be found on the surface of the Gortan Sea. There were no tides.

"Where is he going, Mendel?" asked James.

"He is going to get us a lift ashore."

"On what?" asked James.

As if in answer, a loud gush of water burst free of the grey water and sprayed the beach. They all crouched low and waited.

Cathy Peck drew her swords and was just about to offer David Peck one of them when she changed her mind and thrust the hilt into James's palm. "You've probably more chance of doing some damage than him." She sneered.

David Peck stood empty-handed and puce-faced.

Another gurgling sound rose up from the depths followed by a deep resonant roar. *Mmmmmoooar!*

The Harrisons picked up an assortment of rocks from the shore and braced.

"Another Skater?" asked Helen, in a shaky voice.

"Nah," said Craig. "They run across the surface not..."

His words were cut short, however, by the emergence of a massive, bald head. Water poured off the ears and nose as a giant's head rose steadily out of the water.

"A giant?" asked David Peck.

"Eeee no," said Eethan, scampering up the beach. He shook his white shock of hair and picked up Mendel's shell. He shut the lid and fastened it onto Bero's collar with a few carefully selected strands of weed. As he tittered his way up the beach, he explained, "It's a Skurder."

"A what?" shouted Craig.

"Eeee Skurder," repeated Eethan, as if Craig was a complete imbecile.

As more of the Skurder revealed itself, James could see that it wasn't as big as he first thought. Despite having a head that wouldn't have looked out of place on a hundred foot tall giant, this Skurder creature had the squat body of a crab.

"Thees Skurder is much smaller than thee ones in Scotland," assured Eethan. "Less nasty too."

"Yeh, right," said Craig. "We've got these things round the coast of Scotland?"

James thought Craig sounded more like himself but he knew that his best friend was putting on a brave face.

"What are we supposed to do, Eethan?" asked David.

"Wee ees supposed to climb aboard and ride on eets back to the shore," explained Eethan. He screwed up his eyes in Cathy's direction. "Just don't..."

"Yes?" prompted Cathy.

"Just don't insult eet," whispered Eethan.

The Skurder opened its human-like mouth and exposed a row of serrated teeth that were brown and crooked. James also noticed that the Skurder had no eyes. The sockets were deep but covered in leathery grey skin.

Wee Joe tilted his head. "How come it doesn't have any eyes?"

"Shush," snapped Helen. "We don't want to upset our big friend now, do we?" Her voice brightened.

Wee Joe shrugged, as if he couldn't care less.

Wading out to board the creature, they all stopped suddenly. They bumped into each other as they halted.

A pair of crab-like protrusions slithered free of the Skurder's nostrils. Each snake-like appendage sporting a bulbous red eye on the end that blinked in their direction.

"Eets eyes," whispered Eethan, with a wink.

"Yuck," muttered Helen, quickly covering her mouth.

James widened his eyes at her and pressed his forefinger against his lips.

"Eeevery one aboard?" said Eethan, in a very polite manner.

James made room on the Skurder's broad, barnacle-encrusted carapace for Bero as the old dog skidded and skittered on the slimy surface.

The Skurder roared and then wriggled its horrible legs.

Cathy Peck pinched her nose. "What a stin..."

"Manners," Mendel reminded.

Buuurp!

The creature's massive rift caused James to quickly pinch his nose. He grimaced as the smell of part-digested goodness-knows-what wafted over them. *Rotten kippers and dirty drains*, thought James.

Noses pinched, or in Jal's case, nose-slits closed, they cut through the waves at a good pace until they neared the shore. As soon as they could see the bottom they jumped into the water and swam, the cold and wet being preferable to the stench of the Skurder's bad breath.

"He really needs to brush his teeth sometime," panted Helen.

"Eeeee…" wailed Eethan.

In the same instant the Skurder moaned and produced a long pair of claws from beneath its bulky body.

"Quickleee!" urged Eethan.

Knee-high in seawater, they all tried to push their way to the shore before the Skurder unravelled its claw things, which now looked more like a pair of hairy whips.

"Helen has upset eeet. Eets whips ees poison," warned Eethan, pulling Helen by the hand as hard as he could.

James still had his mum's sword and, with a quick whisk, he managed to cut the tip of a whip-claw clean through just before it touched Helen's legs.

"Rrraaa!"

"Now you've done it," said Craig. "Ah!" He tripped over a submerged stone and splashed under the water.

The entire group had staggered up the shore, apart from Craig and Bero.

James waded back in as the Skurder lifted higher out of the water, its whip-like appendages now squirming above Craig's head.

Bero was still doggy-paddling, woofing and yelping, Mendel's shell bobbing under his muzzle.

I hope Eethan made it watertight, thought James.

"Insult it, James!" shouted Mendel.

"Hey! Over here, grimy gub!" he shouted, disappointed that grimy gub was as big an insult as he could muster.

The Skurder looked confused as it turned its attention to James.

"It probably doesn't know what gub means," choked Craig. He grabbed Bero and waded towards the beach.

"Mingin' mouth, then," jeered James.

The creature lunged then paused, again looking confused.

Everyone began shouting Scottish insults at the Skurder.

"Dunder-heed!" blasted David, running along the beach away from James.

The creature growled.

"A… hawd yer weesht!" barked Cathy, running in the opposite direction.

"Ya big numpty!" yelled Helen.

"Bowfin' breath!" added Cathy.

James was now a good fifty yards up the beach. "Look, it doesn't know what to do."

"Baldy bane!" roared Wee Joe, obviously enjoying himself.

Looking dejected and now well out of range, the Skurder slumped back into the water and disappeared beneath an eruption of bubbles and foam.

Everyone was scattered over the beach, panting while slowly re-grouping next to Bero and Eethan.

"I feel sorry for it," said Helen.

"You're the one who said it had bad breath," said Craig.

"Yeah, well," sighed Helen. "It did."

"It got us here, despite its halitosis," said Mendel. "As Eethan said when we boarded, they are very sensitive creatures."

"Hali... What?" said Craig.

"Bad breath," said Cathy. "What do they teach you in Drumfintley School?"

"Not a lot," muttered Craig.

Drumfintley School seemed like a distant dream to James. Soaked through and exhausted, he caught up with his mum and dad. Instantly feeling guilty, however, he glanced back at the three Harrisons walking, shoulders slumped, behind him. "What are they going to do?" he said to his mum, quietly.

His dad looked to his mum for an answer but she was focused on some unknown spot on the horizon, far away in some distant thought.

"Let's get back home first before we get into all that, Son," said his dad.

"But they hardly know their own dad, and with Mrs. Harrison..."

"They can stay with us," whispered his mum.

"Cathy, don't you think we should discuss it?" protested David.

"What, you'd rather palm them off with some man who never bothered with them in the first place? Jean told me all about Mr. Harrison. A selfish pig, like the rest of you."

"It might not be our choice," said David.

"Too much like hard work; is that it?" she jibbed.

"No... I..."

His dad seemed to have run out of steam and James was just sad. Sad for the Harrisons, and sad because, whatever he said, his parents always managed to twist it into an argument.

"Theee Hedra look readee to attack theee city again. Where ees Cimerato?" asked Eethan.

Eethan had been walking right next to the Pecks, unnoticed.

"Over there!" shouted Jal.

Cimerato had taken the remaining Manimals and Yeltans to a grassy knoll quite near to the shore of the Gortan Sea.

"That was an old Manimal settlement, built long before Gwendral," explained Mendel.

"Why has he taken them there?" said James. "Surely it would be easier to defend the city, even if it *is* in ruins?"

"I think I know why he's taken them there," said Mendel.

CHAPTER TWENTY-FOUR

THE GRASSY KNOLL

Cimerato sat down on a block of granite covered in purple lichen. He knew that he'd been lucky to survive Dendralon's attack, but he was inconsolable when it came to the destruction of the city. Gwendral had been his ancestral home for over nine thousand years.

"I've counted up the survivors, and we have one thousand six hundred Manimals, four hundred Yeltans, twenty eight Yukplugs, two Humans and one Mertol." Elgry moved officiously, traipsing through the tired and the wounded, flicking his papers and rearranging his bags.

"Sit down, Elgry, you're just going to annoy people prowling round like that," said Cimerato.

"Only trying to help," said the Secretary. "And I'm sorry about your father. We all are," he added.

Cimerato sighed. He would have to subdue his sadness and frustrations. He had to harness his anger, forge it into energy and then demonstrate the sheer will needed to lead and win. He would defeat these Hedra, no matter what the odds.

"They're back," said a high-pitched voice.

Cimerato watched Ephie Blake waddle through the tattered ranks followed by the cleric, Father Michael. She was pointing towards the Gortan Sea.

Cimerato had seen the dragons of Hest fly back to their mountains and had assumed the worst.

"They're still alive," said Michael. "James, Craig and the rest of the group."

"What about Mendel?" asked Cimerato.

"I presume so. I can see Bero and he still has something round his neck," said Ephie. "I'm just worried about Dendralon and those things." She pointed up to the ridge that overlooked the Plain of Gwendral and the Hedra. "They're regrouping."

"Ephie, Michael, I need to find something," said Cimerato. He scanned the remains of the Citadel. "There is little hope that it could have survived but I must try."

"Hope springs eternal," said Michael.

Cimerato could tell he was about to offer some other little nugget of wisdom when the Mertol roared out.

"Bak!"

"What do you need to find?" asked Ephie.

Cimerato watched the Mertol head down the knoll towards the approaching group from Drumfintley. He spotted Eethan and Jal. "I need to find a cup."

"A cup?" asked Ephie.

Still staring down at James Peck and his mother, Cimerato began to explain. "This knoll was once an ancient Manimal settlement. Every settlement had a talisman, a good luck charm, if you like. It was supposed to protect the town or city from evil. This knoll is all that is left of a town called Malicia. My father told me that there was a cup buried underneath the grass and rocks here. The cup, which is edged with rubies, can be used to help the Manimal race if they are faced with extreme danger."

"Why haven't you used it before?" asked Michael.

"We had the Magic Scales of Gwendral to take us away from danger. The magicians had long since abandoned the Manimal cups, but it was said that they could conjure up some kind of monster or apparition. They were merely a scare tactic that our enemies eventually got used to, but..."

"So you think that this cup along with Mendel's magic might scare the Hedra off?" asked Ephie.

Cimerato pulled Ephie and Michael away from the rest of the gathered Manimals. "Much has been forgotten about these relics but it may be the only hope we have. Look," he pointed beyond the ridge towards the forest of Eldane, "other creatures are coming to see what pickings there might be now that the city has fallen. Tree Trolls and a group of Osgrunfs have been spotted at the tree-line. Who knows what else may appear next?"

"Where is this cup, exactly?" asked Michael.

"It is supposed to be in a well. It will be long-covered by now but we must try."

Michael seemed to be deep in thought.

"What is it, Michael?" asked Ephie.

"Can you find me a couple of twigs, Dearest?"

"Twigs?" she bleated.

" Yes, twigs. It may be a good time to try some water divining."

* * *

By the time James and Craig reached the grassy knoll, there seemed to be a great amount of digging and excavation going on.

Cathy Peck saw Ephie and asked, "You're digging defences, right?"

"Not exactly," replied Ephie, a wooden shovel in her hands. She stuck it into the soft earth and carved out a divot. "We are looking for a well, apparently."

"Dig here!" exclaimed Michael. In his hands a pair of thin twigs, their points crossed, bounced erratically above the grass.

James saw the Yeltan leader, Garlon, spring over to be beside the Reverend. The Yeltan began to dig a fresh pit and soon uncovered a neat ring of stones, piled on top of each other.

"I knew it would be a Yeltan who found it first," said Cimerato. The tall Manimal turned to James and the rest of his group. "All safe?"

"Yes," replied Jal, "and one less Hedra wizard to deal with."

"Dendralon is dead?" said Garlon. He shook the dirt from his hands and walked a little closer to the assembled party.

"How can you be sure?" asked Cimerato.

"Oh, I think we can safely say that he is dead this time," assured Cathy.

"Scoffed up by a fifty-foot dragon after his head was choppeded off," said Wee Joe, adding smugly, "by my big brufa!"

"Technically, it was Jal who did the head-chopping-off thingy," said Helen.

Wee Joe gave her a sharp dig in the ribs.

"And Mendel?" asked Cimerato, already examining the stone well revealed by the Yeltans.

"Still here, my good friend," said Mendel.

"Where?" Cimerato scanned the assembled group, his eyes eventually resting on Bero, the Golden Retriever.

"In the shell. He's a fish again?" said Helen.

"I'm afraid so," sighed Mendel. "And..." the old wizard seemed to be gathering his thoughts, "I no longer possess my magical powers."

"Your magic has gone? I don't understand. Are you sure?"

"Quite sure," said Mendel. "You've taken the right course of action, Cimerato," he added. "I take it you're looking for the Cup of Malicia."

"It was you who told me what to do should anything disastrous ever befall Gwendral," answered Cimerato.

Mendel splashed loudly in his shell. "Boys?"

James and Craig stepped forward. Cathy, however, placed a hand on James's shoulder.

"Boys," continued Mendel, "I need you to go down this well and retrieve a golden cup."

"Why the boys? Why not Cimerato or Jal? Why not you?" snapped Cathy.

"Ignoring the last question, Cathy, their size and enduring friendship are my main reasons."

Cimerato explained, "They will need to be lowered around one-hundred feet before they reach the ledge; is that not correct, Mendel?"

"It is," replied the wizard.

David Peck pushed to the fore, edging past Jal. "I will go, if you like?"

Everyone turned and stared at him.

"If you like?" pressed Cathy. "If you like?" she repeated. "Not exactly a clear, definitive statement, David."

Ephie Blake shook her head and was just about to speak when Michael caught her arm. "Ephie, best keep out of it..."

"No," said Cathy, "Let's hear what she was going to say."

Ephie flushed. She stared at David Peck; the Drumfintley scout leader, the local expert on wildlife, the man who rallied the village defences against an invasion the year before. "You seem to have lost something..." she hesitated.

"His *get up and go*," said Helen.

"Ha!" blasted Cathy. Her eyes narrowed as she circled her husband. "Your get up and go got up and went a long time ago. Didn't it, David?"

James hated this kind of public humiliation. She always did this kind of thing and it made him cringe. There was no need.

"I was only trying to help," said David.

Mendel's voice seeped into their heads, "Thank you, David, but as I said earlier, the boys are a better choice, due to their size."

"I would have gone," said David.

"Sure you would." Cathy sneared. She unsheathed her swords and began examining the blades. "Here, take these." She offered them to the boys.

James stared at his dad and then at his mum. "Why do you think we might need these?"

Mendel interjected, "Better safe than sorry."

"Woh there!" said Craig, still nowhere near his normal self. "What's down there, apart from a magic cup that will scare off the Hedra?"

"Mendel?" pressed James.

"There may be a few of the local fauna lurking about."

"Fauna?" asked Craig.

"Wildlife," said Helen. "Don't you ever watch the nature programmes on the telly?"

"Nothing that shows you the kind of *fauna* we've had to deal with," snapped Craig.

It would have been at this point, James decided, that Jean Harrison would have said something encouraging. He missed her, and could tell by the Harrisons' faces that they were thinking along the same lines.

Selecting his sword, James tucked it into his belt and caught hold of the rope. "What kind of fauna are we talking about, Mendel?"

"Jurpnas or perhaps a few Rartons," sighed Mendel. "Nothing that should cause you too much of a problem."

"If you slice off a Jurpna's antennae, they become harmless," added Cimerato. The tall Manimal clipped an oil-lamp onto James's belt and then lowered them into the darkness.

"What about a Rarton?" Craig shouted up, his voice beginning to echo off the stone walls of the well.

"Let's just hope they're not about," said Cimerato.

"Chin up!" shouted Ephie.

"Which one?" whispered Cathy.

"Oh, I heard that," said Ephie. "Do you have to be so…"

"Honest?" replied his mum. "And another thing…"

But as the voices above them faded, the world below the grassy knoll came into focus. James could see a ledge below and his mind raced with imagined Jurpnas and Rartons. "You okay, Craig?"

"Yup," said Craig.

There was no wisecrack or sarcastic comment.

James wriggled his feet until they found the dusty ledge. "This lamp is pretty useless but it's still easy to see down here."

"The slime trail of the Rarton is luminescent," said Mendel.

"Mendel?" James was surprised to hear his voice.

"I can still find my way into your head, boys, so don't worry too much about…"

"Sssssssssss!"

"What was that?" whispered Craig, taking a step back.

James felt his heart racing. His hands were sweating, and his mum's sword almost dropped onto the floor of the tunnel. "Why can't we call our magic weapons anymore, Mendel?"

"Dendralon took them from you," said Mendel.

"But he's gone now, Mendel," said Craig, ducking below a protruding rock.

"Sssssssss!"

"What the heck is that sound?" said James.

"Sounds like a Rarton," said Mendel.

"You mean the thing Cimerato said we wouldn't meet?" James's voice trailed off as the Rarton came into view.

Craig gripped onto James's shirt. "Is it sleeping?"

The creature was about the size of a dumper-truck and emitted a weird, yellow glow. It resembled a scaly pig with a single horn and, as Craig suggested, it seemed to be sleeping. It snored loudly.

"I can see the cup," whispered James.

"Oh yeah," Craig whispered back, "It's behind the Rarton. You go get it, and I'll tell it a bedtime story."

"Hardie har har," hissed James. This was more like the friend he knew and loved.

"Is that an eye?" asked Craig.

The Rarton had an aperture above the horn, right on the top of its ugly head. It blinked open.

"Sssssssss! Whatssss do youssssss wantsssssss?"

"It talks?" whispered James.

"Yessss Issss talkssss…"

"We'd like to borrow the cup…if you don't mind," said James.

"Whysssss?"

James saw now that its mouth was on the side of its left arm. A set of teeth glistened each time it said something.

"Whysss do you thinkssss?" answered another mouth, on the other arm.

Mendel's voice was a faint whisper in James's head. "Keep it busy. Ask it a question."

Craig must have heard Mendel too because he asked the next question. "How does the cup work?"

"Thissss cupssss?" The Rarton unravelled its arms to reveal a whole new set of mouths. A myriad of gleaming teeth shimmered in the half-light.

"Yeah, that cup." James pointed at the golden cup with his sword.

The Rarton spat a spray of foam across the floor of the tunnel.

The boys edged back toward the dangling rope behind them.

"Keep going forward," said Mendel, "It's only phlegm and carbon dioxide."

The boys edged forward again, their legs cooled by the bubbles as they approached.

James felt his legs tingle. "Are you sure it's only bubbly spit?"

"Ah, wait a minute. *Rartansis tengalis…* It… It has a spit that can morph and…"

"What?" urged Craig.

At that moment the foamy substance that covered the floor rolled into a ball and formed the shape of a beetle, a white foam-like beetle that pulsed with green light.

"Bloomin' marvellous," whispered Craig.

"Nossss cupssss for youssss boyssss!" hissed the Rarton.

The newly formed beetle pounced and James had to hack down with his sword. "Mendel?"

The sword sliced straight through the big bug but it just resealed itself and jumped onto Craig's chest.

More foam snaked round James's feet as an assortment of other insects took shape and began to climb up his legs. "Mendel?"

The boys' swords swung uselessly as the bugs simply joined back together and solidified again. They didn't bite or stab or anything but the more bugs that caught hold of them, the more difficult it was to stay upright.

"Don't fall onto the floor," said Mendel. "I've remembered..."

James braced against the surprising weight of the foamy bugs. "Remembered what?"

"Sing!" shouted Mendel.

"Sing?" Craig yelled back. "Bloody sing? I can't stand up any longer, never mind sing."

Through the tangle of bugs James saw that the Rarton was moving towards them, an array of munching mouths snapping as it slithered closer.

"Sing!" blasted Mendel.

"Oh I do like to be beside the seaside," squeaked James.

"You what?" snapped Craig.

"Join in!" shouted James. "Oh I do like to be beside the sea..." he continued.

"Oh I do like to stroll along the prom, prom, prom..." they wheezed, "as the brass band plays: 'Tiddly-om-pom-pom'..."

The Rarton began to hiss, as if it was in pain.

The bugs began to drop off...

"Keep singing," urged Mendel

"So just let me be beside the sea!" they blasted.

"ARGH! Sssssssss..."

With a burst of purple steam, the Rarton exploded and the foamy bugs fizzled into the floor.

"Oh, I do like to be beside the sea..."

"That's enough," snapped Craig.

James opened his eyes. "It's gone?"

"Yeah," said Craig, "and you can't sing."

"Never said I could," replied James. "Thank goodness for Mrs. Miller, the music teacher."

"Yeah," said Craig. "That's about the only song I know."

"Me too." James's eyes drifted to the golden cup. A row of red rubies sparkled as he reached out. "The Cup of Malicia, I presume."

"Let's grab it quick before that other thing comes round the corner," said Craig.

As soon as James touched the cup's smooth surface, however, a pair of red antennae wriggled down from the ceiling above them.

Swish!

James hacked them off and watched them drop to the floor.

"Well done, numpty boy," jeered Craig. "You know something, there's more of your mum in you than you think."

A tiny black wood-louse joined the squirming antennae on the floor at the boys' feet.

"Those antennae were attached to that?" whispered Craig.

"Yeah. Weird," agreed James. He picked up the golden cup and made his way back to the dangling rope with his best friend.

Cimerato's face appeared above them, silhouetted by the bright Denthan sky.

"Pull us up!" yelled James.

CHAPTER TWENTY-FIVE

THE LOST SEEDS

James and Craig sat down beside Helen, Wee Joe and the rest of the Drumfintley contingent. They opened the hemp bags thrown down at their feet by the Yeltans and rummaged around for something to eat.

"Ees good, that fruit ees," said Eethan. He sat cross-legged at the edge of the exposed well, picking his nose with his thumb.

"Do you mind?" said Cathy Peck. "We don't want to see what you've got up there, so give it a rest."

Eethan looked bemused but soon backed off to a safe distance.

James sat close to Bero and Mendel's shell.

"Here you go," said Garlon. "That's the second time I've had to fix that trinket."

"The brandy barrel!" said Helen. "I picked it up from the Dragon Chamber," she explained. "I didn't think you would be able to put it back together again, Garlon."

"It was a challenge." Garlon handed it to James.

"Excellent," said James. He prised open the lid of the shell and poured Mendel inside the refurbished brandy barrel.

Craig fixed it onto Bero's neck.

James caught a glimpse of gold and yellow through the slightly opaque window of the barrel. He began munching on some mossgeld, an edible kind of vine that hung down from the trees in the Forest of Eldane. "I'd forgotten how good this stuff tasted," he muttered.

Craig and Ephie nodded in agreement, too busy scoffing the delicious dried fibres to look him in the eye.

"What do we do now, Mendel? I mean with the cup. And how are we ever going to get home?" said James.

There was a long pause before Mendel answered. "The cup will summon a demi-god called Frasfer."

"And that's a good thing because...?" asked Craig.

"The Manimals think it will scare off the Hedra," said Cathy.

"You said it was a demi-god?" asked Michael.

"That's right, Dear," said Ephie. "That's what Mendel said."

"Oh," replied Michael.

Jal wandered into their midst and gazed out across the Plain of Gwendral at the darkening sky. "The Hedra will attack at first light."

"And why would they wait until it was light?" asked Cathy.

"Yeah," said Helen. "I thought you Hedra had infra-red vision? Surely it would make more sense to attack us when it gets dark?"

Jal laughed. "We have our rules."

"Rules?" asked James. "They... I mean *you* have rules about not attacking in the dark?"

"More like superstitions, really," answered Jal. He hunkered down and settled in beside them. "We would never attack when there is a risk of upsetting the gods."

Helen stood up. "And this Fraser..."

"Frasfer," corrected Mendel.

"Frasfer... This demi-god is one of the gods you fear?" Helen pressed.

"Oh yes," said Jal.

"Never mind all that," snapped Cathy, tugging the last piece of mossgeld from David Peck's fingers, "James is right, for once. How do we get back home to Drumfintley?"

"You would just leave all these Yeltans and Manimals to their fate?" asked Ephie.

"Yip," said Cathy.

"Charming," whispered Ephie.

Michael gave her a little stare that said, 'Be careful'.

Mendel continued, "First things first, Cathy. We will conjure Frasfer at dawn. By that time, I hope the Mertol will have returned with something that will help you get back home to Scotland."

James scanned round for the big Mertol in the half-light. "Where is he?"

Michael stretched out towards Ephie with a handful of mossgeld. As he did, however, a tattered, brown envelope fell from his inside jacket pocket.

"What's that?" asked James.

Michael was just about to put it back in his pocket when Cathy snatched it from him.

"Excuse me!" protested Michael.

Before anyone could stop her, Cathy opened the envelope and removed two very old and faded pieces of cloth.

"It's just a keepsake," said Michael.

"It's tartan," said Cathy. "What do you want this tat for?"

"It's not tat," said Michael. "It's very old."

There was a splash from the barrel.

Everyone looked round at Bero and then back at Cathy. She handed Michael the scraps of tartan cloth.

"I found one piece in the Holy Land, while I was a student," said Michael.

"You mean you bought it in some souvenir shop," said Cathy.

"No, I found it in a clay pot near the Sea of Galilee."

"So, you found both pieces there?" asked James.

"No," interrupted Mendel. "He found the second piece next to the Jesus Rocks, didn't you, Father?"

"Well, yes..." said Michael. "I always had a notion that there was a connection."

"Connection?" asked Cathy.

Michael sighed, as if he'd been compromised into some kind of explanation. "There is a school of thought..."

"You mean, it's your idea?" interrupted Cathy.

"A school of thought," continued Michael, "that says that the Celts originated in an area of what is now south-east of Russia, around the Caspian Sea. They migrated westwards until they finally reached Ireland, Wales, Cornwall and, of course, Scotland."

"What's that got to do with your tartan keepsakes?" asked David.

"Well…" continued Michael, "their migration over the centuries can be traced in the place names beginning with GAL… Galatea, Galicia, Gallipoli, Galada, Gaul, Galway, Galloway… The Greek historian Diodorus Siculus, writing in 50 BC, describes the Celts as wearing tartan 'striped or chequered in design, with the separate checks close together and in various colours.' Galilee is described in the Bible as 'Galilee of the Gentiles'. Some believe that the original Galileans might have been Celtic."

Cathy guffawed. "Ha! So you're saying that Jesus wore tartan?"

Michael seemed to shrink back into the shadows. "No. But it's not at all as far-fetched as it might at first sound."

"All very intriguing, and not without some element of truth," said Mendel, "however, there are more pressing matters at hand."

"I'll say," said Cathy.

"Well, I thought it was very interesting," said Helen.

"Helen," said Mendel, "do you still have Dendralon's pouch?"

"Pouch?" Helen traced her small fingers over her belt. "Em… Was I supposed to take his pouch?"

"Have you got it, James?" pressed Mendel. "No, I'm sure it was Helen who…"

Cathy Peck rounded on Mendel. "Stop getting at her, will you. She's been through enough without you ripping into her."

"I was not ripping…" Mendel sighed.

Cathy's eyes narrowed. "You never asked anyone to get Dendralon's bloody pouch. You just asked us to stop *him* from getting it."

"Eh…" Helen looked very agitated. "I picked this up but there's nothing inside." She shook the empty pouch in front of James's face.

"Oh no," whispered Mendel.

"He's dead," reminded Craig. "I mean how many times do we need to kill him?"

"He was gobbled up by de big dragon," said Wee Joe.

"His head was," corrected James.

Craig stabbed Cathy's sword into grassy knoll. "Exactly. So how can he still be a threat?"

"Eethan, you will have to swim back to the island and look for those seeds," said Mendel. "We need the seeds that were in the pouch."

"But how can he possibly find…?" interrupted Craig, clearly on the edge of exploding.

Eethan bowed respectfully and turned.

James and Craig got up to follow him.

"Eh…" said Cathy, "I'll have my swords back, boys."

"What about the seeds?" said James, whisking the golden sword from his belt.

"Let's leave that to Eethan for now. We shouldn't jump to any bad conclusions," said Mendel.

"We could really do with our magic weapons," moped Craig.

Eethan skirted the Drumfintley group, giving Cathy Peck a wide berth.

Cathy Peck eyed the little blue man's thumb suspiciously

The wizard-goldfish sloshed around in the barrel. "Eethan, before you go…"

"Yees Mendel?"

"Eethan, I need you to help young James, here, with a bit of magic."

"Ees my pleasure. What ees we doing? Turning hees mummy into a tree?"

"Very funny," said Cathy, running her swords back into their scabbards with a violent flick of her wrists.

"No, not this time. I'm thinking more along the lines of a replacement spell."

Eethan became very animated, stamping his feet and circling on the spot.

None-the-wiser, everyone continued munching their mossgeld, all eyes on the little man.

"Ee loves thees kind of spell. What ees we replacing?" said Eethan.

"I'd like to see if we can do what Craig has suggested. I'd like to see if you can reassign the Denthan sword, Firetongue, and the Denthan spear, Greenworm, to the boys again."

Eethan came to a sudden stop. "Yees, but eet weel take time wees do not have. Ee likes doing magic for yous Mendel, but thee seeds…"

"I know. If Dendralon has found a way to retrieve the seeds…" said Mendel

"He's dead!" blasted Cathy. She mimed Whindril swallowing his decapitated head. "Head in dragon's tummy!"

Mendel ignored her. "Eethan, join hands with James."

James and Eethan joined hands and approached the barrel that swung from Bero's neck.

The sky was peppered with stars, and there was a great fire burning in the ruins of Gwendral. On the far off ridge, James could see hundreds of Hedra campfires glowing like fireflies. He shivered. "Right. What now, Mendel?"

"Say these words: reclamify da thirth et da greeth."

"Da…" James began.

"Reclamify da thirth et da greeth!" said Mendel, even louder than before.

James and Eethan said the words and waited.

Eethan smiled and closed his eyes. A faint blue light flickered in his chest.

James squinted down at the glow and then closed his eyes too.

He felt a warm sensation trace his spine.

"Now visualise Firetongue and Greenworm," said Mendel. "Picture the weapons drifting through the air. Firetongue to you, James, and Greenworm to Craig."

James could see the weapons in his mind's eye. He felt the familiar hilt settle in his hand.

"Argh!"

He pulled away from Eethan and tucked his hand under his arm.

Craig had screamed out too.

"It will take a few minutes," said Mendel, calmly.

James opened his eyes in time to see Eethan scamper off in the direction of the Gorton Sea, but in his hand…

"Greenworm," shouted Craig.

"Yes!" said Mendel. "You have the weapons back. And this time, because it was Eethan and James who summoned them, they should remain at your call, even back on Earth. Natural magic, you see."

"No, we don't see. And that's if we ever get back to Earth," added Cathy.

Craig wandered over to James and patted him on the back. "You're a regular little wizard now, aren't you?"

"Hardly," said James.

"Well," said Craig, proudly examining his green tattoo, "You did all right." He pointed toward the dark void that marked the Gortan Sea. Eethan had almost submerged beneath the waves. "Is he off to see if Dendralon has pulled off another resurrection stunt then?"

"I guess," said James.

Craig studied his feet. "Seems unfair that Dendralon could have survived when…"

"I know," said James, thinking of Craig's mum. "Not fair."

* * *

Although the water was freezing, Eethan swam through the depths with ease. Passed the swaying kelp-like forests and then over the rocks and deep trenches until, about a hundred yards from the island, he slowed and broke the surface. He soon found the small beach where they'd fought with Dendralon. Covering every inch of sand and sea-weed he looked for any sign of the Hedra wizard's body or the large Eden Seeds, but there was nothing. Sniffing the sand he eventually came to a spot where he was convinced the dark wizard's body had lain. A few faint furrows and indentations indicated that Dendralon's body had been dragged, or more worrying still, had pulled itself into the sea. Eethan knew that there were any number of creatures capable of devouring the body or indeed eating a few discarded seeds. "Eees no good," he muttered to himself. "Ees gone… Wees stuck here now."

* * *

It was the sound of Hedra trumpets that woke James. Cimerato had kept a careful watch over his kin during the night but Jal had ventured as close as he dared to the Hedra positions. James had seen him crawl, lizard-style, towards the campfires that dotted the far off ridge before he'd fallen asleep.

"We've hardly slept at all," complained Helen.

"Greenworm," called Craig, anxious to see if the trusty spear with the emerald sheen would appear in his hand.

When it did, he rolled the shaft over his forearms, watching it spin up to his elbow and back down to his waiting fingers. "It's good to have Greenworm back," he said.

James felt the cold breeze cut into him. A bitter wind was coming down from the far off mountains and, as he stretched, his stomach grumbled in complaint. "How long have we been gone from Drum-fintley, Craig?"

But Craig's face had glazed over. "Two…three days?"

James suddenly remembered that Jean Harrison was dead. It was obvious that his inane question had been eclipsed by Craig's own horrible realisation of this fact. The pain was etched on his best friend's face.

"I'll fix us some breakfast," said James, unable to look at his friend's expression any longer.

"Yeah," muttered Craig. "Whatever..."

The rumble of war-drums followed another blast from the Hedra trumpets.

"Is there any sign of Eethan or Jal?" said Helen.

"I'll find out," said James. He wondered if Helen and Wee Joe's separation, a whole year deep in an Indian jungle, had somehow acclimatized them to the loss of their mum. They didn't seem to be showing the same pain as Craig.

Wee Joe was up and already squirting dozing Manimals with his water-pistol.

"Good boy," said Cimerato, "that'll wake them up."

As James gathered some dried meat and mossgeld, Garlon tapped him on the arm. "Here, James, take this..." He handed James a small vial filled with black liquid. "Pop a single drop into the Harrison's breakfast. It will dull their pain for a while."

James examined the bottle and smiled. "Thanks, Garlon. I'll see..."

"Just thought it might help."

"Thank you. I'll just see how they bear up first." James didn't want to be rude but he was uneasy about drugging the Harrisons.

Michael was attempting to shave using a kind of razor shell. Elgry, the Manimal secretary, was giving him instructions. His face was covered in a kind of cuckoo spit that Elgry had scooped up from the long grass.

"Any sign of Eethan or Jal?" asked Michael.

"Talk of the devil," said Cimerato.

The huge eight-foot Hedra, Jal, had reverted to two legs again and, at his side, looking very tiny indeed, was the unmistakable figure of Eethan.

Bero nuzzled into the back of James's bare legs and wagged his tail.

James reached back and patted the dog. "Good boy."

Mendel's voice filtered into his thoughts. "Is Eethan empty handed?"

James shouted out. "Eethan. Did you find the seeds?"

Dolefully, Eethan shook his head.

James wondered why they'd appeared from the direction of the Hedra on the ridge.

"Any other news?" asked Mendel.

Jal obviously heard the wizard goldfish. He addressed the barrel. "I spoke with a friend of mine, Relfarth. He said that Dendralon had spoken to him in person yesterday."

"When?" asked Mendel, anxiously.

"Oh, well before Whindril had her snack," said Jal. "I told Relfarth to spread the word."

"And will he?" asked James.

"Yes, he is quite happy to see the back of Dendralon. Many of the Hedra feel the same."

Elgry wandered closer. "So why do they want to attack us? Gwendral has fallen."

Smoke was still bellowing up from the ruins behind them.

"There are still many of the Hedra who think that, in ruins or not, Gwendral is rightfully theirs. You have to remember that we wandered the stinking Southern Marshes in exile for thousands of years. There are also many soldiers loyal to the memory of Feldon our King. Some of them still believe he's alive."

"He's another one who lost his head," said Craig, remembering the Hedra King's demise at the hands of a giant Salt Troll.

"Yes, but in their minds they are only a few hours on from that point," said Mendel. "It is not surprising that the news of their King's death has not reached them all. A mere ten hours has passed, in Denthan time, since the sun, Tealfirth, exploded."

"So are they going to attack?" asked Ephie, her big wax coat wrapped round her.

"Yes," said Jal.

"Then, we will have to use the Cup of Malicia," said Mendel. "Eethan, prepare the area needed."

"Yeees, Mendel."

CHAPTER TWENTY-SIX

FRASER THE DEMI-GOD

D awn was well under way, and the Hedra were on the move.
Ephie brushed some crumbs off her battered-looking coat.
"I hope your cup works, James."

Beyond Ephie, James's mum and dad were niggling at each other and his thoughts were still a mishmash of the collapsing citadels and dragons. "What was that, Ephie? Sorry…"

"I said, I hope that cup can conjure something up that will scare them off." She pointed to the neat rows of grey-scaled Hedra that poured down from the ridge onto the Plain of Gwendral.

"Mendel seems to think that it can."

"We might have to fight again," said Helen.

"We might," agreed James. He called on Firetongue. The crimson-bladed sword filled him with bravado and energy. As he held it, however, he remembered the anger that Craig had displayed before, when he'd touched Greenworm, and he wondered again if these weapons, like the Yeltan drinks and powders, somehow affected their personalities. He turned the sword back and forth and smiled as it glinted in the half-light. "I'd forgotten how amazing this feels," he whispered.

"Nothing will feel amazing until we're back home," said Helen, in a small voice. "Nothing will ever feel amazing again."

"Sorry, Helen. I didn't mean to make you upset, I..."

"Eethan's ready," she said.

"Yeh... Of course," James mumbled. *What a prat I am.*

At the edge of the plain, Eethan paced out a circle he'd marked with some loose stones. In the middle, sat the Cup of Malicia. "Ees ready, James," he shouted.

"Fine," said James. He slid his way down the knoll towards him. "What do I say this time?"

Eethan chuckled. "Ees easy. Just touch the cup wees me and say: 'Frasfer'."

"Frasfer," repeated James.

"Not yeet. When ee..."

"When we both touch the cup at the same time," James finished. "I've got it. No problem." Slightly out of breath, he crouched down within the circle and looked at Eethan. They were a good hundred feet ahead of the Manimal lines, at the base of the grassy knoll.

His mum walked down towards him with Cimerato and Jal at her side. She still looked every inch the warrior-queen.

A sudden gust hammered into them and they braced.

James saw the Hedra's advance waver. "What on Earth...?"

Cathy Peck stepped inside the circle. "We're not on Earth, James. What the heck is that?" She pointed up at the brightening sky, her black hair flying behind her.

In the bleary dawn sky, James saw a huge, irregular moon slow and then stop. The Gortan Sea was whisked into a lather of waves and foam. The grass that covered the knoll whipped about their feet, and the wind, cold and from the north, strengthened.

Through his narrowed eyes, James saw Bero bounding down the hill, Craig and Helen at the big dog's side.

"Mendel?" asked Cimerato, staring wildly at the massive lump of rock in the sky.

"Now Denthan has a moon," said Mendel.

"It doesn't look like any moon I've ever seen," said Craig.

"Oh, and how many moons have you seen then?" said Cathy.

Meekly, Craig answered, "You know what I mean."

"It looks to me like this could be part of Tealfirth. Luckily for us, it must have been slowed down by the gravity of the other planets on its way here. It could have smashed into Denthan and..." Mendel drifted off in thought. "If there are other planets out there, the magic performed in the Dragon Chamber must have saved the entire Denthine System."

"Is it going to fall on us?" asked Helen.

"No, Helen. Not now, but it looks as though Denthan will change. There will be tides and different kinds of weather to deal with."

"Never mind all that," shouted Cathy. "What do we do now?"

"Yes, of course… Continue with the spell. The Hedra are obviously confused by this phenomenon too."

"Some have gathered on the shore," said Craig, pointing with Greenworm to a large group of Hedra that had broken ranks.

James waited until everyone had cleared the circle and then touched the golden Cup of Malicia at the same time as Eethan. The little blue man nodded and James projected, as loudly as he could, the name he'd been told. "Frasfer!"

Rust-coloured clouds raced over the morning sky and thickened above them. The wind died away. There was an almighty flash as lightning forked down and split the cup in two.

"James!" yelled Cathy.

James and Eethan fell back and then edged out of the circle away from the thing that grew taller in front of them.

A huge hand slammed down onto the ground.

As James tried to roll out of the way, fingers as big as tree trunks dug into the ground beside him. "Ahhh!"

Someone caught hold of his shirt and pulled him out of harm's way. It was his dad.

"Just caught you in time there, Son."

"Thanks…" James felt for the hilt of his sword.

"Let's pull further back," his dad urged.

The ground rumbled and ruptured to reveal the biggest giant James had ever seen.

"I hope he's on our side," said Helen.

"Yeah," said Craig. "And good one, Mr. Peck; James would have been squished for sure just then, if you hadn't yanked him back."

James's dad smiled and dusted himself down.

James saw Craig look across at his mum, decked in her golden armour, and then back at his dad. "I don't think you're a big useless coward, Mr. Peck."

"Oh, thanks, Craig," David replied, a frown forming on his face.

"That thing is Frasfer?" asked Helen.

"Yeah…" James craned his neck in an attempt to see the giant's head.

"It must be two hundred feet high. What do you think?" said Craig.

"Yeah… Easy." James groaned.

* * *

Everyone in the Drumfintley group had fallen in with the Manimal ranks halfway up the grassy knoll. The giant, Frasfer, stretched and growled, his gaze fixed on the Hedra beyond.

"What are the Hedra…? Sorry, I mean what are your kin up to?" asked Cimerato.

Jal squinted up at the misshapen moon and then back at the ridge. "Well, they're not running away, but they are not advancing either. I feel…" Jal paused and shaded his yellow eyes with a big scaly hand. "I feel as if they should have made a move by now. There is still a size-able force down on the shore. I don't know why that would be…"

The Yeltan, Garlon, edged into the conversation. "They have found something that gives them hope."

Everyone looked at him disdainfully.

James saw a knowing look flash across the Yeltan's pallid face. "They can't have any hope against that." James pointed at Frasfer, who was standing some hundred yards down the hill.

"I think Garlon's right," said Jal.

At that moment, there was a disturbance at the top of the knoll. James turned back towards Gwendral and the summit of the grassy knoll. "What the…?"

"It's the Mertol!" shouted a Manimal.

"Excellent!" exclaimed Mendel.

The lumbering, fifteen-foot high Mertol called out, "Bak!" It was carrying something.

Craig, Helen, and Wee Joe all strained to see what it was.

"What is it holding?" asked James's dad.

Cathy Peck eyed him suspiciously.

The Mertol called out once more but stopped short when the giant, Frasfer, turned round and looked down.

James thought the Mertol looked scared.

Still covered in dust, the Mertol's fur, which was not dissimilar to an orang-utan's, was even more matted than ever. The pits in its face flickered open and shut as it placed something on the ground behind a large rock.

"Get me closer to the rock," said Mendel.

The Harrisons were already sprinting towards it, Bero at their heels, his tail wind-milling.

Craig was the first to pass the Mertol and reach the large rock. "NO!"

James's heart was pounding. He skidded to a halt behind them.

Helen edged out from behind the rock. She faced James, her eyes already full of tears. "It's not Mum."

"Ah…" said James, feeling useless.

"Bak!" The Mertol stooped down and caught hold of Bero's collar. The barrel swung as Bero left the ground. The Mertol glanced nervously at Frasfer and then picked up the object he'd retrieved from the fallen city. It whirred and spun just above his outstretched palm.

"The Key of Artilis," said James. He quickly turned to the Harrisons and said, "I'm sorry guys. Chin up."*Chin up, bloomin' chin up. Why do I say the most stupid things at times like these? I never say 'chin up'.*

Mendel's voice slipped into all their thoughts. "Magic attracts magic, children, and your grief will, one day, be quelled."

James didn't know what the wizard was on about.

Mendel seemed to sense their confusion. "The Mertol has found the Key of Artilis…"

"That's the magic attracts magic bit, we get it," said Cathy.

"And even though the children's loss is great right now…"

"It always will be great," barked Craig. "I don't want it to be quelled, or whatever you said. She was our mum!" He stormed off towards the front of the Manimal ranks.

"Nice one, Mendel," whispered Cathy.

"Mendel?" James asked quietly. "Now we have the Key, can we all go home?"

"We are one step closer," said Mendel. "We can bend time. We just need the Eden Seeds that Dendralon had in his pouch."

"But that's impossible…" began James.

"Wait!" urged Mendel.

About a half-mile away from the knoll, on the shore of the Gortan Sea, a cheer rose up from the Hedra. The wind caught hold again and lightning forked down from the sky. The Hedra fell back as something big rose up from the sands beside them.

"They have a cup too?" interrupted Jal.

James spun round. "No way."

"Yes, way!" said Wee Joe.

Jal pointed down at the shore. "Look for yourself."

"It can't be," said James.

"It bloomin' is," said Helen.

"Another giant?" asked Wee Joe.

Bero woofed then growled. The hackles rose up on his neck.

James recognised this giant. It was horrible. As tall as Frasfer only...

"It's missing a head," said Helen.

"Dendralon was missing a head, last time I looked," said James.

"It's Dendralon," said Mendel.

"What's left of him," added Jal.

"The new tide must have washed his body ashore," said Mendel.

"They have used a Hedra cup and the body of their leader," said Jal.

"That's just great," said Helen, more tears rolling down her cheeks.

Instinctively, James gave her a hug. "Frasfer will sort him out. Dendralon can't even see. He's just a big zombie thing."

Helen gave a small laugh and wiped her face. "A two hundred foot zombie thing."

"Yeah, well..." James smiled.

"Jal!" shouted Cimerato.

"I know. I can see it," replied Jal. "He has no head and..."

"It's not that," said Cimerato. "There's a Hedra chariot racing across the Plain of Gwendral towards us. The driver is carrying a white flag with a scaled hand."

"They want to talk," said Jal.

* * *

As James wandered down the hill to get a better look at the Hedra coming towards them, he heard Craig move in beside him. He turned and with a red face said, "I'm sorry, Craig. I don't know what to say, sometimes. I mean about your mum and stuff. And Mendel... Well..."

"It's all right. The old guppy just caught me at a bad time."

"He didn't mean any harm. The old guppy, that is," said James.

"James and Beldam!" shouted Jal.

"Cathy Peck, to you," snapped his mum.

"Cathy." Jal smiled. "I would like you both to come with me."

"Fine," said Cathy.

James nodded. "Okay, but what do you think they want? I mean, they've got a two-hundred foot Dendralon."

"And we have Frasfer," said Jal. "I know the Hedra that approaches. He is the one that I made contact with last night."

"Relfarth?" asked James.

"One and the same," said Jal. "Come. The Yeltans have put a chariot together. They've hitched some Yukplugs to it."

"Call that a chariot?" said Cathy.

"Can you drive it?" asked Jal.

Cathy circled the chariot, pointing rudely at the Yukplugs. "With those things pulling it...?" She sighed. "I'll try."

James and Jal jumped up onto the footplate. He watched his mum take the reins.

"Ya!" she bellowed, racing the chariot straight through the Manimal ranks. They had to dive out of the way to stop from being run over.

"Nicely done." Jal beamed.

Awkwardly, James waved back at his dad and the Drumfintley group.

"God speed!" shouted Michael.

A bump almost threw James from the footplate. He lost his footing. Jal nipped his skin through his shirt as he pulled him back on board.

"Awch!" yelped James.

"You're back on, aren't you?" snapped his mum. "So don't moan, and hold on tighter."

As they got closer to the oncoming Hedra chariot, James could see the two Raptors harnessed to the rigging. One was mainly purple, with red feathers while the other, smaller by far, was decked in golden flecked feathers that shimmered in the breeze. *They look quite beautiful when they're not trying to eat you*, thought James.

"Whoa!" yelled Jal.

Relfarth, was smaller than Jal in height but much more stocky. They gave each other a kind of salute and pulled up, side by side.

Cathy drew her swords and eyed the Raptors.

"They will not harm you, great Queen," said Relfarth.

Cathy gave him a particularly snidey glance.

James could see the giant, ghoul-like form of Dendralon, swaying slightly, as if waiting for some command. There was no sense of Dendralon actually being present, just of some giant mechanical toy effigy ready to do its master's bidding.

"I have a proposal," said Relfarth.

"Propose away, my friend," said Jal.

"To the rest of the Hedra, it must look as if we are at odds here, Jal," said Relfarth. He circled their chariot and flicked the Raptors with the reins so they roared in a threatening manner.

"I understand," said Jal.

"There are many Hedra who say that they would follow you."

"Me?" said Jal.

"Yes," replied Relfarth.

Cathy Peck tapped her sword on the side of the chariot and hauled the Yukplugs into line. "Ha!"

"Mum," whispered James. "Not too threatening."

Relfarth stared at his mum for a long moment and then continued, "I propose that our two mascots join battle. Whatever giant wins will determine the outcome of the fight between our forces."

"But you could overrun us quite easily," said Jal.

"You know as well as I, that our kind fear Frasfer. They would think it bad luck to take him on directly."

"That was our hope," said Jal.

"Let them fight." Relfarth circled. "We found Dendralon's body on the shore. I suggested using the Hedra cup we took from the Southern Marshes to transform the corpse."

"Did you find any seeds on the body?" asked James.

"Seeds?" answered the Hedra.

"Shhh! Be quiet, James," barked his mum.

"But..." James moaned.

"So be it," said Jal. "Let them fight. The giants will dictate which side issues the terms of the peace."

With a sharp nod Relfarth pulled his chariot round aggressively, bumping into their Yukplugs and spraying them all with dirt.

The Yeltan steeds yelped in pain, but Cathy pulled them round and raced back to the Manimal lines.

"The seeds?" protested James.

"First things first," said his mum.

They bumped and lurched back over the plain until they halted in front of the towering figure of Frasfer. He resembled a Manimal in every way. He even had the same white-slit eyes. James looked over at the hideous form of the headless Dendralon. Even in death the wizard had returned to haunt them. One hand tight in a fist, the other open and bearing a set of Hedra claws that must have been five feet long, Dendralon's corpse still looked a formidable opponent.

"What happens if Dendralon wins?" he asked, as they dismounted the chariot.

"Then," began Jal, "we are back to where we were before. "We have nothing to lose."

"You knew that Hedra well, didn't you, Jal?" said James.

"Well enough. We used to stand guard over Feldon, the Hedra king. We were his champions."

Cathy Peck marched over to David, who was deep in conversation with Ephie and Michael.

James found the Harrisons and Bero on the left flank and joined them. Mendel splashed loudly in the barrel and announced that he was feeling better than he had in many a year.

"Dendralon may have taken my magic," Mendel continued, "but he has restored my youth."

"How long do goldfish live for?" asked James. He stared into the barrel through the little plastic window.

"About twenty years or so. I think the record is forty three."

Mendel's scales did seem to have taken on a brighter sheen and there was a little wisp of a beard under his lower lip. "Never really noticed the beard before," said James.

"It's always been there," said Wee Joe. He tapped James on the shoulder as the giants began to walk towards each other. "How will de big Dendralon know where he's going without a head?"

James shrugged. "I hope he doesn't know. He might even squish a few Hedra."

Helen drew him a disapproving glare. "Jal says they are not all bad."

"I've yet to be convinced on that one," said Craig. Greenworm spun round in his hand. He twirled it and then pointed to Frasfer. "He's got a massive Gwendralin sword. Dendralon stands no chance."

As the giants closed in on each other, James noticed something. "Did you see that, Craig?"

"What?"

"Look at Dendralon's outstretched hand; there's sparks or something dancing round his claws."

"There can't be," said Helen. "He's dead. The real Dendralon's dead."

As Frasfer struck down with his sword, the giant Dendralon sidestepped him and kicked Frasfer's legs from beneath him. Frasfer crashed down onto his back and Dendralon knelt on his massive chest. The headless wizard's claws found Frasfer's neck and began to close, crimson sparks hissing from the tips of his fingers.

With a roar, Frasfer rolled out from beneath Dendralon and found the hilt of his sword. He swung it at Dendralon's back but it shuddered off of the creature's grey scales. Like huge grey slates, the scales shattered and slid off Dendralon's back to smash on the plain. Dendralon, however, managed to find his feet. He pointed at the approaching Frasfer and a stream of red liquid shot out of his fingertips...

"That's impossible," protested James.

Frasfer thundered backwards, unsteady and flailing wildly.

"He's going to crush us! Run!" roared James.

The Harrisons and Bero all retreated a further hundred yards, just missing the juddering head of Frasfer as it smashed into the grassy knoll.

"I thought this was supposed to be a piece of cake," said Craig.

The giant, headless Dendralon staggered, blindly, towards their positions.

"He can't see," said Mendel. "He is only depending on some residual magic."

"What?" said Wee Joe.

"Dendralon's body must still have some magic flowing through it," explained Helen.

"Precisely," said Mendel.

"Watch out!" bleated James.

Dendralon tripped on Frasfer's outstretched legs and tumbled down towards them.

"The big rock!" shouted Craig. He pulled Wee Joe in beside them and braced.

CRASH!

He headless body of Dendralon landed on top of them.

"Argh!" James closed his eyes.

"Bak!" An orange, matted hand scooped them out from the gap between Dendralon's toppled body and the rocks. Bero bolted out after them, barking and growling.

"Bak!" The Mertol pulled them further back.

This time it was Frasfer who took the advantage when, with a deafening yell and a twisting action, he freed himself from the giant deadweight of Dendralon and knelt to the side. Picking up his sword he stabbed down just as Dendralon's body pushed up. The oversized Gwendralin sword buried itself deep in the giant Hedra wizard's back.

"Ooooew…" said Helen.

"Good enough for him," spat Craig, still full of pent up fury.

Dendralon's massive, clawed hand reached up to the sky, sending a shower of multicoloured sparks and flames into the gathering clouds before, seemingly spent, the wizard's zombie-like corpse slumped down and shuddered for the last time.

James had to sidestep Dendralon's closed fist as it clumped down onto the hillside beside him. "Whoa! He still nearly managed to kill me."

"He's got to be dead this time," said Wee Joe, squirting his plastic water-gun at the huge, scaled fingers.

Free of the fight, Frasfer knelt down and then rolled onto his back and closed his eyes.

Strangely, the two giants began to shrink down to normal sized beings. Creaking and slipping across the grass, they returned to the way they had been before the magic of Denthan had taken hold of them.

"Frasfer was once a soldier of Malicia," explained Mendel. "He has performed his last duty."

The Hedra jeered and wailed in disapproval, but the one known as Relfarth tore across the plain in his chariot and raised his fist.

James turned to Jal. "They're going to attack. They're not going to keep to the agreement."

"No," said Jal, "Relfarth will bring order. He has the respect of his troops."

But the Hedra were advancing en masse.

"They're going to attack us," pressed James.

"I don't think so," said Cathy. "James, go stand with your dad and the rest of the Drumfintley group."

"Do as you mother says," added Mendel, his voice drifting into James's head.

"Wee Joe's in danger!" said James. "He's too close to Dendralon's body. No, Joe!"

"He's fine," said Mendel. "He is going to retrieve something. Jal must speak to the Hedra."

James felt anxiety grip him as he glanced between Wee Joe and Jal. Wee Joe was prizing something from Dendralon's closed fist.

"Eees thee Eden Seeds," said Eethan.

"They were in his hand all the time," said James. He could see that Jal had begun walking out to meet Relfarth on the plain. "What's going to happen now, Mendel?"

Mendel's voice assumed a serious tone. "Jal has a chance to lead his own race into a new kind of dawn."

The Denthan sky began to brighten as the clouds parted.

"What do you mean?" asked James. Cimerato and Eethan walked out behind Jal.

"Relfarth has asked Jal to become the new Hedra King," said Mendel.

The whole Hedra force, still a sizeable army, closed in round the grassy knoll. The darker creatures of Eldane; Osgrunfs and Tree Trolls, and even a few Centides, began to slope off towards the safety of the great forest.

"You mean when Jal went into the Hedra camp last night to make a deal with Relfarth?" asked James.

"Yes. But it will all depend on Cimerato and the rest of the Hedra accepting the proposal," said Mendel.

"The proposal?" asked Craig.

"Let's go and listen," said James.

"Not without me, you don't," said his mum. Cathy Peck clinked along beside the boys and Bero.

James's heart pounded, as he got closer to the vicious-looking Hedra. The charioteers pulled the colourful Raptors back. They screamed and barked menacingly, obviously keen to attack.

James's sweaty fingers traced the hilt of Firetongue.

"Relfarth," said Jal. "Our champion has beaten yours."

"He has," answered Relfarth, matter-of-factly.

The gathered Hedra hissed and murmured.

Relfarth turned to face them. "Enough!" The hissing and shouting died down a little. "Many of you know of Jal," he pointed to the giant Hedra beside James. "Do you forget that he was once King Feldon's champion?"

"He betrayed us," shouted someone from the crowd.

"No!" said Relfarth, "It was Dendralon who betrayed us. Jal had the good sense to see the truth. We have lingered in the Southern Marshes for too long. It is time for a new beginning."

"We should take the city!" shouted another Hedra.

"What city?" replied Relfarth.

There were more hisses of dissent.

James glanced back at the ruins of Gwendral. Smoke still seeped skyward from the toppled citadel.

"Dendralon destroyed the very thing he promised us," continued Relfarth.

"Jal and I have spoken of a new way," said Cimerato.

There was a deathly silence.

"His armour is still covered in Hedra blood," shouted another Hedra.

"And yours in Manimal blood," barked Cimerato.

Jal, taller than most of the Hedra, jabbed his sword into the ground. "I will lead the Hedra nation on one condition…"

There was an eerie silence.

"The Hedra and the Manimals must work together to rebuild Gwendral, and then share it."

James heard the Manimals behind him chatter and mumble.

"As equals," shouted Cimerato.

More derision and hisses from both sides.

"Or do you all want to keep on killing each other until there is none of you left?" said James, instantly wondering why he had said it.

All eyes fell on the thirteen-year-old boy with the crimson sword.

James thought he should continue. "I have fought alongside and now respect both of these…" He searched for the right words. "Two." They have saved each others' lives on more than one occasion. I am told that there are many more Hedra as brave and as just as Jal." He paused as a small Hedra, similar in height to himself pushed through the ranks and approached. It was the same Hedra boy he'd met beside the giant crossbows the day before.

"This boy…" the young Hedra pointed at James, "spared my life. It is time for the Hedra to show mercy."

"A young king in the making," said Cimerato.

Relfarth raised his hand. "Perhaps we should make these two boys the joint rulers of Gwendral. They seem to have more sense than all of us."

"No way!" blasted Cathy Peck. "He's with me." She pointed at James.

"And with me," added David Peck, stepping up beside his wife.

James waited for his mum to issue the obligatory put down, but there was none.

"He's with both of us," said Cathy.

"And we're going home to our own world," added David. "We have our own lives to rebuild. You need to sort yourselves out."

James felt his chest expand with pride.

"Nice one, Mr. Peck," said Craig.

Bero woofed and wagged his tail.

The young Hedra boy looked down at Bero before pointing to Jal. "I will follow this Hedra warrior and help to rebuild the city."

"And I!" said Relfarth.

And I," said someone else from within the Hedra ranks. "And I, and I, and I…"

Soon the whole battlefield resounded with the Hedra's shouts of support.

Cimerato stood next to Jal. "Those who are not happy with this new beginning are free to go." He turned to the Manimals and Yeltans behind him. "That includes everyone. They can leave now, unharmed, and without blame. Watch how we rebuild the city as two peoples with many different skills and return when you feel you can."

The sound of the two gathered armies was deafening as they yelled out their approval. James. However, noticed a few groups of Hedra and even some Manimals skulk off during the celebrations. In the main, however, weapons were thrown down and the two races mingled. Hedra streamed past him and the Drumfintley group, climbing up the grassy knoll for a better view of their new home, Gwendral.

Mendel's voice filtered into his head. "It is time we found a quieter spot. All who wish to return to Drumfintley… Please follow Bero now."

"Are you not going to stay here and help them?" asked Helen.

"No," said Mendel. "They need to find their own way of working together. Jal and Cimerato will keep order. I know the peoples of Denthan are in good hands."

"And the dissenters?" asked Michael.

"And the Tree Trolls and the Centides?" said Ephie, puffing as she tried to keep up with Bero.

"There will always be those who do not approve of the agreed way; those who even relish death and destruction, those who only care about their own survival... But they will find themselves alone and closed off from the greater good. There will always be a need to keep the walls of Gwendral strong. This union of Manimal and Hedra, though, is a true victory for Denthan."

"Never mind Denthan," said Cathy, "How do we get back to Scotland?"

"You've given enough up for this world, Cathy," said David.

James could see his mum biting back her words. She looked at Wee Joe, Craig, and Helen.

"You have all given up far too much, and for that, I am truly sorry," said Mendel.

"Poor Jean and Archie," whispered Ephie.

"God rest their souls," Michael whispered back.

They had stopped short of the shoreline where a long strip of brown beach separated them from the Gortan Sea. James craned up at the newly formed moon. It hung, as if poised to fall at any moment, in a deep purple sky. All around it, wisps of clouds cut white slashes in the heavens. "What now, Mendel?" asked James.

"Ees time to go home," said Eethan.

* * *

Ephie Blake plumped herself down on a springy tussock of beach grass. "Eethan, how exactly are we going to get back to Drumfintley from here?" Unanswered, Ephie stared out over the Gortan Sea; choppy and wild, the great expanse of water stretched out before them. James could just make out the small island where they'd fought Dendralon the day before. It made him think of Whindril and the dragons of Hest. The mountains behind the ruined city of Gwendral had grown dark as thick clouds massed round their peaks.

"Eethan!" blasted Cathy.

The little blue man almost jumped out of his wrinkly skin. "Ees thinking..."

"Ees picking your nose again, you little minger," she snapped.

"Now, now," said Mendel. "Let me focus."

They all waited.

Mendel's googly eye touched the inside of his window. "Wee Joe?"

The plastic brandy barrel swung slowly.

"Yes," said Wee Joe

"Do you have the Eden Seeds?"

"Yip." Wee Joe held them up for everyone to see. "Got dem from the dead wizard." He stared down at the funny looking seeds. "They look agusting."

"They're not for eating," said Helen. She looked up and waved.

Behind them, the Mertol approached, something spinning above his outstretched hand.

"And we have the Key of Artilis," said Mendel. "The Eden Seeds will open a portal back to Drumfintley with the right magic. That's where you come in, James."

James felt his stomach churn. "Will Eethan help?"

"Yes, yes… and the Mertol too. The key will take us back, or should I say forward, to the right time. It would look rather odd if you were all to go back to Drumfintley two years older."

Helen patted Bero's soft, golden fur. "And there's no chance for Mum…?"

"I'm sorry Helen, it doesn't…"

"…work like that. I know." She sobbed.

James felt his own tears well up.

Michael gave Helen a small hug.

James caught his mum and dad whispering and wondered what they were talking about. *At least they aren't shouting*, he thought.

"Wee Joe, throw the Eden Seeds into the Sea," said Mendel.

Wee Joe hesitated for an instant and then threw the seeds into the waves.

"Why?" James protested.

"James, think hard on the seeds," said Mendel. "Just imagine them drifting down to the sandy loam beneath the waves."

"What?" he gulped.

"Just do it," his mum barked.

"Okay, okay…" He closed his eyes and found that he could almost see the seeds, like a movie in his head, zigzagging down through the clear water. "I… I can see them."

"Ees good, James," said Eethan. "Eee can see them too."

"Bak!" The Mertol placed the spinning Key of Artilis in front of Bero.

"Craig?"

"Yes?"

James opened one eye. He could tell that Craig's thoughts had been elsewhere.

"Take the key and put it in James's hand," said Mendel.

James felt a rush of air over his hand. He knew the Key of Artilis was spinning above his outstretched fingers. His spine tingled. The blood seemed to boil in his veins. In his vision, the Eden Seeds landed on the seabed. They burrowed under the sand, and then white light shot up through the water and towards the new moon. When he opened his eyes, the two seeds had formed a huge, glowing archway that rose over the waves.

"The water is shallow here," said Mendel. "You must all walk into the archway. All except the Mertol, who will keep it open while we pass through."

"BAK!" The Mertol's paunchy face was moving. The slits that covered its cheeks opened and closed in intricate patterns.

"James, you must walk through the archway last of all. Bring the Key of Artilis with you."

"We're all going to walk through together," said his mum. Standing to his left, she ushered Ephie, Michael, and the Harrison children into position.

Eethan began chanting in a strange language. "Eethna che ta nar thi tempa."

Over and over, the words rattled round in James's head.

He watched Bero walk into the shining archway first, the barrel swinging under his muzzle. Then, in step, they all followed.

Still chanting, Eethan slid through the opening too.

So there he was, the Key of Artilis magically spinning and changing shape above his hand, his mum on his left, his dad on his right. *It could be a new beginning for us all,* he thought. As if hearing him out loud, his mum hugged him into her.

James glanced back at Denthan one last time. He saw the Mertol and, behind that, the figures of Jal and Cimerato surrounded by thousands of Manimals, Yeltans, and Hedra. The two leaders raised their swords in salute. He felt his dad's hand close round his, and then they walked straight into the light.

CHAPTER TWENTY-SEVEN

A WALK IN THE PARK

Gauser, the village drunk, woke himself up with a particularly loud snort. "Snooorrr... Ah... Wit the...?" He rolled off the park bench and thudded onto the cracked tarmac path, a green bottle of Buckie spinning round, loudly beside his left ear. His thick, smelly overcoat had softened the fall but his head thumped as if a Galway giant was grinding it into the dirt with a size forty pair of boots. As his red eyes squeaked open, a blast of warm air thundered into his face. His straggly hair blew back. Throat burning, he had to shield his eyes from an incredible light. "Ah, to be sure, I'll stop de drinkin', Lord! Don't punish me no more!" He sobbed.

Gauser rolled under the park bench and squinted out at the thing that had appeared above the bandstand. Like a huge, glowing wishbone, it burned as bright as the gates of heaven in the dull Drum-fintley dawn. The middle of the giant wishbone rippled and splashed like the water on Loch Echty.

"Mary, Muther o' Jaysus!" he cried. He found the neck of the wine bottle and held it like a club, hoping beyond hope that he would never have to use it. Aliens were walking out of the light onto the grass. "Ah knew it, so a did. Ah bludy knew it."

* * *

As the cold air caught his chest, James began to cough and splutter.

"Here, Son." His dad gave him his inhaler but he was too amazed and relieved to care about his asthma just then.

Distractedly, he took the blue puffer, handing his dad the Key of Artilis in exchange. He staggered forward. Ahead of him, Eethan scampered onto the main playing field of Drumfintley Park. His mum walked forward to join Father Michael, Ephie, and the Harrisons.

As he turned round, however, he gasped in fright. Something else had followed them through the archway. Something big.

Cathy Peck drew her swords and braced.

"What is it?" said his dad. The silhouette grew bigger.

"BAK!"

The whole group gasped as the unmistakable figure of the Mertol lumbered towards them, its pitted face shining in the light of the archway.

"There is *no way* that thing is coming here," said Cathy. She walked towards the fifteen-foot tall creature and began to shush it back into the archway with her drawn swords, clicking them together above her head.

The Mertol cowered and whined. It pointed back at the shimmering gateway formed by the archway and shook its matted head. It gnashed its black teeth together as if it was trying to explain.

"It cannot return," said Mendel.

"Who's that over there?" said Helen.

James saw that she was squinting across the grass at one of the park benches.

"Oh… Brilliant," said Cathy, turning away from the Mertol. She called out, "Gauser, come out from under there."

Gauser dropped an empty wine bottle and pulled his grimy jacket even further over his head.

James felt a strange sensation, like someone knocking into him, and then the giant, glowing arch began to waver. Bit by bit, it fizzled out in the early morning drizzle until, finally, there was a small *puff,* and it was gone.

The Mertol sloped past James and focused on the terrified Gauser.

"Mary, Muther o' Jaysus!" yelped the old tramp. He began to shake.

"It's okay, Gauser," said Father Michael. "It's just a…"

"It's just a what?" said Cathy. "It's just a fifteen-foot magical carnivore from a different world that could eat you whole in about three seconds?" She stormed past them all and yanked Gauser out from under the flaking, green bench. "Sit there and don't move."

James listened for Mendel's voice, "Mendel, a bit of advice wouldn't go amiss," he prompted.

"Well, we're back and that's the main thing," said the wizard.

Everyone stared down at the brandy barrel. The sky was becoming brighter, and James could just make out the outline of Ben Larvach through the mist. "We could wipe his memory, if you tell me how," he suggested.

"His memory was wiped clean a long time ago." Cathy Peck picked up the empty wine bottle and dropped it into the black council bin. She sat down beside the old trembling tramp. "Anyway, who's going to believe *him*?"

Strangely, James recognised the black bin as the first place he'd ever set eyes on Mendel. He could still picture the little goldfish in his fairground plastic bag, the scales glimmering beneath the rubbish.

Ephie Blake sighed and gave Father Michael a knowing look. "Gauser wasn't always this way, Michael."

"No?" Father Michael screwed up his eyes in disbelief.

James's dad explained without looking at anyone in particular. "Gauser, or should I say, Mr. Gaudie, was my R.E. teacher at one time."

"And mine," added Ephie.

"He was what?" asked James. "Here, at Drumfintley School?"

"But for the grace of God, go any one of us," warned Father Michael.

James thought they looked a strange bunch. His mum was sitting next to Gauser, who stared, wide-eyed, at the Mertol. His dad shivered beside Father Michael and Ephie, and the Harrisons… A wave of sadness caught him, and he just managed to fight back a huge sob. They were all back home. They should have been whooping and cheering, but they couldn't. It just didn't feel right.

He felt Bero's warm fur brush against his legs.

Mendel's voice echoed over Drumfintley Park. "Eethan and the Mertol are going to leave us. So say your goodbyes for now."

"Where, exactly are they going to go?" asked Cathy. "I mean they don't exactly fit in."

"They would in Stendleburgh," said Craig, biting down on a grin.

"Yeah." James risked a smile.

"Ees fine, James's mum," said Eethan. "Eee ees used to disappearing into the hills and trees. Scotland ees my home too."

"Yeh, but it's not bloomin' his, is it?" She pointed to the Mertol.

"He ees good at hiding too."

"Bak!" yelled the Mertol.

"Shush! For goodness sake," said Ephie, nervously scouring the park for any sign of the locals.

Gauser began to shake a little more vigorously.

"Come on, Mendel," said Cathy. "What's it going to eat?"

His scrawny legs dangling over the bandstand, Eethan kicked his heels together. "Sheeps and chickens."

"Oh, well that's all right then," mocked Cathy, "We'll just tell Glenhead Farm to allow for a certain percentage of their sheep turning into Mertol poo."

"Thees won't all be from dee one farm," said Eethan, sticking his thumb up his nose. He winked at Cathy.

James knew the little blue man was winding his mum up on purpose now.

Cathy drew her swords. "Why you little…"

But Wee Joe broke ranks with the Harrisons and wandered across her path towards the Mertol.

The huge creature bent down and picked Wee Joe up in its ape-like arms. It grunted and yelped tenderly.

"Yous gonna come back sometimes, aren't you?" said Wee Joe.

"Bak," answered the Mertol.

The pits in the Mertol's face rippled in intricate patterns and James thought he saw a smile of sorts.

The beast lowered Wee Joe and was just about to turn away when Wee Joe caught hold of a lump of its fur. "Here." He pulled the green water pistol from his belt and handed it up to the Mertol. "It's for you. Mum said it gave me good luck." Wee Joe lowered his gaze. "I wish I'd given it to her."

The Mertol tilted its filthy head and made a strange hissing sound. Then it reached down and took Wee Joe's gun before merging into the rhododendrons.

"That was really kind of you, Joe," said Helen. "Mum would have been… She would have been…"

"Really proud of you," finished Craig.

James could see that the stuffing had been knocked out of his cocky friend.

Bero woofed as Eethan performed an extravagant bow. "Ees weel see you all again, one day soon."

"Never, would be a day too soon, as far as I'm concerned," muttered Cathy.

"Bye, Eethan," said James. "Don't let the big man eat too many sheep."

Eethan's chortles and giggles soon faded as he slid into the bushes and disappeared.

James saw Gauser's wild eyes searching their faces.

"Mindfreeze?" suggested James.

"Well remembered, James," said the old wizard. "Now concentrate on Gauser's eyes and say the word. It's all a matter of focus."

James moved closer to Gauser.

The old tramp's eyes shifted wildly.

Then, just as Gauser caught his gaze, James said, "Wwmindwwfrewweezeww!"

He turned to Bero and the barrel and whispered, "It came out all bubbly again."

"I think you're stuck with that now. Bit of a carry over from the way your mind assimilated the magic," said Mendel.

"For goodness sake, Mendel," snapped Craig. "We don't need to know the bloomin' science. Did the numpty boy get it right or not?"

James smiled at his best friend.

"He did," said Mendel.

Gauser was in a trance-like state.

"Now," pressed Mendel, "repeat after me, James: I'm giving up the drink because it's making me see things. A big helicopter landed in Drumfintley Park and dropped off the Pecks, Father Michael, Ephie, and the Harrison children."

James, somewhat bemused, repeated the words and then listened as, still glazed over, Gauser said them back in his lilting, Irish brogue.

Mendel splashed loudly. "Now snap your fingers and say: it's good to be back."

"It's good to be back," said James.

They all waited.

Gauser jolted upright and scanned the skies. "A helicopter, eh? Posh."

"Yeh," said Craig, "It was one of those reality TV shows, Gauser. They treated us like kings. It was just like going to another world."

James held onto his straight face as long as he could.

"And in fancy dress I see." Gauser was scratching his chin while circling Cathy Peck in her golden armour. "Let me guess…" He screwed up his eyes and then nodded confidently and said, "The Queen of Narnia."

"Close," murmured James.

"Well, she's hardly a wee green man from Mars, now; is che?" spat Gauser.

James wiped Gauser's spittle from his grubby shirt. "Funny you should say that because…"

"James," warned his mum.

Even Helen began to chuckle.

Gauser staggered around for a few moments until he found another unopened, green bottle in his coat. He twisted off the lid and sniffed it before, absentmindedly, dropping it in the bin. "The Queen of Narnia, eh…" Gauser wandered off towards the swings. "More like the Wicked Witch of the West…" he muttered.

Cathy's eyes narrowed.

"Now, Dear," cautioned David. "It's not worth you…" he stopped mid-sentence.

Cathy fixed him a death-stare.

James cringed.

"David, James. Home!" she blasted.

Father Michael sighed. "Shall we go home too, Ephie?"

"Oh, yes please. I can't believe we're back. You know, it's a lot colder than when we left."

"Autumn can be cold here. Milder in Galway," said Gauser. "I'm off to the shop." He wrapped his heavy coat around him and staggered off towards the park gates.

"Autumn?" Ephie shouted after him. "What's the date?"

"I dunno, September… Near de end, I tink." He bellowed.

As Gauser wandered through the park gates, James saw everyone look down at the barrel.

Mendel cleared his throat. "Well, at least it's the same year. Eethan set the exact time we would return to. The Key of Artilis responded to his chant and the Eden Seeds gave us the portal."

"So, you're blaming Eethan?" said Cathy.

"He's not blaming anyone, Mum," said James, meekly.

"Nobody's going anywhere yet," said Cathy. She looked across at the Harrisons and then addressed the adults. "What are we going to say? Where have we been? How are we going to explain Jean?"

Father Michael cleared his throat and reached down to pat Bero. "I'm not sure yet. The kids could come with us for now. What do you think, Ephie?"

James could tell by Ephie's face that she was horrified by the prospect of looking after three kids.

"Of course, Dear," she replied.

"Maybe Craig and Bero could come with us, Mum?" said James. "Split things up a bit. Make it easier on Ephie and Father Michael."

Craig walked over and dug him in the ribs. "I heard that."

"No," said his mum. "It wouldn't be good to split them up. It's all or nothing."

James couldn't quite believe it. Had his mum just offered to take the Harrisons in?

Helen tapped Cathy Peck on the arm. "You might want to ask us what *we* want."

Cathy stared down at her.

"Sorry, Dear," said Ephie. "Tell us."

"We should say that mum has gone to visit someone far away," said Craig. He kicked a pile of leaves and added, "After a while, they'll realise that she isn't coming back."

"What about your dad?" asked David. "We'll need to contact him."

"You'll be lucky," said Craig." We've not heard a peep in over a year."

"Ah," sighed David. "Still."

"The rectory is bigger," said Father Michael, decisively. "We'll collect some clean clothes from your house, Craig, and take it from there."

"Fine," said Cathy. "We'll just stick to the reality TV show rubbish that Craig blurted out."

"Oh, I'm not sure I can lie very well," said Father Michael.

"Say it's a secret. Say it would spoil the programme if you revealed what happens. Say you've signed a confidentiality clause," said David.

Cathy eyed him suspiciously. "Good at lying, aren't you, David?"

James heard Mendel splash loudly in the barrel. "We better get home, then."

"About time too," said James.

"I hope someone's fed Mufty," said Wee Joe.

"Oh no," said Helen. "He's right. We must be a good three months on from when we left."

"Sergeant Carr had a key," said Ephie.

"He'll help us with the reality TV story," said James. "We can tell him the truth about Mrs. Harrison too. He'll understand."

Come on then," said Cathy, resplendent in her golden armour. "I want to get out of this gear before anyone else sees me."

"See you later, Craig," said James.

"You mean when we all move into your place?" said Craig.

"You never know," said James.

"Don't be a numpty," Craig whispered.

"Bye," said Wee Joe.

"Here," said Helen. She handed James the brandy barrel from round Bero's neck. "You'd better put Mendel back in his tin bath."

"That would be nice," said Mendel. "Very nice indeed."

* * *

Three months later, James sat down to write in his diary...

We've all stopped school for the Christmas holidays. Craig is in my room with the tin bath and Mendel. Helen and Wee Joe are in the spare room and Mum and Dad have actually been forced into sharing. Weird. I can't really explain it entirely but they are definitely getting on better now that the Harrisons have moved in.

They had a memorial service for Jean Harrison. Bizarrely, Father Michael had those keepsakes of his, the tartan bits of cloth, turned into a proper Drumfintley tartan. It was made official and stuff. The worst bit was that he gave Dad, Craig, Wee Joe, Me, and even sergeant Carr, specially made up kilts to wear. He said that we were all in some kind of Drumfintley club or clan or something. Mum got all stroppy as to why he didn't make kilts up for the girls in the group and he ended up spending even more money getting the Drumfintley tartan for them. Anyway, we had to wear the things to the church. Sergeant Carr has helped a lot with the legal stuff and the story that poor Mrs. Harrison went missing after a canoeing accident in Peru. Although the whole thing is horrible, it's been quite nice to have some brothers and sisters. I didn't realise how much they all fight, non-stop. Mum and Dad said some nice words about Mrs. Harrison at the service and Father Michael got quite tearful. We all did.

Bero has moved in with Father Michael and Ephie, where he's pestered by Patch most of the time. Oh, and Mum said that there was no way any smelly hamster was coming into her house, so Mufty is there too. She tried to get me to put Mendel there as well, but there was a bit of a riot and she gave in.

The villagers in Drumfintley still nag us about the Reality TV show and keep asking us what it was about and when it is likely to come on the telly.

Mendel still talks to me most days about my magic and stuff. He's taught me six spells now and he's always winding Craig up with his big explanations. He says Eethan and the Mertol are both living on the island of Harris, off the west coast of Scotland. Dad says we can all go and visit next summer, but Mum isn't too keen. She says we've all had enough of all that stuff.

There was never any word back from Mr. Harrison, so it looks like Craig might actually become a kind of official brother at some stage. How weird is that?

Craig says that, although the Rectory was much more peaceful than our house, he actually prefers it here. He's already had a few cuffs round the ear from mum for his cheek, but in a strange kind of way, I think he enjoys the challenge. At least that's what he says. Wee Joe whacked Mum on the leg with a toy sword the other day and she had to drive round the by-pass four times before she calmed down. In saying that, she never really calms down. There's always lots of shouting and nagging, but that's just Mum.

We often get together at the rectory and talk about the Hedra and the Manimals. Craig reckons they'll be at each other's throats but Mendel says that Cimerato and Jal are both strong and that they will rebuild Gwendral together.

All in all, it's nice to be back home.

James yawned and closed his diary. Craig was in the spare room playing computer games with Wee Joe.

"JAMES!"

His mum's voice still made him jump.

"Yes, Mum?"

"Get that gormless guppy some fish food from the shop. Take out the bins on your way, and on the way back, tell your dad that he's fixing the slates after playing the big man at the Scouts tonight."

Under his breath, James muttered, "There are three other slaves here too, Mum."

Strangely, as if she'd heard him, there was another blast from the kitchen. "CRAIG!"

James heard a thump from next door. He skidded round the top landing and opened the door of the spare room, so Craig could get the full list of commands. Craig had fallen off his chair.

"Get that computer off! Get the two wee ones to sleep and STOP BANGING!"

James held up three fingers and mouthed, "Three commands. There are always three. Get to it, numpty boy!"

"There must be some way we can have a whip-round and send her off somewhere nice," said Craig.

"Like Mars," added Wee Joe.

Helen looked up from her book and chuckled.

James shook his head and smiled wistfully.

Poor us, thought James.

Poor old us...

ABOUT THE AUTHOR

ABOUT THE AUTHOR

BORN IN HELENSBURGH and educated at Glasgow University, Sam studied Zoology, working his way through his uni-years by playing in various rock bands in the UK, America and Holland. He began writing songs in the late 70s, poetry in the early 90s and eventually his first novel - 'The Magic Scales' in 2005, part one of the Denthan Trilogy. Sam is currently writing more children's books. He still continues to perform his workshops and presentations in schools, libraries and at book festivals. Sam works closely with the charity Asthma UK to raise awareness of the condition through his work with children.

List of titles...

The Magic Scales – Book 1 of the Denthan Series.

The Second Gateway – Book 2 of the Denthan Series.

Return to Denthan – Book 3 of the Denthan Series.

Contact Sam at: samwilding1@gmail.com

www.sam-wilding.com

Lightning Source UK Ltd.
Milton Keynes UK
27 April 2010

153422UK00001B/22/P